Praise for *The Half-Life of Guilt*

A PopMatters Best Book of 2024

"In this beautiful and layered novel Lynn Stegner takes us on a passionate tour of self-discovery and family history written so closely and with such astonishing sincerity that the entire novel becomes a kind of surprising tenderness. Stegner has the writer's gift of creating a dear victory from the uneasiness of pristine places. This is a rich, rich book."—Ron Carlson, author of *Return to Oakpine*

"*The Half-Life of Guilt* is a powerful tale of family loyalty, romantic love, and the long reach of a single, shocking childhood tragedy. Lynn Stegner has a profound understanding of how sisters relate—or fail to relate—and how the truth of the past can be lost to our misperceptions. This sobering and insightful story is beautifully told."—Elizabeth Crook, author of *The Madstone* and *The Which Way Tree*

"Lynn Stegner is a beautiful writer. This fiercely wrought family saga will take your breath away with its sharpness and depth."—Rick Bass, author of *For a Little While: New and Selected Stories*

"*The Half Life of Guilt* adroitly braids paired narratives: a risk-filled present journey down the coast of Mexico and the fraught past of a family in northern California. The twins at the center of the story—Nina and Clair—compel our close attention, and the novel somehow manages to be both action-packed and contemplative. Lynn Stegner gives us scientists and vintners and idealists and cynics: troubled creatures all. And she does so in prose as vivid as her scenery; the dead remain wholly alive."—Nicholas Delbanco, author of *Why Writing Matters*

"As Stegner explores both personal responsibility and our responsibility to care for the natural world, she illuminates the ways we love, fail to love, and repair our failures. Her unique sensibility makes for a fascinating read."—Andrea Barrett, author of *Natural History* and *Ship Fever*

THE HALF–LIFE OF GUILT

THE HALF-LIFE
of GUILT

a novel

LYNN STEGNER

HIGH ROAD BOOKS | ALBUQUERQUE

ISBN 978-0-8263-6688-7 (cloth)
ISBN 978-0-8263-6899-7 (paper)
ISBN 978-0-8263-6689-4 (ePub)

Library of Congress Control Number: 2024933507

Founded in 1889, the University of New Mexico sits on the traditional
homelands of the Pueblo of Sandia. The original peoples of New Mexico—
Pueblo, Navajo, and Apache—since time immemorial have deep
connections to the land and have made significant contributions to the
broader community statewide. We honor the land itself and those who
remain stewards of this land throughout the generations and also
acknowledge our committed relationship to Indigenous peoples. We
gratefully recognize our history.

Cover illustration by Felicia Cedillos
Designed by Felicia Cedillos
Composed in Adobe Caslon Pro

For Margaret

CHAPTER 1

From above, the airstrip is a dark scar on the land, an unnatural feature in the sprawling Vizcaíno Desert with its soft shadings of buff and dun. To the south spreads a vast patchwork of salt pans, milky pastels of green, turquoise, pink, and the sharp white glare of the crystallization ponds. Stippled in between the saltworks and the smallest of the lagoons to the north is the town of Guerrero Negro, ashen and lifeless beneath the midday sun. But the lagoons make brilliant forays of emerald green that wander far into the great dry country as if to reassure it. The deep water of the Pacific from which the lagoons find their source is a simple blue, and though the high sun has faded sky and ocean together, both are so quiet and measureless as to suggest an infinite goodness. Against the long western length of the Baja peninsula, this sea lies, giving, taking, a point, a cove, a bight, a bay. The California gray whale migrates along this coastline—south to breed in the lagoons of Baja, Mexico, north to feed in the cold, rich waters of the Bering and Chukchi Seas. March—many of the whales have already left the lagoons to begin the journey north.

From above, the scene is as static as a still life, just swaths of color—those that are natural, shapeless, and those that are manmade, defined by sharp corners and lines and dots for buildings or machinery. But at noon something metallic flares, and a muscular little plane awakens the scene, sweeping down suddenly and running the length of the airstrip before returning slowly to its midpoint opposite a knot of people. There are only three flights a week out to Cedros Island where the saltworks make use of the island's deep-water harbor for the export ships, and every flight is full and late, and every flight requires the painstaking adjudication of room for passengers, room for goods.

Each seat that is taken from the plane frees up space for another vat of entrails that is carried through the open rear door by small brown men wearing white. When they extract two seats in tandem and swing in a quarter side of beef swaddled in wet burlap, using a grappling hook to secure it to a ring attached to the ceiling, Clair feels they have reached the apotheosis of despair from which the vehicle of Fate will now plummet to the tarmac and re-incarnate as the C-47 waiting before them. It still bears the faded painted pentimento remembering the Tarzana Air Circus.

To say *this is the place, the moment, when everything changes*, when one direction becomes its opposite, when one feeling meets its nemesis, love to hate, as it does in the heart; when day becomes night, and night then vanishes in a torrent of light, as it does in the desert—that is not an easy thing to know and then to say—without fear. Usually things changed like ships turning at sea, imperceptibly and with heavy reluctance, as if called back to port for some neglected formality. But she thinks she can name that place and that moment. It is here, it is now.

Again, the man walks toward them, unhurried, the heat wavering around him so that he is just another one of the mirages they have witnessed all down the Baja peninsula. He is wearing a cap of some sort, like a chauffeur's cap with a purple insignia, PSP for *Productores de Sal del Pacífico*, and his dark shirt has buttons—is not a smock like those worn by the others. He holds a clipboard against his hip, then brings it to his chest as he reaches their small group, Clair and Mason off to the side where the others, with a mixed dose of disdain and respect, have abandoned them. The flight was scheduled to depart at one, and it is now after three. Every fifteen minutes or so, instead of carrying the vats of *tripas*, or the bushel baskets of vegetables and fruits to the plane, or the bindles and bundles of the island's residents, this man calls out the names of a few passengers—"Villareal, Muñoz, Caponegro"—and without expression, they hurry across the tarmac and climb aboard. Again, Mason reads the triplicated tickets, the dry wind ruffling the copies, and finally she puts her hand on his forearm and he lets it drop. She is hoping now that there will not be any room for them. The light is assaulting them, like the glare from tilting sheets of metal, yet fixed at the center of the light the open rear door of the C-47 seems an entrance to a tunnel that will lead them into deepest darkness.

Mason begins to pace, eight steps south, eight steps north back to her, yo-yoing patience and impatience, surety and abandonment.

"Does it help?" she asks him.

"I don't know," he says, his hand exploring his lower back.

"I could try to find some ice." She lifts her chin back toward the flat-roofed building no bigger than a gas station, which serves as the terminal.

"Seriously?"

"It's an idea, that's all."

He glances at her, perhaps considering an apology. The light makes two bright coins of his spectacles that magically vanish when he swings his gaze with disgust at the C-47. "This contraption might take off any minute for all we know. I don't want to give them the satisfaction." He starts off on his eight-paced tour away from her. "We'd better wait."

"I don't want to," she says too quietly for him to hear. It takes more courage to say this than to contemplate being a passenger on the C-47, to say what she doesn't like, doesn't want. Her consolation has always been that others have what they want or need, and taking something for herself is almost impossible. It may be that she has finally forgotten how to want; that pleasure has become a concept fraying to nothing, like those disconsolate pennants, already desert-bleached and wind-shredded, snapping to celebrate the grand opening of the hotel in San Quintin—a hotel entirely empty but for them and a dour cadre of minions scuttling the back hallways. Yet here she has at least said something she does not want. She does not want to wait. For this plane, for this man, for things to get better or maybe only easier.

"You've taken a lot of photos. Don't you have enough?" she asks him on his return trip, allowing fear to overtake duty.

He quivers his head at a slightly cocked angle as if he's heard her wrong.

"Well, don't you?" she asks again, this time adopting some challenge in her voice, because suddenly she is tired of their mission, tired of always going on, tired of being the one whose job it is to jolly everything and everyone along; to say that it will all work out, that it's not as bad as it seems, even when it is worse than she can admit. Tired of waiting for something she can't yet identify. Tired of waiting to live. Tired of having a mission and not a life.

He is wearing his mustard yellow shirt with the cuffs rolled to his elbows and, crossed over his chest, the mail courier bag in which he carries his passport, Tourist Card, money, and a small journal for notes that only he can read—the handwriting, if it can be called that, so idiosyncratic that it looks like a lost alphabet whose sounds no one knows any longer how to make. She has always liked the yellow shirt, something he bought himself in Morocco—before they knew each other. Do they know each other now? she wonders nervously. Maybe as much as one can know another . . . The faint stripes of elegant white embroidery combined with the worn edges of collar and cuffs somehow persuade her that he won't ever lie to her. And in fact, he never has. But she does not like his handwriting. It makes no effort to be accessible; it is private and self-serving and exclusive. It means to say *keep out* as much as it pretends to the conceit of mystery. "Do I have enough? What about the docks, Clair?" he asks without really asking. "The ships, the mountain of salt? What about the whole bloody company-town scene?"

"Okay."

"What about the whales?"

"Okay, okay."

She wants to touch his face, to wake him up from his quarrelsome mood, but he tacks on an impassive look and turns away. Also, she realizes, she wants to hurt him, but not nearly as much as she wants to love him out of the anger he can't seem to give up. This might turn out to be what the problem has always been—anger.

But then softly he adds, "What about your work, the plant transects?"

"Right," she seems to agree. She does care about that, about the mission.

She glances at his belt, and below, remembering the night before, the slowness of his entry; she was not to move—last night's little game—and he had still not acknowledged her apology. It seems . . . unlike him, though now she is wondering what exactly *is* like him, and again, whether or not she has any idea who he is.

It is doubtful that they, these officials, know who Mason Comstock is, despite the hard case of camera equipment—or that they would even care. Plenty of *touristas* arrive with expensive gear, to fish or camp, to photograph the elephant seals battling for breeding privileges, to use up the hours of unavailing lives spending their money in other men's countries. But how many come to Cedros Island? This place belongs wholly to Mexico, an inner sanctum where things are done that you don't want others seeing you do. How many more inner sanctums can there be? The afternoon sun detonates off the aluminum camera case and instantly she shifts blinded eyes south toward Guerrero Negro, Black Warrior, where the night before they found a small clean room, painted in colors so bright and so badly by someone in a hurry and indifferent to the debt of perfection, that they did nothing to blot out the desperation of the place, only heightened it. Someone had had hopes once—of tourists, money, domestic complacencies.

Visually the town seems to be sinking into the yellow-gray flats, its flotsam of low-set buildings like crates and boards and furnishings from a wreckage half-submerged beneath an undulating sea of heat. She can see the short ugly lighthouse, the glint of a panel truck; no movement that can be counted on or believed in. She thinks of a *Twilight Zone* episode she watched as a child, a town somewhere in New Mexico mysteriously emptied of its citizenry. Alien abductions and the pulsating silence of abandonment. The unrelenting flatness of the landscape bends everything down to a rule. It is the landscape of death—the sameness, the visual tedium, the indifference—a world where people might go to disappear, people who would not be missed. West across the lagoon and forming the boundary between the Bahia and the mainland are the great white dunes mounding up. Then the blue sea. The desert around the airport radiates out into a dun nothingness, though, if she tries, she can make out small dark tufts of something living trying to make a go of things. Maybe creosote or ocotillo or the inescapable cholla. Anyway, nothing beautiful. She is missing the easy beautiful things, the orderly green stitching of the vineyards of childhood. This is not a friendly place.

But it can be beautiful, she reminds herself. Only a few days ago, it was beautiful.

Mason is on his knees, throwing open the camera case, fitting a lens to the Leica M6. Then he starts shooting, mostly the man with the clipboard, approaching, returning to the plane, conferring with the men who are loading the supplies for Cedros; but also pictures of the mountain of goods still waiting, and then, swinging around, of the second airport official leaning against the doorframe, smoking. It is some category of attack, for there is a maniacal intensity in his eyes, though, like the other travelers, he has managed to void his face of expression. In that one respect, it, too, is flat like the land with its salt lagoons, the line of the horizon lost in the broad brushstroke of heat and light. An immense futility begins to settle within her.

"Stop," she says under her voice. "Please."

He doesn't respond except to aim the camera at her and snap one off. It feels a little like being slapped and she actually winces. The Leica is quiet, but not so quiet that she can't hear each of his threats pelting the air. Some line has been crossed, a last wrong step taken, and he is frightening her, even while, on some level, she is also aware this is an act of childish frustration and impatience that will pass.

Standing nearest them is a stubby middle-aged woman who looks Indian, a descendent of the local Cochimí, Clair supposes. Her nose is straight and flawless, with large, perfectly flared and symmetrical nostrils, the skin glistening with sweat, like a bronze cast. Above the high cheekbones are two solemn eyes that glare without actually glaring at Mason as she pulls her boy to her. The boy has dropped his head; Clair notices that he has a cleft lip.

"Will you just stop?" she says again to Mason. "Can't you see it doesn't do anything? They don't care. This woman might care because of her boy, but no one else cares. This isn't our country. You're playing the ugly American. You've become the ugly American. I just don't know what's going on with you. Is it your back?"

Touching his palm to his lumbar spine, he paces away from her. "This bloody country," he says.

Mason is always walking away. He is a fine-boned man with fingers that feather over things—cameras, breasts, the guitar he plays now and then—and all of what strength he has moves like coaxial cable through his body charged with intensity of purpose. That purpose seems to always lie somewhere else. He never cares much what he eats or where he sleeps, but he is curious about the men who have caught the fish or the women whose hands have formed the tortillas or the machines that have excavated the lagoons—he is interested in the action even though he puts an end to that action in film. It is one of the things she likes best about Mason, the way he goes to sources, to first acts. Clair has decided it is a form of control, that capturing on film, that exhumation of sources. If you know where and how something began, then maybe later you can contain its consequences, frame them and fix them, prevent escape. An obvious concept, she has to admit, if only by reason of perpetuity, which to her thinking is a welcome thing. Like her father, she likes what lasts, especially the beautiful ways, the beautiful ideas. But even if the world were full of beauty, there were plenty of people ready to despoil it.

"Pineda, Anza, Ugarte, Maldonado," calls the man with the clipboard.

Mason takes his picture, and the man neither attends to it nor ignores it. It is as if they do not exist, and that drives Clair to a kind of unsettling nerviness because as much as she does not now want to board the plane, it is worse to be excluded from the rest of the assembled humanity, from the piles of goods and consumables, from the stuff of the world. Something invisible is killing them off, unanticipated forces, a virulent sun. The wind, dry and restless, gusts into them and stings their eyes so that she is convinced that the salt is there as well, in the air. The salt is everywhere. And salt kills as much as it preserves.

If they could just board quickly, not think any longer about all of it, just get it over with . . . She fingers the scar on her ear and again remembers the night before when he had forgotten about his back. *When the fight-or-flight response has been stimulated, endorphins are released and the perception of pain diminishes.* From what long-ago book did that now surface? Mason was not fleeing; he was attacking, feeling no pain. And today Clair has become a flight risk.

At that moment, brimming up and over a shallow barranca at the edge of the runway and out onto the tarmac comes a small herd of goats, their little bells tinkling. The men loading the C-47 set down whatever they are carrying and wander languidly toward them, laughing a little, separating as they approach the animals and forming a kind of human corral with their hands extended to their sides, palms out, and a soft *chucking* sound coming from their throats; the goats dropping their heads, indecisive, veering left and right, and finally cutting back toward the barranca. They are a solemn people, their laughter unexpected and . . . comforting. In the distance, Clair makes out a figure so far away that it's like a piece of white cloth torn away and sailing on the desert thermals. The goatherd. Probably a boy. She thinks of Ethan. Her boy.

Ethan. Over the course of his six years, she has taken fewer and fewer risks, even though she had once announced that she would not let having a child alter her lifestyle. Her life—of course—but not her lifestyle. Yet she has noticed the quiet deductions, the trips she doesn't take, the recreational drugs she usually declines, the Volvo wagon that has replaced her Alfa Romeo Spider.

Another seat is removed from the C-47. It is looking more and more like one of the things she should not do because of Ethan—board this plane. There it sits on the tarmac, nose up toward heaven more steeply than seems right, making anticipatory pleadings, while the seats that have been unbolted and lifted out gather along the edge of the tarmac like chairs in an open-air theater awaiting an audience that everyone seems to know will never come. From around the far side of the terminal a stray dog ambles out of the shade and weaves aimlessly toward them until, passing the line of seats, it sniffs one, hops up, and promptly falls asleep. There are a lot of strays in Mexico.

The air ticks with heat, and the heat becomes time, and the time is everywhere and nowhere, a sudden menacing surfeit of the incomprehensible. There is too much time suddenly. How is it that everything has wound itself down to this? How is it that time no longer makes sense? She has lost sight of the shore of herself . . . she feels . . . at sea . . . lost.

Mason removes his spectacles and rubs his eyes. Ordinary eyes, narrowly set—she often cannot picture them, their exact color, or whether they have the limbal rings that make eyes more beautiful, or if there are flecks of contradictory color—but she always feels their concern. Absently, he says, "By the by, I'm English," long minutes after her remark about the ugly American, and she decides that it is best not to respond to this stupid and feckless invocation of a past he has long rejected, and which she knows so well that she can recite it as if it's one of the children's books Ethan used to insist she read again and again. By the time he was four, Ethan had memorized them, line for line, so that he could pretend to be the parent reading to the child he resented having to be. Maybe there was some of that same resentment in Mason. A holdover.

She can remember the exact moment that she fell in love with him. Or rather, the image that tightened her heart beyond release. It was a newspaper clipping about the Greenpeace fight to prevent the Brent Spar, a buoy designed for storing and off-loading oil, from final burial in the North Atlantic Sea. The oil company had identified a deep trench along the North Feni Ridge as the optimum dumping site, deep enough not to cause trouble for shipping traffic, and purportedly not so abundant with life that any great loss would be incurred. Diverse life, perhaps, but not abundant life. Mason was part of the media flotilla that had headed out to the buoy to cover Greenpeace's three-week occupation. There were heavy swells, birds littered against the flat gray sky. In the clipping, Mason is sitting along the port side at the bow of an inflatable, a camera nesting under his chin in the neck opening of his lifejacket, and his hand, with its delicate long fingers, is splayed over the tube, trying to hang on—vulnerable, clinging, half-effective, but determined. It seemed to define him completely. 1995, spring—three years ago.

There are two kinds of ambition, the kind that wants to best another and the kind that seeks to do the best one can. Mason wants to do the best that he can, and there is something pure and icy about it. Nothing can melt his resolve.

He is a tense man, a man who fidgets under certain circumstances, bouncing a knee, or winding and unwinding his ankles, or unconsciously nudging back the cuticles of his fingernails. When he is particularly edgy, he taps his index finger on the inside of his ankle—he often sits with his left leg crossed up and resting over his right thigh. He paces. He talks with his hands, not in passionate gestures, but with his fingers in a sign language only he can read. When he needs her, he calls too often or not at all, leaving long messages that sound vaguely like remonstrations to her or to himself, she is never sure. Once she noticed penciled into his calendar the letters "DNC" three days in row. "What does that mean?" she asked him. "Do Not Call," he said without further explanation.

None of it bothers her, only endears him to her, this tense and driven man who in the end will probably fail at the causes that prompt his pictures, but not at the pictures themselves. The pictures are successful monuments to the ends that are gathering like the last muster around them. Soon it will be our turn to end, she thinks, our loves, our lives, our species.

Still, Mason is irritating about his work, the kind of environmentalist who gives environmentalism a bad name, who makes legislators balk and friendlies close their checkbooks; the kind of photographer who is resistant to ordinary human needs. He once spent three months in a sea kayak paddling the Inland Passage. He had packed the bow and stern with waterproof bags of rice, living on that and whatever fish he could catch. He has to be reminded to hug her, but he seldom fails to slap her bottom when she leans over the sink to brush her teeth in the morning—when she only wants to wake up in the privacy of her own body and set her feet on a path into the day. Why is it, she wonders, that he thinks he can have the one without the other? Or is it only that lust is so much easier than love?

Ends have a way of reaching back for beginnings, as though, had she been more careful, had she properly noticed something back then, the end might have been avoided. Not this C-47, which suggests the most mundane of endings, the one each of them will negotiate alone one day. Something else seems to be ending. Who was she to say whether what was to end was a good thing or a bad thing? Somehow the bad things were harder—much harder—to give up, as if they are deserved, while the good . . . the good is often what you think you managed to get away with.

"Zuniga, Cosio, Torres."

Mason gives a snort of derision. "Aero Fatale."

"Please," she says to him, "it's already hard enough." The air is so dry that her mouth is pasty, her lips torn strips of parchment, and she digs through her backpack for one of the pieces of hard tart candy, Jolly Ranchers, she's been sucking on to keep the saliva coming, finds a red one—watermelon—then decides to offer it to the boy. His mother nods and, furtively, the boy takes it, his small fingers dirty and eager. But in that instant Clair worries how he will manage the hard candy if his palate is as divided as his lip. To his mother she says, "*Está bien?*" and points a finger toward her own mouth.

The woman's face darkens and that is the end of their international commerce. Now unsure what he can do, the boy begins to cry, puling softly against his mother's side, the Jolly Rancher cocooned in his fist.

Even here in this culture, faraway and less simple than it seems, it is best not to notice things, the mistakes and tragedies, the unattainable wholeness, the imperfections that throw belief into question and God out of favor.

Mason, observing the misunderstanding, squats before the boy and assures him that the candy will not hurt him and then, rising, he tells the woman in Spanish about a group of doctors who travel around the world solely to correct this problem. The woman smiles. She knows of it; they already have a plan to meet with them.

DIVIDED THINGS ARE supposed to fuse—palates, fontanelles, hearts and houses, nations. But sometimes they fuse in ways that are not good, not healthy; not knit together like the held hands of lovers after a fight, or the plates of an infant's skull, but like tectonic plates, one sliding beneath the other. Then, along that subduction zone, there are earthquakes and volcanoes, the lifting up and the tearing down of mountains, the emergence of islands and the submergence of continents of life that might have been or that still want to be. A geologic agreement has silently taken place, one is held down by the other, and eventually where they touch the protests begin and never seem to end.

Nina . . . She probably thinks of Nina too much. It is almost entirely involuntary. But they are twins, after all. Nothing can change that.

THEY ARE THE last standing at the edge of the tarmac. The man with the clipboard reads their names without looking up, "Bugato. Comstock." The brim of his cap is low on his forehead, but she can tell that he doesn't bother to read their tickets. They are the Americanos, the only ones here, and there is never any question, the Americanos always pay. He doesn't ask what they are doing, going to Cedros, to a place that, in no conceivable reality, is a tourist destination and that might not even have a hotel, perhaps only *cuartos* for itinerant cannery workers or visiting family; or why, if they are going to this disagreeable place, if for some reason they must go, they are only staying four nights. What job can one accomplish in three days and four nights? He doesn't ask what this graceful young woman with her worried eyes is doing with this *cabrón* and his *cámera cara*. That is how she knows they must look, the roles that have taken them over. He doesn't follow them to the plane; he's already heading back to the terminal, already saying something to the man leaning in the doorframe rolling his cigarette butt between thumb and finger with a kind of nostalgia, both their jobs done now and the plane, with its human and sundry cargo, fragments of the abruptly concluded present.

Clair and Mason gather up their bags and walk alone to the open door of the C-47.

CHAPTER 2

Whatever hen you are a twin, the world is your sister. *Nina.*
Clair was the first out and the biggest, and so far as the
doctor knew, the only one. But then came Nina, and Nina did
not come without a fight. There was a lot of blood, several transfusions, and
it may be a certain unconscious resentment. Louise Bugato was not fond of
surprises. She did not love easily, but once she did, she loved with a deep
and durable promise. Her people were Bavarian, three generations in California, and they kept the transplant's loyalty to origins and its customs.
Like her mother, Louise ran a tight ship. So: twins. But there was only one
of everything back at the house and so now a scramble of last-minute duplicate purchases and because it was September and picking season and Henry
was needed in the fields, a nursemaid to help. But Henry was beside himself. Twins!

Nina was the prettiest, her features falling expertly into place, her
demeanor calm and watchful, despite her embattled entry into the world.
As the second born—born almost an hour after Clair—she was the per-
fected version, as if in that hour God had made quick amendments to His
initial effort. Although they were fraternal twins and there were clearly
two sacs, they looked so remarkably close to identical, yet not close enough,

that the pediatrician began to talk about a new category of twins, near-identical twins or half-identical, she had read about, the babies sharing 75 percent of the genetic inheritance. A tightly timed sequence of cellular events, the egg fertilized by two sperm, and then immediately, the egg dividing, not dying as it ought to have, and then two separate placentas, two babies, two lives bound forever by the thinnest of threads, infinitesimal timing.

They were warm-skinned babies with ginger tones in their dark hair, and as they grew and their hair thickened, sunlight made a game of spinning titian filaments. For a while, Clair stayed the bigger of the two, but by the time they were three there was little difference in their height and weight. "Nina is catching up," their mother remarked to the pediatrician during a checkup.

"Well," said the doctor, reviewing the two charts, "it's not that. Clair has slowed down." And she showed the mother the graphs, Nina's growth rate angling up and Clair's beginning to flatten.

Mrs. Bugato smiled with cosmic satisfaction. "Twins . . . everything's got to be fair."

Nina was the prettiest, but she was not the most loveable. She seemed to expect people to come to her, parents and friends, even the dogs, and whenever they did not, it was as if an invisible emissary had carried instead a tiny somber weight to her shoulder so that by the time she was five, she seemed already to bear a grudge against the world. Her dark eyes acquired a look of wary calculation, and she developed a habit of asking questions to keep others from finding ways in, questions with answers that might go on awhile and to which she paid only sideways attention. She seemed always to have a secret and she laughed at odd moments, and long after they had stopped being babies, for no apparent reason or gain, her voice would climb and pinch into babyish inflections, like a psychological *non sequitur*.

But Clair . . . Clair was *obvious*—running to her father when he came in from the cellar or the vineyards, or wrapping her arm around her mother's leg as if it were a pillar made for just that purpose, for hanging onto, or jumping in bed with her parents as soon as they awakened each morning. She was not exactly demanding, just so happy that they were there when she was there, great living comforting god-toys, happy that she belonged to them and to that mountaintop west of Napa Valley where patchwork vineyards fell from the summits in quilted folds and billows. Children seem to have no religion. Their parents are their religion, and they are born zealots. Gods, sometimes monsters of God, but always godly.

Did she remember that Nina was still back in their shared bedroom, or notice that Clair was winning some unannounced competition? It came so easily to Clair, winning, that almost from the beginning, it felt entirely natural, like air to breathe and sleep when you were sleepy and food the instant an aimless pang of hunger quickened into something like anxiety. Would there be food? Of course there would be food. Food and comfort, victory and fellowship.

One morning she returned to their bedroom almost as soon as she had bolted from it. She felt uneasy. Suddenly it did not seem right that Nina never piled into their parents' bed each morning to jump about and hide under covers and generally demand the affection that a whole night away in sleep had rendered vaguely unreal and unreliable. Parental love. Nina was out of bed too, standing at the dresser, her back to the door. There was a knife in her hand, one of the harvest knives that were kept in a wooden box, its thin, sickle-shaped blade as shiny and lithe as a fingerling cutting through fast water. They were not supposed to play with the harvest knives, or even to enter the field house where the picking equipment and sulfur and other dangerous things were stored. Harvest knives were very small and very sharp, so that a good picker might reach up under the canopy of leaves with one hand to cup a bunch of grapes and with the other, and the slightest flick of his wrist, sever it from the vine. Any child could hold one in her hand, they were so light. But no child was supposed to.

Nina was cutting something into the top of the dresser. Clair came up behind her to inspect the carving, just a line of small o's, and then x's over them. Nina was not the artist that Clair was. She preferred to build things, like the boys down the road, with Erector Sets and Tinker Toys, not draw pictures or fashion things out of clay. And when it came to stories in books, she was remarkably . . . *dumb* about why things happened the way they did. It was so surprising to Clair that she almost didn't believe it. But it hardly mattered anyway, because Nina had no interest in Clair's explanations. If it was something she didn't know, then it wasn't worth knowing.

"Nina?"

"What." There was nothing in her voice, and that worried Clair. The skin under her arms began to tingle. There was no point in telling her sister that she would get in trouble.

"What are you doing?"

"Nothing. Thinking."

"What about?"

She shrugged. "Things."

Clair was trying to figure out how they would hide the o's and x's. Maybe they could put one of their mother's runners over the markings, or color them out with brown crayon. *Burnt Sienna*, that was the color she would choose. "Like what things?"

"None of your bee's wax."

"Why?"

Nina swung around. "Well," she said, her tone utterly different now, informative and friendly, "when I have a thought and I'm done having it, I cross it out and have another. There are lots of thoughts. Thoughts can't do anything bad. Uncle Sal told me that. They're just bubbles in my head that pop."

This seemed so perfectly reasonable, or it was said in a way that implied that there was nothing *un*reasonable about it, that Clair said simply, "Oh." And then, after a pause, "Like what thoughts?"

Nina smiled brightly, and even to Clair at that young age, she saw how very pretty her sister was and felt proud, and maybe scared, too. Her prettiness was a force in and of itself, apart from her, apart from the two of them together. "Like pierced ears. I was thinking about pierced ears."

Some of the girls who belonged to the Mexican pickers, girls their age and even younger, had pierced ears and in them wore the tiniest jewel studs—rubies and sapphires and emeralds. Clair had been longing for blue stars on her ears, and the girls had been after their mother to take them to the shop in town where it could be done. But Mrs. Bugato said not until they were at least eight, which was so far away that the girls knew it would never happen. She may as well have said when you're grown-up, which was also a faraway place that they would never get to go to, like the North Pole or Disneyland or Lake Berryessa.

"We have to wait," Clair said—it was a statement—running her fingertip along the crude line of x's.

"I don't see why."

"She said."

Nina gazed thoughtfully out the window. "If one of us has pierced ears, she has to let the other one."

This was irrefutable logic, Clair knew. With twins everything had to be fair.

"I'll let you go first. I don't mind waiting a little," Nina added. Once again, this made sense to Clair: if Nina was going to get something out of it then there was really nothing left to question. And Nina possessed an uncanny talent for patience and timing. The whole deal suddenly acquired the weight of plausibility and with that, broad permission. It was like going to the beach where the instant you set foot on the sand, customary rules no longer applied. You could take off your shoes and get wet and sandy, and run off, a long ways off, and throw things and dig up things, eat with your fingers and pee in the water.

Sometimes when things hurt, their mother put ice on it. And so Clair was told to fetch a tray of ice. Nina's thought was graduating into something more than a thought that she might think and then cross out. When she returned, Clair lay down with her head against the pillow, and Nina held cubes of ice to her ear lobes, one in front and one in back.

After a few minutes she said, "Now I'm going to make the hole for the post, so don't move." Clair watched her sister. There was a calm concentration about her face, an authority in the way her small pink lips tightened to the task. Nina was the meticulous one, her side of the room always tidy, her toys lined up like obedient soldiers awaiting instructions, her playtime plans premeditated and sequenced in a way that convinced Clair and their friends that she knew what she was doing and ought to be in charge, and so she was often in charge.

Clair felt something warm against her neck and it was running down, and she touched it, and it was the brightest red blood, so much of it that Nina straightened, a strange look of surprise in her eyes, followed by something like fear and a smile that was . . . unsound. The smile seemed to be trying to undo what she had just done. She had the good sense to holler for her father, but it was Louise Bugato who came; then the great fuss of words, a towel pressed to Clair's ear, the flurried ride to the doctor's office down in St. Helena. The lobe was hanging by the last little bit of itself, and had to be stitched back to the rest of Clair's ear. The doctor positioned a green sheet over her face, and then folded back one corner by her ear, so that she could not see his expression or what he was doing, she could only hear the tools clinking softly in his hands and his breath coming and going in a series of sighs, breath that smelled vaguely swampy. "It's just a teaspoon of blood," he said several times, in between telling her how brave she was and what a fancy little scar she was going to have to brag about, and why—*really*—had she let her sister do this? Then in the car winding back up the mountain, her mother asking what could have *possessed* her.

After that, whenever she was nervous, Clair fingered the fine white scar as if it might offer up some truth she couldn't quite make out.

A WINERY WITH its own vineyards was a grand place for a child to grow up on. There was always something happening and plenty of people around, field workers and cellar workers, and then the monthly tastings with neighboring winemakers and their wives or husbands, the borrowing of equipment and picking crews, the barrel rackings, the bottle lines that arrived in a big white truck, the dark, high-shouldered bottles of Cabernet Sauvignon laid down and stacked in long low walls, and the moldy vinous smell of the caves dug into the hillsides. The Mayacamas Mountains were developing a style recognizably distinct from the valley wines where the soil and drainage and climate were different, loamy and deep. The soil on the western slopes was volcanic, porous with an orangey hue. Iron. It drained more readily and held fewer nutrients, so the vines had to compete. Competition was a good thing, Henry told them; the grape flavors were concentrated and the yields lower but the grapes more prized for their character and complexity. Their vineyards were above the fog line but not the frost, and their harvest always came later than the valley floor, later by two weeks, with maybe lower sugars but higher acids, and Cabs that were reticent, taking longer to age and open up, to give themselves over to the deep sensuality of their innate character.

It was the early seventies and subregional fraternities were beginning to form, terroir to terroir, microclimate to microclimate. Each growing area had its own problems, and those problems were only just being sorted out and talked about. Bugato Vineyards were up on Spring Mountain, a twenty-minute drive from St. Helena. "Well, what are they doing over at Mt. Veeder? How is Mayacamas dealing with the high acids this year? The bunch rot? The hard tannins are shutting down the flavors . . . how to soften them, reduce the aging time . . ." Except for the wine judgings, the competition between the growing districts and the wineries was mostly collegial. In those days, putting Napa Valley on the international map was the primary objective, and whatever sibling rivalries there might have been were easily driven beneath this larger purpose. They were mostly small wineries often founded by people who had had earlier incarnations as lawyers, doctors, entrepreneurs. Henry Bugato had been a banker in San Francisco when he and his brother, Sal, a restaurant owner in the city, decided to buy a hundred acres in the Mayacamus Mountains and plant grapes. The Bugatos were originally from southern Italy, and Henry's father, Mauro, never let them forget the wines of his homeland, Lacryma Christi from the slopes of Mt. Vesuvius, and the dark drama of Primitivo, the same but not quite the same as the Zinfandels of California.

Yes, a world of vineyards and wineries was a fine place to grow up in, where farmers were artists and artists rode tractors and the Paris newspapers complained about the California growers who never had to chaptalize and where you could drink the wines in half the time it took the wines of Bordeaux to mature; where the wines were big and ripe and dramatic, saying everything that the grape might say on its best day, in a perfect year. The French said, *"La beauté du Diable"*—The beauty of the Devil.

"What does that mean?" Clair asked her father.

"It means that something is too good to be true."

By the time they were six, the twins could use a corkscrew like master sommeliers.

THEY WERE ALWAYS referred to as *the twins*—a singular entity that demanded a unified response. Everything had to be equal, everything had to be shared, and if something was not equal or not properly shared, it must be publicly, officially evened out so that whoever was on the short end of the current negotiation would know that swift measures were being taken that would put things right. Their fancy clothes were the same, but different colors; their candlewick bedspreads identical; their doll cradles pink and white. For Christmas, Clair got Malibu Barbie and Nina, Busy Barbie; their wagons were respectively blue and red, as were their battery-powered toy VWs that terrorized the dogs. Stuffed animals might be different, but they had to be approximately the same size, and neither could have more than the other sister. Louise believed in chores, in being a "good citizen of the house," no matter the age—so the twins were assigned daily jobs that were theoretically equivalent in duration and effort.

One morning Clair was to dust the living room furniture and Nina told to water the potted plants on the patio. But Nina always seemed to take longer than anticipated, or she dillydallied, and then Clair might be told to help her, or even assigned a second chore to give Nina a chance to catch up. Clair could see her sister through the window aiming the hose into the air, or up at the wild doves that liked to nest in the wisteria vine trained along the eaves. Every now and then she might let the water find a potted lemon or the box of red geraniums under the big picture window, but when she caught Clair watching through the window, she shot the water at the glass and laughed at Clair's startled face.

Clair ran outside. "Why'd you do that?"

"You were watching me."

"So?"

"I don't like you watching. It's not nice." Nina's eyes never wavered. She said this as if everyone ought to know, and Clair immediately felt bad.

"Well I only want you to hurry up so we can go find Daddy and sit on the tractor."

"I don't like ugly people watching me."

"But we're the same."

Nina's lips thinned into something like a smile. The sun was behind her, but Clair could see the stripe of white that was her teeth. "Not quite." Not quite was what everyone always said about them, *not quite* identical, a phrase that seemed to contain miles of difference that Nina regularly paced out and measured and enforced. She did not want to be anything like Clair; she was ashamed of her niceness and the weakness it hinted at, and she was frequently glad to explain this sad fact to her sister.

Clair glanced back at the window where the hose had sprayed. The force of the water had kicked up potting soil from the geranium box, so the glass was not only wet but spattered with bits of dirt and bark. "She's gonna be mad."

Nina stuck the hose in the next pot and casually said, "If you clean it, I'll do the watering. Then we can find Daddy."

So Clair cleaned the window with rags from under the kitchen sink, and soon enough the two girls made their way down the hill into the lower vineyard where their father was working. On the way, Nina took her sister's hand and Clair gave two skips, one for each of them. She was happy. Their baby brother had arrived that year, and his presence, along with their mother's preoccupation with him, had cinched the lines between the girls. Nina did not often take her hand. They were always together, but not quite. Some of their friends had made-up sisters or brothers who thought or did things, often things that might have gotten them into trouble, bad impulses or naughty behavior, like taking change from the coat pockets in the hall closet to buy candy from the Oakville grocery. So it was a great advantage, Clair decided, not having to imagine a sister who looked so much like you and who could be and act so contrarily. She already had one who was real. From the beginning, Clair's job was plain: to be the good girl.

It was May, and the flowering vines were giving way to fruit set, so that at the end of each slender shoot clusters of tight green balls, the size of baby peas, had grown. The mustard weed had formed a yellow haze down the center of the rows, and in some of the wetter depressions were lingering patches of lime yellow oxalis. The wild marigolds took the margins; poppies and lupines grew here and there as reminders that it was still spring, and they were still king and queen of California wildflowers. Henry Bugato was bending over, inspecting a vine, his head half-concealed beneath the canopy of grape leaves. Clair never noticed his skin, except when someone remarked upon it, a friend or an overheard adult, but that day beneath his straw hat, it was noticeably describing of her father. The amorphous areas of light and dark pigmentation that, to her, were like land and sea on maps, or good and bad, never seemed to bother him. She liked to trace her finger along the edges of one to the next, good to bad, land to sea, and he in turn tolerated her explorations. She was learning the topography of his face. They had even begun to name the light continents and the dark seas, to dream of voyages little girls might make one day. In spite of the pigmentation, he was a beautiful man with a quiet smile, never so big that you couldn't trust it, and never so restrained that you wondered about his true feelings; and his soft eyes, even if he had wanted, could not hide the simple native intelligence he brought to everything.

Clair ducked under the canopy and forced her father to regard her. "Hi," she chirped, and he let his fingers wander blindly to the tip of her nose, as though it were a pink grape. As though nobody could really see anyone except through the touch of fingers.

"Almost ripe enough," he said, musing. "I just might have to sample this one, see how sweet it is."

She clapped her hand over her nose and peered up at him. The sunlight was coming through the brim of his straw hat in tiny diamonds, so that his pigmented face was twinkling with stars.

Straightening, he hoisted her up and swung her onto the tractor seat where Nina had already staked a claim. "Scootch," he told her.

Nina didn't budge. Instead, she asked him about the fruit set, the twins having already acquired all the lingo of making wine, and that led him away from the issue of sharing the tractor seat to harvest speculations, at least for a minute or two. But eventually he told her, "When you're big enough to take up the whole thing, you can have it. For now, share it with your sister."

"No," she said, looking determinedly ahead and gripping the steering wheel, as if she were driving it down the row. "No, no, no."

He smiled gently. "Nina for no. That's a word you use too well and too often, little one."

Clair did not want to get her sister into trouble. With their father, they would never get into much trouble, not like with their mother, but as a rule she did not want their parents to take sides. Everything had to be fair, even when one of them was wrong. She squirmed out of his arms and wandered down the row, picking up dirt clods and tossing them at the trunks of the vines. She had wanted to sit in the tractor seat, she had been looking forward to it all morning, but it seemed more important to Nina, and anyway, there were other things she could do and maybe like just as well, though at that moment it did not seem possible. A knot of misery grew in her throat.

Released from his Solomonic duties, Henry followed the course he had already begun, stopping to check the occasional vine, cupping the green clusters, palming up the canopy of leaves to ensure that there was enough protection from the sun. By the time they reached the bottom of the row where the oak trees began, Clair had begun gathering wildflowers for the vase on the kitchen windowsill. Even at that early age, she was enchanted by plants, plants of any kind, and she had a remarkable facility for remembering leaf configurations and the particular places where each green thing liked to grow, what it seemed to need from the little disk of world surrounding it.

Suddenly, behind them, Nina pushed the button that sent the wailing call of the tractor across the vineyard. Henry had had a horn installed that year because of a nasty accident last season on one of the steeper slopes. The tractor had rolled, crushing a worker's leg, and he had lain there the better part of a morning, waiting for help.

Henry stopped, dropped both arms, slowly turned and pointed to the ground. Nina climbed down and tramped back up to the house. Clair watched her sister yank one of the clusters of baby grapes from a vine and toss it where her father would be sure to see it. Before that could happen, Clair would have to collect the cluster and throw it away.

Why didn't Nina care about making them mad? Why did nothing nice matter to her? She didn't even like being hugged; she was always watching from some corner, or acting like things didn't interest her. She was always up to some secret something.

Henry Bugato was a tall man, beautifully educated in Jesuit schools, then Carnegie Mellon, who possessed a mannered, old-world bearing that he had deliberately adopted from his father, Mauro, to honor him. He never raised his voice, and it was well-known among the workers that the angrier he was, the quieter he became, so that a whisper from Henry Bugato was as thunderous as a sonic boom. He had a mellifluous voice, the voice of a tenor who happened at the moment not to be singing but who kept the phrasing and syncopation of song. There was nothing nicer to Clair than late afternoons finding him in the barrel room with Eric, his assistant winemaker, who lived in a cottage on the property with his wife, tasting from each barrel and keeping up a running commentary on the developing wine while the assistant made notes in the cellar book. She could hear her father's voice long before she had sorted out where exactly he was, winding her way between the stacked barrels and puncheons, his voice a trail to treasure. But the barrel room was not a safe place for a child because what if there was an earthquake and one of the barrels came loose, and rolled off and crushed her? So when she did find him, the first thing he did was to lift her up to safety and then would come the gentle reprimand, "Clair, you'll end up flat as a flat worm," or "How will I find you when the barrels come tumbling down?"

But later that afternoon she did not go to find her father in the cellar room. Instead, their mother took them shopping for spring clothes. There were other winemakers coming to the house for a meeting, and Louise wanted to give them enough time without the Bugato offspring underfoot. Clair was in the dressing room, trying on birthday dresses, and it was Nina, not her mother, occupied with the fussing baby, who brought Clair things to try on—pastel dresses with lace and puffy underskirts. She was being so very nice to Clair, so attentive and motherly, calling her Clairsie and cocking her head like an eager and trusting puppy.

"But don't you want to try some on?" Clair asked when the last batch arrived.

"I'll pick what you pick," Nina said. So she was in a good mood, she wanted Clair to get something they might otherwise fight about.

"But a different color," Clair said, pressing the yellow one to her chest.

"I like the blue anyway."

"Okey dokey."

"Hunky-dory."

"Peachy keen."

"Holy moly."

They laughed themselves into hiccups until the store clerk herded them out of the dressing room and back to their mother, who had finally managed to placate the baby. Nina stuck her fingers under his chin and tickled him so hard that he began to scream again while Clair pretended that it hadn't really happened. His name was Tony. So far as she could tell, he wasn't much fun yet, except that he did make goofy sounds with his lips and he was crawling all over the place, like a piglet. Now and then, she liked to imitate Tony, which got her mother's attention. For a while, she might even play along, pretending that Clair was still a baby, too. Nina was especially scornful of this game, and usually had to leave the room whenever it began.

So the near-identical dresses were purchased, one yellow, one blue, and they went home. The meeting was just breaking up. Henry was loading the dishwasher with the wine glasses they had used to taste Cabs from the last vintage, and a dozen or so vintners were clogging the front hall, their faces rosy with alcohol and camaraderie. When they had finally left, the last one a little wonky on his feet and being towed off by another, the girls tried on their new dresses for their father.

"Princess one, princess two," he declared and off they went while dinner was cooked.

Everyone was tired after dinner; everyone wanted the day to end. But it was a day that would never, ever end. Not for Louise, not for Nina and Clair—it might have grayed and tattered and found some cubbyhole to fit itself into, wadded up in a drawer in the back closet of the mind where clothes you would no longer wear found refuge, former selves and unpleasant memories, things you ought never to have done or seen or tried. And not for Henry—not especially for Henry who didn't seem to have a drawer or a closet in the back room where no one ever went any more. For Henry, everything was eternally present, demanding the same accounting day after day, with the same results year after year.

The baby would now eat spaghetti, along with the rice and pureed fruits and vegetables Louise regularly prepared from scratch. Sitting in his highchair, he squeezed it up into his rubbery mouth, swallowing a tiny portion in a way that seemed purely accidental, then out it would come into his plastic pelican bib where Louise, practical about such things, would spoon it back up for a second ascent. The girls watched with fascination his happy barbarism, red sauce smeared across his face and one noodle clinging like a tracing of a future big smile from the corner of his mouth clear round to his ear.

"Anthony, old chap," Henry said, "you've disgraced yourself." Henry liked to address his new son in highbrow borrowings that seemed especially to please his wife as though she were solely responsible for introducing aristocracy into the House of Bugato.

Tony answered with something like a high-pitched extended *Ha*! and then broke into his version of song, his fist crammed into the corner of his mouth and a babbling repetitive eruption, *labba-labba-labba*. Nina egged him on and Clair collapsed in laughter, and then their mother said, "Enough," because she was exhausted, she said, and don't "you girls" have anything better to do than to get the baby all charged up at the end of the day? A bath would calm him down. A warm bath always calmed him down.

"Go and fill the tub." Or had she said, "Go and fill his tub" or "the baby tub?" No one could remember. "I'll be along in a minute." Everyone remembered that. She was busy swabbing off the worst of the spaghetti and lifting Tony down into his walker chair, the one that he could maneuver by himself around the house, his fat little toes and feet slapping the hardwood and sending him wheeling about. Henry cleared the table and began emptying wine glasses out of the now-dry dishwasher so that he could refill it with the dinner plates. He held one of the glasses up to the light where it winked in flawless clarity back at him and, satisfied, hung it from the stemware rack. He had been meaning to set up a different water-heating system for the house and winery, one that didn't have to be set so high, and that hadn't happened yet. In the meantime, the tanks had to be sterilized, the cement floors hosed down, the glasses washed free of residue. But he hadn't gotten around to it yet; he had been meaning to, he said later, but he hadn't gotten around to it. There was always so much to do at a winery.

Clair flounced down to her parents' bedroom where there was a full-length mirror, wanting to see all of herself in the new dress before having to take it off for bed. She could hear the water running in the hall bathroom and, more distantly, her parents talking in the kitchen.

It took a long time for night to come to California, for the late afternoon yellows and pinks to withdraw from the sky, emitting what she imagined was a soft fizzling sound, and so even though it was late, the big window that took up the south wall of the bedroom was not black yet but the deepest peacock blue. So that was behind her, peacock blue. In the mirror her yellow dress was especially pretty, with the blue behind her. She remembers that, yellow and blue. And then going into her parents' bathroom to rummage through the caddy that held her mother's makeup, finding the lipstick, the orangey one, the one her mother wore to fancy dinner parties. Clair remembers running it back and forth across her lips and, before she left, studying a tampon from the box on the back of the toilet and thinking that it was some kind of fat straw and liking the crinkly sound of the paper, like wrapping paper, but also knowing somehow the way children do that she should not ask her mother about it, that it was still too big a mystery, maybe a bad and dirty mystery, else why would it live only in her mother's bathroom?

She could hear Tony's walker pinballing down the hall. The walls were scuffed with dashes and darts wherever he had run into them just above the baseboards, and Louise was already planning to repaint once he was walking on his own. She liked to keep up with things, minor repairs and the like. Not a day went by that she wasn't deadheading flowers, or polishing a piece of silver she had inherited from her grandparents, or changing the hem on a skirt to keep up with fashion. Once a year, she sorted through everyone's clothes, culling and bagging them for the Goodwill truck that parked down at the edge of town every weekend. Sometimes an item of clothing would go missing from Henry's side of the closet, last week a pair of brown cords she was famously tired of seeing him in, and he pretended to be angry, and she pretended that she didn't know what had happened to them—the dryer ate things. "It does," Clair assured her father because she, too, had been missing something favorite, the sock with the ladybugs, though that had eventually turned up in Nina's drawer.

Behind Clair on her parents' bed was a pink duvet. Not candy pink, but cameo pink, faded and old-looking. So there was that color too—pink.

From the kitchen, the sound of a glass breaking. Her breath caught; someone would be in trouble. But no, her mother was laughing. Maybe they were kissing. Things were always happening when people kissed, glasses broke and stuff went unnoticed. The pantry door squeaked (he was going to fix that, too), broken glass swept and rattled into the metal dustpan, voices, softer now, murmuring. The bath water still running. Tony singing his *labba-labba-labba* song, then one of his sudden *Ha*'s shot down the hall, and back to the *labba-labbas*. The walker charging another wall, plastic on sheetrock, *thwump*.

Now it really was getting dark, and she decided to put on more lipstick and show herself off to Nina, but this time the lipstick broke. She had pressed too hard. Opening the window, she tossed the orange bullet out into the night. The crickets and tree frogs were so loud that she stood for a moment or two, just listening. They were ringing or singing or screaming at each other all at once, and it did not sound alive but like machinery gone haywire and sending up an alarm. The air smelled of wet dirt with something sweet but not nice-sweet on top, dying flowers, but it was too early for them to die so she didn't know what it was, she only knew that it was not a good smell, not a spring smell. Not far from the house stood four young redwood trees that her father had planted, the color disappeared from them now. They were just black cutouts with a gray lacy fringe along each bough, the four of them pointing straight up and keeping their line as they nailed themselves into the sky. Up in the sky, the stars were fizzy and bright. Something big flapped down from one of the tall Douglas firs that stood beyond the redwoods and she closed the window. An owl maybe.

And then there was a different screaming, singing, ringing, screaming, a crazy mad sound, the sound of air shattered and space wobbled and time stopped, especially in her head, and her ears hurting as she's running out of the wobbly room and down the hall where the steam is coming from, and then in the bathroom, through the steam, Nina, her hand or her hands on the faucet going one way, going the other way, and Tony's walker taking up the middle of the cramped room, but Clair does get past it, does see what's in the tub, it's just the color red, that's all, the most amazing red bubble puddles, small ones and big ones with streaks swirling curling feathering off. Her father is behind her now slamming into the walker, into her, and she feels the water splashing, hot water, and it seems he has Tony in his arms, but it's not Tony, it's something lumpy and red with peels of pink coming off. Behind him now her mother with her arms empty and strange and shaking down to fingertips, and her eyes as black as the trees that were already nailing themselves into the night.

Yellow, blue, orange, pink, black . . . *red*. Red was the memory of that night, the color that took over all the other colors.

Before they fled with Tony, Louise glanced with a look of horror and confusion at Clair, at the lipstick gashed across her mouth. "I don't understand." That was all she said. *I don't understand.*

THEY ONLY HAD to eat one of Eric's wife's meals, instant oatmeal, not the cooked kind their mother made in a pot on the stove that took so long and held its shape even with milk cratered around it. Susan was her name. She was pregnant. Susan wouldn't look at either one of them, but the next day it was only Nina she wouldn't look at. By late morning, they heard tires crunching through the pea gravel, two car doors, then the front door opening, voices in the entryway, Susan saying, "Oh god!" and not long after there was the sound of the front door opening and quietly closing again. The girls were sitting on the floor of their bedroom playing a board game, *Chutes & Ladders.* Nina looked up. "Hi," she said. Someone passed, no one answered.

Soon their mother called them to the kitchen and set two plates with grilled cheese sandwiches before them, two glasses of milk, fruit salad in a big bowl. Much too much fruit salad for two girls, enough fruit salad for all the children of the world. How long had she stood there, peeling and slicing and chopping up fruit, her hands trembling, her hair uncombed, a runaway look in her eyes? After she had put the food down, she straightened and paused and smoothed down her apron, the way a waitress does after she's delivered the order to the table and asks, *Do you have everything you need?*

They didn't see her for two days. She had done her duty and was released now to flee into the shelter of madness.

All that first day Henry kept them with him wherever he went, into the vineyards, the winery office, the caves where he inspected ullages on the older vintages, one bottle at a time, but he didn't seem to be paying much attention because the ones with low fills went right back where they had been in the rack with the others that were not flawed. Two sheriff's cars came up the drive and, not long after they left, the cleaning lady's Ford showed up though she had already been to the house that week. Finally, Henry walked them up through the vineyards and around the courtyard to the kitchen door, stooping to brush his fingers across the oregano and thyme growing between the cobbles and stopping again at the door as if an invisible beast had knocked the wind out of him for a minute. There he stood, staggered, his right hand gripping the frame, unwilling to reach for the door knob. At the stove, he heated up a can of alphabet soup, keeping his back to the twins until it was time to serve the bowls, the crackers, the glasses of milk for them and wine for himself, no food. It was nothing like dinners their mother prepared and so, in that respect, more fun, like camping, or like the times when the babysitter cooked and then let them eat more than the allowable number of cookies.

In his quietest, gentlest voice he said, "It's time for you girls to say now what happened."

"Where's Tony?" Nina asked.

Clair said, "The water was red."

Henry winced. "Before that."

Nina had just spooned up some soup and was blowing across it. "It was too hot." And then after slurping the soup into her mouth, "Mama said to fill the tub."

"Too hot," Henry said to himself.

Nina nodded.

"But you were helping your mama."

Clair fiddled with her spoon. Nina stared across the table at her father. Finally she nodded.

"She was trying to help," Clair said with a rush of encouragement as if this was the way out of all of it, out of the dark spell that had taken over their family, the spell of silence, of strange people coming and going, of nothing being paid the old kind of attention.

Her father was looking at her with sudden alertness. The pale parts of his skin were pinking and the dark patches were the color of grapes. "Where were you?"

"In your room . . . mostly. I wanted to see my dress in the big mirror."

He dropped his head. "Lipstick . . . ," he said to the floor.

"It broke. I'm sorry. Will you tell mama I'm sorry?"

"She doesn't care about lipstick. Who gives a . . . a tinker's damn about lipstick, Clair? Why would anyone care about lipstick?"

"I'm sorry."

Now he turned to Nina. "Nina, what about the little tub, Tony's tub? Why did you let the water fill the whole tub? How did you lift Tony into the tub? How did you do that all by yourself? Clair didn't help you?"

"I don't need Clair's help. I don't need anybody's help."

His twin hands had been folded in a calm, almost affectionate bundle on the table, but now he pulled them apart and lay them very carefully, as if they were breakable or hurt or in need of a time-out, palms down and fingers splinted straight out, each one separately on top of each thigh. Nina was intent on spelling out her name with the alphabet noodles, assembling the letters on the table beside her bowl, then swimming her spoon through the soup for the next letter. It was only the A she needed now. "Is that why you didn't wait for your mother?" he asked, trying to corner her eyes. She was still fishing for the A in the yellowy depths of the soup.

"Sure."

"Sure?"

"Yeah, sure."

"But is that why?"

"Is what why?"

Something flashed across his face, a shadow, and Clair thought of the owl from the night before, the shadow of its great wings against the pale shadow of the night.

Henry whispered, "How did you get his clothes off?"

Nina glanced up brightly. She had captured the A now; it was floating all by itself in the hollow of the spoon. "Oh, they came right off. The diaper, too."

Clair was watching her sister, her eyes so sparkly, so pretty, so proud. She had the purest features, like a doll's. Nina placed the A at the end of her name and, using the edge of the spoon, neatened up the letters.

"It wasn't poopy," she added without looking up, as if, had it been, she might have waited for her mother. And nothing bad would have happened.

Slowly Henry rolled his head back and forth, his eyes closed and the eyeballs bulging behind the lids. He took a sip of wine and set the glass carefully back down, then he decided to take another, longer drink, and then he just ran his thumb back and forth along the bottom edge of the glass, faster and faster. Over the counter, the clock was ticking, and outside Clair could hear the crickets and the frogs setting up their alarm, and down the hall, the loud and forbidding silence of her parents' bedroom door shut all day was booming up from the depths, from the dark earth underneath their house clear up to the base of her throat and filling it with a hard hollow shape as big as a walnut.

"Is Tony okay?" she said. All day she had been afraid to ask, and Nina had seemed strangely uninterested. But everything had happened so fast that hardly anything seemed to have happened, or could possibly have happened enough to be real and bother any of them, so why *should* Nina wonder?

"Tony?" His lips moved in a strange way. "Tony is gone. Anthony Mauro Bugato," he said, reeling out the words as if he were introducing a character in what was now a storybook, a little prince, a perfect boy. His voice was very soft, very beautiful, a trilling, a little song of sounds, but Clair heard, too, something like astonishment. "My boy is gone."

For a long while no one said anything. Henry poured himself more wine and the girls ate their soup. The clock kept ticking, slow unwilling ticks forward, and out the window it sounded like a jungle with the treefrogs and crickets and the piercing cry of a single screech owl and then Boomer, one of winery dogs, giving voice to the wild, naked, and improvident night. The indoor silence grew bigger. Silence, she learned that night, was not something gone but something too big to hear.

Full of twitches and worries, her lower lip quivering, Nina's face was not looking like her face. "Daddy?" she said.

"What?" He did not lift his eyes from the table, but then, as if finally he had to, as if there was yet another father in the room even bigger and older than he himself who was telling him to, he drew his head up and regarded her with spent indifference. "What is it you want to say? Nina." Adding her name did something, broke something—the silence, the spell, the ticking clock, all their hearts all at once.

"Nothing."

"Nothing?"

"Nothing. I . . . I spelled my name," she said as if in afterthought.

Henry rose from the table, gathering their dishes, and when his back was turned, Nina used her spoon to smash the letters she had taken such pains to align, and her face had gone back to the way it usually was, pure and untouched.

CHAPTER 3

Because he knows that she doesn't like it, though she has never told him why, Ethan insists on a bath whenever Clair goes away. It is how he punishes her. Instead of resisting, she lets him have his way, but she always sits with him in the narrow tiled room, reading aloud or listening to him talk. Usually he prefers to shower the way a man does. In spite of his intelligence, he still likes to have the toys around him, the boats and rubber creatures of the sea, and she likes to hear the stories he makes, the elaborate confabulations with their intricate and telling plotlines. This one is about a shipwrecked rat throwing a beach party—*Rattus rattus*, Ethan calls him because he is already learning some of the Latin names for animals. The island ogress has gone away in a "dark mood," and the only thing to do is to have a big party and eat up all the good coconuts so that there won't be any food when she comes back. And maybe *Rattus rattus* will build a raft and go away before she comes back, so that there won't be him either. And the ogress will have a "dready" feeling before she even sets foot back on the island because something tells her that she has made a "wretched" mistake going away.

"But *Rattus rattus* comes back, doesn't he?" she says, making a pouty face. "He brings mangos and papayas, and they plant the seeds so that they don't have to depend only on coconuts."

Ethan tips the bow of one of his boats so that it begins to fill with bath water and, just as it's about to sink, lifts it carefully from the depths, drains it, and nudges it toward the faucet end of the tub. "Maybe." He scrunches up his face. "But not the papaya. Papayas are too tropical. This island is in the temperate zone."

"Ah, of course."

Tucking him into bed that night, she fingers the damp hair off his forehead and smiles down at his face, so openly serious. He hasn't learned yet that seriousness is something to hide or apologize for, and she hopes that she can resist being the sort of mother who jollies her children out of gravitas, as if it's a bad mood or a virus, something to be got over. Again, in spite of all he knows and can think or say at this early age, in spite of the quick and easy interpretations that suggest an adult, he is still only six and snugged up to his chest is Mr. Dickens, a thuggish bulldog whose stuffing has begun to escape just around the lower lip so that he looks to be foaming at the mouth. They have agreed that Mr. Dickens needs stitches but they have not set the date yet for the procedure. Ethan needs to plan things out precisely, to know long in advance when important events are to occur, in order that he has time to study all the variables and methods and prepare himself properly. He is a nervous child, rangy and strong for his size, but given to hypochondriacal worries that extend to Mr. Dickens or his mother or sometimes his cello teacher, Mr. Bergen, but lately mostly to Mason.

"There are rattlesnakes in Baja," he tells her. "One that doesn't rattle, so you can't hear it. Mason should be extra careful."

"I'll make sure he is."

"I don't like Mason," he adds, glancing away and scratching Mr. Dickens between the ears.

"He likes you."

"How do you know?"

"He says so."

"You go on trips with him. He makes you."

She tries to poke some of the stuffing back into Mr. Dicken's lip. "He doesn't make me," she says. "I want to go. To help him with his work. But this time I'll be doing some work, too, you know, identifying and counting plants on an island called Cedros."

Instantly Ethan cups his hands over his eyes, and she realizes her mistake. He seems to think that she can't see him if he can't see her, and right now he would rather she didn't see his face shipwrecked with feelings. "Why do you want to leave me? Why don't you want to take me with you? Why do we have to have Mason around? We were happy before Mason. Mason is a scourge on our land." *Scourge*—another new word. Even though she knows now the unexpectedness of gifted children, the rapidity of acquisition and the startling combinations, it is still thrilling—and a little frightening—to hear how his mind works.

"I like that word, *scourge*. But the truth is, Mason is not a scourge. He likes you very much and I like him very much. But I like you best."

"Only when you're here."

"No, I like you best no matter where I am. I love you. Nothing changes."

He is silent for a while. "Everything is gone when you're gone. I'm gone."

"But how does that happen? Why?"

His eyes widen and he says simply, "I get smaller and smaller and then I vanish." Something in his voice, fear maybe, but fear buried in a fist, causes her to drop into silence, to count his fingers and memorize his freckles and lean in to smell his skin, as if in fact he might vanish, this beautiful improbable boy.

"You can't vanish," she says, laying her palms on her chest, tapping them rhythmically. "You're here in my heart, and here in my head," she says, tapping her head now, "and here in my eyes that love to look at you. So you can't ever vanish because my heart would stop beating and my head would stop dreaming and my eyes would stop seeing all the pretty things in the world and all the handsome fellows in the world, too, like you. Plus, I would miss you. I do miss you when I go away or you go away to the mountain to see Grandma. But I always know we come back together. We always come back to each other."

Soon, the disguise he's made of his hands relaxes and, as if he's forgotten what they were there for, he begins rubbing his eyes sleepily, then the hands fly out to his sides, and he stretches into an arch. "Mama-sweetie . . ."

"Yes, O Best Beloved?"

"It hurts a little inside my left scapula."

"It does?" She rolls him over and massages inside his shoulder blades, doubting the authenticity of the hurt but not of his need to need her right now. Every ache must be taken seriously. She is happy, relieved. With his phantom pain, Ethan has given her a way to make it up to him so that he might then forgive her and they can separate across solid ground. And the next morning after Mason's appointment at the chiropractor, they will head south to Baja for two weeks, another adventure together but one in which each has professional purpose this time. It imposes balance on their relationship. Fairness. She has never gotten over the necessity for fairness. And here is this boy-child with his nascent wings offered up to her because they are not yet possessed of feathered power and the loft of time to fly him away.

"Mama-sweetie," he muffles into his pillow.

"Yes."

"Mama-sweetie . . ."

As much as she thinks she likes this term of endearment, a recent neologism, she can hear in it the assumed equality that a fine and fast mind claims as an entitlement. "O Best Beloved" from the *Just-so Stories* is her way of saying to him that the two terms are not really true-life, they are storybook namings. His endearment is also a reflection of their one-to-one life. With Tom out of the picture from the outset and Clair a single parent of a child who comprehends more than he should, Ethan decided a year or so ago that she is his sweetie as much as his mama. Or he decided that she needed one. Mason represents his first brush not with Oedipal issues themselves, but with a challenge to what has so far been a walkover. There's another dog on the field, a bigger one who gets to sleep in her bed and spirit her away. Living with Ethan, Clair is always having to function at full tilt. He is like a plug that begins to spark in proximity to outlets, everything anticipatory and hungry and reaching. In the mornings before she's quite awake, she can sense him in his bedroom sitting cross-legged on his floor, a buzzing nucleus of pursuit, books and games and maps orbiting around him.

The next day when she opens his door, he keeps his back to her and won't look up from the book in his lap. Message delivered. She tries not to smile.

"Mrs. Holian is here," Clair tells him.

"Excellent." He slaps the book shut and heads to the front room where he finds his usual live-in sitter, a small cheery woman whose own children are grown now. The two of them sit down to plan out his day. Every now and then he glances around to locate his mother. Clair has already loaded the car to minimize the departure transactions, so when she hugs him it's only her purse she has over her shoulder. She does not want him to see her taking things away or to witness the taking away itself. In preparation for this long absence, she has purchased fourteen different gifts, each one small and precisely chosen, each appealing to one of his many interests, wrapping them in different paper—something Ethan would of course notice, the effort, the particularity—and then filling up a shopping bag. Every morning when he wakes, he gets to choose one gift, and when the bag is empty, she will have magically reappeared. She can't bear for him to think that he has been forgotten or that each day she doesn't think of him in a new and special way. The bag of gifts is still sitting on the couch where it was rejected the night before as sorely inadequate to the task of making up for her imminent defection. But now he wanders over to it and stands awkwardly beside it without actually looking at it or touching it. She decides that it is better not to mention the bag of gifts; that he will claim it as soon as she leaves. Already posted beside it is Mr. Dickens in guard-dog stance and still foaming at the mouth. Ethan's own mouth is twisted up with boy bravery, and he is wearing a shirt he knows she likes but that he himself does not like. She tells him that she will call him often, then again realizes another mistake, because they then have to parse and define the word *often* before she can leave. Hugging him, she can smell on his skin the faint milky acid of anxiety. She's late to Mason's.

THE NEW BLUE van is in Mason's driveway, he's in the driver's seat, but he doesn't seem to notice her until she taps on the window.

His face is pale, he's staring straight ahead through the windshield as if there's an invisible vise holding his head and neck in place. Without moving his torso, he works his hand along the armrest and powers down the driver's window.

"What's wrong?" Clair says.

"I think he broke my back."

"Miller?"

"Miller was out. Family emergency. Some eejit named Bonebreak. Thinks it's funny, a name like Bonebreak for a chiropractor, thinks he's a farcist. We had to have a chat-up about it before he ruined me, bloody eejit." Whenever Mason is angry or hurt he drops into the vernacularisms of his youth.

"I don't understand . . . is it really his name?"

"Yes, yes, for god's sake, it's his name, his surname. Ever heard of such idiocy? And I chuckled and snotted myself right onto the table. It was fine until I stood up and went face down. Out cold. The pain's like an axe. He may as well have sunk an axe. L4, L5."

"How do you know that?"

"How I know is that the good doctor was kind enough to illuminate the particulars of my new problem, the one I didn't have when I walked in mostly perfectly fine. And now I'm mostly perfectly *not* fine."

Clair gazes around the expansive front yard and garden beds, then up into the branches of the two big oak trees setting off the property, her mind scrambling from one possibility to another—going, staying, going later, finding another chiropractor, pain pills . . . Mason has a long-term lease from a couple that have taken high-paying jobs in Sacramento, and in exchange for general caretaking, he gets a substantial break. It is a beautiful house—tile roof, iron balconies, arched windows in the style of the Spanish grandees, clay court in back—one of the nicer houses of old Palo Alto. It has always seemed wasted on him, even while it somehow suits him, the sort of place certain people don't notice because those certain people have grown up privileged and are accustomed to nice places and nice things. At the same time, he understands innately standards of maintenance and in that respect he's the perfect tenant. Inside, the house may be littered with the carelessness of having always had plenty, his clothes may puddle in corners and the partially read books and periodicals may mount into cairns on side tables and counters, but Mason grew up with the second sense of looking after fine old homes, recognizes a proper plumber when he meets one or the laconic proficiency of a right-good carpenter. The owners know this about Mason, about the so-called farmlet in Cornwall that is actually an estate and from which it seems he receives an annual, which is also why, by some reverse logic, they charge him so little. He is their equal. Plus, she has noticed that, among Americans, the English accent confers an automatic promotion.

So they could stay here, they could simply hole up in luxury. She could use the break, it occurs to her suddenly. Even without the trip to Baja, she needs to get away from her life. Even from Ethan, his intensity, his endearing but never-ending dissections, his fantasies and fabulations. She can't remember the last time she wasn't working at full throttle or just trying to be a good mother. *Don't kid yourself,* she thinks. *You mean trying to be a perfect mother.*

"Get me a bag of ice," he tells her. "Empty out every tray and fill some ziplocks. And the ibuprofen, don't forget that."

"But you can't even move. How can we go? We can't go."

"Of course we're going."

"Mason."

"Clair, get the ice. Please."

"We could go tomorrow, first thing." She loops her fingers through the curls of his hair and slowly draws them out. He keeps it longish and she likes it that way. It makes him look passionate and somehow Russian, a composer or a revolutionary. "I'll take care of you. I'll spoil you rotten. I'll kiss your toes and feed you grapes."

Just for a moment, he leans his cheek against her arm and she notices that he has bothered to shave. "We ought to make San Diego by tonight."

There's no point in arguing, in reminding him that no one is waiting for them anywhere; they don't even have reservations along the way. They are free agents.

The house is reasonably tidy. Taped to the fridge is a note for the cleaning lady telling her to take the perishables and toss the rest, excepting condiments. In the bathroom just outside the shower, his broken-down slippers sit, a long-ago gift from his sister with whom he speaks only at holidays. The slippers prompt the first tears. Along the outside in bas-relief are the faint bulges where his toes have pressed against the leather, the brown dye worn white. He won't buy new slippers. What he does with the money she doesn't know, but he won't spend it on himself. She grabs the ibuprofen, and then a bottle of codeine she notices leftover from recent dental work. The English and their teeth. Also, from the bar downstairs, a liter of scotch, and for herself, for them right now, the butt-end of a bottle of Pinot Noir. Fortification. It's going to be a long day.

BEFORE THEY REACH San Luis Obispo where they plan to get burgers, he stops the van, labors up and out of the seat, and stands with his back to her, "making water," as he says, into the roadside ditch. He doesn't want to have to deal with a restroom, with doors and humanity; doesn't want to have his pain witnessed by strangers, doesn't welcome sympathy of any sort. When it comes to his body, Mason is a minimizer not because he's stoical, but because his own illnesses or injuries infuriate him. They interfere with his work, surprising him with limits he chooses not to register. At forty years old, he still seems to think that time can't and won't lay a glove on him.

The pain is chopping up his breath and creasing his brow. His shirt is damp where the ice has been resting against his lower back, and Clair braces up and positions the ziplock for him as he eases himself into the driver's seat, swallows a codeine, and starts up the engine.

"I can drive, you know."

"Steering wheel helps," he grunts. "Something to hang onto."

But she also knows that it would take an act of God for Mason to relinquish the steering wheel.

She cannot imagine how this is all going to work out, how he's going to hike around the lagoons and the island. Briefly, guilt instantly cauterizing the thought, she even wonders how he will make love to her. It has been weeks and she's missing his touch. There are things they could do, but she assumes that he won't feel up to any of it; nevertheless, she glances involuntarily over her shoulder at the backseat couch, two pillows stacked at one end.

Mason ordered the van months earlier from a dealership, specifying the highest quality seats with the best back support, a thirty-six-gallon gas tank instead of the standard twenty-four, and a bench couch that opens flat to make a double bed. His back problems started a year ago on the kayaking venture through the Inland Passage where he was photographing Grizzlies. Now the van is packed with camp and camera gear, an ice chest, milk crates purloined from the rear delivery door of a local grocer and containing instead canned goods, beer and wine, lantern, flashlights, cookware, a Coleman stove. Fishing rods are strapped to the drycleaner hooks. There are also half a dozen grocery bags of dry consumables, and three five-gallon jugs of water, a box of books and film, personal duffels. It already looks nested in; it has become at least in attitude and intent, their home. In spite of everything, she is happy for that, for the traveling home he has made for them. Mason is a thoughtful, careful planner when it comes to work trips, even while his home base is a comfortable chaos of encyclopedic interests.

When they reach the L.A. County limits, Clair climbs over the gear, pinches out her contacts, and stretches out on the couch. She doesn't even want to see the sprawl; her eyes are burning from the smog. It takes them two hours to cross the basin in rush-hour traffic and neither one of them wants to stop or knows how to stop, where to exit, where to re-enter. Mason doesn't like advanced civilization and so hasn't made any effort to understand it. In urban centers he is a reluctant tourist, and when he is working in the field, when he is in the middle of nowhere, he is as easy and comfortable as a wild animal. L.A. is a slow-motion explosion of everything he abhors. There are eight lanes of cars on each side of the interstate, all moving at seventy-five miles per hour, jostling for new positions no better than the last one. Every now and then helicopters swing down from a murky heaven to film the traffic, and between the aggressive drivers, the drumming descent of the copters, and the AM radio stations broadcasting accidents and gridlocks, the whole scene feels like a war zone. It will be better to keep heading south.

Somewhere east of Redondo Beach on the 405, Mason asks her to pour him a scotch. He's not much of drinker, beer mostly, but probably because of the basin, the back pain, he elects the hard stuff. Fishing cubes from the ziplock lodged behind his back, Clair drops them into a metal camp mug, and they share several solid blasts.

"It'll be all right," he says. "A day or two of this, just driving, ice, *drogas*, I'll be good as new."

"O-kay, but I know you."

"Feels fine now."

"Scotch," she says, drawing in the corner of her mouth like a mother whose scolding is secretly a form of praise.

"I'm not squiffy," he tells her with his boyish English grin, the one that lets him get away with so much, the tiny curl off to the left of his upper lip, sexy and mysterious. "Just nicely lubricated," he announces to the wind-shield and the road ahead.

She's feeling hopeful. The scotch, the long day driving out of their lives, out of time, has conjured a sense of suspended rightness, of being where she ought to be with the man she is destined to love somewhere, anywhere, on the globe. The road south begins to rise up out of the basin and, gazing back to where they've been, she watches a lavender haze materialize over the landscape and the lights of the megalopolis prickle to life in the twilight and it's even pretty, now that they are leaving it, the burnt rosy overtones of the smog, the fog belt along the coast holding it in place, like a white dam, and on the other side of the dam, flat blue water and the coming night just beginning to deepen the blue.

Between L.A. and Costa Mesa, Mason decides to call up Daniel Mar-kovsky who lives in Laguna Beach, rather than trying to make it all the way down to San Diego and the border. She studies Mason's hands on the steering wheel, his long fingers, and thinks about a night cluttered with someone else around them, someone she's never met and with whom she will have to be charming or easy or clever. Mason likes to show her off, and it's a part she has not yet failed to perform. To be enviably his. She knows that she is pretty, not as perfectly pretty as Nina, but pretty in a vulnerable, ethereal way. That is what men have told her, that she is too trusting and seems to need protection, though it has sometimes been from they themselves, at least from those who know the instinctive allure of a bared neck, of something like innocence gone on too long.

His hands are soft; it always surprises her how soft his hands are. In theory, he is not a soft man.

On impulse she reaches over, takes his right hand and tucks it up high between her legs, his fingers slipping instantly under the center panel of her panties. She is wearing a cotton skirt because that morning she checked the weather reports and knew that it would be hot, but now she's wondering if that was the only reason. It doesn't take long for him to bring her. He never looks at her, never cracks an expression, not after that first flicking scribble of excited intrigue around his eyes; he orchestrates and plays her pleasure with implacable expertise, and she feels that she is his, that she belongs to him, and that heightens the eroticism. His possession of her. Afterward, with the tip of her finger, she touches his shorts where a dime-sized spot has appeared and under which she can feel him pressing up.

"Later for you," she says.

"Good."

"You taste as fresh as the sea," he adds, sampling one of his fingers.

She leans over and kisses the delicate place behind his ear. "The primal sea of me."

"Funny girl you are."

"Funny and brilliant."

"Bees knees. Wouldn't have a bird who wasn't brilliant. Birds and bees. What more can a bloke ask?"

Yet she feels a little miserable after this bit of derring-do, of showing off what must be a false comfort in her sexuality, else why the bravado? A little too contented for another kind of comfort that might be called happiness, bigger and life-sustaining, or life-threatening, so she tells herself that it pleases him so much as a man to bring her to this happy crisis, that it is in its way a gift to Mason, not to her.

DANIEL MARKOVSKY IS an old Peace Corps buddy from Ecuador, the one among them who went native. Inevitably there is always one who goes native and the Corps, despite repeated occurrences, never quite knows how to deal with this. The Peace Corps is still a gentle enterprise and doesn't plan for AWOL conversions or officially sanctioned punitive measures. Daniel and Mason were working in the school partnership program, living in small communities and through benevolent but devious means, suggesting to villagers that having a school just might be desirable. Always better, always more successful, to let the local *padres de familia* think that they had come up with the idea themselves, Mason tells her. Otherwise, all the money and materials that the Cuerpo de Paz provided may end up financing a building that became a structure for storage or chickens or, in one case, a whorehouse, or that lay empty, left to molder into the fast ruin of good ideas gone begging. They were living in the Andean jungle south of Cuenca with the Jivaro, or the Shuar, as they think of themselves. When the two-year tour was up, Daniel re-upped. And when his second two-year tour was up and he was required to go back to the US, he didn't. The Corps commissioned Mason to go down to Limoncocha and somehow persuade his buddy to quit his now-defunct post. So he sent word into the jungle and two days later Daniel showed up at the little roadside tienda Mason had specified. It had a few tables; Mason knew he'd be there a while. It was after dark, and the tienda had closed, but the woman had offered to fry up some *llapingachos*, chorizo, and eggs while he waited for his amigo. Eventually Daniel wandered in, wearing a straw hat and a couple of heavy flaps of fabric strung around his waist, and of course the ridiculous, shit-eating grin that took up most of the landscape in his range of expressions. With so much skin showing, he seemed taller than he really was.

"And I'm supposed to tell the *Jefe* what?" Mason asked him before he sat down.

"Why don't you tell them I'm in love?"

"Love."

"Conquers all, I hear."

"Love."

"I've got a hut-full of *cuy* and a woman."

"Is it the *cuy* or the woman you're in love with? For clarity's sake."

"*Cuy.*"

They asked for cervezas; the woman was already bringing them over. It was obvious that she did not think much of Mason's friend and was regretting the after-hour meal and the bonus fried plantains. During the fourth round of beers, she untied her apron and told Mason to lock the door when they left. He handed her a folded sucre bill and nodded his assurance that her tienda was safe in his hands. Wherever he went, Mason engendered respect. He had a way with underlings and employees; he had the way of a *Patrón*. He had always been entirely too sure of himself.

"You've got your own private breeding pen."

"A veritable corral," Daniel admitted. "Takes up half the hut. And she's a wonderful cook. You'd never know it was guinea pig. 'Course, we don't mind knowing."

"We." Mason slowly twirled his beer bottle, smoothing the condensation top to bottom with each click. "Your family's worried. The Corps is stymied. You've bollixed up their whole works."

"Did I mention her *chicha*?"

Mason shrugged. "Alcohol is alcohol."

"Look Mason, it's real here."

"What's real? Nothing's real."

"Life. Pure life. None of the shit. None of the shit-for-brains either."

"They think you've gone round the twist. Your version of Moonies."

"The country's gone round the twist. And I don't mean Ecuador. Do you know what's happening in the Amazon basin? Do you know what we're doing? What Texaco's up to?"

"Yeah, I know." Mason swabbed up what was left of the eggs with a potato patty and dabbed his mouth with one of the paper towels the woman had folded and laid out for them. A string of white Christmas tree lights outlined the window, providing the only illumination in the room, and from outside they must have looked, he said, like characters in some equatorial adaptation of *A Christmas Carol*. Or maybe like Gauguin with his friend, trying to fathom why he would abandon civilized life in Europe to paint heathens in Polynesia.

"At least let the Quito office know what your intentions are."

"Intentions? You sound like the father of the bride. My intentions are honorable, sir."

"Sure they are. But it's time to shut it down," Mason said sadly. "Home with all its violence beckons."

"Shit, Mason."

"Yeah."

"Shit shit shit. Shit fuck piss corruption snot."

"All of the above."

"She'll never come."

"No."

"I think I love her."

"Try the pet stores. They sell guinea pigs."

"I mean it. I love her. I love their way of life."

Clair imagines Mason tipping his head slowly to the side, a habitual gesture that precedes shows of rumination, and studying Daniel. Mason's voice—when it came—would be rhetorical, faintly mocking: "Nice Jewish boy from Brooklyn, a degree from Brandeis, father a doctor, mother a mother, three sisters, two cats, and a dog. Everyone on your side. Even your old prof Collins, met him last year. Total coincidence. Collins didn't want to give you that D, but he said you never took direction. Brilliant kid who never took direction, Daniel Markovsky. Time to take some direction, Danny boy. You have no selection in the matter. And sooner or later, the US government will give you no quarter."

"I do have a choice."

"Not this time. Anyway, what's left to be mad about? They're all on their knees. They want you back. Whatever this rebellion is, it's run its course."

Daniel lifted his beer and set it back down without drinking from it. A wan smile. "I had a fine run at it, didn't I?"

"Fine indeed."

THEY MUST HAVE looked at each other then across the scapes of culture and metaphysics—that is what Clair imagines moments before they arrive at Daniel Markovsky's—looked and seen and understood that so much of life is crushed beneath the weight of possession and ornamentation.

MASON HAS FILES of great white hunter tales, and the scotch, the long drive, the talk of exotic primitive love all have her feeling euphoric, as if anything is possible. "What does he do now?"

"Writes for the *L.A. Times*. When he got back to the states, he found a job with a pissant weekly in Orange County, but he was digging up so many of the big stories that the *Times* finally hired him just to muzzle the competition. Now he has a standing sinecure, investigative environmental pieces, occasional op-eds."

Markovsky's place is a small stucco bungalow with a banana palm out front and, strung across the back porch, a white Venezuelan wedding hammock, its tassels brushing the porch planks. That's where they find him. On a bench beside the hammock stands a half-consumed Dos Equis, and down three steps to the patio a kettle barbecue puffs smoke. She is vaguely worried that it might contain guinea pigs, but Mason says, "Still running up a bill at the local pet stores?" and Daniel yawns, "Naw, they figured it out when it got up to four a week. Horrors! The kid who works the counter treats me like a cannibal now."

"You still go in?"

"Visitation rights." He lifts his chin toward the barbecue. "That's post-industrial fowl." When he notices her hanging back by the corner of the house, Daniel sits up quickly and extends his hand. "Mason didn't mention he was accessorized."

"That doesn't surprise me," she says, introducing herself.

"Lucky fellow."

"I'd like to think so," she smiles. "But luck can turn."

"Now I know he's lucky," Daniel says to her with a bright appreciative grin. "A girl with an attitude."

The attitude, she knows, has been manufactured for Mason's benefit. He likes a strong woman, someone who doesn't necessarily need him, or needs him only when he's in the mood to be needed. She knows she's not strong, not in the ways he thinks, but she doesn't understand exactly how or why she *is* strong. It must have to do with Nina; everything had something to do with Nina, half of the whole they had tacitly agreed to from the beginning, with Clair squaring things up, always squaring things up. Because Nina didn't care about balance; probably, Nina would have gladly crushed her, even though, had truths been let out of their cages, many more would have crushed Nina.

Daniel Markovsky is a small fit man but so pale that he looks like someone recovering from an illness, his eyes shining from deep sockets. A dark tuft of hair lengthens his chin and seems to enlist the wispy mustache to produce an image of giddy revolutionary intellectualism. His bare feet have a waxy quality. One of his wrists is bound up in a brace and while he fishes another two beers from the cooler on the porch for them, he explains that he's developed carpal tunnel syndrome, typing, and that he's currently in a sidecar status with the *Times* until matters improve. As proof, next to the beer on the bench, there is a manual typewriter with which presumably he's not supposed to be consorting, but there is, in fact, a piece of paper rolled into it and plenty of text filling the white, a stack of finished pages under a rock weight beside it.

"What are you working on?" Mason asks him pointedly.

"My *me*-moir."

"Aren't you a little young?"

"Never too young to die, Mason, you ought to know that. You just don't believe death applies to you."

"Spell my name right, will you?"

But the first thing Clair wonders is whether Daniel Markovsky is in fact dying. Because he looks somehow . . . infirm. Then again, she thinks, we are all actively dying.

He and Mason obviously have a lot of respect for each other, but when they get together they're no longer Peace Corps rubes sponging up third-world culture and wringing out righteousness, they're captains in all the good wars the world was busy trying to ignore or suppress. Clair decides to take over the salad preparation, let them get some of their news out of the way, along with the ritualistic sparring she thinks men need before they can speak honestly to each other. A baguette on the counter has already been sliced lengthwise and dressed with butter, garlic and herbs. The bungalow is so spare and, at the same time, so randomly jumbled that it looks as if he's just moved in, but she knows that isn't the case. When the chicken is ready, they eat off plates in their laps, Daniel balanced on the slung edge of the wedding hammock, facing the two of them with an unbroken expression of childlike glee in their company. They are like a Christmas present he didn't expect. He seems fascinated by her and fascinated by Mason's having her, too. He wants to know if she's wearing a bra and Mason simply stares blandly at him, as if he's heard this incorrigible intrusive chatter before and it isn't worth a response.

"Does it make a difference?" she asks him. "You're not a cultural anthropologist." Nevertheless, she peers down her shirt and replies informatively, "No, apparently not."

Daniel doesn't quite know what to do with this information; he has cornered himself with his own impudence and turns awkwardly to Mason with a neutral question.

The air is silky and moving like silk, too, in undulations from the sea. It is an older neighborhood, so the houses are all different though about the same size, same price range, the fences chest-high and swaying in and out against leaning overgrown juniper hedges and rotting boards. They can see into other yards where domestic activities wind down the day—an old woman gardening next door, a couple of little kids in a sandbox that is actually mostly dirt, a man and a woman arguing about when to light the charcoal. Behind them, from the street, the *clack-clack* of a skateboard taking the sidewalk seams in rapid succession. Now and then the smell of jasmine, of mown grass, of someone's compost bin . . . onions. Summery and suburban, gloaming gently into night, a species at its leisure, nothing bad is meant to happen in a place like this. She excuses herself to call Ethan, then returns to the porch, feeling wholly present and available, as if, right now and into the still-faultless days to come, ones that will begin and end in another country, another reality, she gets to live a different life and be someone she's never let herself be.

"How's the lad? Still sore?" Mason asks.

"He's fine. And now he'll sleep."

"You, too," Mason observes.

Daniel doesn't ask her about her son or her marital status, and she doesn't ask him about the empty house, the empty clutter that so obviously expose a contingent existence. No lover, no kids, no pets. The freedom to leave anything anywhere—objects abandoned exactly where he was when he had stopped using them, or when he needed to free up his hands for a different object—a turkey baster on the bathroom sink; a pair of gym socks hanging over the arm of a chair; bug spray on the mantle; a hand mirror on the coffee table. He could jump ship any time. They don't know each other well enough to inject a stranger's questions into the soft flesh of the truly personal. Whether or not she's wearing a bra doesn't count; it is a bit of boyish salaciousness, harmless as a peephole and somehow charming for its lack of guile. It occurs to her that this approach has probably got him into a lot of beds from which his unprepossessing looks might have otherwise excluded him. He is a like a puppy no one has the heart to train or refuse.

But he does ask her about her work, and then, to annoy Mason, what she sees in him.

"Passion," she answers, deciding to be candid. The whole day has roused a mood of candor, of calm urgency, as if they've been told that they have only weeks to live, and everything must be tried, said, savored.

Mason gives an affirming tip of the head. "Thank you, dear."

Studying them, Daniel raises his eyebrows with theatrical surprise. "Oh-oh. You're in love."

Mason snorts and Clair glances away before heading back into the kitchen to replenish his ziplock of ice, rattling out trays from Daniel's ancient and frost-choked freezer.

"Don't let him talk you out of it," Daniel calls to her from the porch. "He's good at talking people out of things, like love."

Note to self, she thinks. And maybe why they have only told each other about their feelings on rare and arbitrary occasions, so sudden and informal that they can't be relied upon or held to, yet for all that, utterly credible. Tom used to tell her he loved her, even while he was making plans to bug out on her and the pregnancy. He told her so often, in fact, that it became a formulaic closing emptied of meaning, sounds you no longer heard for hearing them so habitually. She might not trust the saying of it now. And the attention it draws worries her and violates something rather deep. It's one thing to acknowledge love as part of a larger bundle of thoughts or feelings or acts—*I do this one thing partly because apparently, I seem to love you*—but to let it stand awkwardly, nakedly alone brings to mind criminals who are stripped before incarceration. See me, don't hurt me, lock me up if you must, this body, this heart. But be just.

In spite of her cautious reticence, her thoughts are fine and straight and pacing out at exactly the right intervals, like dance steps. She does love Mason Comstock. *I love you*, she whispers in her mind. She admires what he does, and he what she does. Her son is the best thing that has ever happened to her. Her body is lithe as a dancer's and she wears it well and knows it, wears it comfortably. In Baja, in the smooth wet sand of the golden morning before the work begins, she will run along the beaches because she loves to run, and Mason will look around the edge of his camera and perhaps with some surprise, recognize her as the woman he cares for. They will not need history or the business of lives or the trappings of house and home to tell them who they are together. They will not rely upon a social fabric to bear them as upon a litter to the final pyre of marriage, all the love used up and the gluttonous life of years gone. They will have the sand and the sea and the salt on their lips to tell them what needs to be heard. They will have eyes and hands and breath, and no need of words. They will tell secrets with skin and cradle secret hopes. She will straighten his collar if it wants straightening, and he will comb his fingers through her hair without asking, and they will know when one of them needs the butter passed, or something to laugh about, or help with saying things that are hard to say, or not saying the things that don't need saying.

While she's arranging the bag of ice against Mason's back, Daniel disappears and reappears with the hand mirror that was on the coffee table. From a vial in his shirt pocket he shakes out a small rock of cocaine, chops and edges it into six lines with a razor blade, then spindles a ten dollar bill until it's tight enough to use as a straw.

"You do this often?" Mason asks.

"Not often."

Mason is dubious. "This isn't Ecuador and that's not a coca leaf and there's no shortage of food hereabouts."

"Hey, cut me some slack. It was a gift. Anyway, house rule—never buy it."

"Who likes you so much to give you coke? This stuff looks decent too."

It has been some years since Clair has accepted convivial coke, but she can tell that it is, as Mason observes, very good stuff, the color not bleached white but faintly citrinous.

"Pure as driven snow," Daniel assures them, arching his pale brow to inquire if she wants any, then passing her the mirror and spindled bill. "Actually, you should meet this guy, Rubio Cantú. Lives in, let's see, Puerto Vallarta, Acapulco, Cabo, Cancun," he counts on his fingers. "Right now he's slumming in Mulegé, but he comes up to L.A. for a girlfriend who's finishing at UCLA. Buckets of money. I met him at a party. He rents a house on the Strand in Manhattan Beach from some star athlete who's out of town during the season. Rubio's a real sweetheart of a guy. Sophisticated too, obviously brought up in high Latin society."

Clair finishes and passes the mirror, Mason inhales his two lines, then sends the mirror back to Daniel. "Dealer?"

"Probably. But also probably just a hobby. Doesn't need the money. His father runs the biggest land-moving company in Mexico. In fact, cleared the way for the Transpeninsular Highway you're about to head down. Among other projects . . . dredging out Cabo San Lucas—that was one of his, too. But the thing you may be interested in is this, Mason—it's the same company that dug out the lagoons around Guerrero Negro for the salt. Seventy square miles. And now PSP has its eyes on San Ignacio, the third sister of the three sister lagoons. *Adios* Gray whales."

"That's exactly why I'm going down there."

"Right. So, you should talk to Rubio. He'll give you the inside line."

"He would tattle on daddy?"

"In a heartbeat."

Clair asks, "Why?" It is exactly the kind of thing she never seems to understand, betrayals and grudges, and it is somehow related to her famous inability to get jokes or to recognize a shady character when she meets one. If it is not innocence, then a form of innocence that she has made a deliberate choice of for so long now that its strings and wires no longer show. Even she believes it to be real, the puppetry that protects her from knowing how human beings really are, how she herself might be behind the curtains and backdrops. It began with Nina and it continues with Nina, a fine-print clause in their unspoken contract as twins. Everyone gets the benefit of the doubt, even when there is no doubt.

"I don't know," Daniel is saying. "But there's definitely bad blood. He practically spits over his shoulder when anything to do with the old man comes up."

After they make a plan to stop on their way back in two weeks, they stay up late into the night, talking along electrified currents powered by the cocaine, all of them of course brilliant and witty, snapping out glib phrases and conjuring dazzling interpretations that, it seems, ought to be chiseled into stone before they are forgotten. Until, that is, Clair begins to feel she is chewing her own teeth and that there's a very good chance that what they have all been saying to each other might sound dead obvious and just plain stupid in the morning. "I'm to bed," she says, heading for the guest room.

Adopting a weirdly falsetto voice, Daniel tosses out one last impertinent question: "What are you going to wear to bed, Miss Clair?"

She hears Mason say, not unpleasantly, "Bugger off."

In the cool white sheets, their voices but not their words drifting in from the porch, Clair enjoys the luxury of ignorance, of not having to know everything and of trusting Mason to take care of whatever needs taking care of. She feels that she belongs with him, that she is where she ought to be at this moment in this unplanned place, on this unmapped journey away from all that is familiar.

In truth, she is wearing no clothing to bed because it is how he prefers her, naked and credulous, and even if nothing happens between them tonight, everything that matters will be happening. She will feel his ribs arching against the palm of her hand, the soft swale of his belly, the shy warm hollow inside his hip bone; and he will feel her breasts pressed into his back, the puff of hair below, her knees notched behind his, her breath alongside his neck, coming and going. A configuration of love so contented that she would be happy to die in that contentment of passing through, and on, and gone.

CHAPTER 4

I t is entirely possible to live an everlasting death. At some point the human heart refuses to commit treason against itself. It loves not the misery it feels, but loves so abidingly what left misery in its wake that even that tracing of stardust, of light always dying in a measureless emptiness, is better than the going on or the leaving behind.

Henry Bugato was not making but remembering memories now, a supplicant in the religion of despair, and a saint whose god has vanished without parting instruction or a gesture of farewell.

How to live? How to see colors that have drained from their vessels, to hear music muted to unintelligible murmurs, to tell the ripeness of grapes that have turned to stone? The breath and belly of actual experience drew away from him, and what remained was as brittle as dry parchment upon which there was nothing really worth writing or, if written, succeeded only in tearing into the thin skin of the life left to him.

He embraced his wife and tended his vineyards and tasted without tasting the wine; he read to the twins stories, he fed them food, he took their hands when a father's hand was asked. But these acts found no purchase in his heart, for nothing new could take root there, no living experience could grow in the hardpan of loss. At night he drank whiskey because it was faster than wine. He forgot to bathe, he forgot how to feel. He fixed things, ran things, but took no pleasure in the wholeness or rightness of those things. In his garden, the roses and hollyhocks, the irises, the peonies and poppies—all flourished, but when he wasn't working among them he never saw them, never smelled them. Their beauty he hated simply for existing, for beauty was an affront without Tony. He did his job, paid the workers, spoke gently to the girls often without noting which of the two stood before him. He had the hallway bathroom gutted and made over into a shower. There were no more Bugato children. Death had cured them of making lives. The barrel room and the field house, the cellar, the caves dug into the hillside, the garden shed, and the barn all were fitted with keyed locks so that no child could come to harm. He stopped listening to opera, and the books he read were practical now, books for vineyardists and enologists, books for repairing decks and tinkering with farm equipment, books about native flowers, drought management, solar systems, phylloxera, grafting, dog training. Useful books meant to expand knowledge and improve matters—except for the biographies. He developed a taste for biographies as if, in reading about the lives of others, he might replace or even forget his own. Henry no longer occupied his life as the man of the house occupies his home, his chest expanding as he considers what he has built and what flourishes. Now he stood impoverished on its threshold or outside its windows, like a day lodger working for keep, or a beggar too ruined even to ask for a handout. And the desolation that with time might have mineralized into philosophy never found that smooth hard form to last through the ages, never ceased to be a breathing emptiness still beating with the just departed.

For Tony, he planted a small four-acre vineyard—*Tony's Vineyard*, the label said—for which he charged so much that only the most dedicated Cabernet drinkers knew of it or could afford it. Mostly, though, he gave the bottles away to those he judged worthy, but there were few he judged worthy, and so, like the boy, the wines died unenjoyed at maturity. No tractor was allowed in Tony's vineyard, no field hand not invited by Henry himself, no bad thing, no loud thing, no lugs abandoned at the ends of rows attracting bees and dirt, no tools forgotten or ill thoughts remembered, no trucks or tire tracks, no talking during harvest, no sound but the soundlessness of spreading leaves and growing grapes, of winter rain and the ticking of summer heat. He did the pruning himself, bundling the canes and carrying them across his back like a bent picker from a thousand years gone. And from beneath the flat gray sea of his sorrow only one unkindness surfaced: he did not allow the girls ever to enter Tony's vineyard.

He missed his boy child, missed what he stood for, fathers and sons and fathers again, future from past, and the arms of man embracing time, redressing mortality, putting to rights the cosmic scales with a life for a death. He had had . . . Tony had had, no completed personality, but he had had fingers that grasped, and he had made sounds in the night that quickened the air of the house, as the sound of a small wild animal can electrify the night, and he had held the roly-poly bugs with implausible tenderness. He sang with his hand pressed to his mouth, and he had a smile so big that the whole world rushed in, and the bottoms of his toes were as plump as pink tadpoles dotting the shoals.

For a while, people, friends, talked about what had happened, *the incident*, they said. "Why isn't there a bigger word?" he asked his wife one morning. "It's not right. There should be a bigger word, or no word. Why isn't there a different word?"

"There is," she said. "No one wants to use it."

Louise soldiered on. If she had run a tight ship before what happened, now she became petty about everything—smoothing the wrinkles in the couch fabric after anyone had been sitting on it, wiping the narrow top edge of the baseboard with a towel that matched the color of the paint so as not to leave any contrary color, cleaning and dusting, vacuuming and mopping, each object in the house fitted to its exact place—the knick-knacks, the throw-pillows, the edges of rugs, the brooms and mops that hung like bound men from a scaffold. It was two years before they touched each other in bed, and then only because Louise had read that they ought, and so they did as they ought. Afterward, after she had showered and when Henry had gone into the bathroom to clean himself, Louise changed the sheets, stealing down the hallway to the laundry room and starting the washer before they went to sleep. It was as if the whole of her days was dedicated to erasing any evidence of a family living on, of a family daring to live on. If it was a form of pleasure, what they had done with each other in bed, then she must make as though it had not happened, or as if it had happened to other people, patients who were her charge and for whom she would do what was prescribed. Pleasure itself had become a form of difficult therapy.

And the twins . . . after what happened, Nina had to be protected with something like love, but not love. Excruciating fairness. Clair could not now be freely loved; it would have been too easy, to love her, to decry Nina. So the love that Louise and Henry felt for Clair was held back, reconstituted and redirected to Nina. If Clair went to her parents' room in the morning, she was sent away. She was too old, they said, to be coming in so early only to wake them, only to trouble them with childish play. If Nina struggled with a book report at school, Clair learned to conceal her A. If Nina could be coaxed into helping with the cooking but never the cleaning, Clair was told to wash the dishes, to find satisfaction and honor in any job well-done. If Louise was caught idly stroking Clair's hair as they sat on the couch watching the television, it was not Nina who, like any sibling, might have bristled with jealousy, but her sister who objected or who leapt up to make it stop, so deeply had the roots of guilt dug themselves down. But guilty about what?

About herself, Clair—just that, all of that. *Being Clair.* Or rather, not being Nina. And glad not to be Nina; glad for all the advantages of being not-Nina, and then guilty of that gladness. Of that winning.

No affection could come her way without twice that going first to Nina. Nina had to be defended from truths that none of them could have borne. Every family sooner or later builds its own house of justice within which might occur behavior that, in another family, would be iniquitous. Clair became the keeper of the family justice, and because the scales were always inclining naturally her way, she had to weigh down the other with added goods; to overpraise her sister, to depreciate herself. She had to keep her parents in line, she had to deny pleasures, she had to learn to prefer the lesser of two likings, to seize the smaller of two pieces of cake, to take the movie house seat whose view was obscured by the woman in front, or the bedroom without the big window, for now that Tony was gone, the girls slept in separate rooms. She had to want to stay behind even when she didn't want to stay behind, when there was only space for one more child in the Rec department van going up to the lake, reading instead in her room all that hot afternoon, trying not to think about the cool water and all their friends and the popsicles that would be handed out and the little fish that they would be catching where the creek came in. She took her illnesses outside to the woods and her sadness to bed with her at night. She vomited behind trees, she muffled her coughs into a pillow. Her infected tonsils went on far too long, long enough for her to have lost many pounds before the doctor knew to remove them. Anyway, Louise was impatient with illnesses; they were not part of any plan and certainly not compatible with running a tight ship. As for disappointments, Clair cultivated a talent for saving tears until, in solitary binges spent in the back corner of her closet, she cried herself into hyperventilation, her lips, the edges of her hands, her fingers going numb, stiffening into palsied appendages that no longer belonged to her. It was a satisfaction, the numbness, the otherness. She learned to stop being some of who she was or who she wanted to be, to live half a life, to be half a girl, because Nina could not stop being Nina and who Nina was was not especially likable. It was easier for Clair, easier for them all, if Clair just held back or closed off, marking her failures, forgetting her successes. And she could do it; she took pride in knowing that she could do it; she could do it long enough and well enough to regret having done it.

"Clair is too solitary. Clair reads too much. Clair used to be so bubbly—what's happened to her?"

"A phase," said Henry.

"Clair is always apologizing. Why is she always saying she's sorry? It's irritating, how often she says she's sorry. It makes everyone feel bad."

"She's just a sensitive girl," Henry would say. "A humble girl."

"Humble? She thinks the world is her fault! What kind of girl thinks she's responsible for an entire world?"

"Her sympathies are . . . broad."

"Well," Louise huffed, "she ought to weed her own garden, not everyone else's."

"She does have a big heart."

"I tell you, Henry, it's maddening, all this apologizing! Who does she think she is, after all?"

"Brünnhilde," Henry murmured.

She acquired a certain affectionate distrust, loving the world in spite of its inevitable failures. The distrust she concealed with the most improbable belief in everyone, in what they said or did, or said they would do, so that nothing could expose the sadness inside, or the fatally failed belief in goodness that Nina had caused. Her parents were no longer gods and what they uttered no longer divine intelligence, because the scores that they kept were faulty and the words they used false. A child could spot the truth at a glance. And so Clair learned not to glance in the direction where Truth stood, like a boy with a telegram no one dared accept, his hand unhurried, his gaze cast to the side, holding a telegram no one wanted to read.

"She's developing a stoop, have you noticed, Henry? She stares at the ground when she walks, she never looks up. What can you say about a seven-year-old who never looks up?"

"She's thinking. She's a thoughtful girl."

"Nina doesn't stoop or apologize for everything under the sun."

"No, Nina doesn't."

"Nina holds her head up."

"Yes, Nina does."

In the Bugato family, it was this complicit arrangement that helped them weather the years after Tony. But it was not an arrangement that the rest of the world recognized or had agreed to, and within a year of elementary school, the twins were put into separate classes, Clair in the faster class and Nina in the one reserved for those children who needed more time. She was strong in one thing, math, but the rest of the subjects were a slog for her. It was Nina's misfortune that this class was located at the front of the school where everyone must pass to reach the other classrooms. They were the first ones out for fire drills and recess; the first ones in line for dodge ball and the tether ball courts; the first ones on the bus after school—but they were last in everything that mattered.

And friends . . . friends did not know of the Bugato family strategy either, did not know that all things must be equal between the twins, which is to say, unequal in Nina's favor. Clair had two or three close friends who saved her a seat at the picnic tables during lunch or who invited her for sleepovers or who sent her letters on pink stationery when their families took them away for vacation. But Nina ran with a half-dozen kids from her class, none of whom particularly liked each other, their allegiance based on a form of schoolyard sociology that recognized an unspoken order with the "slow" class, as it was known, taking up the lower caste. Bound by shame and mutual distaste, they would have done anything for the group but nothing for each other individually. They had the instinct of a pack of well-fed dogs, looking for trouble that none of them needed. Any one of them, promoted to the faster class, would have turned instantly on their former classmates.

Not once did Nina indicate to her sister that she cared one way or the other about being in the slow class. She was one of its leaders, and the boon of underlings seemed to compensate for the ignominy of Classroom 1.

First and second grades passed. By third grade the twins were back in the same classroom, but it was a situation that lasted only a month. The school psychologist separated them, it was never explained why. Someone may have implied that separating siblings had become standard procedure; someone may have taken a few steps down the same path that Clair had already traveled miles earlier.

About that time, Nina began locking Clair out, or locking her in—in the linen closet or the steamer trunk or the storeroom; or out of the house. How was it that Clair let her sister lock her in the linen closet? They had been playing a hiding game, only instead of throwing open the door in discovery, Nina threw the latch and stood outside while her sister screamed. Whatever it was that Clair wanted at a given moment, her sister needed to refuse her, then give it to her, but only after an episode of desperation had set in, Clair screaming from the closet or the trunk or crying outside in the rain. Then, at the point Clair was giving in to despair, when, one winter afternoon, she had turned away from the door and was heading down toward the winery buildings where she hoped to find an open door, Nina relented. And, oh, the relief, the strange gratitude toward her persecutor who had rescued Clair from that selfsame persecutor's own deeds. Relief, gratitude, and resentment so stifled that it could only be trained inward.

"Where are you going?" Nina called. "Let's play Barbies."

Emptied now of feeling, Clair regarded her sister, there in the doorway, her arms crossed over her chest. Nina gestured for her to come in, to follow her, but for the first time Clair turned away. A drubbing rain, cold and leaden. The stick arms of the vines were black and bare, and down the rows rivulets were forming. Her father was in the cellar room, but it had been a long time since he had swung her up to his chest to let her smell the wine in his glass as he moved from barrel to barrel with Eric, the loyal acolyte, at his side. Louise was in town at one of her fitness classes. She had become fanatical about staying in shape, about being thin and elegant and playing the part of a baroness in Napa Valley's fast-developing wine aristocracy. It gave her something to do, a post and billet on her tightly run ship, with meetings to organize, tastings to hostess, vintage releases, and charity auctions.

"I was just kidding," Nina said behind her. It was her baby voice, her sweet-girl voice. But they were eight now; it didn't make sense. The baby voice started after Tony, and no one knew what to make of it. "Are you mad at me? Don't be mad. I was only kidding!"

"No you weren't." Clair's back was still to her sister. Everything she had on was soaked, her wavy hair veining darkly around her face; everything felt bad in a final way, as though it would always be so. Inside, a gray apathy pooled and gelled while across the vineyard the rivulets were finding each other, and now muddy canals of water were foaming down the rows toward the woods. Everything seemed to be going away from her, a mass exodus, retreating from a world that had somehow lost its center. Its heart. She herself seemed to have lost heart. The rain clouds caught sailing east over the western ridgeline, torn up and shredded between hills and vales so that the tops of redwoods sometimes shot like arrows out of clouds, not from the earth, and the thick snaking branches of the oak trees were ragged with mist and hanging moss, figments in a ghost story. One of the tractors sat abandoned by the shed with its bucket loader, a great wide mouth open in dismay, dropped to the sodden ground. The chickens were huddled in their coop beside the barn, clucking anxiously, but one of them had somehow got loose and was standing with ridiculous but also sad and desperate superiority inside the loader's hungry mouth. The rain fell in vertical ubiquity, a weight that could not be denied and that Clair seemed to feel across her back, and inside, too, crushing her heart until it was as pressed in on itself as a small wary animal.

"Why don't you like me, Nina?" she asked indifferently. Still, she would not turn to regard her sister.

"I like you, Clairsie. You're my best sister. Don't be silly."

"You don't like anything."

"I do too. Come on, don't make such a big deal. Why are you making such a big deal? You always do that, you make a big deal out of everything. I was just kidding. Let's play Barbies, come on."

"I don't care about Barbies. I don't want to anymore."

"Clairsie, Clairsie, Clairsie," she sang in descending notes.

The rain was steady and hard and everything she said she almost had to yell. "I don't care about anything anymore. Leave me alone." The yelling felt good, felt right, like batting the softball so that it shot level and true past everyone. Nothing could hurt her if she didn't care, if she expected nothing, if none of it mattered.

Down the drive at the cellar, a side door opened and into the gray rain a yellow slip of light escaped, and for just a moment, Clair felt hope tearing through her chest. From the porch, something stirred, a crouched shape—Boomer, old now with splayed hips, staggered inside, the door closed, the light snuffed.

"Okay, I'm sorry. Does that make you happy?"

A knot formed in her throat and then she was crying. "Are you? Are you really?"

"Sure."

It made a tiny difference, Nina saying she was sorry. "Really?"

The cellar door opened again, and they could hear their father's voice as he finished up for the day with Eric.

"Sure, okay? But come inside now. What are you, nuts? Hurry up before we both get into trouble." The baby voice was gone. Nina was back, commanding and calm. And she was right: Clair had to get inside and changed before their father discovered that she had been locked outside, that Nina had misbehaved, that Clair had not succeeded in protecting them all from what none of them wanted to admit.

Only when Clair had reached the door did Nina add, "You always make such a big deal. You are *such* a baby, Clair."

"I guess so," she said, going to her room.

So never again would things be fair between them, not the way they had been before Tony, not frank and transparent equity, a doll for a doll, a dress for a dress, a hug for a hug. A different ledger, one that took into account dark matter and dark energy that wobbled stars and moved planets, a cosmic ledger in the Bugato universe—that was where things were inventoried and tallied now.

WHEN THEY WERE twelve, just weeks before the end of sixth grade, the captain of the St. Helena Fire Station began showing up at their house. He was a short barrel-bodied man with a knobby head and nose, and wild eyebrows that tufted up inquisitively. But Louise, in her gym-fit confidence and rising status as one of Napa Valley's grandes dames, was not susceptible. Henry openly liked the man, and that made it impossible for Captain McClarren to intimidate him.

In California, fire is a grave concern. It seemed that there had been a number of small fires, mostly around St. Helena. They were all doused, but then of course there was the matter of responsibility, of damages. A shed had gone down, so had a pallet of shake shingles waiting to be someone's new roof, plus the wooden backstop at the baseball field, a bin of trash behind the Foster's Freeze.

"Are you suggesting that our daughter is responsible for these fires, Captain McClarren?" Louise asked.

"Not responsible, Ma'am, not saying that yet. But she has been seen in the vicinities of these fires, before or after."

Henry asked, "Which one?"

"Couldn't say," Captain McClarren replied. "Aren't they identical?"

"Not exactly," said Henry.

"Firestarters . . ."

"Firestarters? Is that some special term?"

"It is, Mrs. Bugato. And they, your daughters, they are at an age when it is not uncommon, particularly if there has been some kind of stress. Has there been anything that might have set one of them off lately? Some trouble in the family?"

Louise briskly answered, "No."

A respectful pause lingered between them, then Henry said, "None that I can think of, Captain."

Clair, listening from the hallway, could hear the clink of cubes as her mother poured out more iced tea.

"What about school? Any trouble there?"

"Of course not," Louise snapped. "They're good students, good girls. Both of them," she insisted.

"My wife is correct, Captain, they are both getting along well, well for two girls about to head off into the jungle of junior high."

Captain McClarren chuckled and for a moment, courteously regarded the carpet. But he would not let it end there, on a light polite note; he would not let himself or the matter be dismissed by civility because there were damages to consider and responsibilities to assign. "Any friction between them, between the sisters?"

"They're twins," Louise declared as if this was all that needed saying.

"They are close," Henry agreed. "Close in that way that the rest of us can't decode. They have their own special way, twins."

"Devoted to each other," Louise said.

"That's where the hottest temperatures are. Feelings, you might say, make friction," the Captain remarked, adopting the modulation of a wise and experienced elder. "Speaking as a fireman."

"Yes," Henry said, "I see what you're saying."

"Are we finished here?" Louise asked. "I have a meeting."

Then Henry said, "There was some talk about a boy."

Captain McClarren released a loud puff of sudden old-world comprehension. "A boy!"

"They're too young for boys, for any interest in boys. Not even in junior high yet, not even teens. And they are *de*voted to each other. I can't imagine what you're saying. Henry?"

"Just that there was some mention of a boy, a squabble one day out in the vineyard. They walked away from me, they didn't want me to hear."

"But that's no reason to go and start fires. My word, the egos you men have!" She could be heard gathering up the pitcher and glassware, terminating the idea, terminating the men. "I have a meeting." Louise was marching toward the kitchen, toward the hallway where Clair had been hiding, and quickly she slipped back to her room without hearing the conclusion of Captain McClarren's inquiry.

But he was back three more times, his big car with its fancy door seals parked at the top of the drive. And even though Clair knew about the magnifying glass, even though Nina had shown her one day in the tall yellow grass how to focus the sunlight until smoke threaded up, then the sudden flame popping to life; or once to burn a beetle she had captured in an old can that died before their eyes, its funny little hair legs frantically twitching; and another time their mother's blouse where the concentrated beam left a black-rimmed hole the size of a nickel; even though Clair had witnessed her sister's mute fascination with these tricks of small power, small hate, she did not want to believe that Nina had set the fires that brought Captain McClarren up the mountain to the Bugatos'. She did not want to believe it so much, so deeply, that she never asked Nina directly, and Nina, for her part, did not bother to enlighten her. This, too—the not asking, the not telling—was part of their covenant as twins.

They paid the damages and Nina slumped through several visits with the school psychologist, a fat older woman whose upper lip was always perspiring above a messy stack of files. The fires stopped. The magnifying glass disappeared to the bottom of Nina's drawer. She wasn't cured of whatever it was that drove her out with her glass in the sun, but somehow she had been curbed.

To Clair, it was always strangely surprising that Nina never told her about these misadventures, the fires and other intrigues. She kept whole parts of herself away from Clair, and went with a different crowd, older kids who did dramatic things—hitchhike into town or ditch school or crawl through the culvert to where it drained into the creek and then what they did down there she couldn't imagine. There was just so much about Nina that Clair could not imagine, underpinnings of activity from which she could not seem to build anything plausible. People assumed that as twins they were close, but what closeness they had was a function of a deeper hidden dynamic, a form of reciprocity relating to survival. They never, for instance, ratted on each other.

And there *had* been a boy. From Nina's crowd and a year older. The crime was not that Nina had caught them messing around in the woods behind the school, kissing. The crime was that he had defected from her group for something as stupid as liking a girl, a girl who happened to be Nina's sister. She seemed to feel that Clair had brought dishonor on him, that nothing was as low, as distracting, or as humiliating, as a crush.

"But haven't you ever liked someone?"

"No," said Nina. "It's gross. Anyway, who has time for that?"

"It doesn't take any time at all to like someone," Clair said. They were strolling up and out of the vineyard, away from their father. This was nothing they had agreed to, leaving so that he would not overhear them. It was simply instinctively obvious that they keep big news, like crushes or crimes or naturally any arguments, away from adults. "Well, I liked him right away. He's nice. He gave me something, a four-leaf clover that he pressed inside a sketch book."

"It's not real."

"Yes it is."

"Do you have to be so stupid, Clair? Is there some rule that says you always have to be so stupid?"

It was probably so; they had often tricked one another by holding two clover stems together, the ordinary three-petaled with a single torn from

68

another, to make it look like four. "Anyway, it doesn't matter," she said. "He's nice." She was thinking that he had taken the time to press it, to try to make it seem real for her, and that seemed as real as realness itself, his trying, and he had written at the bottom of the pressed page, *To Clair, from Jeff.* "Jeff Burnham," she said aloud. She even liked his name.

"Don't say that! Don't say his name. He was with us, not you and your goody little friends. It's embarrassing. And you kissed him, you wrecked him."

"It was his idea."

"Oh, pathetic, pathetic! That makes it so-o worse." Her cheeks had pinked with feeling, and her pretty dark eyes were flickering. Nina almost never cried, but it seemed that she might now.

"Well, I'm sorry. But what do you want me to do, stop liking him just because you think you're the boss of anyone who hangs out with your bunch of, of hooligans?"

"Hooligans?" Nina laughed. "Oh my god, when were you born?"

"That's what Dad calls them, your friends."

"Hooligans! Wait'll Jeff hears that!" She was swinging her head slowly, grinning into space, apparently imagining Clair's upcoming public humiliation.

"Okay, fine. I won't like him anymore. Is that what you want?"

"Right. I believe that. You can't help yourself. You're helpless, Clairsie, god, are you helpless!" She placed her hand on Clair's shoulder. "You know, I feel sorry for you."

The hand on her shoulder felt like a piece of raw meat, heavy and coldly clinging, and she ducked out from under it. "Look, let's just say I don't like him anymore. Let's just forget about it and agree on that. He's yours."

"Are you kidding? He's one of you now. He's, he's pathetic." This was Nina's favorite word at twelve; everything was pathetic—food, homework assignments, outfits that other girls wore, boys that sisters liked. "A pathetic loser."

But this last would not stand because Clair really did like Jeff. "He is not. He's cool," she insisted, using one of her sister's other favorite words. People were either cool, or they were pathetic.

"Not anymore." She leaned and picked up a stick, tossing it at the new pup who had replaced Boomer. The pup yelped, tucked tail, and vanished behind the field house. "What'd he do, show you his *thing*?"

"No!"

"Yeah, right, I believe that." She stopped, leveled her eyes at Clair, dropped her voice. "Everyone else has seen it."

"You're making that up," Clair said, barging away from her sister, away from these things she couldn't stand to hear. Because she really did like him. Even his name in print seemed to magically jump off the page at her.

But she did not go to the woods with Jeff Burnham again. Passivity toward her own likes and interests was always the last refinement of these fights with Nina since it was possible and increasingly easier to set aside something she wanted rather than battle Nina over it. It meant more to Nina and more seemed to be what was at stake. Whether it was the object of contention or the object of affection, or the winning itself—it all ceased to matter. And after a while Clair learned how to convince herself that it was undignified to scrabble, and all in all a very risky business indeed to reveal wishes or dreams, to like anything that, in the end, she would be obliged to give up.

CHAPTER 5

They enter Mexico midmorning through the San Ysidro border crossing after stopping at a travel facility that offers instant Mexico insurance, Tourist Cards, fishing licenses, and currency exchange. Once he is on the trail, Mason is like a dog sniffing everything in its path, rapidly subtracting whatever lacks relevance, and so typically he gathers one each of all the brochures and maps in the display rack, which, Clair knows, he will scan and lose track of almost immediately. But they will live on in shadows, tucked into the visor or between the seats or in the door compartments until something catastrophic comes along and purges them, something like a car wash. Or a hunt for something suddenly vital that has gone missing. It is the same way with his feelings, held back in shadows until something comes along and releases them.

The ice is replenished, the water jugs topped off, some American candy—peanut M&Ms—purchased just because road trips require junk food, though the peanuts are half a takeback. Then they are in the van covering the last few miles to the border.

Behind them and to the west is the Tijuana River estuary, softly green with narrow wandering canals of milk-blue water and, above, small squadrons of birds lifting and settling in unison. A peaceful promising mood envelopes them. The air is still cool, the sun rising and not yet a force, and the light has a playful, just-washed clarity. They have been listening to Bach's *Mass in B Minor*, and their quietude has been infused with the aural incense of the ecclesiastical.

When she was a child, within a year of Tony's death, her family stopped attending mass; she can't recall the reason—maybe only the long twisty drive down to St. Helena—but she has always assumed that her father had lost the heart for it. Or he had decided that no god could exist who could let such misery loose among its flock, like a wolf that takes away in a single strike the will to live, and quickly after, the ability to live. Several years later, Clair began to accompany a friend's family to the local Catholic church—not for the religion, but for the collective attention paid to belief and fellowship, and a room full of people thinking about goodness. It was a comfort. She liked the singing and the way people valued her just for being another body in the room. Belief in general had fallen out of favor. Her attendance worked to confirm some of their own choices, having a potential convert among them, and so young, too. She began to imagine that she might be special, she might be *holy*, singled out for mysterious signs, like stigmata and annunciations. She would sit in her room with her palms open to the ceiling, praying and waiting for the spots of blood to appear, sometimes feeling the premonition of blood, a tingling anticipation the size of a penny. It would have made up for Nina, those penny-sized drops of blood, a loftier compensation than domestic peace. Or those pennies might have paid for something Clair seemed to feel she had caused, for Nina, too, had fallen out of favor. It occurred to her that what had happened to Tony might not have happened at all if Nina had not already had five years of Clair to contend with; five years of competing with a noncompetitor and still losing.

THE MASS SOARS around them—the *Osanna*.

About God, Clair has never been sure, but godliness now and then seems possible. She does not believe in miracles, but she believes that they happen, in the same way that she can't intellectually countenance destiny but when Mason crossed her path she was sure it was meant to be. Her postdoc studies at Stanford had nothing to do with destiny and everything to do with old-fashioned hard work and a lifetime love of plants, but when it also meant Ethan could attend the best public school in the country, one with classes for gifted children, that counted as destiny. So her faith, such as it is, she thinks of as "checkered."

The highway funnels toward the border where a phalanx of lanes choked with cars slows to fits and starts as each vehicle with its occupants is stopped and inspected. Borders make everyone nervous. Mason pats her leg, a gesture that vaguely annoys her; he has been all over the world making photographic records of environmental problems and so exudes the confidence and courage of experience with just cause. But she can't help feeling that there is something she has done, some crime that she can't quite remember, and that a petty official, looking for an altogether different crime, will discover by pure accident. She just wants to get through and be on their way.

They choose one of the lanes designated *Nada Que Declarar*—nothing to declare—which moves far more quickly than the others, expecting to be waved through. About Mason there is nothing overtly threatening, though on occasion the steadiness of his gaze can turn another's eyes to the side or down, a talent he has cultivated to success when traveling in foreign countries. Tall, but not so tall that it is an aspect about him she can't forget, and athletic, but not designedly so, with a thoughtful, almost philosophical bearing, he was undistinguished when she first met him, even mildly disappointing, the kind of man she would not recall from a crowd or a photograph. Except that she had. Something solid there . . . something hard and *primary*, like a color pigment that needs nothing else to make itself and that cannot be broken down. He never angles for attention or affection, but once either is his, he is secretly passionate in that possession, hoarding it and hiding it and resenting it too. Its power.

Ethan's father, Tom, was a big gregarious man who sneered whenever he felt uneasy. He was contemptuous of everything, even his own happiness, as if it had cost him nothing. In the end it had cost him everything. Clair's mother had been a little too enamored of Tom and, during the breakup, had spent most of the phone calls consoling and blandishing him, though he was the one leaving. At one point, in a moment untethered from convention (maybe she'd been drinking), she had even suggested he give Nina a call—anything to keep him in the family. What it was that she had liked so much about Tom was never acceptably clear, but Clair came to think that it was simply how jolly he was, a flurry of wasted energies and half-done schemes but always with the big ideas gassing up the room, like nitrous oxide, everyone laughing, everyone willing to buy the lie. After Tony, Henry was a study in gravitas. Having Tom around must have been a relief, never mind that, in the end, nothing he said or did could be counted on.

Tom went back to an old girlfriend who was a little older and who would not take him seriously because she took nothing seriously, a retro-hippie bitter about the standard fare—families, bad luck, chronic laziness, the job market—and so Tom was spared having to try to be better than he was. Clair had heard that he was giving walking tours of San Francisco where his fluency in three languages undoubtedly paid off. At night he waited tables at one of the trendy new restaurants where the male patrons wore T-shirts under cashmere jackets, and the women intentionally unkempt their hair. Tom didn't really mind not being taken seriously because he must have known that there was something boggy down there, something unreliable. A man who fled his own child. Early in their relationship, he would give Clair massages that did not—as they ought to have—lead to sex. Foreplay had always been his forte and the rest, when it eventually happened, was fast and undistinguished. No, Tom had never been much for the follow-through.

Glancing over at Mason, she is relieved to see his expression so calm, so present and confidently waiting that it is like a screen seconds before the movie begins and sides will have to be taken, hearts lifted, hearts broken. Ready for anything.

But Mason's back is worse today, and with the Mexican official, he ends up sounding gruff and uncooperative. His English accent draws notice, as does the big new van packed with camping gear, tools, and film. They are asked to pull off to the side for a more thorough inspection. When Mason strains up and out of the driver's seat, the official stands back, opens his palms, one to each side, and smiles a smile that wobbles not so comically between curiosity and mockery.

"Señor, you are not well. Why do you wish to visit our beautiful country when you are not well to enjoy it?"

"I intend to be well soon. *Pronto*," he replies.

Smiling, Clair hopes to encourage credibility. Even though they have done nothing wrong, she feels in the wrong because they are suddenly in question.

The immigration official—Norberto Duarte, his name tag reads—beckons another official with his arm straight out from his chest, the back of his hand facing the man, fingers in unison tapping his palm with bored impatience. The lesser ranking of the two men prowls through the van while Officer Duarte smiles behind his questions. He is very handsome, tall beside his compatriot, and the whites of his eyes are practically neon with health. Even the small taut muscles of his face look somehow fit and ready for action.

"And what will you do when you are well?" He pauses to locate a stubby pencil from his shirt pocket, the kind that golfers use to keep score, then jots a few things down on a small pad. "In our land."

"Recreate," Mason says.

Duarte shifts his gaze to Clair. "We are here for pleasure," she says. "Not business." This is a phrase she has learned crossing the border into Canada. *Business or pleasure*, the friendly Canadian official always asks. Pleasure, she has been told, is always less menacing, less suspect, than business.

Presently the underling emerges from the side door of the van with a single box of film. "Very many," he says in Spanish, holding it up, smiling.

There are entirely too many smiles darting about. Even Mason's face is blank until a rictus grin thaws to life and just as quickly refreezes. "Amateur photographer," he says.

"You are English. You are American," Duarte says, nodding now to Clair.

"We are both US citizens," Mason says. "Land of plenty and all that."

"Yes, so I have heard, so I have heard," he murmurs, glancing north over the cars, a tile-work of hot gleaming hoods, waiting to enter Mexico. "And it is cold in England, no?"

"Damp. The women are cold." The first chink in his armor, this currying of male locker room favor, and also the first time Clair notices something like unease.

Again, Duarte smiles insincerely. He is so young, but his job has lent him an older, tired authority, as if he has seen more than he wishes, heard more than he can take.

Finally Clair's anxiety gets the better of her and she blurts out, "But what are you looking for? Why have you stopped us? Everyone else has been waved through."

"Looking? We are not looking for anything." He shrugs, gently tips his handsome head in what is clearly a sarcastic bow. "But we find things. Señorita." The *señorita* is pointed, accusatory. It is a Catholic country, and she and Mason are obviously not married. And why is it so obvious? she wonders.

"What is it about us?"

Mason, standing a few feet from her, hobbles over but does not place what she worries might be a condescending hand on her shoulder. "It's the van. They're nervous about the van. That's all. An *effing* van."

"But we are *entering* the country."

Norberto Duarte shrugs again. "You will leave it, too. With this van." He sniffs. "And many pictures."

Pivoting without warning, Mason makes his way, bent-backed, to the driver's side door. "Probably a dose of *turista* as well." He swings his head toward Duarte. "So. May we enter your fair land, Officer . . . ," he squints theatrically at the officer's name tag, "Duarte?"

The smile evaporates but no expression replaces it. She realizes suddenly that he must hate his job, hate Americans with their big new cars, their drug-hungry money, their colonizing compulsions. She has been reading about all the beachfront property between Tijuana and Ensenada that not-so-well-heeled Californians are buying up through special "partnerships" with Mexican banks at what are comparatively, maybe even literally, dirt-cheap prices. Property that few Bajacalifornianos can themselves afford.

A brown and white dog appears from nowhere, wanders up to Duarte, nudges his hand; Duarte bats it away, and taking no offense, the dog trots off, zigzagging among the cars. He wears no collar and his left hip has a caved-in look as if it has had a close encounter, begging car to car.

Poised submissively off to the side, Clair studies her sandals, her strong thin feet and narrow ankles accustomed to running, exactly what she would like to be doing right now. Running. Everyone in cars passing into Mexico rubbernecks them, these two detainees under scrutiny. Without explanation, Duarte decides to launch into a conversation with the other officer, a long apparently funny exchange because the other one can hardly keep from slapping his thigh in between glancing over at them with sheepish, sadistic speculation, as if they are the subject of the narrative and he needs to corroborate how they look and that they are still present, their fate in the balance. Finally, Duarte seems to rediscover them, raises his eyebrows, lifts his chin once, sharply, and sends them on their way.

"Were you trying to irritate him?" she asks Mason when they are back in the van. Her hands are still shaking.

"Me? He was doing his level-best to irritate us. That's the protocol, rattle the blighters until they expose themselves and their nefarious intentions."

"Why didn't you just speak Spanish to him? You speak beautiful Spanish. Why not make nice in their own language?"

"I speak Ecuadorian Spanish, a much higher, purer form than the lingua franca hereabouts. That would have added hours to our wait. He might have thought I was some kind of mule for a Latin American drug lord. This is Tijuana, Clair. Everything happens here. *Everything*. But especially coke."

She glances out the window, remembering last night's cocaine. It was good, but not worth it. She's feeling a little strung out.

Tijuana itself looks like a town after a hurricane has barreled through, a scabrous litter of cinderblock hovels, casitas, homes left half-finished but already lived-in and overcrowded, clinging cheek by jowl to the blasted hillocks and gullies, the claustrophobic canyons, the treeless, scarified slopes, and along the border itself, shacks and hovels like windblown trash pressed up to the corrugated metal fence—and then, here and there, a cadre of walled or fenced compounds where presumably the wealthier live with their satellite dishes cocked heavenward, the paint colors everywhere flaring, aggressive, the commercial signage a chaos of desires, demands, unsavory diversions. "Sometimes, Mason, you are so . . . *English*."

"Why, thank you, dear. Wouldn't want to disappoint." Unflappable, he steers the van through a scramble of rumbling beaters, most of them, as far as Clair can tell, ready for the junkyard, and none of them obeying any of the traffic signs. She does not like him addressing her as "dear."

"Well, you do disappoint. Sometimes," she adds to soften her irritation. She runs her hands over her cotton skirt, smoothing and tidying it, anxious to reach the coast where she thinks she will be able to breathe again. They are not off to a good start, but she wants matters to improve; she wants the feeling they had as they approached the border, the mass playing and the green estuary off to the west and the open fields flowing down the bottom hem of California. "What were they talking about, the two of them at the end? What were they saying about us?"

"Officer Duarte was telling his *compadre* about a new nightclub in town. Very risqué. A woman and a pony. Then the other one was bragging about the money he won at the *lucha libre*, the wrestling matches they have down here. Free-form. His man was 'the Blue Mystic.'" Mason sucks one of his teeth, a habit she is beginning to find annoying and that signals some residual form of dismissive English arrogance. "None of it had anything to do with us."

"Oh," she says, disappointed on several scores. But now she can see the sea in the distance, an opening sky with a fan of sunlight fractured and glittering across the water, and she feels a little less anxious. "Why would they want to hassle us?"

"A sport and a pastime, sport and pastime." He makes a broad waving gesture that takes in the city, the day, the morning traffic. "The day is young. Maybe they were cutting their teeth on us. Forget about it."

It takes a long time to escape the fringe neighborhoods and tailings of

Tijuana. For six miles the road runs west along the flood control channel and then the border fence, a strangely flimsy silly barricade against mutual otherness that marches down the beach and many yards out into the surf. The haphazard jumble of settlement, the garbage, the complete apathy toward beauty, is exhausting to Clair, as if she feels not only responsible for its existence, but also for its remediation. All she wants to do is crawl into the back of the van and close her eyes until it has been drawn from them like old skin from new, and they are truly free of it. The vegetation, such as it is, is no different from what they found south of San Diego, but it feels somehow frayed and struggling and mean with jealousy. Many of the streets are dirt, but dirt without any gravel or weight in it, and fine dun-colored smudges linger after passing cars, and already the vents have admitted enough to coat everything in the van. The air is fouled with exhaust and noise, because in Baja, mufflers, according to the guide they picked up in San Ysidro, are a sign of weakness, a condition so many locals want to avoid that there are road signs reminding drivers that by law, mufflers are required. When they reach the coast and turn south, they pass through the first toll booth, about a dollar in pesos. Offshore, Isla Coronado floats serenely on a jeweled blue carpet, distancing itself from the mainland chaos and general disgrace that is humanity. From that point south for the next thirty miles, the beaches are partially hidden behind condo developments, fishing villages becoming resort towns, and various infrastructure facilities, including the Rosarito generating and desalinization plant. But they are heading south, away, and that is sufficient for Clair.

In La Fonda they stop for fish tacos and ice to replenish the ziplock still lodged against Mason's lower back. Clair picks out the shards of wilted greenery in the taco, but is still worried about contamination, and Mason is amused by her fastidiousness. His familiarity with the globe and its multitude of comestibles, together with his impervious gut, give him an advantage he enjoys flaunting, but which makes her feel childish and finicky. On the way back to the highway, he buys tequila and beer from a tienda that looks about ready to close down for good, the shelves mostly empty spaces punctuated by dusty boxes of translated American products, undersized compared to their cousins across the border, or crates of avocados no bigger than eggs, and tiny grapes well on their way to becoming raisins. Everything is smaller here, expectations, dreams; everything is nearer its end. He takes one of his codeine pills with the beer, ignoring her concerns about mixing alcohol and pain meds, and invoking the bad water as reason enough. They both know that there are three, five-gallon jugs of potable water in the back of the van. They have stopped conversing.

Even though it has nothing to do with why he is here in Mexico, Mason wants to photograph some of the famous surfing breaks north of Ensenada, which they can see—long crescent lines moving on an oceanic conveyor belt toward the playas. He prefers to work alone. When she has accompanied him in the past, it is as if she is not there anyway, so she decides to take a run, cool off in the surf, and then read in the only shade there is beside the van.

Burning through hundreds of frames to harvest one useable shot is an approach that is foreign to Clair. Her work is careful and final, second chances no more reliable than second selves. The data that she collects is fixed in time and place and, in some sense, already dead when it reaches her desk, receding into the past and decreasing, tick by tick, in value. So by training and nature, she is a perfectionist.

Down the beach, his shape blurs and shrinks and, at one point, seems to float, mirage-like, above the in-washing waves. His safety seems never in question. She cannot now imagine the world without him in it, and that is becoming the source of a deep and unnerving happiness. She feels trapped by it, like an addict already worrying about her next fix, already doubting the one she has now, already sunk deep into a vein.

The morning light, once bright and clean, turns some unnoticed corner, and something vaguely infirm enters it. Colors in the under-spectrum have disappeared, so that there are only two or three contributing to the available light—yellow, white, gray. The surfers are too far out to believe in, mysterious black ink marks on a blue blotter, and the beach is too vast, too empty to feel playful, as beaches ought. Unexpectedly, she misses her sister. Beaches seemed to free them of their status as twins, as rivals. They were good at the beach, good to each other; sisterly. The two of them facing the towering waves and the great empty universe of the sea racing way from them toward the horizon. She can remember taking a bad tumble once beneath a heavy vertical wave, not knowing up from down and hearing the gritty wash of sand, feeling the surprising weight and finality of water, and then Nina dragging her by the straps of her suit to the surface, pop-eyed with fright. She hadn't laughed then; she had regarded Clair, a thorough once-over, her eyes as serious as a doctor who might have bad news to deliver. Then the eyes cut away. Nina did not like to be caught caring. Or maybe she was half-hoping that the news was bad, and she didn't want to expose her disappointment.

By the time the highway leaves the coast and bends inland and then south, it is after 2:00, hot, and no longer a promising day but something that must be got through with set-teeth and forced patience. Her eyes are burning from the glare and aridity. Staring out the window, she begins to think about marriage, if this is what happens once you enter that country, billowed up with celestial hope and ornamented with promises you are already forgetting even as your finger grows accustomed to its tiny gleaming noose; and then everything just gets a little less easy, a little more like something you have to think about, toothpaste in the sink and dirty socks under the front edge of the couch, bills that one of them failed to pay, gestural habits that were once so cute composing signs and signals you're not so fond of reading over and again. Hot drives in foreign countries an ordeal, not an adventure, not a lark, not a strand in the DNA of their destiny together.

She has never been married. She would like to be married. She would like to marry this man. To give him joy, to see that joy in his eyes, to have and to see the other side of giving. And to have someone securely on her team; someone who might worry if she didn't come home one night; to give to her son a father, which Ethan claims not to want so vehemently that she knows it has to be exactly what he wants. It is one of the occasions on which he makes a deliberate and aggressive display of his intelligence, brandishing weapons to hide war wounds he's not old enough yet to brag about. *I'm tough, real tough, like Mike Barber in the movies . . .* a line that floats up from one of the children's books she reads to him. "I don't need a father. Why would I want a father? Who needs fathers?" She's begun to worry that his attitude is developing into a phobia.

But about marriage Mason is vague, a shape to make out now and then down an empty beach.

She glances over at him, as if to make sure he's still there in the driver's seat. "What are you thinking?" she says. "I've got a penny here some-where." She pretends to pat pockets for change.

"I'm fine."

She is looking at the side of his face, his set mouth; beyond him, filling the driver's side window, the burnt yellow mountains. "Fine? Now I know you're not."

"Okay. Right you are. You owe me a penny."

She smiles without showing her teeth. "No penny. You haven't told me yet what you were thinking about. Details, details. After which, payment will be made."

"My father. Hare hunting with my father." Abruptly, there is a deadpan warning in his voice that only makes her more curious.

"That's far away, Cornwall."

"Not far enough."

"Why Cornwall? And hare hunting?"

"Because of that stray, that *perro vagabundo*. The brown and white one."

Funny, she hadn't really registered the dog, at least not to keep remem-bering it. "So?"

"It was obviously used to getting something from Duarte, a morning treat, but Duarte ignored it because of us. Didn't want to look soft in front of the Americanos. Machismo," he adds.

About Mason's past she thinks she knows a lot. When they were first together, he used to talk about Cornwall, about his life on the farm with his father and sister, the stone house, the clotted cream, the thistles. She knows that his birth was difficult, a breach; that the doctor had to yank one leg, then the other, and finally hook his finger in Mason's mouth and pull and wiggle and wedge him through the opening; that the mouth was so torn he could not nurse, and so, according to family lore, they did not bond, mother and child. Forever after, the doctor was referred to as "the butcher."

Well past the time when he should have, they noticed that the baby still had not begun to walk. One leg was not developing like the other, and only then they discovered that his hip had been damaged during the difficult birth, and so his leg had to be set and imprisoned in a metal brace with a boot attached to the end. For reasons he can't recall, the brace was named "Fanny," as in, "Where's Fanny? Time to put on Fanny!" Mason wore the brace until he was almost four.

Once not long after they'd met, Clair ran into Mason on a street corner, a chance meeting. He missed a step and half stumbled. It didn't have to be because of her, but she thought it probably was. She had felt flattered and then embarrassed for him. Now though, she wonders if it was because of his past, his misdeveloped leg, not because he was excited to see her and a little nervous. She thinks of the expression, *he stubbed his toe*, meaning someone—a man—had had an illicit relationship, an expression her mother used when gossiping in front of the twins about a neighbor who took regular excursions from his marriage. But there was nothing illicit about their relationship, hers with Mason, and he was naturally loyal—didn't seem to have it in him not to be loyal. It could be that, for Mason, love itself was illicit, something dangerous and forbidden, frighteningly unknown. What did it matter who its current emissary was? In love, things could get at you, and Mason was always behaving as if things could never get at him.

She knows that his mother, a small demure woman, was herself so torn up during the delivery that had lasted two full days that she had, in fact, died once during the delivery only to be brought back, they said, like some defector from a state they had all sworn allegiance to—the state of life. The doctor had said, *it's over*, before it was really over. Then she died a second time for good when Mason was a year old, having never quite recovered from the damage done during his birth—again, according to family lore. His head was too big, they said, and that became both metaphor and mockery, the first from his father and the second from his older sister. So it was just the three of them, father, son, sister. Five years older, Emily assumed certain manageable aspects of Mason's care, a situation that effectively deprived them of a proper rivalry and generated an almost militant reflex against anyone, but especially a woman, trying to look out for his best interests. He knew what was in his best interests, thank you very much. He could take care of himself.

Surreptitiously, she considers Mason's head, calling up various melons and playground balls to measure it against. A perfectly normal head, she decides, though a chord of guilty silliness vibrates momentarily just beneath her breastbone. A perfectly wonderfully brilliant head. It was awful how the stupidest ideas and casual cuts could grow into family factoids everyone instantly stops questioning just because some aunt or second cousin after too much Guinness one night came up with a clever but mean epithet. Everyone had loved Bridget Comstock; *impossibly nice*, everyone said. The boy was no consolation. And what did that mean, *impossibly nice*? That it couldn't be trusted or that Bridget Comstock had remained nice in spite of . . . what?

Louise Bugato used to accuse Clair of being too good to stomach, and now she wonders if they aren't the same implausible conditions. Goodness. Niceness.

She reaches over and squeezes the sides of Mason's neck where the tension usually gathers, and he rolls his head appreciatively. "What's it like?" she asks, "hare hunting?"

"Cold."

The air conditioning in the van has been struggling to maintain a tolerable temperature. "It's hot. Tell me a cold story, then. Maybe it'll have a salutary effect."

He smiles grimly, and she can tell that he is pleased with the way she thinks, but sad about what he remembers. "Not much to tell. It was a cold damp day."

"What day?"

"The day I'm remembering. The day in question."

"The day in question."

"Yes. That one. The only one. The day all was revealed."

"Okay. So . . . it was cold."

"That's what you want for good scenting, wet ground with the air colder than the ground. Chimney smoke not rising."

"And . . . ?"

"So, there was mist, scarves of it stretching and staying low down along the creases and combes, and blue smoke muffled around the stone chimneys. I could hear the rumble of the surf from the north and west, not loud but just . . . off there. I used to think that it was the earth mad about something, the lot of us on top, trampling about, ruining things."

"But what happened?"

"We went out with the locals."

"The locals."

"Farmers and graziers, some town folk. Dad being a sort of gentry, we had no contact with them except when it came to hare hunting. It's good scenting country, Cornwall, and the hares are plentiful. Cornish folk like to get together and work the dogs across pasture and plough. It was all about the dogs. The chase. We saw the locals often when there were no hares, in mid-summer, just to work the dogs back and around, sometimes up into the Bodmin moors where there aren't wires, only a few stone walls staggering along."

"What kind of dogs?"

"Beagles. A beagle is a fine animal, fine and friendly." Mason smiled, leaning back in the driver's seat and nodding to himself. "As game as they come, too, but independent. They like the chase. I had raised one of ours from a pup. Jules. Had some basset in him, quite a lot, actually, which is why he ended up mine. Not a pure beagle. But bassets, they're better at scenting, at staying the line and not getting distracted by fresh quarry, because they can't run as fast across the open fields and uplands. Jules was mine. But my father took a shine to him, or maybe it was both ways round. At any rate, they kept royal company every night at the hearth, Jules' head flopped across his boots and the titbits dropping accidentally so often you'd've thought the old man had palsy and couldn't feed himself properly any longer. The day before Jules joined the others, his first hunt, I was sitting at the table in my room, pasting photographs in an album. No one had ever bothered to sort them up, the family pics. There was a hamper of them in the closet, and I had decided to take it on. It was November. Long nights. I was bored. It's a bit of fun, you see, spotting scraps of yourself, a squint about the eyes, or a stubborn cowlick, a way of holding your hands, all the genetic ticks and tags scattered through the gang of us. Something to belong to," Mason says, deliberately turning his face away from her toward the desert.

"Then dear old dad popped in and blew a bloody gasket," he adds in a strangely apathetic singsong.

"Why?"

Mason shrugs, his eyes dead to the memory, lids lowered.

"No, no, there had to be a reason. You're not telling it all."

"Might've been the pics of mum," he says, biting his lip.

"Your mother? But why wouldn't he . . . I don't understand."

Another shrug. "I say something, he says something, I give him a right royal salute, and the next thing I know, I'm a cheeky mongrel, and he's yanking off his braces to flog me."

"How old were you?"

"Old enough to hate. Twelve."

"Did you fight back?"

"Not if I wanted to suck another breath." Again, Mason turns his head to the side, away from her. "The first time you hate, or know that you hate . . . that's something you don't forget. Jules crawled under my chair, and that was what finally stopped the old hide. Jules wasn't defending me, never growled, not a whimper. He was just there, looking up with those doleful basset eyes. Judge and jury."

They haven't seen another car for miles, and the solitariness of their journey, the fact that no stranger is there to witness them on the road, has the effect of transporting them back to Cornwall as if nothing lashes them securely to this time and place, to this road, to this heat, so that they are in yet another country, the undiscovered country behind them and in the past. She does not seem to see the landscape around them; she sees instead the boy with photographs of a mother he never consciously knew and whom he is charged, in whisper and innuendo, with having done in. A demure and impossibly nice mother, a boy missing a mum on a dark day in November, and photographs no one had had the heart to look at after.

She asks, "Did you look like her?"

And Mason nods, as if admitting to the crime. "Like her and not at all like Himself. Except for the height. And the temper."

"The next morning Dad was knackered. He should have called the meet, but he was the Master and the others looked to him. So we went to the village green, we were supposed to go and so we went where we were supposed to go, to the meet, with Jules on the seat between us and the others kenneled in the back. It was the only thing we shared, the love of Jules.

"In the village, the Huntsman was waiting, the Whippers-in, green coats and caps in the middle of the gang and the followers milling around, puffing breath, jabbing hands in pockets, some of them nipping at flasks. Dad, too. Hair of the dog. Everyone in trainers or hockey shoes because it's shank's mare, a hare hunt. No horses. And they can go on for hours and over miles of humpy cow pasture and moors with stone and ledge, hedgerow to hedgerow, moss-backed stones. It'll bugger you out."

"And you? What were you?"

"I was to play a sab."

"Sab?"

"Saboteur," he says as if she ought to know. "To make it more sporting. I was on the side of the hare. There were two of us, a mucker from the next hamlet over, some years older. Nice lad. Had a thing for Em. Our bit was to distract the dogs, whistling maybe, or spraying scent duller, splitting the pack, clapping to make the sound of the whip—whatever it took, but not so's the Huntsman could see."

"So English," she murmurs, "arranged sabotage."

"A life is at stake," he tells her seriously, and she refrains from saying, *but it doesn't have to be, it's a sport.*

"And so we set out. The Huntsman cast the hounds, and I worked downwind. Jules made his way to the front of the pack, but we all knew it would be the older ones who took the lead once they were closing in. It was Jules who struck the scent, the basset in him. God, I was proud of him. He was my pup, my flap-eared beauty. Jules struck the scent. We all took the field, the dogs barking, the whips whipping, the pack swinging back and around together, like a school of fish, and the hare darting by, along the hedgerow, jinking to one side and the other. But it must have clapped to the ground because the pack lost the scent. Then the milling, the consternation. A brown hare is not easy to spot against a brown November scene. And if it has the opportunity to foul its scent in a pad of manure or exhaust from a passing car—anything—it will. They're faster than a dog, but the dogs will outlast them.

"The Huntsman cast the hounds again, they scattered, tails up, trying to puzzle it out, everyone, the whippers-in and the followers watching for the hare to break. And break it did, not ten meters from where I stood. My father gave the horn three short notes, one of the supporters pointed with his cap, and then the first dog struck the line and they were all barking and the hare running in wide circles, wider and wider. When the pack came back 'round where I was following downwind, I shouted *on-on-on* to send them off in the wrong direction, away from the line. Ah, but Jules knew I was lying and he held the line, and so now the pack was split, and then the second sab split it again. The Huntsman collected the pack, and we were back at it. Over and over again.

"By noon we had two hare, but some wanted another. By god, it was the longest hunt. Cold, and down where we were then, misty, hard to see, with stone and hummock, stumps and bogs, everything made, everything wanting to break a bone or turn an ankle. Eventually the pack struck one, and now it was the older dogs at the lead, Jules somewhere at the tail end. I was following still, whistling, clapping. There is a small river in that country, the Hayle River, and the hare was chased up to the bank of the Hayle, jinking left and right, wanting to avoid the water, once squirming under some roots. Then, by rights, the hare was given law, and chased down again. Those are the rules, to give law. Now it was my father's turn to shoot. Suddenly the hare leaped into the river. That meant the end of the hunt, and I was glad enough. I turned to glance back up the pasture where Dad and some of the followers were still coming down, and made a movement with my arms, crossing and uncrossing them to say, *it's over.* I looked away. His gun went off." Mason paused to breathe.

"How I knew that he had shot Jules I can't tell you. It was like the smell of wind before it quite reaches you, before it overcomes you, only it was a scent I struck in my heart before I knew even what I was turning for, turning to the left, to the open pasture with its matted dead grass and its sodden stench of earth and shit, the pasture that swung down to the Hayle. The other dogs were still scrambling and searching along the bank for the quarry, and back behind them a brown and white shape, not moving, and his white so pure, so startling and not believable, not anything I could stand to believe, lying there in the brown pasture."

"I don't understand," Clair says. "What happened?"

At first Mason doesn't answer. He reaches with his left hand around his side and rattles the bag of ice just to have something to do, it seems, then he rubs his lower back. There is no expression in his eyes, his pupils are like gray clearies no one is likely to notice or want to play for in a game of marbles. She wonders how he does it, how he empties his eyes of feeling and interest and gloams them over so that no one can see in.

Suddenly, ahead of them and to the right, is a line of upright beer cans that quickly vectors to the side of the road, to a broken-down Suburban. Its occupants are spilled out of the vehicle, children playing in the ditch beside the highway, and a man, maybe their father, with an oil can, has his head under the hood, another man drinks a beer beside him, and two women sit on the rear bumper, training their listless gaze on the van as it slowly passes.

"Should we stop?" she asks.

Mason says, "Everyone in Mexico knows how to fix a car." And so they keep driving.

The mountains that form the spine of Baja are a dirty sulfurous yellow, and the sun, crawling down the western sky, has made them incendiary mountains of lithified flame before which Mason is silhouetted, a dark cut-out of a man driven and driving south. In that moment, it occurs to her again that maybe she has no idea who he is or if she can trust him with her happiness, least of all her sadness. With live feelings.

"But what happened?" she asks again.

"The dog jumped up just as Dad fired. He didn't see my signal. Didn't see me. Didn't see the pack scattered. Didn't know the hare was in the Hayle River. That was what he said back at the house when we buried Jules, him weeping like an effing baby and jabbing his finger at me as if it were my fault. Never said he was sorry. Never said that hate was stronger than love. Never had to say it after that day. Never let me have those pics of her. He hid them away or threw them away, but I never saw them again. Never mentioned the wooly I was wearing, one of mum's, except to tell me to take it off and clean myself for dinner. Maybe I wore it that day just to dig at him. Maybe it *was* my fault."

Something in Clair needs to make it all okay, the nervous, hand-wringing girl standing in the corner; to make the world and the way it works not really the way it works; to make it okay, a good safe place, a safehouse. "So it was an accident."

"That's not what I said," Mason answers in a voice so leveled out that she hardly recognizes it. It is like the road unwinding ahead of them, vacant and black.

She decides to consign his tone to some other part of her brain, the part that seals over things rapidly, both by pretending it was said to someone else not present in the van, and by giving a short laugh, as if an embarrassment has just been committed, and she's not sure who's responsible and doesn't, really, want to know.

"Why," he pretends to ask her, "would Jules jump up? How could Jules jump high enough to have caught that bullet? A beagle with more basset than beagle in him. Think of his legs, his stubby legs, his big clumsy paws. Think of the pasture, slung down the hillside to the Hayle, and Jules at the lowest bit of it in the boggy hollow where the runoff collects. And him, my Jules, jumping for what?" Mason jerks his face sharply toward her, then back at the windshield and the road unwinding before them. "What was up there in the sky for him to jump for? Not a hare. The hare was in the Hayle River, swimming for its life. Jules had his nose to the ground where a hound keeps his nose, plowing for quarry. No. My father shot him to take someone I loved away from me. To square things. Because of the pics. Because we were thick with each other, blood thick and sick of each other, and only Emily to water the whole muddle down. It must have been hard on her, now I think of it."

"Hard on all of you."

Now in silence, they drive on. Not a lot changes, she thinks . . . people chewing off something important to get away, to have something new in a new place. A chance. But memory . . . is the memory of pain worse than the pain itself? It seems so. It seems to get bigger, more knotted up. Mason has a life now that is his and his alone. His father is far enough away, so far that the past has mummified around him. Then there was her own father whose memories destroyed him. And Nina, there is always Nina with her unremembered memories. There will always be Nina to sort out, like those hampered photos in the stone houses of November.

She stares out the window. It takes so long for cactus, for any plant, to grow in this landscape that the highway construction twenty-five years earlier is still evident in the scar of mostly lifeless shale and dirt bordering the road. A few members of the cactus family have begun to colonize the scarified ground—barrel and hedgehog cactus, some black-edged cholla, no beavertail, a few stunted cardón in the distance, and here and there a struggling ocotillo. No desert flowers. Recovery is slow in some places, especially where resources, like water and nutrients, are insufficient. Recovery is slow for some people, too, and for the same reason.

THEY ARE SILENT through Ensenada, trying in some unspoken wounded communal way not to notice its junky assault on their senses—the trash, the ragtag businesses, the tourist kitsch, and bad jokey signs, the insistent but somehow languid and wasted bustle, as if everyone is sun-drugged and can't remember why they're hurrying, but hurry they will. Over the next hundred and twenty miles, they talk about their work, or talk not at all, both of them tired and Mason's back not just an ache but beginning to randomly spasm. He wants to do something nice for Clair, he wants it to be possibly even romantic, where they end up on their first night in Mexico—that's what he implies in so many words. He has always been clumsy about gestures of romance, not because they aren't real or meaningful, but because they are so real, so meaningful that they overload his system. When the road descends into the comparatively fertile valley of San Quintin, where actual palm trees grow and water meanders, where there are salt marshes and greenhouses, even a vineyard, he drives straight out to Playa

Santa Maria and gets them a room at a fancy new resort built along the edge of the sand. The plantings around the entrance are so recent they are no bigger or taller than a boot, though the pennants strung in celebration of the grand opening have been hoisted long enough to be already frayed and faded. A single clerk stands behind the lobby desk, a young woman wearing an embroidered poppy-red peasant blouse, who takes their money with a solemn sense of purpose and hands them a key. Then a middle-aged man who looks like her father or uncle carries their two duffels and leads them down a tiled corridor. The place smells faintly of kerosene and fish. Although it is still light, candles burn in wrought iron wall sconces along the way. The man explains to Mason that the power is out, but it always comes back on, *pronto*, he assures them. In the room, he indicates a carafe of water with an upside down glass capping it. Bottled water, he calls it. *Saludable*, he tells them. When the door closes, Mason says to no one in particular, "Yes, and where are we supposed to think that water came from? The faucet. Which, oh, that's right, is not saludable."

He's standing in front of the glass doors that frame the sand and sea, his hand on his back, and she comes up behind him, pressing herself into him, kissing the side of his neck, lifting his hair where the collar has matted it and running her fingers through it. "Let's try to have a nice time, okay?"

"Sure."

"Scotch."

"Scotch neat."

The power never does come back on, and they decide to skip dinner, eat from the American snacks in the van, and sleep at nightfall. Dawn, before Mason is awake, Clair slips out the glass doors for a run. The fog has come into the bay, not quietly or stealthily, but shoved in by rough and confused onshore gusts. She can't see the ocean, its measureless size, only the thin line of the surf now and then, and the curving white margin of salt foam each wave pushes in. It is this margin of white foam that she follows south. The fog is white, too, and surprisingly cold, the beach long and barren, and because she can't see where she's going, everything begins to feel aimless and primordial. They seem to be the only guests staying at the hotel. The wind has sculpted the dry upper sand in smooth broad mounds and hollows that she knows will be different tomorrow and different the next day. Nothing permanent or reliable. The hotel is new but feels old and left behind, rejected, and the old things, like sand and sea, keep changing. New things that are already old and old things playing at newness.

Everywhere along the wet rippled flats are sand dollars. She collects one to take back to the room. In the fog, the sand is dull and tawny, with a fine grittiness pleasing to the bottoms of her feet. Occasionally she feels something stony, and realizes that it is a clam digging down, away from light and air. She has run longer than she meant to, long enough to feel the beginnings of strain in her calves, and so she turns back north. The tide is ebbing, and the broad flats are pocked wherever the retreating waves have briefly uncovered a clam. For a while, because of the shape of the shore, the fog withdraws beyond the break, and now she notices up the sandy slope fence posts set at irregular intervals along the top edge of the beach. Perched on each one is something dark the size of a small dog . . . there's a spot of red, too. She climbs the slope, and when she nears one of the posts, she sees that it's a buzzard. They are all buzzards, on every fence post, like sentries or living gargoyles. She has never seen so many just roosting and waiting. Slowly, Clair backs away, trying to catch her breath, to calm down. They are big birds, solid and sobering. But there is nothing about her they find interesting, not one of them even lifts a folded wing or straightens its drooping neck. If they are sleeping, they are also watching, and if they are watching, they must be waiting for something to die. To wash up on this beach and give them something to do, the job of cleaning up after lives that have ended.

Before she can tell Mason about the buzzards, he says, "Where have you been? I'm in bloody agony. Get me some ice. I can't even move without this damn thing going into spasm. First, codeine. Ibuprofen."

She's rummaging through their things for the bottled water, and he says, "I don't care about the water. Any water." And so she pours the carafe water into the glass and tips it up to his lips. He's lying flat on his back with his eyes pasted to the ceiling, trying not to move.

"What's the word for ice?"

"*Hielo,*" he groans.

She repeats it, then rushes out of the room down the tiled corridor to the front desk. The same young woman is there, alarmed by the way Clair looks, by her expression, her bare feet. There are still no other guests in evidence. "*Vielo?*" Clair asks urgently. "My friend, my amigo," she adds quickly, "needs *vielo*." Then she pats her own back and mocks a look of pain. The young woman shakes her head, frowns, calls for Franco, the same man who carried their bags the night before but who today is wearing some sort of long leather apron. They are the only two employees she has seen so far, but she senses others in the dusky back hallways, waiting. It takes Clair and Franco another five minutes to unravel the mystery of *vielo*, first blundering their way through similar words, *viejo*, and then he tips a sympathetic head and explains in torn English that the power is still out, that the hotel still has no *hielo*. His soft feminine mouth is only faintly amused, and if he doesn't quite know what to do with this *gringa*, whether to give in and like her or to fall back on cultural ridicule, his eyes remain steadily kind.

Soon after there's a knock on their door—Franco with a block of ice wrapped in canvas. Tiptoeing past Mason to the small patio, he sets it down on a flat rock where they chip it down to size. Franco has a shy fatherly face that carries its own story of pain, pain that he will never reveal, and she finds herself wishing that he would come with them to help Clair take care of Mason. He seems the sort of creature who can silently take care of everything. And she is feeling very tired, tired of taking care of things, tired of the years of taking care.

All day she lies on the other bed, watching Mason in his drugged stupor, watching the fog drift past the glass, trying to read, sleeping a little, studying his face and comparing what she sees to what she has previously thought about this face. They are not the same. The individual points do not add up to the final argument, and yet she is completely convinced, completely in love.

Mason can't move, and so twice she helps him pee into the empty ice bucket, a charge that feels like monastic duty. The contaminated bucket must now be stolen. She rinses it in the tub—*too yellow*. She makes him drink more water, then he drops instantly back into sleep. His mouth parts and slackens, one of his hands twitches. He's only forty but the pain makes him look older. And she can't help thinking that he is not exactly a handsome man. Awake, fisted up with purpose, his brow strong and broad and his eyes as alert as two search lights, he is irresistible—a rebel, a man of passion. But not today—today everything feels in question. Her own secret border patrol is rummaging through her life, holding up this, examining that, asking questions.

She takes a shower, observing her body in the steamy mirror, a thin curving peachy blur of flesh, a dark cap of wavy hair that rests just above her collar bones. But for Ethan, Mason is all she seems to have now. And it may be that Mason simply hasn't enough to offer and will have less and less as time ravels out. Anyone that sure of himself must be defending against something; must be living on principal. It worries her.

In the late afternoon, Franco knocks on the door again, this time with food wrapped in foil—burritos—and in a red ceramic bowl he has carefully covered with a kitchen towel, *posolé*, plus two sugar-coated *galletas*. Twice more he brings ice. The power is back on and so the hotel has its own *hielo*.

"*El Señor*," Franco says to her on one of these visits, his voice as soft as a girl's, "you are to love him, *sí*?" He nods to agree with himself.

"Yes. *Sí*."

"*Mi corazón, mi* heart, *esta quieto* . . . it is standing still, *para usted*. For you."

"But why?"

Taking a step back, he opens his palms, and she half expects to see the stigmata, but it is a simple gesture of obviousness and inevitability, as if she, before all others, must see the situation she is in, the kind of man she is with. The destiny of it. She is in love, and that makes her pitiable even to strangers.

From the other bed, she devours the burrito, watching Mason doze. In his dreams, several expressions she has never witnessed visit his face, one a pouty sort of woefulness that breaks her heart, and then the look of a scared boy. The fog has lifted and far out in the smooth wet sand she notices a woman and a boy, the boy darting forward and back, swinging a mesh bag in his hand. At the surf line, the woman uses a pitchfork to dig up pismo clams the size of her palm, the boy opening the mesh sack for her to drop them in. Overhead, seagulls. Behind them, a flock of sanderlings trotting in tiny unison like a single pointillist creature moving in and out, following, then just escaping the low waves, in, out, in, out, their beaks frantic and probing. For some reason she is embarrassed by their silly panicked hunger. *How pathetic life is, how ravening . . .*

From the pay phone in the lobby, she places a collect call to Mrs. Holian whose report is brief and positive. Then Ethan is on the line.

"Mama!"

"Hello, sweet boy. Do you know that I adore you? If I were there I'd squeeze the stuffing out of you."

He giggles. Usually his intelligence keeps him from banal forms of joy. She is so happy to hear this joy, so hungry for it, that she giggles back. She tells him about the buzzards—Ethan has a morbid but enchanting curiosity about ghoulish things.

They talk for five minutes. As she's wandering back to the room, she marvels, *this boy . . .* and suddenly wonders if her own mother still feels a little jealous or even resentful. Almost immediately she decides that, of course, she must.

Another day, another night, another foggy run down the beach past the buzzards. This time, men in rubber boots with long poles and long lines are surf fishing. Mackerel. They do not turn to look at her, she is just a thin white ghost from the country to the north, an intrusion to ignore, to put up with. There is a glint of silver out in the mess of surf, and the men, speaking rapidly, surround the beautiful and remarkably muscular fish flashing sunlight as she jogs by.

On the third morning, Mason is ambulatory, but the codeine seems to be making him touchy—touchier than usual. The plan is to camp one or two nights in the central desert as they travel east over the spine of the peninsula before the highway turns west again and back to the Pacific. It is two hundred fifty miles to Guerrero Negro, and they have plenty of time to do some exploring. The road drops into a barren canyon where they notice a strange crew of people—not Mexicans—with picks and small hand shovels, mesh screens, plastic boxes, working along the sedimentary layers.

"Fossils," she tells him, "paleo-peeps," because this is peripheral to what she knows and does, inventorying the past, comparing it to the present, what's missing from what was, and what has replaced it, or what never was. Mason nods, accepting her authority. He is comfortable, learning from her, a trait that most of her male friends and former boyfriends and colleagues do not reliably share.

In El Rosario, they stop at the Pemex station for gas, making sure that it is unleaded—*Extra*—then pick up fresh food—food in peels, plus a chicken hardly bigger than a game hen—and keep going. The smallness of everything in Baja is already beginning to tell her things about her own country, about sustenance and dreams, about resources and expectations, about waste. Embarrassments of riches. They are both a little shell-shocked from the time in San Quintin, and don't talk. But when they enter the *Valle de los Cirios* and the road parts a forest of them—cirios, boojum trees, (*Fouquieria columnaris*, she enunciates in her mind), which grow nowhere else on the planet—Mason pulls over to the side of the road and, in silence, they both climb out to wander among the strange plants, each one with its own personality, its own take on being a boojum. Their dirty yellow skins are hard as enamel, but dull, and compete with the cardón for the tallest plants on the peninsula. They are like inverted carrots, all of them thorny, some bristling with short stubby branches or, if it has just rained—and it must have—furry with leaves. The tallest, most mature of them have crowns of crazy arms, three, four, five of them waggling at the sky, with supplicating hands of white flowers at the ends of each. Mason is thoroughly amused by them and has her snap several pictures of himself beside one, gesturing an imperial introduction. They are right out of a Dr. Seuss book. Eventually, Clair returns to hide in the van; it's hot, the sun as heavy as a sandbag across her shoulders, and the ordeal in San Quintin has caught up. She watches Mason through the open window, cavorting among the boojum, and wonders how much codeine he's had. His affection for the world's goofiness always charms her, it is so unexpected, so contrary. And these are very goofy plants, rocketing straight up fifty, sixty feet, and defying all experience with symmetry and sensibility. They have individuated with a ferocity that she has never before encountered.

"How," he says, when he is back in the driver's seat, "how can something so silly-looking, so improbable, come to be? They're stupidly complicated. Can't decide what to look like, what to be, *how* to be or even when to be what. Look at that one over there, frizzed with leaves. It's pure farce."

"Yup."

"Yup?" he snorts. "That's what our resident botanist has to say? Yup."

"Every single aspect of the cirio is an adaptation to catastrophically narrow resources. That's bound to make you a little . . . weird."

"Weird."

"Think of it psychologically. Think of it as a plant's version of affect regulation. It controls the way it looks to the world to get along with the world and its . . . moods. And to get what it needs from the world. To survive."

"Moods."

"Down here," she says, "the world is in a perpetually bad mood."

"This analogy is beginning to make me feel a bit . . . itchy. Mind if we change the topic, love?"

"Go right ahead."

"You're in a quirk today."

She swings her head away from him and gazes out into the desert, and then at one of the cirios standing off by itself, so solitary, so accepting, that leans like a dancer toward the ravine where the fog, practically the only source of water, draws inland from the west. Its arms reach up and out, and its little white flower hands grasp at nothing. It reminds her of a half-mad homeless woman she saw once, dancing by herself in a rain storm in Union Square, all the tourists smiling with embarrassment as they passed and Clair trying not to cry.

They camp that night in the sandy bottom of an arroyo. The landscape is well-vegetated with cacti and other plants. All day long, off in the distance or stumbling across the road, they have seen small bands of grazing cattle, lean by American standards, and many of them horned. *Herbivory.* They have entered *Las Virgines*, a natural park where cattle from the local ranches are discouraged but not actively barred because there's no money to pay someone to keep them out. Clair notes the flowers, dozens of varieties the size of nail heads that have had a chance to grow because here the cattle are scarce. Up close, the land is surprisingly filled in, but everything has a spine or a thorn, and so it is not easy to walk, let alone to sit. The sandy arroyo they spot from a rise in the road several miles down a sidetrack seems a prudent place to stop.

Mason's back is better, less precarious. He arranges the Coleman stove on a flat-topped stone, wedging a piece of elephant tree bark to level it, then screws in the propane line and strikes a match. Clair has filled a pot with some of their potable water and sets it to a boil, peeling potatoes and onions to fry up with the chicken; peeling carrots and cucumbers and oranges for a salad, raisins to garnish. The air is still and peppery with the scent of the desert, though now and then something incongruously sweet brushes past, and she wonders which of the cacti are flowering. In the west, the light is blushing through popsicle orange and pink, towering cardón silhouetted against the changing colors, and the air still enough for them to see not just bats but moths, too. There are no visible insects, not even ants, but the bats are finding something. While their dinner cooks, Mason scrawls indecipherably in his journal, and Clair scrambles up the bank to look around. Caterpillar cactus surrounded by cryptobiotic crust; an elephant tree growing out of the crack in a fall of granite; cholla, ocotillo, coyote scat, desiccated and furry; javelina tracks; and the sounds of a woodpecker pounding away on a cardón, of crickets and finches and, when the air stirs wistfully, the dry rattle of dryland plants. It is a lonely world, an audacious world, this place of so little. It hardly seems worth it to try to live here, every plant and tree, every insect and animal accepting a challenge that seems plainly foolish and unwinnable. Yet they are winning, each in its own way.

They sit on stones to eat, their utensils clinking against the metal plates. In the distance, the woodpecker has stopped knocking and a hush, like held breath, surrounds them. That is when she notices that Mason is staring at her with soft open eyes. His hands are not negotiating his meal now, though his lips are slightly parted as if anticipating the next and now forgotten bite of food.

"What?" she whispers.

"What yourself." He doesn't stop gazing at her, but his eyes have widened.

"Thinking what?"

"Thinking, that's all." He forks up some carrot salad and looks away, then back at the food on his plate. "Thinking how pretty you are."

For some reason she doesn't smile, doesn't feel gratitude. Self-consciously, she runs her fingers through her bouncy hair. And just to be mischievous, she asks, "What if I were in some horrible disfiguring car accident?"

"What if you were?"

"Would you still love me? Assuming you do."

The pause is entirely too long. She saucers her eyes, not sure whether to be amused or furious or wounded, brought down by something worse than mortality. Truth. Or maybe only male truth.

Finally he says, "I would hate you. I hate you now. I hate you for letting me in on all this, this truck with love. I would hate you with all my might, and I would keep on hating you for the god-awful misery of love." He is clenching something back, an intolerable apprehension that knits up the corners of his eyes and moves his lips with odd uncertainty, as if many more words can't seem to break through and out. Then suddenly, it's gone, the storm in his face. He looks exhausted and sore. "What? You think you're just another pretty little chicken? Go ahead, have all the accidents you want. And while you're at it, go gray and get fat and shuffle about in your wrinkles and pink mules, and crack a can of hash and serve it up to me three times a day. You think it'll change anything? You think it ought? Never mind disfiguring accidents, why do you think it ought to change anything? Why do you worry? What is it you think you've done?"

She's never told him about Tony.

"Is this your way of saying that you love me?"

"So be it," he says, not looking at her, looking, instead, at the potato he's gently lifting onto the back of his fork and just as gently carrying to his open mouth.

THE NEXT DAY they don't travel far. They stop to take pictures, or for Clair to hike up some arroyo, stretching her legs, collecting and pressing bits of plants, a hobby habit that has nothing to do with the plant survey on

Cedros. Mason lies supine on the couch in the van, knees propped, nursing his back, reading. When they make camp that night, it is the same routine—stove out, food peeled and prepared, journal notes, Clair's sunset walk from which she returns with a few more plant specimens that she lays between paper sheets in the big, wood-bound plant press, screwing down the four edges after the last addition. But the feel of it all is different—ominous. Gray, frustrated clouds fist along the eastern mountains; the wind is impulsive, swirling, abruptly falling, and she begins to feel an unease about the place, as if something terrible has happened there, and they have come upon its aftermath whose impression still hangs like a miasma. It might be the configuration of the rocks, of the red wall sheering to the east, of the humped land behind them, mostly gravel with a few spiny and half-dead cacti. Or the way the load of dirt obscures the horizon so that they can't see out and away; the empty barranca, like a trench dug for a mass grave, that the hill drops into . . . everything feels *wrong*. She would swear that there is a sound, too, a sound they can't hear, but that is penetrating their bodies in slow flattened frequencies. She will feel foolish mentioning it to Mason; she is sure that he will make fun of her. But the feeling is so strong. The instant they have finished dinner, she admits, "I don't like it here."

"No?"

"It feels . . . bad. Somehow."

"Does it?"

"Yes." It will put more strain on his back. It is almost dark. Their stuff is scattered around them like shrapnel from a small incendiary device. She is not very good at asking for something that is just for herself. If it were for Ethan, or Nina, or Tom, or her mother—anyone else behind whose needs she might camouflage her own, or even if she could cobble together a practical reason to rationalize a move—these kinds of covert maneuvers she is good at if she has to be. Nibbling at the edge of a fingernail, punishing herself merely for asking, for needing, she says, "I'd rather not stay here."

And then Mason does something marvelous. He rises in silence and matter-of-factly begins packing up the camp kitchen. "I didn't much fancy it myself."

CHAPTER 6

Nina had her breakdown when they were fifteen. My breakdown, she came to call it, as if it were separate from her, a possession over which she had control.

Louise was the only one who was surprised—surprised enough to argue with the doctor about the necessity of medication, even after the two-week hospital stay. To Louise, medication equaled dependency, which equaled weakness, which meant you were vulnerable, to what, who could say. Imagination would fill in the blank with monsters bigger than any version reality might supply. "She's never needed pills before," she argued. "No one in the family has ever needed pills. This is just a bump in the road."

"She needs help, Mrs. Bugato."

"Nina has never needed help. She's the strong one. If this were Clair, then I could see, maybe . . ." She patted Clair's hand and let her voice drift off. The psychiatrist glanced uncomfortably away. She was a little too hip to be the head shrink on a psyche ward, this psychiatrist with her lab coat draped over black patterned leggings, her shiny French flats, the lacquered hair sticks knitting themselves through a glossy coiffure. But somehow for Clair it lent a sizable measure of credibility. She didn't have to do this, was Clair's thinking; she didn't have to hide out with a bunch of wackos; she actually seemed to want to *ease suffering*. Maybe she even had something more than a profession, maybe it was a *calling*, which made it sound almost spiritual. Maybe she believed that people could change, actually get well, lead productive lives, get over the crippling sense of omnipotence that led to runaway responsibility.

"But now she does need some help."

"Forgive me, Dr. Wells, but you must be used to dealing with adults," Louise said, waving her arms grandly toward the walls of the office behind which Clair imagined hordes of crazed adults pressing in like bug-eyed Zombies. "And Nina is a teenaged girl. *A teenaged girl*." Her voice leapt an octave. "They're always having fits and phases."

No doubt sorry she had requested a predischarge family meeting, but required to do so by convention and rule, Dr. Wells glanced again with nervous apology at Clair, and in a moment of multiple calculations scribbling visibly across her pale, room-cloistered brow, she decided on candor. She had a way of hesitating before the final words in sentences and then dropping her voice, as if, like many of the adults Clair had experienced, she was reluctant to utter the truth, though in her case and as a psychiatrist, often the final word did pack a wallop. "Nina is severely . . . dissociative. But that is a significant improvement on the psychotic state she arrived in. We do not want to go backwards. She has progressed from something like catatonia to running into the arms of anyone who enters the ward, even the janitor."

"What exactly are you saying?"

"She hugs everyone. A much healthier a-ffect," she drew out the *a*, like someone having his tonsils checked, "than nothing, than catatonic depression, but still . . . troubling. People in the sort of state she's been in are hypersensitive to . . . inauthenticity. It is important to be gently, consistently honest and straightforward with her. The world for Nina, the parts of it that she encounters in these first few months must be . . . reliable. Without pretense. Rock solid. She's like a child at this point, meeting a new world. She has been through something that, for her, was terrible. Well," she added in afterthought, "for any one of us." Dr. Wells flipped randomly through Nina's file, not reading it, just neatening and calming the pages so that they squared up with the others marking time on her desk. "Solid ground and simple honesty," she concluded, "that's what she needs now."

It was then that Henry, seated off to the side and slightly behind the female Bugatos, spoke. "Yes, I can see that." He was looking at the carpet between his shoes when he began to speak, but at the end, he swung his head up toward his wife. "We can do that, can't we, Louise?"

"That's not the point, Henry. What I am trying to understand, what you have not made plain to us, Dr. Wells, is what exactly is the state she's in, or was in? I think that we ought to know what we're dealing with here." Louise kept patting the outside of her purse in time with her words, sending up a soft drumbeat that suggested a tribe not quite far enough away preparing for battle.

Apparently considering how to respond, or even whether or not to respond at all, Dr. Wells stared at Louise's hand before emitting a weary sigh. "It is a form of depression, but profound. Deep enough that it pulled her down into a psychological black hole, if you will. Her thoughts, all of them, have negative themes. There's a strong element of . . . self-conviction." She dropped her eyes to the open file on her desk, and Clair had to wonder just how many of these *family meetings* Dr. Wells was obliged to conduct each week, and whether or not she had trouble keeping track of each patient's troubles and symptoms. "Persistent anxiety," she read.

"But why? What's the cause? She's been getting along fine at school. Her room is always neat and tidy. She's beautiful. I know I shouldn't say that, I'm her mother, but she is. And as thin as a model, too. She could be a model."

"Yes, I noted her weight."

"So then you know she takes care of herself."

"That's not what I said."

The meeting maundered on, Louise's drumbeat faded to a nervous *pitty-pat* of fingertips, and finally the Bugato family collected their wounded warrior. While there was no longer a medical reason to justify keeping Nina in the hospital, there were certainly psychological and emotional issues that needed sorting out, including, (news to one and all) bulimia.

She would have to see someone for a while. Dr. Wells had referred her to Dr. Roth who maintained a practice for adolescents in the city of Napa. Twice a week. No termination date.

WHAT HAPPENED EXACTLY, the sequence and details, made no sense to anyone except to Clair. And—assuming Nina put it together enough to tell him—Dr. Roth, eventually.

A week before Nina's breakdown, they had been on a school-sponsored camping and hiking trip in Big Basin Redwood State Park. It was the beginning of their sophomore year, and these trips were designed to help students bond before the semester got under way, though as often as not, they set up the inevitable cliques and rivalries with a vengeance that smaller doses of time and intensity might have modulated into something approaching social normalcy. September in California is the driest month, the green a full season gone from fields and hills, the creeks a trickle if they aren't already reduced to rocky channels and patches of dampness, and even those plants that have been saving a postgreen yellow have given in to gray. Months of desiccation have strained the renowned extravagance of California's flora, and every living thing has lost half its size and become a somber memento of itself. The trails are dusty, and in the shade under the Redwoods, in the chromatic simplicity of that season, the air is incongruously warm.

The school chaperones had divided the sophomores into groups of six, so that they wouldn't be "moving the caterpillar one leg at a time." This new band of teachers did not yet know to keep the twins apart; had not yet experienced the subtle disturbance that set out from the girls, like deep temblors from a quake-prone world into whose interior no one else had dared venture. Apart, Clair would have been at the front of their group. As a runner, she was generally faster than her peers, and more competitive than she liked to admit. But with Nina in their little group, she deliberately held back, poking along behind the last hiker, a girl named Ginny Thorpe with whom they had grown up, grade to grade. Ginny was not a popular girl, but inevitably she was always there at the fringe of a clique of popular girls, doggedly insisting on proximity. Her parents were wealthy, and she was an only child. The one thing she had going for her were the latest fashions, the trappings and ornamentation of status without the thing itself. Nina was fond of tormenting her in one way or another and Ginny, pragmatic and dumbly shrewd about such matters, assented to it. She looked like a Pekinese, her round wide-set eyes gooey with perpetual supplication, and pale wispy hair, which she was in the habit of twisting round her fingers while she talked. And she talked constantly. Clair felt a unique distaste for her.

"So I told the dad that I hoped they would pay me for the overnight part, too," Ginny began, "and he says why should I pay you to sleep. But, I mean, I'm away from my house, my room, and that's something, you know, not to be in your own house. And anyways, my friend, she babysits for people who come up from the City for weekends, and she gets paid for the sleeping time, too, only it's half the charge of daytime hours. That seems fair to me. But these people, they are, like, *perfect parents*, and their kid is perfect, too, *perfect Pete*, I call him, even though he's not perfect—in fact, he's a whiner and a half, and I should charge double."

"What does he whine about?" Clair interrupted.

"Oh, how should I know? Everything. Nothing. Yesterday I set his bowl down on the table, and he starts whimpering and patting the table because he thinks I've hurt the table. He thinks everything is just one big part of himself. You know how little kids are, if you hug them they think they're hugging themselves, or if they notice a spoon in their own hand, *their own hand*, somehow it's part of their body just because they feel it touching them. Weird."

"Is it?"

"Yeah. To think that everything's connected to you? Yeah, it's weird."

"Really?" She didn't care about the conversation, didn't care one way or another what Ginny thought, she only wanted to wedge in some doubt and pry up whatever confidence Ginny had managed to lay away because she was such a wannabe, so pathetically passive, always wagging along after Nina who had somehow evolved into one of the class leaders, albeit on the shadowy side of things.

The trail was winding up through the Redwoods, the light so snuffed by the great trees that it was a warm quiet dusty twilight in the middle of the morning. Here and there a bit of sunshine made its way through the lacy foliage, and then the fine trail dust that their footsteps lofted up became visible as floating clouds of amber light. They had all had breakfast around the park tables and fire pit, tidied up their sleeping bags and tents, filled their water bottles, and set out in a dozen different directions. Nina led their small band of hikers, Nina with one of the chaperones, someone's parent, tramping along about three-yards behind her, the chaperone gesticulating with her lean yuppie arms and offering up "fascinating" data about Redwood trees and water consumption, which, according to her, could be five hundred gallons a day and all acquired through the tiny flat needles of the "mighty and magnificent" Redwood whose wood was virtually imperishable and, though soft, never rotted.

Suddenly from around a corner came something, something dark in a fast-wobbling swinging motion, a long cloud of dust agitating in its wake. It was the size of a baby goat, a kid, and whatever it was jumped up at Nina. All Clair could see were black arms and the pink undersides of two feet. And it was screaming because they—the girls, the chaperone—were all screaming. Everyone was screaming. But Nina wasn't screaming. Nina seemed to be trying to breathe, even while her arms went instantly around the baby chimpanzee. The creature kept lifting its whiskered chin against her neck and blinking its little wet round eyes. Nina's face was a portrait of beatific wonderment. Behind them came a human couple staggering around the corner, breathless and startled by the group of girls. When they saw Nina with the chimp, they slouched with relief, folded in half, and panted, facing the ground.

The woman flicked her hand up at Nina. "Thank god."

"You caught him," the man said.

"No," Nina said strangely.

Between heaving breaths, the woman managed to say, "He's very mischievous."

"And very smart," the man added.

Nina said, "I didn't catch him. He came to me. He came right to me and not to anyone else."

The man reached out to take the chimp, but the small huddled creature clung more tightly to Nina, pressing its neck against hers, its pale brow wrinkled with uneasy love, but love nonetheless.

By then everyone had gathered around. Some of the girls tried to pet it. From the back of the group, Ginny Thorpe stared at it with a kind of impatient contempt, like a scavenger late to the feed. Meanwhile, their chaperone, who took her volunteerism seriously and who had little tolerance for dings and dents in the smooth body of her day's plan, had one of those sensibly friendly, isn't-this-amusing-but-not-really adult conversations with the couple. She wanted to get on with their hike. The day had a definite schedule, and *this* was not on that schedule.

Nina began to ease away from everyone. "What's his name?" she asked quietly. The chimp had burrowed his face into the hollow at the base of her neck and was making cute nuzzling chirping sounds with the occasional demanding *hoot*. It had been years since Clair had heard her sister actually giggle.

"Oh," the woman said, smiling, "we call him Butler. He likes to answer the door. And he dresses like one, wouldn't you say?"

"Butler. That's no name, Butler. Why would you name him that? That's a terrible name for a baby boy."

The woman frowned, took a step closer to Nina. Butler swiveled his little furry head left and right, then reflexively nuzzled in closer to Nina's neck and grabbed her hair. Obviously having reconsidered her options, the woman asked, "What would you name him?"

"Jack."

"Jack," the woman repeated, cocking her head slightly.

"Jack."

It took the chaperone and the man a solid ten minutes to pry young Butler from Nina's arms, and Nina was no help at all. She didn't even mind that his furry old-man hand was tangled up in her hair or that he was yanking at it with playful desperation. When the woman began to remonstrate her to be more *cooperative*, Clair accidentally trampled her foot. Nina glanced at her sister with astonished gratitude.

For days, Nina descended into silence in what seemed a determined though somnambulant march as someone who has been on a great journey, a journey that began in vigor and lively thought on a morning radiant with promise, and now the traveler, nearing home late on a dark night, must summon the last of her reserves to set one foot before the next, and another and another until, at length, coming to a stop. She was like Eurydice after the turn, no lover now to follow, and so no doubt, either, only the disappeared true love and the descent away from hope and life. Her expressions slowly evaporated, leaving behind a masklike face, though her eyes seemed to be holding on to an image that had unexpectedly vanished, and her lips opened and stayed parted as if she had witnessed something that had left her stricken and mute. In her room, she played one song over and over, a simple mournful Irish air. Louise complained. Then the silence became more complete.

Her right hand plucked at herself, preening bits of imaginary unwanted things from her clothing and hair. Finally, one afternoon Clair saw her standing in one of the vineyards gazing at nothing in particular, nothing and everything, with that same mesmerized absence. Her face was as smooth as a sleeper's with a vastness taking up her eyes the way too much of an infinite vista can sweep away all you have ever known or seen, like a great wind. A stranger, passing, might have thought her blind.

Clair grabbed an apple from a bowl on the kitchen counter and wandered out. The apple was supposed to divide her attention. Clair always tried to approach her sister with options and alternatives in hand.

There had been a run of late hot summer days and the fog, lingering offshore for over a week, had finally drawn in and raveled north from the bay. White tendrils of it were drifting past Nina and coiling back around her, as if just discovering her, as if wanting to make her a part of itself, of the ghostly creature that could swallow whole cities, whole valleys, whole lives. For a few minutes, she was gone, then there she was, exactly where Clair had seen her from the house and in exactly the same posture.

"What are you doing?" she asked, taking a loud bite of the apple.

"Nothing."

"That much I can see." For some reason she was angry with Nina. With Nina like this. "Seriously, what do you think you're doing?"

Nina was gazing at the air in front of her face as if it were a seeable thing. "I'm standing behind Nina. And Nina is trying to talk to you. I'm listening to Nina try to talk to Clairsie."

"Cut it out. I don't know what you're doing, but it's giving everyone the creeps. Dad can see you." It was true: Henry was poised in the cellar doorway watching the two of them.

This news sent an electric shock through Nina. She skittered her eyes, but just as quickly seemed to give up on something that she had already mostly given up on, and it was only a reminder that she needed. A reminder to keep giving up. She actually gave her head a single, not quite imperceptible shake—*no*, sending away the new thought, the crazy idea. Carefully, she lifted a contraband cigarette from the Altoids tin she kept in her pants pocket, lit it, watched the ash grow, forgot to smoke, forgot to turn away from her father's field of vision to hide what was forbidden. "It's funny," she said in a wispy voice, staring at the inch-long column of ash, "how things dying still grow into something."

Trying not to noticeably hurry, Clair ambled back to the house, tossing the half-eaten apple.

Each day it took Nina longer to do the simplest things, like putting on her shoes. First, she had to study their "*predicament*," the two reverse plots they mapped out on the floor, the laces struggling away to either side, and the openings where her feet were supposed to slip in, waiting and waiting. Presumably, the shoes would take her places where things would be expected of her. Things like talking. But talking had become, she told Clair, "humongous."

"They don't walk without you in them," her mother said, passing the door. "Time for school."

On the edge of Nina's bed, Clair sat ready to leave. They really did have to go. The van that came to pick them up at the end of their road, a half-mile-track off the main road that wound down the mountain, would be out there soon. Their friends would be in the van, along with others who lived in the remoter reaches of Napa County. They were a clan, the outliers, and it was verboten to be late.

"Hey, come on. Get your shoes on."

"Boots."

"Fine, put your boots on." Nina was in a fashion phase that required Vasque hiking boots, no matter the rest of her attire, and Goth eye make-up.

"They are in a predicament," Nina said.

Clair puffed her cheeks. "Okay, well, let me help you then."

A look of alarm electrified Nina's eyes, only to be replaced by something far worse, something frighteningly infinite. She began to pluck at her clothes again.

"Just stop it, Nina, will you? Will you just stop this crap? No one cares about your predicaments or your boots or the make-believe crap you keep picking off your clothes. There's nothing there, by the way."

"Jack was here." She pressed her hand against her neck.

"Butler. His name was Butler. And anyway, what does that monkey . . . ?"

"He isn't a monkey." Then something wholly unexpected happened—Nina's eyes filled with tears, magnifying them so that they seemed to be gazing up through deep water.

From Clair's own deepest depths a kind of wretchedness rose, like sump water backing up. "Okay, okay, let me help you."

"There's nothing you can do to help me."

"Don't say that."

Unseeing, her eyes dry and curtained over now, Nina stared back at her.

"You can't do this," Clair warned.

Slowly Nina dropped her head and resumed plucking at herself, her gaze drifting to her bare feet, even while her hand methodically, mechanically continued to pluck.

Clair could not remember ever feeling so angry with her sister, so cosmically exasperated, so betrayed. "You can't do this, Nina. Not to me. You can't do this to me. Everyone's always coddled you, always given you whatever you wanted because you never take less, you won't take less, everyone always doing half your share of the work, always covering for you and, you know, you know . . . you know, we had a . . . a kind of deal, and you just can't erase it and everything else the way it is, the way it's always been. You just can't do this to me now." She could hardly breathe,

the words were piling out so fast. "One year, one year. Is that too much to ask? One year and then it's over. I'll have an actual life. A life of my own. So just put your fricking boots on and let's get this day over with, and this year over with, and then we can go our separate ways." It was only then that Clair realized how frantic she was to get away. Their parents had always planned to send the girls to separate prep schools for their last two years of high school, to help them become "individuals." Without once admitting it to herself, Clair had been leaning toward that with inexpressible hunger, a prisoner who cannot let herself for a minute contemplate the day of her release, for to do that would be to render all the days that must lead up to it unendurable.

Nina never did put her boots on, not that day.

Two weeks later when they brought her home from the hospital, she had an inspired sweetness about her that none of them had ever encountered. She was as pure as a flame, and just as insubstantial. She brushed her hand lightly across the oiled wood panels of the front door, she touched the objects she had grown up with—the alarm clock, the tea kettle, the porcelain figurines in the sideboard—she smelled her clean cotton pillowcase, she jingled the wind chimes, she blinked at the autumn garden, withered and yearning for the first rain. Dr. Wells had told them to be honest and straightforward, to be authentic, but it was unnerving to be all of these things with a girl who had become, apparently, someone else entirely. It seemed as though it was Nina who was pretending, who was not being authentic. If you couldn't quite believe what you were seeing, how could you pretend that it was so and then behave accordingly? To do so would involve some version of a double negative making a positive. Collective amnesia, that was what was required. They all had to forget what they knew about Nina, even Nina—forget what her life so far had taught them about who she was and who she was well on the way to becoming. Plus, she was still hugging everyone—in the mornings when they arose, whenever anyone entered a room or went out the front door, and especially before bed. These hugs were longer, more considered, and seemed to carry whole texts of weighty meaning. They were like telepathic bedtime stories, silent and compressed and *deep*. Henry just stroked the top of her head, looking sad. Louise put up with them, her mouth jittering between discomfort and reluctant joy. Louise had never been much of a hugger.

"I'm not going off to war, Nina, I'm only going to sleep," Clair told her one night. Throughout the embrace, she could feel Nina's spine, the individual vertebrae with their crucifixion ribs laddering up her back, and it irritated her, how thin and unfortified her sister had become. All their lives together Clair had protected her, but not in any of the ways that this new girl might need and for which Clair had no training or for that matter, inclination.

Nina leaned back, her hands still slowly draping down and along her sister's arms, and gazed peacefully at her. Her eyes had grown bright and uncomfortably intense, like the eyes of a religious convert or an EST trainee or a starving Biafran. "Sleep can be a dangerous world."

"It's not a world, it's a necessary and natural state. It happens every night, in case you haven't noticed."

"I have dreams," Nina murmured, glancing off into the obscurity of their childhood home.

Clair shrugged. "So do I. Everyone does."

"I mean terrible dreams. Night terrors, Dr. Roth calls them. What if you were a little kid? What if you spent every night with gory scenes and beasts and people doing gross things? What if you kept losing the one thing that was the key to everything and can't get back in, you can't ever get back to the door that you don't even have the key for anyway, the door back into the world that you're not in now? And it's the only world you know?"

"Well, you're not a kid. They're just dreams. No one wants to hear someone else's dream." Again, that same wretchedness rose from the depths of Clair. Her sister was broken, and Clair couldn't help hating her for it. Hating her for this new responsibility it laid on her doorstep; hating her for changing the rules they had all agreed to ten years earlier. "Remember Uncle Sal," she added, lifting her brow in playful caution and trying to send the wretchedness back down, to make a funny conspiracy of it all. Uncle Sal was always recounting his dreams for them, as if they were great movies he wished they could have seen with him. The girls never failed to marvel at the crushing boredom someone else's dream produced in an unwilling audience.

Nina smiled. "Uncle Sal." And went on, nevertheless, to report her dream. She had become a talker, a bean-spiller, which Louise put off to the therapy—a side-effect, like hives or difficulty breathing.

For five months Nina went to see Dr. Roth. Apparently, he did want to hear her dreams. The hugs became less frequent, less urgent, less affectionate, less needy, until there was only a graceful if hasty simulacrum before bed. Everyone seemed relieved. Nina was getting back to herself. The Bugato household made sense again.

One day Ginny Thorpe was over, hanging out with Nina in her room and picking up some children's books for her regular babysitting charge, Perfect Pete, whose parents wouldn't expose him to anything so violent as nursery rhymes. Nina had decided to get rid of her childhood possessions—toys, books, memorabilia. "Why do you think they always name the boy Jack?" Clair heard Ginny remark. "Jack and the Beanstalk, Little Jack Horner, Jack be Nimble, Jack and Jill, Jack Sprat . . . it's all Jack."

"That may be the first intelligent thing you've said all year, Ginny," Nina coolly mumbled.

There was a leaping giddy gratitude in Ginny's response. "Well, it's true, it's true, isn't it? They're all Jack!"

Jack. So it was . . . And so it was that the baby chimp had hugged Nina, had chosen Nina for protection, and had assumed she was no worse than the next girl on the path, perhaps even slightly better, but certainly no more envious, no more violent, no more a murderess than the one coming along one step behind. In all of that randomness, a particularity had keyed its way into Nina's very being that day, opening the door to something like forgiveness. Because while no one mentioned Tony—*ever*—Tony was there like a held chord in the lowest register, *basso continuo*, a not-quite-conscious vibration, never silent, never absent.

After Ginny left, Clair crossed the hall to her sister's room and tapped on the open door. Nina was dusting the objects on her dresser—a music box, a small basket of hair ties and clips, several polished stones she had bought for herself from a rock shop in town, two baby abalone shells, thin as ears, a tray of eye shadow in the darkest shades, and a book on Egyptology. When she had wiped one side of the dresser, she nudged the objects gently over, using her forearm, dusted the other side, then rearranged her belongings into their initial positions.

"So," Clair began, "so you're okay these days."

"Yeah, I'm okay."

"Have you gained any weight? You look like you've gained a little weight."

"Yeah?"

"That's what it looks like. To me. Like you've gained a little weight."

"Okay, if it makes you happy."

"Only if it's true."

Nina had lifted the pillow from her bed and was refolding her nightgown, which she always kept underneath. It was an old white nightie with pink starfish on it, frayed and ready for the garbage, but Nina didn't want to give it up. She'd had it for years, a gift from their mother. "If what's true?"

The question was confusing to Clair. "If you're happy."

"You want me to be happy, Clair? Or do you want me to be Nina? I mean the one in your head, not this one." She flattened her hands against her chest. "I can be either one, whichever floats your boat, but doesn't rock it. Right?"

"Look, I only came over to see if you were okay." She searched the empty hallway, suddenly wanting to flee. "If you're happier now."

One of Nina's hands was resting palm-down on the pillow. "You just couldn't stand it, could you? It all worked out for you, when you think about it. I got everything, that's your idea. More than my share, more than's fair? Maybe. But none of it was real. You think I couldn't tell? You think all your frantic evening-things-out made it better? Fixed it all up?" She fluffed the pillow and lay it over her nightgown, making sure that the pillow hid it completely, the nightgown she wore into battle each night. Watching the excessive care her sister took with her old rag of a nightgown began to break Clair's heart. "But I'm not complaining," Nina shrugged. "You can't ask people to lie about everything.

Some things, but not everything. Not feelings. Not really. They always leak out."

"But I love you, Nina. Really. And mom and dad love you. We all love you to bits." She was sobbing now. "That's why this whole thing, the hospital, the shrinks, it's so upsetting. We just want everything to be the way it was."

"Sure you do," her sister said. She held out a box of tissue and Clair took one, her hand shaking as if it had just committed an unplanned crime.

"Your hand's shaking."

For some reason Clair shoved it under her arm to hide it or stop it, and it was then that a strange stillness enveloped them: Nina, her mouth slack with the heaviness of understanding, observing Clair, and Clair—confused, ashamed, the wretched sump water all around her now, why, she couldn't say—Clair looking back at her sister.

Finally, in a voice that was so quiet, so level it was closer to humming, Nina said, "Maybe two or three pounds," and then she turned back to purging her childhood from her room and cleaning whatever remained.

CHAPTER 7

It is their fifth morning in Baja, and they decide to make miles and reach the oasis town of Mulegé. They are not tired of the desert, but suddenly the idea of a tropical oasis sounds alluring, something to be desired for the purpose of desiring. She wants them to *want* together, to gulp the world, to surrender completely. There are mangroves in the estuary, according to the guide, and date palms and banyan trees—banyan trees . . . it sounded so mythical—and tropical fruits, mangoes, oranges, and of course the Sea of Cortez with its warm turquoise water and exotic fish—dorado, sailfish, marlin, yellowtail. She has never seen mangroves, a small personal fact that she doesn't want to confess to Mason who seems to have seen everything; does not want to reveal this kind of inadequacy even though it gratifies him to be the first to show her all the particulars of all the corners of the world. Or not wanting to tell him expresses her competitiveness, a relic from life as a twin—never reveal your weaknesses. They—she and Nina—could not even compete fairly. Clair would rather communicate indifference, for it was the strongest position of all.

Also in Mulegé, a shower. A shower would be awfully nice, particularly as not having one is making her shy about sex. Mason has no such qualms. "I like the literal woman," he says. Sometimes he makes love as if they are committing a last deed together, and afterward she has to remember how to breathe, even while she'd rather not, she'd rather stay in the no-place-time between the union that has just happened, the delicious and consuming bedlam of it, and the ordinary steps away from it that they will each have to undertake alone.

Inexplicably—or perhaps it is simply the nature of back injuries—Mason feels worse. He had a nightmare sometime in the hours of sleep, and he might have tensed and strained his muscles during the ordeal. Though lean, he has a beautiful strong back, softly rounded with muscles and tendons that run deep. If it did not trigger spasms, she would offer a massage. Edging his teeth and staring off the pain, he starts down the Transpeninsular Highway, the day just risen. A wind stirs across what moments earlier had been the cool unbreathing stillness of the desert, the only sounds wild doves up in the hills, sad and nostalgic, and the clicking of grasshoppers warming up their instruments for the day's mating rituals. Coming at them, a blistering day—they can already tell, they can already feel it across their shoulders. It took only seconds for the last bit of coffee, poured into the sandy soil, to evaporate. When the sun had cleared the high mountains forming the backbone of the peninsula, it discovered their little campsite like a one-eyed predator—fierce and unflinching. Nothing they might marshal against it would have the least effect. In no time the soft pastels of the desert sunrise have become nearly hueless, and they are both grateful for the interior of the van that, at the very least, keeps the glare outside. They are running low on gas and decide to forgo air conditioning until Catavina, forty miles away in Las Virgines, the boulder-garden area of the desert, where a small settlement includes a Pemex station.

But in Catavina they find the Pemex closed. At the abandoned station, two boys materialize from the shade, small shades themselves that scuttle out to tell them that there is a *Viejo*, an old man, who sells gas from a barrel just before the trailer park. It is their self-appointed job to send disappointed travelers to El Viejo and to collect what tips they can. Mason doesn't disappoint them, though once again she notices how surprisingly awkward he is about tips and other gestures of gratitude. His pause is too long, a graceless shrinking away from the moment of commerce that every adult male in the world ought to know, and his fumbling for pesos too real to be an act. The boys are waiting, their eyes politely uncommitted to the outcome, the hand of one of them fretting the knotted rope holding up his britches.

Under a thatched canopy, a *palapas*, the old man is sitting in a molded plastic chair, the kind that they have seen in all the outdoor cafes that weigh nothing and stack easily. He is staring straight ahead as the van bisects his line of vision and rolls to a stop. Mason climbs out with difficulty, and the old man, taking no notice of this Americano's discomfort, instead, lifting his chin toward the van, utters one word: "*Nuevo.*"

"Yes, new," Mason agrees.

The old man shakes his head. His gas is *Nova*, regular, not unleaded, and so low in octane—79—that even he does not want to sell it to them and risk profiting from their future misfortune. Stakes are higher in the desert. In a hot desolate landscape it is problematic to be conventionally inhumane, to cheat a little here and there, to sell bad gas, to give bad advice or shaky directions because you are too proud to admit that you don't know, or too lazy to get it right, or too sunk in your own misery to extend an affable hand. Someone you don't even know might not survive your moral lassitude.

"I'm willing to risk it," Mason insists, speaking Spanish.

The old man shakes his head again and in perfect English says, "Catalytic converter." The Mexican love of cars translates to an intimate knowledge of parts and functions, a longing, like sex, that is half-satisfied by familiarity with automobile lore the way pornography does half that other job, even though most of the vehicles on the roads of Baja are too old to have the fancier anatomic components, like catalytic converters. Mexicans would as soon shoot one of their own goats than wound the viscera of an internal combustion engine.

Mason scratches his head and frowns pleasantly. "Well, Señor, it is my rig. *Mi carro.*"

El Viejo fails to smile. He is done with them, there is no money to be made.

It is now that Clair realizes that the avowed "little" Mason knows about cars is actually pretty much *nada*, and she's glad for the old man's refusal.

"Bloody hell," Mason says once they're back on the highway. "But listen, it's a thirty-six-gallon tank. I special-ordered it." He gives the gauge a friendly tap. "And an eighth . . . that's four and a half gallons. We can make it easily to Rosarito on an eighth of a tank. Easy-peasy."

"I love your confidence," she says, intentionally looking away, out the window. But she doesn't love it, too, because whatever that confidence is grappling with or defending against, it has begun to worry her. He had also special-ordered double doors for the backend, but the van arrived with a single. "Are you sure they gave you the thirty-six-gallon?"

"I paid for it," he tells her as if that settles the matter.

He is being remarkably, stupidly overconfident, or all-powerful, thinking that his having done his bit is all that needs be done to make something happen, to complete human transactions. Almost smiling, she says, "But we haven't really done the math. I'm just wondering."

"About?"

"The tank. The gas tank."

Mason picked up the new van on the afternoon before their departure. The actual size of the tank is the kind of detail that ends up where his awareness begins to tatter off. He's a 90 percent kind of guy, leaving the 10 percent to chance or to the attention of lesser beings, because his own attention has already dried up. They've never let the tank zero out; they've been filling from somewhere around half, because of the desert, because of the menace of space and aridity and heat, and neither of them has calculated liters to gallons, and then correlated that to miles and kilometers. With a sudden sense of unease, it occurs to her that she can't count on Mason, not always and not about all things. Why it is that she has trusted him so far makes for an even bigger question. His self-assurance, his experience traveling about the world, his facility with languages, his capacity to survive on rice and fish, his effing English accent. *Brilliant*, she thinks, borrowing from his small collection of catchall Englishisms. Hemingway was right: the English spoken language has fewer words than Eskimo. Inflected phrases carry all the meaning.

The sky holds no clouds and hardly any more color than an ashen blue, now that the sun has blanched the world. Colossal boulders jumble across the land, boulders the size of VWs, with cardón and cirio, Joshua tree and candelabra, many varieties of agave, and the smaller cacti, like barrel, struggling between the granite. In one place, El Pedregosa, a hill-sized pile heaps up like an island of stones in a dry mythic sea. It is so weird and random, this island of boulders, that Clair tries to imagine it as a real place through time, through seasons, with heat and rain and the smell of steamy wet stone, the desert greening up, and soon enough she feels optimistic again about their destination, an oasis. A contradiction. An outpost of Eden in a punishing landscape.

At the trailer park, they replenish the ice so that even Mason, his zip-lock full and once again numbing his lower back, looks reasonably con-tented.

After a while, to the east, a vast dry lakebed, white as chalk, spreads out beneath the sun, giving off its own glare from the fine white silt, the over-whelming light from above blinding in unanimity. The road goes on, lift-ing and dropping. A sign says "*Zona de Vados*"—dips. It isn't clear whether these vados are where they are because the road is following the contour of the land, or whether they are intentional low points to allow water to cross the roadway without destroying it, but there are troughs of dried mud at the bottoms of some of them where the rains have carried off the desert. Vados . . . the need to point out the obvious mystifies her. It was all that lay beneath the surface that wanted for some sort of documentation, that land where the past, well-disguised and speaking in tongues, plays out again and again. No, the dips in the road ahead are self-evident.

Down they go again, and then at the top of a long steep grade, far off to the west, they see the Pacific, as peaceful and unreal as its name.

They pass through a couple of settlements, *ranchos*, the first with a café that is long closed, judging by the weedy tamarisk sending exploratory tendrils through a broken window, and the second at a junction that has a gas station but no unleaded, no *Extra*, and a café down the road that insists it is open in the evening. Then, another trailer park. Several houses with tin roofs and adobe walls, ragged fan palms guarding the doorways.

Evidence of people, but no people. Now and then, lean leggy cattle wander indolently across the highway. The ubiquitous *perros callejeros* with their small yellow eyes watch from just this side of wildness. A *mercado* with some of the products it used to sell in more hopeful times painted onto its façade—*tecate, carnes, frutas, verduras, hielo.*

Finally, Rosarito. Pemex station, café—closed—trailer park, crops of jojoba. The pueblo itself is entirely dirt, a hot-feeling reddish dirt—dirt streets, dirt dry *acequias*, dirt structures. No one has bothered even to whitewash the adobe. Outside the settlement, in long irregular rows of bushes, is the gray-green of jojoba. Her gaze flees toward it.

Mason pulls into the station, and Clair jumps out to work the pump—but it doesn't work. Neither of the pumps work, *Nova* or *Extra*. No one mans the box where an attendant ought to be. There is a small silver trailer, the old humped kind with two wheels and cinder blocks under the hitch, just past the station where a handful of people, maybe field workers, wait to buy food from a window belching greasy smoke. She hurries over to ask about the gas pumps. The ragged crowd, entirely men with heat-glazed stares and broken straw hats, make her so nervous that she hears herself begin with school-girl French before lurching back into English. In heavy Spanglish, a young man at the back explains that the power is off every night, but today it does not go back on. No power, no pump. He shrugs, regarding her somewhat sadly. Without prompting, one man mentions a plane, but it is so enigmatic that it sounds like a rumor or even a koan . . . *there is a plane that some of us have been imagining, this plane, it might help you* . . . The rest of the trailer's customers are keeping their backs to her. She asks the younger man when he thinks the power might come back, and he tells her mañana, but a question mark hangs in his voice, and the look in his eye is not encouraging. No one seems exactly indifferent to her, but they are also behaving as if this *gringa*'s trouble might be contagious.

At the van, Mason can hardly move, and his temper has worsened. She can see the veins standing in his neck. "Brilliant," he says. Fisting his right hand, he brings it down like a gavel on the dashboard. "And these lay-abouts," he adds with disgust, backhanding the air in the direction of the men waiting for lunch, "they're about to be worthless."

"What do you mean?"

"After lunch, siesta. Nothing interferes with siesta."

They're both hungry. The gas gauge says that they have no gas, that they have, in fact, less than nothing in the tank.

"You know, we did just drive in here," she says, standing at his window.

Like the young man waiting for food, Mason shrugs too. Now his eyes have a lusterless, given-in quality. It is uncharacteristic of him to give in.

"So maybe there's just something wrong with the gauge."

"It's a new van."

"But this new van is still moving down the highway. Something down there is motivating it."

"Fumes."

"If it's a thirty-six-gallon tank we should probably still have some gas. Thirty-six gallons ought to have gotten us to Guerrero Negro, right?"

"Sure. And how much are you willing to bet on that? It's bloody hot out there. It's an effing wasteland." It is, in fact, over a hundred in the shade. She cannot even rest her arms on the doorsill as they talk.

Bruised by his tone, she says, "It's not the end of the world," though in truth she's beginning to feel desperate—more desperate than she did back at the hotel in San Quintin. At least there she could run, she could call Ethan, there was an ocean. There was a man who helped them, who brought food and ice, who regarded her with kind eyes. Mason is popping codeine like aspirin. His mood has gone south and bunkered in, and the nightmares . . . the nightmares are a new feature manifesting what, she doesn't know. "Why are you this cranky, Mason? And why with me? Of all people, why with me?" Her eyes are desert dry and the incipient tears burn.

"Lovely. Now we'll have a bit of a sob-fest."

"You're being an ass."

"Right."

"What's gotten into you?"

He slings his head away from her. "Well, let's see . . ." Using his index finger, he mimes short tabulations on the passenger seat: "My back's a mess, we're out of gas in a third-world country in the middle of a desert,

I'm hungry, and . . . *oi*, dear old Dad kicked off last week, and I've got all *that* mucking up my guts."

"What?" Her voice, what remains of it, emerges between a gasp and a whisper. She straightens, takes a step back, and her hands, suddenly as useless as wet pompoms, drop to her sides.

Mason stares straight ahead into the wavering heat of the desert where the wind has come up, conscripting dust into whirling dervishes. The sun has transformed the silver trailer into a misshapen gibbous creature of blinding light. At its window, the little waiting crowd is like a mirage of humanity, wavering and uncertain, feet no longer seeming to connect with the surface of the earth as the men above it ascend like a band of angels.

"Why didn't you tell me?"

"I'm not keen on discussion." His faintly threatening words of caution are made worse by the singsong delivery, something out of a Hitchcock thriller.

"But Mason . . ."

"I said."

The nightmares, the tales of hare hunting, the childhood memories . . . it all makes sense now. "Well. I'm, I'm sorry."

"They also serve who up and die," he intones bitterly.

"Still, your father . . ."

"Is this a discussion? Sounds like the makings of a discussion."

She stares at him, the nervous silence slipping into something irretrievable. She has no idea who he is. "But he was your father. There are things to say, to feel, when your father dies."

"I'll say something when I have something to say."

Minutes pass while she fantasizes going home alone, the mechanics of hand gestures that might communicate *my . . . consort has gone round the twist, and I am in need of transportation north to the US*. Finally, she says to Mason, "Have it your way."

They decide that Clair should get herself under the van to see if there is anything on the outside of the gas tank that indicates thirty-six, not twenty-four. Mason's back prohibits crawling around in the dirt. If it's the bigger tank, then they will make a run for Guerrero Negro and gamble on something being wrong with the gauge. If not, then they will begin asking around for help, pay someone to drive down to Guerrero Negro and bring back gas, or else wait for the power. But that might be waiting for Godot. When the man at the lunch trailer had mentioned a plane, and she pictured herself in a two-seater bumping down a dirt runway with a stranger in a greasy straw hat, leaving Mason with his bad back in the van, she had instantly rejected the idea. There was no guarantee either of them would survive. Mason has already popped another codeine.

Lying on her back, she scooches under the van's left rear, beneath where the gas cap fits. At the trailer the workers waiting for lunch slide their eyes to watch. She's suddenly keenly aware of what she's wearing—a pale yellow and white cotton top, sleeveless, khaki shorts, leather sandals. Legs are very long, she reflects, when they are only legs V-ing out from under a van. Glancing down the length of her body, she can see the soft knoll of her pubis beneath the khaki and already feels violated by eyes she can't see but knows with certainty are watching her.

The gas tank is a rounded-off square of heavy hard plastic, black, with grooves where metal straps secure it to the chassis. At the inside edge, in small, raised numbers, 36. She can hardly believe that someone took the time to mold numbers into the tank, that she found them, can touch them, and that they read 36, not 24. Stupidly, she raps her knuckles against the tank to hear either the hollow retort of bad news, or the *swish* of liquid. When Mason hollers down to her, she explains her idea and he says with a derisive snigger, "It's not sheetrock, it's not like finding a stud."

Codeine, she decides, the codeine and his father's death. What else can she decide in the middle of nowhere? When you have no choice, you make bargains in your head; you figure out how to survive; you wall up the feeling and busy yourself with small productive actions. Anger is an unaffordable extra.

Not eager to move, Mason stays put while Clair is the one who lines up with the others at the trailer to buy tacos, using her fingers to indicate four, and not bothering to specify contents. No one else seems to be making choices. The trailer serves only one kind of anything. Perhaps it is the same every day. The shapeless woman peering down at her through the grill smoke, her face glistening with challenge, is openly disgusted with the fact of her. The clean, healthful, shining, presumably rich American fact of her.

The young man who had told her about the power says something in Spanish to her, lifting his chin almost imperceptibly toward Mason, a shadowed presence in the driver's seat. She does not understand, but she can tell it is insulting to Mason, no doubt because she is the one standing for food and she was the one crawling under the van, and no real man lets his woman crawl under an automobile. And even though she knows how much pain he's in, there's a part of her that agrees with the young man. This is more trouble than she has bargained for, and a lot less fun. She has been hoping, apparently, that with Mason, for maybe the first time in her life, someone else will take care of things, someone else will protect her, look after her interests, think of her first, square things in her favor.

In the hot shade of the van, they sit and eat, Clair picking out the lettuce and other unidentifiable greenery before taking a bite. The dark gray meat left at the bottom of the tortilla is gamy with a funny texture.

"What do you think this is?" she asks. "It's like rubber."

"Goat." He takes a thoughtful bite. "But maybe dog."

"Christ."

They make it to Guerrero Negro and to the first Pemex station near the junction. The only other customers are two parties of Americans, hippie types in jeeps, who act as though they live on the premises, slouching against one of the pumps, washing hair with the station hose. One of the attendants comes over when Mason's pump exceeds 128 liters, worried that it is pumping fuel onto the ground, then he and Mason talk about the size of the van's tank, and she can hear a trace of masculine pride in Mason's voice.

"Thirty-six-gallon tank, twenty-four-gallon gauge," Mason says. "You'd think they might have thought of that. You'd think someone might have put two and two together when they wrote up the order. Idiots."

"Maybe there's just something wrong with the gauge," she says.

They go on to Mulegé.

Stretching out on the seat in back, Clair sleeps.

One hundred seventy miles. Late afternoon. The highway snakes steeply down off the eastern desert escarpment and there below them is a cut of green water bordered by date palms and mangroves, with the town taking up the north side of the river and extending along the estuary. Alone on a hilltop to the south is the old stone mission. East in the late and searing saffron light, the Sea of Cortez forms a swath of radioactive blue.

Narrow dirt streets crossing at odd angles lead them to the central plaza. It is a dusty green town with red-tiled roofs and white Spanish rococo structures, haciendas and courtyards of brilliant flowers; close, cluttered, busy where the open markets display their goods. Tourists are out strolling among the ceramics, bright clothing, mangoes and figs and dates, fish in bins of ice, hammocks and straw hats, outdoor cafes under palm thatching. A boy trots alongside their van, eagerly reporting casitas for rent, slapping the side of the driver's door in a cocky rhythm to win them over. They follow him to a cluster of thatched structures near the river and take one for the night. Mason tells the boy to find ice and cold cervezas. After showers, when the light is finally dusky, they walk back toward the plaza to find some dinner.

Approaching the Jardin Corona, wandering along in the shade of an arcade toward an intersection where three small streets pinch together, they become aware of a commotion ahead. Two cars are blocking one another and a third hangs back waiting for resolution and the tiny intersection to clear. Someone is honking his horn, a Bajacaliforniano, and another has thrust his hand wildly out the window—he is trying to park and the other one is insisting that it cannot be done. Several American bystanders are drinking under a *portale*, one of them pointing at the mess, narrating the scene for a latecomer. This is what passes for entertainment. Locals weave between the flummoxed cars as if they are merely parked and unoccupied. The driver with the wild hand has thrown something yellow onto the hood of the other car, a mango. Suddenly, a man zigzags backward through the intersection. His thick black hair falls to his shoulders, his shirt is blousy and very white, like a poet's or the son of a medieval nobleman, his black trousers cinch at the ankles, and his *huaraches* are not the cheap ones they have seen hanging from market racks, but heavy and dark with thick rubber soles. A cigarette conducts from between his lips, tipping up and down as he hollers back to someone on the street from which he has just materialized. Clutched to his breast loosely, carelessly, as if a stranger has handed it to him and he has not yet taken the time to register it, is a three-foot high wooden crucifix. The other arm, the one that is still free, is gesturing grandly at the chaos around him—and this man, this crazy figment, is clearly, inexplicably, incongruously jubilant. He gives the trunk of one of the trapped cars two happy spanks, as if it is a big woman he wants to embarrass with flattery.

Clair knows instantly that this man is Rubio Cantú. Without looking for him, without knowing, in the hushed intake that just precedes knowing, she recognizes him; recognizes, too, that this encounter will be one of the freaks of chance that make destinies, and that from here on, they will all be improvising. She can sense the meaning, the consequence of those hollow seconds caught between before and after. Everything will be divided accordingly: before, after. To no one in particular she says, "There he is."

They follow him around several corners and into a dark cantina called El Farolito that does not smell good. It only takes mentioning Daniel Markovsky's name once to win Rubio's total allegiance. "My friends, my friends," he says, touching first Mason and then Clair in a gesture so graceful that she cannot tell where exactly he touches her, but she knows that she has been touched. His English is not flawless or pure, but it is precisely uttered, and with the added ornamentation of the smooth melodic line found in all Romance languages. She likes his voice immediately. His cleft chin. She calculates that he is in his late twenties, a few years younger than she, though there is also something ageless about him.

For a while it is just the three of them, the crucifix taking up the fourth chair. But then a woman arrives, the student from UCLA, and a fifth chair is dragged over. "Ah," he says only, opening his arms, smiling lightly. Her name is Marla. She is the only one among them not in love with Rubio Cantú. It is obvious that he charms men and women alike, that he doesn't try, that it comes from the radiance of his personality, a force that swings outward like a seine net. Marla is impervious; this too is clear. Perhaps they are not using each other, perhaps they are engaged in the desultory commerce of small pay for common goods, as worthy an enterprise as any.

Marla is a fine-looking woman, languid and uncaring, long-haired, long-legged, slightly taller than Rubio, a discrepancy he does not seem to care about. Her smile is as meaningless as the other pallid expressions that drift across her face and bring to mind thin rainless clouds in a flat blue sky. Without inflection, she says to them, "More Americans. We're everywhere."

"Seems to be the plan," Mason says. "Taking over the world. How about your world? Who's taken that over? This fellow here?" It is strange to hear Mason pay court to a man.

She smiles meaninglessly and without releasing Mason's gaze, without glancing at Rubio, holds an unlit cigarette toward him to be lit. When he brings the lighter up to the cigarette, his hand trembles. On the table, around the beer bottle, or gesturing forcefully, the tremor is obscured, and Clair has to wonder whether Marla has required this small favor of Rubio to expose the tremor, the flaw, to Mason.

They have been drinking Coronas, but now they order tequila with lime and salt and four small glasses. The cantina is not full, not one of the tourist places, and the waitress brings the tequila quickly, along with a dish of spicy pepitas, smiling shyly at Rubio.

"What are you studying?" Clair asks Marla.

"Nutrition. I'm a senior. I'm going to be a nutritionist."

Clair remarks pleasantly, "It's an up-and-coming field."

Marla shrugs. Her shoulders are slender and evenly tanned—no swimsuit markings. She doesn't seem particularly concerned about whether her field is coming or going, or potentially remunerative. Both her parents, they learn, are attorneys, Upper West Side, even her brother is doing Harvard Law. L.A. is as far away from "that scene" as she can get without leaving the country, though, as she says this, she is seated in just that—another country. Money is apparently not part of the motivation packet.

Mason is telling Rubio about the project, the gray whales and photographing the lagoons, PSP's salt mining operations in Guerrero Negro and Washiko's loading docks out on Isla Cedros where the water is deep enough to accommodate great salt tankers from Japan. PSP, Productores de Sal del Pacífico, jointly owned by Washiko Company and the Mexican government, is the largest saltworks in the world. They have already irrevocably compromised Guerrero Negro Bay as well as Ojo de Liebre, the lagoon on its southern boundary. With increasing heat in his voice, he reports PSP's new plan to expand farther south into Laguna San Ignacio, the only remaining of the three Vizcaíno Desert bays that is still unspoiled and where in winter the whales can safely breed and give birth. These proposed saltworks, 116 square miles of salt evaporation ponds with all of the infrastructure, the dock, the industrialization, the massive salt trucks, would be even bigger than the existing ones seventy-five miles to the north. "We're doing a feature for *National Geographic*," Mason says. "The guy who's writing it is one of the best. He's already done his bit, and now it's my turn to document the story with images."

Rubio has been nodding, his face grave. "I know about this."

"Dan said."

"I will show you, you will see what he will do for them if they win."

"He being your father."

"My father, yes. Eduardo Cantú. My father who moves the earth for developers, for foreign companies, for governments. He will move it for anyone if there is money buried beneath it, he will move it for the devil himself and hand *El Diablo* a tip for the treasure he has himself purchased. Everything is mixed up, *rápido*. He is the servant you can't rid yourself of because each time he serves he is making you weak to make himself *fuerte*—strong. His voice, it is like *grasa*. Lard." Rubio lifts his hand to taste the salt cached between thumb and index, then the lime, the tequila, then the salt again. Whenever his right hand is untethered to something stationary, it trembles in a way that makes him seem effeminate and delicate, and yet, to Clair, it is strangely heroic. "I hope you do not meet him. He is dangerous. You will like him too well. Everyone likes him. Even I like him the way that any stranger likes him. But he is *peligroso*."

"Not your favorite fellow."

Rubio glances at the crucifix, but again, does not quite seem to register it. "I am not his."

So far no one has questioned the presence of the crucifix. This is how men behave—they do not question the one thing that raises questions, they wait for the other to offer explanation, because to ask is to expose weakness, while to explain is the first sign of defeat.

Tequila is unlike any other alcohol in that its effects appear abruptly, usually when it's too late to interrupt or inhibit the trajectory of the inebriation. And it is not like bourbon or scotch, or even gin, all forms of release that take what exists and warms or loosens it. They are augmenters of one thing or another—anger, affection, sadness—and so the journey is incremental, an unfolding event that lies within control. But tequila is crazy-making.

Mason is going on about his own father, ranting, and Rubio begins to refer to Mason as *mi hermano*, my brother. Their hatred of their fathers has united them. Now and then, individually and quietly, men approach Rubio, "*El Señor*," each softly says, and he calmly rises to go with them, disappearing into a darkened hallway past the open area where the cooking is done, and returning with no explanation, only a happy, hearty greeting, as if he has just quit an obligatory journey that has taken him very far away from home and loved ones. At precisely eight, he looks at his watch and suggests that they go somewhere else to eat. It is unusual for people of this culture to wear watches, and especially to consult one; their sense of time is lax, with so many things vaguely randomly pending, maybe one more desirable than another, making commitment unattractive or beside the point. A gamble. She knows this from some of her earlier fieldwork in the Vizcaíno Desert when she was based in the fishing village of Bahia Asunción; the way her Mexican colleagues might suddenly rise and walk off, or not show up, or work dawn-till-dusk without complaint. Rubio's abrupt redirection of their activities is noticeable, but nothing new to Clair. With a kind of elegant under-attention, he has been conducting business, and now that that has concluded, everyone stands. Rubio lays a generous amount of pesos on the table, and they head for the exit, which is really an opening almost the full width of the wall. But before they are out, Marla touches Rubio's arm and says with a pretty pout, "Hey," and he nods, hands her something, palm to palm, and tells her the name of the restaurant where they will eat. He has made her wait until his customers have completed their purchases for the evening, a delay that inexplicably pleases Clair.

They are not content together, Rubio and Marla; they are not romantically obsessed, there is no urgency, no sense of time racing away or of time disappearing. Goods and manners stand in for love. They are probably just using each other, Clair decides, but neither cares enough to take offense; they have agreed to it somehow. No love, no infatuation. It means that Clair and Mason are not in any danger of being erased as mere distractions. They are four in full measure, plus the crucifix.

The restaurant is a small garden square of exhausted grass and gravel marked off by a makeshift railing of white Christmas lights looped between sticks that are really just somewhat straight tree branches. The ground is uneven, and Marla's chair keeps leaning into Mason's. They have begun to flirt about it, all the accidental bumping and tipping. Rubio is talking with solemn interest to Clair about her work, and she can feel how genuine he is, how serious he wants to be, and how trapped he feels in his money and the cocaine and the leisure that his father's status has webbed around him. In his fashion, he is a grave young man who does not seem young at all, conscientious and considered, but a man who hasn't any purpose. Privilege, having given him everything, has failed to provide the one thing essential in life to movement; it has deprived him of purpose. He would like, it seems, to adopt some of Clair's, to be like a brother who protects her interests, her future, a brother who missed his chance. She is indirectly helping the people and places of his native land, and that cannot have escaped him, for the Cantús have a long and esteemed history in Baja.

She is telling him why it is important to know what plants exist in a place now, and what no longer do, as a way of understanding how the ecosystem has changed because of climate, or human occupation, or the waxing and waning of other species; how decreases in diversity are far worse than numbers of one or another, but how quantitative changes eventually lead to qualitative changes; how suddenly it can all become irretrievable and fine little worlds that have gone unnoticed go on to die equally unnoticed deaths. She uses words like ethnobotanical and selection-driven speciation and ecotone. She says *tipping points* just as Marla's chair cants into Mason's.

Nodding, Rubio leans forward, his right hand crumpled loosely and resting against his mouth in contemplation. His dark radiant eyes are steady, an invisible charge fixing them. "What can I do to help?"

"Oh, I have funding. Postdoc fellowship, research grants." Still, she glances away at the Christmas lights, some of which are fizzing and shorting, feeling suddenly as shy as a young girl waiting to be rescued—except that she doesn't need rescuing, or if she does, it is not from lack of professional support.

"But what do you need? You must need something." His posture hasn't changed. He gazes at her over his softly fisted hand, determined to be of help. Now that his hand is not touching his mouth, it trembles. "I have much money."

She nods once, sorry for him.

"Let me give you something you need. Everyone needs something."

"I need a new vacuum cleaner." She smiles, tossing up an apologetic shrug.

"You do not take me serious."

"I'm sorry. I do. It's only that . . . well, we have only just met." The words are so clichéd that she wants to laugh at herself, except that she means them, too, and does in fact give a little belated laugh that sounds more like a cough.

"We have knowledge of each other before." He sweeps his open hand to include the four of them. "*Destino.* Do you not believe in destino?"

"Oh, I suppose I do without wanting to." Her glass of tequila is empty, and she can't seem to remember when that had happened.

"Why do you not want to?"

"It's easy to believe in destiny when what happens is good, but it isn't easy to believe in destiny when the thing that happens is unwelcome. It makes you feel you're a bad person, that you're being punished. Or, if it happens to someone else, someone close to you, then it's they who've done the bad thing. Then you feel compelled to make it up to them somehow, they're own badness that they've just stumbled into, that they wish they didn't have to know about, and that you've just witnessed. Seeing something bad . . . it involves you. You're more than a witness." All the words are embarrassing. In her mind, Nina kept turning up and sisters ought to outgrow each other, along with the barbarity of childhood with its strange and furious loyalties, the protections that go on too long, the lies so threadbare that everyone can see through them. "I guess I'd like the story to be erasable, otherwise, why try? Destiny means that the ink is already there, invisible on the page, and it's only time passing that makes it legible, time rubbing off all the layers of concealment until you can see a map of your days but it's a map you didn't get to draw. And you can already see your destination, it's there from the start, and count the miles between where you are now and where it waits." She feels herself swallow against something hard and intractable. "What if that destiny is not anything you'd ever want to meet, and the road is a bad road that leads to it?"

Rubio bunches his chin, frowns, gives his head a single shake. "*Otras personas*, they have their own *destino*. You are not the cause of their . . . ," he struggles for the word, touches her arm, "their *efectos*. If a man is broken he has broken himself somehow. If he makes evil, it is because he has evil in him, *la maldad*, and he must release it, like a wild dog running before a chubasco."

"I don't know about evil," she murmurs, "because sometimes it just takes one thing, and other things that only seem to be like it start to magnetize and gather around it and soon, very soon, sooner than is fair, you're not who you might have had a chance to be. One thing happens, one bad thing . . . and then the very next thing that comes along has to confirm that one thing and whatever it's supposed to mean. What it seems to be saying. We look for patterns, don't you think?"

"*Sí*."

"And if they're not exactly there, well, we make them up. A bad scientist will make a pattern out of one piece of data. I've seen it happen—many times."

"You are not a bad scientist."

"No, I'm a good one. But it's tempting, you see. Patterns are comforting.

You don't have to think about a pattern, or feel much about it. It's just there, and you fit yourself into it and everyone else into their own patterns and, pretty soon, they aren't people any more. They're just a tidy little pattern that you recognize, but nothing real has a chance of happening between the two patterns because they're fixed. They're dead."

Rubio nods, regarding the crucifix, which again occupies its own chair at the table, but then his gaze becomes distracted and with two of his fingers, index and middle, he taps the nailed feet of the son of God. "What kind?"

"What kind?"

"What kind of vacuum cleaner?"

She laughs.

He smiles and frowns at once, interested. "You laugh like a child, *sin defensa*—unguarded." It pleases her to hear this, to think that she has not lost something and that she can still be a girl. Also, Rubio seems to need this, for his eyes carry the sadness of too many bad things seen. And she has to wonder about his trembling hand, where it comes from, what it's about, if it's because of some trauma, a stutter that spared his tongue and made a life in his hand.

They order some of the big local shrimp, *langostinos*, and they come grilled with lemon and butter and a delicate but high hot spice, cilantro scattered across. It is the best thing Clair has eaten all year, and they are fingering it up from the great platter centering the table, the tequila disappearing, Venus in the night sky just above a sickle moon, the air a mysterious perfume of desert and sea water and the night-blooming flowers that grow in this strange and ragged paradise, and now and then the corrupted sweetness of the mangroves, while all around the chorus of cicadas rises and falls.

They are drunk. Rubio invisibly, but mathematically it cannot be otherwise—he has had as much as Mason, maybe more. He's just more elegant and languorous. Marla is cool, utterly cool, but twice now she has fallen like a long-legged mannequin sideways into Mason, and with obvious amusement, he has propped her back up, accidentally—or not—touching body parts. Clair is drunk and knows it, because she is willing to feel for the whole world. But Mason . . . he looks unpredictable, his eyes like two dark doors no one has found the keys to yet. This is what happens to Mason—his countenance lowers and darkens, and the commerce of his face closes down.

The bill never does come, Rubio having invoked whatever magic he has established in the town of Mulegé. They go back to the hacienda he has paid for, an expansive adobe on a cliff overlooking the Sea of Cortez, with outdoor lights beneath birds of paradise, agave, fan palms, blooming barrel cactus with their violet-red flower eyes. Inside, cool glossy Saltillo tile, ceramic pots, and small statuary in *nichos*, a chevron of *latillas* across the ceilings, and the colorful tile of the Mexican artisans framing the counters and arched doorways. Here at his hacienda, and for the first time that night, Rubio uses some of his own cocaine, the rest of them join him, and the long night ravels into a second penumbral night, curling like some exotic reptile into the shadow of its own tail.

The last thing Clair remembers clearly is Marla saying that she wants a shower and Mason following her down the hallway, and a few minutes later seeing him standing on the toilet lid, his arms resting along the top of the shower as he leans over to talk with Marla, and the unpleasantly adolescent look on his face as he views her naked body.

"It is nothing," Rubio insists. "Men are boys at this hour."

"And then what? What comes after boys?"

He shrugs, puffs his cheeks. "*Animales?*"

Something between hurt and disgust congeals at the bottom of her stomach, yet she knows that she won't object, won't try to stop what might be happening, won't protect her own interests. It is not in her character to fight for what she might like to keep or have. She'd rather simply turn away from it, walk off the field. This is one of the lessons from her years with Nina, how to vacate the field.

"But with the sun," Rubio is saying, "we are born men again." He takes her hand. "Come with me. It is only the cocaine, nothing more."

They find another room and for a long while listen to music—Cesária Évora, Cubanisimo, Fleetwood Mac's *Tusk*. When she awakens the next morning on the couch in the room where the music was, it takes several minutes for the night before—what happened, what was said—to surface in her mind. Now, already, the day wears an unpleasant oily sheen. She doesn't want to see anyone, but she does want to see what she can see in Mason's face. On the terrace, under the palapas, she finds her companions, drinking coffee, picking at churros and dates. Briefly she regards Mason, and without any inflection in her voice, asks, "Did you sleep with her?"

He gives a short laugh and tears off the end of a churro. "What do you think?"

She pours herself some coffee from the pot on the table, smiles at Rubio, smiles a different indifferent smile at Marla. It would have been better if he had slept with Marla, better than impotent leering, better than any cheap brand of fidelity. She would rather the deepest cut than this idle scratching at surfaces.

Not answering his question, she says, "How's the back?" and takes the seat next to him but slightly behind so that he cannot look directly at her, so that it will hurt for him to try to turn and see her.

"Many things I am," he announces to the sea before them, exaggerating his English accent, "but a liar I am not."

"Uh-huh. And the back?"

"Fine." He draws out the word so that she can hear the question inside it.

"Fine why?"

"What difference does it make? It's fine. Aren't you happy for me?"

"I'm interested. We're all interested." She opens her arms. "Aren't we all interested in how Mason's back is today, and why it's fine, why we're all so fine?"

Imparting a small smile, Marla studies a date without eating it. "Sure, I'm interested." Marla is some sort of moral nihilist, Clair realizes, and maybe the only one at the table who knows how to live, which is to live without commentary and conscience. Nothing about what has happened or is happening matters to her, she's only interested in the energy of the thing, its wattage, and the sad little thrills and spills it might generate. She's just in it for the ride. There's something Clair can't help envying in that, for she would like—as much as an invalid wants pain medicine—not to care so much.

"Healthy living," Mason says.

"Healthy living. Not *drogas?*"

Abruptly, with both hands, he shoves his plate away. "Why don't you just say something nasty and be done with it?"

"I haven't anything nasty to say."

"The hell you don't."

"I don't," she insists.

"Passive aggressive *rubbish.*"

"Passive aggressive?" She sees herself sitting there as if from the outside and doesn't recognize this woman pretending to be Clair. Something like chaos spins up in her mind and a sickening dismay bats about inside her chest. What's happening to them? Who are these people? How is it that they are here, and nothing is right the way it was only days ago? She had known where things ended and began; she had known limits and where things and people fit within those limits. Everything is flying away from them; they are flying away from each other.

"Tell me, Clair," Mason says coolly, "what's it like to be perfect?"

"Oh, it's fucking awesome. You should try it sometime."

Rubio has been smoking in silence, gazing at the water, and now he quietly pushes back his chair and rises. "Let us walk by the sea. It is a good time. The fishermen have their lines in the surf. *Muy bonita,*" he says, "the long lines, the spray of the surf. We will eat mangos from the boy, Angel. He is saving *dinero* to buy a mitt, he is *fanático. El béisbol,*" he murmurs with a nostalgic smile, heading into the hacienda.

And so, like chastised disciples, they stand and follow Rubio, the crucifix resting across his shoulder as he begins to pick his way down the cliff to the beach below. The crucifix, it turns out, is for Angel to give to his mother who is too crippled now to make her way into the village for mass. If there is a crucifix in her home, then perhaps the priest will come to say mass for her, to offer absolution and to give her communion. She is even more devout now that the disease has marooned her. On the way down to the sand, Rubio tells them that the cross itself is of olive wood, very hard, and the corpus is Italian. Angel's mother has people in Brindisi, and Rubio thinks she will like this relic from the long past and from a country she has only visited in her dreams, and through the memories and stories of others now dead to whom she was once related. No, she has not seen a Western doctor, a *médico*. But many times, over the last two years, she has visited the *curandero*, who is a cross between a naturopath and a witch doctor, and it was he who told her that she has what the famous American baseball player had. And so, in some strange sad way, Angel is proud of how his mother must leave him soon. Rubio wants the boy to have his mitt before that day arrives.

The beach is made of sand, pebbles, and an infinite offering of shells, largely murex shells, bleached and broken, and so white that the morning light against them is painful. In one area they pass, fiddler crabs sit by their burrows, studying the world with their eyes up on stilts or scurrying in unison across the damp flats. The fishermen are out with their long rods and lines making perfect triangles with the sea. Farther on they come to a ragged lineup of tents and cars parked beside them, thatched shanties, RVs and trailers that together form an ugly necklace along the curving shoreline. This is where they expect to find Angel selling his mangoes to tourists. Up on the rocky cliff top, Clair can make out the white bark and lacey foliage of an enormous Palo Blanco tree and, just behind it, a hacienda grander than the one Rubio has rented and probably owned by an American expat. She is sure that Rubio can rent even grander accommodations, wear more expensive clothes, have a woman with more . . . *content*, and the fact that he doesn't makes her think more of him.

They buy all of Angel's mangos, maybe a dozen, so that the boy doesn't have to wait to carry the crucifix home to his mother. He turns instantly and runs, his feet slapping through the sheet of water that the last wave has spread across the sand, beating his way down the shore, his white shirt flaring, the cross tucked under one arm and the other signaling back at them his thanks, his freedom, his youth, the silent radiance of the morning lifting like a hosanna all around them.

With a penknife, Rubio slices open one of the mangoes. In the half without the pit, he makes a tidy crosshatch through the bright yellow flesh, then he inverts the peel so that his companions can easily pick out the separated squares. She watches Mason's long graceful fingers as he makes his selection. The sea is breathing before them, drawing in water from the surface of the sand and releasing it in short sighing waves, in, out, in, out. The breathing of the Sea of Cortez is shallow and labored. There is still enough moisture in the air of the young day to make a mist and nothing is sharply defined yet, not the horizon, not the lighthouse on Punta Concepción, and now not Angel, a wavering white form that Clair can't help thinking is just what his name says, an angel.

Beside a small Airstream trailer hitched to a jeep SUV, an old man sits in an aluminum chair. The jeep has California tags. Clair has been obliquely aware of this man all along. He was watching them as they collected the mangoes from Angel; maybe he was already watching Angel when they found him. There is makeup on his face like the kind old white women wear, with a greasy pinkish hue. His eyes look out with an eerie opacity, while the fingers of his right hand, one after another, slowly pace up and down the side of his coffee mug. On a low table, beneath an ashtray supporting a smoking cigarillo, are colorful peso notes, and beside them, a spill of coins. Maybe he was preparing to buy a mango from Angel. Maybe there are other things he is prepared to buy. It is a likely place for locals to ply their goods, this string of trailers and RVs and car-campers from America. She wants to say something to Mason about this man, this decomposing roué with his cloudy eyes and his prowling gaze. She wants to protect Angel as she would Ethan. But she's still too sore at Mason to open up.

The long drive the day before, with the long unexpected night that followed, devolves into a languid tension between Clair and Mason. Neither wants to actively fight and neither wants to make it up. Just now, she doesn't like him, doesn't know him, doesn't want to know him. It's a relief to have other company. Of the day's promise they make very little, wandering through the shops, buying trinkets, embroidered shirts, a wide-brimmed hat. They engage a man with a boat and enter the Rio Mulegé estuary, slowly motoring past the snook fishermen and upstream to see the mangroves, the white egrets standing in mud, the yellow tourist kayaks, the date palms. They eat ceviche from a stand, then go back to their casita to nap before convening later at Rubio's hacienda. Or Mason naps, icing his back. It is not, as it turns out, *fine*. Clair sits outside under the thatch that drops small hard beetles that may or may not be alive.

The desert comes right up to the town of Mulegé narrowly bounded by the river and the Gulf of California, so that even though it is tropical seeming, the awareness of a parched and punishing land closing in is never successfully held at bay. Just past their little courtyard with its fan palms and bougainvillea, its arched wooden gate vined with morning glory, a bright yellow oriole sampling the blue flowers, she can see the thick arms of a cardón and feel the radiating heat of the unprotected dirt. To the west, the craggy range called the Sierra de la Giganta humps alongside the gulf for over a hundred miles, like the back of a great stegosaurus. She hears the distance and abandonment in the wind and, in her mind, she very quickly tallies the meager xerophytic plants that have found ways to survive with not enough.

Even though Mulegé is a pretty little oasis, green and inviting, some quality of sickness hangs over it. Everything faces east, and one should always face west, face danger and death, face the sun not as it arrives but as it leaves. Her father's words. She is more at ease by the Pacific where trouble washes out almost as soon as it comes pouring in, everything open and available for rhythmic purging, the waves continually refreshing themselves, taking away one thing and carrying in something new, the wind clean, the news hard but not defeating. Here, beside this sea trapped between the peninsula and the mainland, an infirm stillness persists. The water is held in one place too long, and seems somehow to fester. The brackish lagoons, the mosquitos, the foul smell of the mangrove roots at low tide, the fish market in the afternoon heat, the doleful cantinas before darkness falls—altogether, they conjure an ominous and pervasive torpor. North of Mulegé where the Sea of Cortez begins and the Colorado River ends in a broad barren delta, she has heard of the tidal bore that drives north through vast mudflats that bake under a mean sun hung from the ceiling of the world. For the first time, she understands the word *godforsaken*.

At dusk, they walk through the town and out to Rubio's. The way has many turns along small dirt lanes and alleys, past walled compounds and adobe dwellings that have been added to with more contemporary materials—plywood to make lean-tos, cinder block and stone for extra rooms waiting, apparently indefinitely, for stucco or adobe mud, little corrals and pens of coyote fencing, chickens. They retrace their steps according to the sequence of dogs. None of the dogs wears a collar, but they do have their territories; people must know where they belong—the Chihuahua mix before angling left at the pit-bull, then the yellow-eyed shepherd, turn right, two moppy creatures that must be siblings, an asthmatic pug, and keep going, the white and black dog that cannot help supplicating, and so on until finally next door to Rubio's something that looks like a whippet, but maybe only a starving mongrel that cowers just inside a lighted gate. Here and there, someone has bothered to put up a sign, a board with an arrow and a hand-painted word, another hung from the low iron fence that runs along a property, a word painted directly onto the adobe, but mostly there are no signs except for the arrows leading to one or another *casa de huéspedes* by the sea. Going home, they will reverse the order of dogs.

Over dinner, they make a plan to find Eduardo Cantú, the earthmover of Baja.

Mason needs Rubio to meet this man, to get into places that he doesn't even know about and that the writer who has already submitted the piece might have failed to uncover. This is how he explains it all to Clair. But perhaps now that his own father is gone, he needs another to hate emblematically, because hatred is part of what drives him, and he needs that energy. She sees this now, this fierce undercurrent. Perhaps, too, he wants to extend his time with Rubio. Perhaps they all do. He is unique; he is generous and reckless, a man willing to make mistakes. He is so serious that sitting at a table with him is like meeting a man who has just returned from forty days in the desert, and who doesn't know how to be any other way than the way that the ordeal has produced. He is not the man, but the ordeal. And then he smiles—a shattering amnesia of joy. His hand quivers and his eyes shine. He leans in so as not to miss the nuance of what Mason or Clair or the man buying coke from him has to say. Trying not to laugh or stare, trying not to feel the embarrassed discomfort that accompanies dignity and sincerity, despair and exaltation, and any of the other high ways of being, even while his intensity infuses everything with meaning; trying, in other words, to believe Rubio, to believe in him, each one of them at certain moments keeps his council and averts his eyes. She sees it, this aversion to authenticity.

He's just a coke dealer, she hears herself try to think.

Another day, another night. More codeine, more cocaine, more tequila and beer, more words that make less and less sense but that also sound in their saying somehow important, urgent. More music and dancing and sexual near misses. And beauty—beauty in the smallest of things that Rubio calls upon them to notice—the scar on a waitress's neck from cattle wire; the wind shearing off the surf; the distant golden pattern that *el farol* makes as he lights one lantern after another in the mission on Sunday morning before dawn.

On the phone Ethan says, "You sound funny, mama-sweetie."

They have stayed too long in Mulegé.

CHAPTER 8

They grew apart, Nina and Clair—or they grew differently. Nina attended a boarding school in the Bay Area, one that attracted wealthy families whose children had not too seriously run amok—underachievers, cutters, idle delinquents, potheads. It was a nondenominational progressive coed campus with some sort of amalgamated Greek glyph over its gate that contained no express meaning and a lot of rules, mostly phrased in gentle italics, as if the school administrators weren't sure they meant them and, anyway, would apologize for troubling the students with anything so banal as rules. The senior trip, famously Draconian among the region's private schools, featured four days solo in the wilderness with nothing but water, a toothbrush, and a tube of toothpaste. Dental hygiene was always on California's priority list.

As an entering junior, the first thing Nina did was sleep with the cook's son, a sweet boy from East Palo Alto on partial scholarship. She got pregnant and got an abortion. It was Louise, ever practical, who took her to the clinic. After that messy fanfare, Nina seemed reasonably compliant, having made whatever statement needed making or gotten whatever needed getting out of her system. She toed lines, even the italicized ones. The whole ordeal may have been more upsetting than she was willing to admit. Worst of all—as she confessed to Clair over the phone—was that she hadn't liked how the boy smelled, which had her wondering whether that made her a racist. She had given a laugh then, nervous and scared, maybe apologetic, too. These sorts of self-discoveries and admissions were grist for the mill of Nina's character, ever since her time with the psychiatrist. In her flat, curious, analytic tone, she questioned everything, and Clair was already predicting that her sister would end up psychologically or emotionally paralyzed—after all, how could one act if everything was always in question?

Clair was sent to New England, into the national rookery of ivy-clad prep schools. Henry's idea. She was supposed to be the smart one, after all. At Penrith Academy, she developed a taste for melancholic winters, the smell of mold, the spit-shine of discipline—and a *dis*taste for socioeconomic caste systems, which, coming from Northern California, she had hardly run across, excepting perhaps in Ginny Thorpe's up-to-the-minute shoe fashions. It took Clair several months to understand the importance of last names, what they revealed, what that meant, and then another several months to metabolize her disillusionment. Also, people didn't smile easily, and making friends was a longer proposition. It was an all-girls school and girls, as she well knew, could be cold-blooded. Some of them had been together at other schools and arrived in cliques as impenetrable as enamel. She became a loner. As much as she had wanted to get away from Nina, from the troubling complication of Nina, from being secretly favored but publicly bilked, it was strange not having the ballast that Nina represented, the counterclaims and counterdemands, the responsibilities that kept Clair tensed and alert and, she had to acknowledge, steady. Parts of her began to wither. Clair had no job, no sacrifice to make, no desires to quash, no ledger to balance. If she chose, she could triumph. She might even hurt someone in the process, if hurting were in order. She could be and do anything she liked. But identifying what exactly she liked or wanted was problematic, the taste for her own pleasure had so long ago dulled. She might weigh one choice against another, but again, the trouble was recognizing and then naming how exactly she felt about one or another and, therefore, which might be preferred.

The whole process seemed mysterious, even impossible. She knew that there was something terribly wrong in this, so wrong that she would not have wanted to tell anyone about it. It was like not having some sort of muscle that everyone else had, and that you weren't supposed to be able to do without—except that she *was* somehow—doing without. Or maybe the muscle was there, had been there all the while, but the nerve that was supposed to wake it up, to fire it into action, wasn't working. Good feelings, bad feelings, love and hate . . . they were all mixed up, indistinguishable.

The first time she slept with a boy was over a holiday weekend. They had each conspired to lie to their respective school authorities about where they were really going—his parents' cabin in the Adirondacks. At the cabin on Friday night, she told him *no*, feeling nothing except a pure and breezy decisiveness. He might have been asking her if she wanted to take a walk or watch a TV show. Having never done anything, she couldn't exactly be blamed for not knowing that sex might be preferable to no sex. So they played cards and drank vodka with lemonade made from powder and ate bowls of popcorn. The next night, when he hadn't even asked, she pulled off her clothes and they tussled about on the hearthrug. She had managed to get pine pitch in her hair from the split wood stacked neatly at the edge of the rug and, at the time, that had captured as much of her attention as the rest of it—what sort of solvent to use and whether or not it would damage her hair.

But his desire fascinated her. Or desire as a state of affairs, for it seemed to know little governance and yet to have the oldest and earliest native home. The desire existed, like another creature in the room, some being who had arrived out of the blue and who suddenly had more rights than anything else present. The Rights of Desire. What she felt for it was respect: they must, the two of them, take proper care of this desire, this charge electrifying the air, this unruly phenomenon that must be fulfilled or somehow dissipated.

His entire body was quivering, a detail she never forgot and years later would sometimes call out from the secret back-corners of memory to excite her. But driving back to Penrith, she couldn't honestly say which had been preferable, doing nothing or doing something. He shut off the engine and for a while looked ahead at the main building with its granite steps and iron railing, its tall, cobalt blue doors. Then, as if he had made up his mind about something, he turned to her quickly and apologized, she was not sure what for—his imperfect performance, or the fact that there had been a "performance." As he spoke, Clair busied herself trying to pick the last of the sap out of her hair. That, more than anything, may have been enough for him to change his mind. He may have been sorry that he had ever bothered with her at all. He was a beautiful boy, popular, confident, his pale skin smelling of soap and health, his thighs strong from rowing crew, but as he walked away from the grand doors leading into Penrith's foyer, having delivered her safely to its threshold, she realized that it had been she who had drawn disconsolate veils over his gallant eyes—and because of that, she would never see him again or hear his breath catch and spill or smell the brave salty newness of his explorations. To be hungry, to *want*, she then understood, did require some order of bravery. Maybe she was simply a coward. Maybe wanting made her too vulnerable to not getting.

The school counselor was unhelpful and clearly in over her head. She had been the field hockey coach before getting the counseling credential that would up her pay, and her general remedy seemed to consist of the pep talk riddled with catchphrases from reflective listening techniques. *It sounds like this is really upsetting you, but this is a lifelong game, Clair. Plenty of time to come from behind.* Clair felt permanently near tears, waiting for the heaviness to leave her so that she might be like other girls.

And so it was that the cold of winter, the pervasive mold, the brittle tedium of discipline, the study hall with its murky windows and blank walls, its pine desks gridded to soldierly perfection, or the library smelling of age and solitude and death, of people with bad teeth and no friends—all these things that no right-minded girl ought to gravitate toward, she embraced. If Nina had been there, these were the sorts of things Clair would have reflexively chosen. Even though she was three thousand miles away, the shadow of Nina crossed every path, every doorway, every choice.

They saw each other at holidays and during the summer between junior and senior years. Nothing ever seemed to change with Henry and Louise. The girls suspected that their mother had had an affair and even that didn't change anything for long. The bit of lost weight and pretty new clothes lasted for a season or two, and then the filling-out returned to her figure. She stopped having her eyelashes tinted, stopped using rose-scented cream, and the pretty clothes, the dresses with floral patterns and the strappy sandals, unsaid their mid-life invitation and quietly retreated to the back of her closet. It seemed almost a relief, to finally check *have an affair* off the list. Louise might very well have been happier *having* done things, but not actually *doing* them. Her life, after a certain point, had become a to-do list.

Henry's teeth went gray from all the red wine. He didn't bother to have them cleaned or brightened, and he didn't bother any longer trying to conceal the drinking. It began now mid-morning with lighter wines, like pinot blancs, graduating by lunchtime to chardonnays, maybe a light merlot, and then in the afternoon when there were tastings to do anyway, he was sipping cabernets from Bugato and the competition. Dusk brought out Lustau sherry in a tiny flute, soon after which whiskey lumbered out of its low corner cabinet to do the real work, and that effectively concluded the day's evolution of beverages, and his own reverse evolution from sapience to amentia. But if he was remembering what it was like to feel festive, remembering the times when they used to give dinner parties, when he was a proud quiet man with honest work and a family business and good friends, friends who were not yet afraid of what he was doing to himself, then grappa was called for, the last liquid refinement before bed, along with the same beloved story of his father serving grappa in his own home in Campania to some of the performers from Teatro di San Carlo following a production of *La Bohème*. Since he had no new stories of his own, Henry was left with old ones, or with stories that belonged to others who had kept living their lives. The alcohol was simply insurance against life, levying indolence and indifference like the taxes he had obediently resigned himself to pay.

Henry was a docile and well-behaved drunk, gazing over from his Morris chair with rheumy eyes, expecting nothing, asking nothing, the intoxication just there beneath the surface, like something decomposing that was drifting up on bloat and gases. For a long time, Henry had been doing just that—*de-composing* himself; everyone could see it. The Morris chair had wide wood arms that supported whatever he was drinking; he kept a cork coaster on each arm to protect the oak. No one else ever sat in Henry's chair. It did not seem especially sanitary, for there was an air of uncleanness about people who were letting themselves go to rot, piece by piece, organ by organ. He had grown odd over the years, a little paranoid, as Louise put it to the girls when, that second Christmas home from boarding school, they discovered a loaded pistol in a canvas bag slung from the arm of the Morris chair.

"What's it for, Pops?" Clair bluntly asked him. She herself had become somewhat obsessed with death, though the school counselor told her it was common among teens, especially girls. Was there, she asked, someone in particular that Clair was afraid would die? "Nina," Clair replied as if there could have been no other candidate starring in the drama of her hatreds and fears.

As for Henry and his gun and why he wanted it at his side, "Oh," he said, looking off, bunching his chin, "impulses."

"Impulses?"

"These workmen, you know . . ."

"Are they mad about something?"

He smiled warmly, as if they were now having an entirely different conversation, one in which she had just introduced some piece of news. "Not that I know of."

"Are you talking about the workmen or the pickers?" she said. The picking crews came and went with the harvest. Often, especially during hot harvests when everyone's grapes ripened fast and pickers were in short supply, there was not one familiar face, which meant that every fall dozens of strangers populated the vineyards, people with unknown backgrounds and dubious citizenships. Louise always kept the girls close to the house during harvest, though the pickers were invariably the gentlest and most softly mannered of the Bugato workers, having their picnics under the oaks and petting the dogs and giving thanks to their limpid-eyed God.

His brow creased with ambiguous effort, Henry failed to answer her question. Clair studied him then, his almost peaceful smile, the quality of absence in his gaze, and then asked to see the gun, a small Glock. He would not let her hold it, but he did show her where the safety was, how to engage and disengage it. There was a proprietary steeliness about the way he regarded the object in his hand—an object of gravity of which he was solely in charge. Yet he held the pistol as if it were a small gray bird that might flit away. Finally, he dropped it carelessly into the canvas bag, took up the remote control, and turned on the television.

His attention had become jumpy and unreliable, responding to questions or remarks several topics later or not at all. The television was on almost all the time now. Neatly stacked catalogues took up the surface of the coffee table, each one fringed with torn pieces of paper bookmarking items he would never actually purchase—chef knives from Japan, fly rods from Montana, stereo equipment, bee-keeping paraphernalia, Parisian fountain pens. They were always the finest of their kind, top-of-the-line. Also on the table sat plates of food, mostly uneaten. He might get excited about cooking something special, usually a recipe from an Italian cookbook, and buy all the ingredients, make a great fuss of putting it together, and afterward describe for anyone who would listen how he had braised or smoked or poached it, the herbs, the special cookware. Though in reportage they sounded frequent, these culinary adventures were rare, a holdover from his Italian childhood. His arms and legs lost mass, he developed a belly that spilled naively over his belt, the kind alcoholics acquired as they traded food for booze without any caloric diminishment.

Henry never did anything that might embarrass his family. Each morning he still showered and dressed in ironed shirts and creased slacks. His fingernails were clean and clipped. But more and more, Eric presided over vintner meetings in the valley as Henry made his slow graceful exit, not yet officially acknowledged. There were always one or two interns from Davis hovering around Eric, practicing their college degrees in enology, passionate young men convinced winemaking could be reduced to science, to flavor wheels and stats and timed exposures to the lees; to French or American oak, burned or toasted oak; to Brix and pH; to fining agents and yeast inocula; to pruning policies and trellising systems; to the latest configurations of crushers and stemmers. Henry was an old-world traditionalist and Eric was his new-age artist—for them, science played a supporting role in winemaking, nothing more. They had always made a good team. Tall, trusty Eric-the-meticulous, and the equally tall, classic Signore Bugato in his white linen shirt and his hurried, unhurried way of moving deliberately about the property from one task to the next, bending or straightening to gaze at something, a mealybug, a trellis wire, late light in the west.

Louise, with her secretary, handled all the winery bookkeeping and paperwork. As history seemed to have it the world over, the field hands and pickers came and went with the seasons. Those who stayed were the cellar workers with steady jobs and families down in St. Helena. The winery even opened a weekend tasting room for tourists and hired Eric's mother-in-law to run it, because she had the sort of maternal authority that managed the over-imbibers without provoking them and without letting them become too drunk to drive—and thus a liability. The winery was doing well, steadily building a reputation, winning awards, high ratings, even Donlon's favor two years running—no easy feat. If Donlon liked it, you knew the wine had "drama."

From high school to college, and still the girls maintained a geographical rift. Clair was accepted at Brown. It was strange to her that Nina chose a college so close to home rather than getting herself as far away as possible. Or that, whenever she could, she left her roommates at S.F. State and drove up to St. Helena for weekends in her junky Ford Focus. It was funny how thoroughly . . . *conventional* Nina was becoming. She and their mother did things together, spring flower shows, poetry readings, and once, on a "lark," as Louise called it, they flew to New York for three days just to see the Matisse exhibit, staying at the Beekman Towers and drinking cocktails in the lounge on the top floor where Louise told Nina things she never told Clair—about romances she'd had before Henry, about her job as a secretary for a construction company, the sorts of people she used to meet, and the dreams she had had that, to this day, said more about who she was than who she seemed to have become. In general, people seemed more comfortable around Nina, even her mother. Despite her beauty, Nina was the flawed one, the humanized twin, and Clair *a goody-goody*, as her mother now and then remarked. People didn't feel they had to try with Nina. They could be themselves.

Nevertheless, around Nina a sadness spread. Everything she chose to do could be approved of, but none of it seemed to bring her joy. This was not to say that she couldn't be funny; she had a dark sense of humor. But that sadness, like the open sea, went on and on, and seemed never to discover a shore upon which to break and spill away. One Christmas during college Uncle Sal gave Nina a guitar, her big gift. They always received one big gift, with a handful of lesser items filling in under the tree—socks, books, a pair of earrings, a sample bag of creams and soaps and facial concoctions—that sort of thing. Nina had been wanting a guitar for over a year, borrowing her roommate's and learning the usual list of starter songs, *Mr. Bo Jangles, House of the Rising Sun, Brown Eyed Girl*. But when she opened the big mysterious package and saw what it was, she didn't just cry, she sobbed and fled the room. Once again, only Clair seemed to understand what this was about. After a few weeks, the guitar disappeared, along with all the other things, the opportunities and people who made assumptions about her worth that she was not prepared to entertain, let alone accept. The psychiatrist had been able to take her only so far down that sun-drenched road.

Nina was still beautiful in that smooth, pure way of hers. Her skin was flawless, her eyes clear and unwavering. She kept her hair long, though it was often bound up in some sort of outdated chignon with lacquered sticks or real tortoise shell combs she had found in secondhand shops. A small tattoo of a black moth appeared behind her right ear sometime during her college years. She smiled not with her mouth but with her eyes, really with the lines at the corners of her eyes. Nor did she ever purposefully exercise, though in the city she walked everywhere. Her voice became deep and apathetic and experienced-sounding, especially when she developed vocal fry. If she laughed, you always felt that you had achieved something rare. There was a smoky aura about her, a film-noir futility that conjured random encounters in cellared establishments after the worst of events had already wound down—lost, strife-torn beings who had seen too much and who had had their feelings wrung out so that they couldn't have lied if they had wanted to. What would have been the point?

People fell in love with Nina regularly—or with whom they thought she was, a creature who had *certain knowledge*. She had a way of letting them see themselves in her, but never letting them see her—smoke-and-mirrors. She was always surrounded by some version of love, but she seemed impervious to it, using her beauty to gain advantage, or to establish a debt, but not to attract genuine love. Human beings are strict arbitrators of conduct even when they pretend otherwise, exacting justice by means of small, unnoticed, ongoing modifications sometimes only evident in the symptoms of anxiety—nail-biting and knee-bouncing, drinking and tobacco use, or driving too fast, door-checking and faucet tightening—she was always tightening faucets—or sex, plenty of sex. Nina's anxieties were practically symphonic, and anxiety was suffering, wasn't it? But how could she let herself be happy?

For different reasons derived from the same Ur-dynamic, neither of the sisters knew how to be happy. Events had driven them into separate corners, and it meant that they were each left with half an existence, the other half, the unacknowledged half, bound and gagged behind closed doors.

They lost track of each other through college. After the first summer home, when university policy allowed students to have their own cars, if they chose, Clair remained in the East, working on an organic farm in northern Vermont between freshman and sophomore years and, thereafter, variously as an intern or field assistant to professors, postdocs, or graduate students doing work in and around the West. The arid regions were her focus, where the land was thirsty and its creatures hungry, a world of perpetual want and struggle.

Nina took summer jobs as a barista, a stocker at the Oakville grocery, a baker's assistant, and once as the hapless wretch whose job it was to clean out the mud tubs at a Calistoga spa. Generally, she stayed close to home. During their junior year and owing to out-of-sync holiday schedules, she visited Clair in Providence. Clair offered her the couch in their dorm apartment, but Nina said she had taken a room off the hill, down in the city. It turned out that during the four-day visit she had been sleeping every night at the west end train station and that a vagrant had flashed her. That was when she'd lost her sinecure on the bench because the staff were suddenly more or less aware of her. There had been a scene. Nina knew her rights. But now she had to spend the last night of her visit on the couch in the dorm room.

"What were you doing down there?" Clair asked. She was sitting cross-legged on her bed, clipping her toenails.

"You didn't ask for this."

"For what?"

"Me to visit. There was no, you know, engraved *invitation*."

"Since when do I have to extend a formal invite to my sister?"

"Since always."

Clair switched feet, looking down to conceal the pleasure she felt in the ways of subtle genetic knowing that passed between them, like a dark light that illuminated things only their two sets of eyes could detect. "Yeah, but it's still not mandatory for you to sleep on a bench." They had spent the last three days playing tourists, even taking the train up to Boston to go clubbing. It had been unexpectedly nice, having someone to do things with, someone she didn't have to explain things to, someone who didn't require fragments of informing background; someone with whom things had long ago been settled. Just to be *known*—that could be enough, if in solitude you spent most of your hours. At the same time, she resented being forced out of that solid, reassuring, and entirely dependable solitude. So far as Clair knew, solitude had never hurt her, though at that very moment it occurred to her that there was still always one person in the room of solitude, wasn't there?—you. And she might be the most dangerous of all.

Nina was standing in the doorway. The room was one of three that opened onto a common area shared by the roommates. "So what's with you?" Nina said.

"What do you mean?"

"I mean we never see you."

We.

"You hide out here in your plant books, or you're the third wheel in a cozy domestic scene, or you vaporize in the desert. What the hell." The deep apathy of experience had flattened Nina's voice even more than Clair remembered, and she found herself distrusting its source. Maybe her sister hadn't seen and done as much as she implied.

Clair had finished clipping and filing her toenails—she was remarkably limber and had her leg and foot angled up so that her toes were lined up just under her nose, like a tight package of short pink uncooked sausages. It was something she had always been proud of, how flexible she was, though, glancing up through her eyebrows to the flat cloud cover of Nina's world-weary gaze, flexibility struck her as an oddly desperate and petty trait to take any pride in. "I don't know what's *with me*."

"I don't know? What kind of answer is that, Clairsie? What don't you know?"

Nina was the only one allowed to call her *Clairsie*. Hearing it now reminded her of the sisterly affection that she had always longed for, the one Nina had mostly withheld, or, Clair suspected, never felt. "I don't know what you're getting at. Also, who gave you the right . . . ?"

"You're depressed or something."

"Depressed."

"Sure. That's what I think." Nina was majoring in Psychology, somehow not a surprise, and now everything she encountered in her fellow human beings could be run down in a Psych 1A textbook.

"Dr. Nina."

Dead-eyed, her sister stared at her. "You're in a free fall. You're apathetic and alienated. It's called depression."

From one of the many water bottles Clair kept around for jogging or to extend the length of time that she could hide out in her room, she poured some water onto a paper towel and used it to dab up the nail clippings and delicate white filing dust. "I'm not depressed because I never get depressed. Depression is a state of no feeling, no interest, no energy."

"Not exactly, but okay, in your own words then. What's going on? What are you?"

"I'm nothing. Engaged in my life. Perfectly happy. I like being alone, that's all. I prefer plants to people. After all, who wouldn't, when you think about it? They just do their best to grow and bloom, and whatever damage they do to another is usually only because they've been thriving. Except maybe creosote." She looked absently out the window. From where she was sitting, she could only see the high naked branches of an elm tree, one of the older ones that had survived Dutch elm disease. She was thinking that you could keep yourself from thriving even if you wanted, if you wanted another to do well, or better; if there was someone you thought was damaged and needed the extra light; if you felt guilty about that, or about something. Guilty about thriving. She watched herself make a little gesture with her hand, a single quick smoothing movement across her knee, as if confirming something that had long ago been ironed out.

"Clair?"

Closing her eyes to change the screen, Clair said, "What I am right now, if you want to know, is upset about you sleeping in a train station, and then not even telling me. Lying to me. Here I was picturing you in a nice motel room . . ." She stopped herself. *That* was the lie: she hadn't once imagined Nina making her way back to a motel room, nice or otherwise, after their nights out. She hadn't continued to think about Nina the instant Nina exited her company, clacking away in cheap pumps, the 2/4 time signature of her footsteps on the sidewalk scooped up almost immediately by the traffic, by the cars and buses and taxis carrying people to homes where there were other people who might worry if at some point in the long night they didn't hear the key in the lock and the door swing softly open and the light of companionship reach into the darkened room, like a prodigal friend at last returned. She hadn't even asked which motel or how far it was away from wherever they happened to have been. Nina came and went. It was a binary system: Nina present, attend to Nina; Nina gone, Nina *gone*. Actually, it was less than a binary system: she wanted to get the visit over with, the time with Nina behind her, a thing that had to be got through, never mind the moments during the visit she could classify as moments of enjoyment.

Oh, but this was bad. Suddenly Clair was feeling bad—very bad about Nina and what it was about her or about their relationship that would advocate sleeping in a cold drafty train station; bad about wanting to get so far away from Nina, and for so long. Forever, in fact. Bad about the way things had worked out, the way that blame had spread through all of them like black ink so that so much that might have been possible could not find a way or a blank page upon which to be written. Of course she would sleep in the train station—or a park or a cardboard box along the sidewalk or in the equally cold drafty arms of a stranger. Every root Clair tugged up from beneath the lives of her family exposed another even deeper root, with pale dirty tendrils snaking off in uncountable directions, the reasons for one thing, the causes of another, the unexamined reactions, the reflexive moves, the resentments, the choices designed solely to build up sedimentary layers of concealment. Fathomless hypocrisy! A conspiracy of cowards!

But not Nina; Nina had done the math. She was only behaving according to what it had all added up to, living as much as possible the truth that the rest of them hadn't been able to bear. Oh god, what had they all done to each other? What patterns had they instantly spun, what characters and characteristics had they so readily etched into their family portrait, what monsters of unnaturalness had their intolerance of natural feelings and accidental acts created? What else but to flee, flee to the farthest point of land, to an opposite coast and a backward gazing sea over which the sun might only and ever rise, everything perpetually starting over? Hadn't they all wanted only that? To start over?

Nevertheless, nevertheless . . . wanting to know just how much truth Nina might be willing to speak, taking almost ghoulish interest, Clair asked, "Why did you do that, sleep in the train station? All those strangers walking by you and looking at you when you can't even know that they're looking at you, the voyeurism and the malignancy, and the trains just coming and going . . . why?"

Nina shrugged and with showy eyes, made a point of surveying Clair's room, which was just big enough for a twin bed, a small desk, a closet no more spacious than a phone booth, and one of those ancient steam radiator heaters under the only window that banged and rattled every time the delivery door to the kitchen, located one floor down, slammed shut. Which it just had. "This is a pretty dismal space," Nina said. The window rattling was just a faint chatter of teeth now. Outside it was gray and still, so still that none of what was left of November's foliage stirred, not even the smallest dead leaves curled in like skeletal claws. There was no snow. Snow would have brightened the sodden turf and provided contrast to all the brick-and-mortar. It might have been a gloomy picture from a forgotten attic instead of the actual living out-of-doors. "How can you stand it here?"

"I live here. It's my home."

"There are, like, only two colors in this world, brown and gray."

"Yeah, well." Clair was now thinking about the *we*. "Who sent you, by the way? Mom?"

Nina squinted up a wry smile. "She doesn't even know I'm here, she's too obsessed with the holiday auction. I sent me. Ever heard of Real Cheap Flights? They post them in the student union. I got a round-trip for two hundred bucks. You should check it out, maybe get one for yourself and come home now and then. Some of us might like that." Why the insistent plural . . . *we, us?* Why was Nina always invoking imaginary comrades to shore up her wishes and opinions? How much more alone could you be if you had to pretend that there were others whose feelings and thoughts mattered, because your own didn't matter at all?

Clair looked at her sister then, the attitude of bland confidence, the willingness to rove about like a tramp, the low-level recklessness that infused most of her conduct and that implied someone trying to accidentally kill herself. Plus, two hundred dollars was a lot of money for anyone their age. "Let's get something to eat," she said. "I'm buying."

Heading down the hallway they ran into the roommates, and so the four of them went together to a pub on Canal Street. As it happened, Clair's roommates were two lesbians who, on meeting, had promptly fallen in love. The roommates made a cute couple, both of them short, funny, fast-talkers from Long Island, one in makeup and impractical shoes and the other expensively nondescript in boy chinos and a button-down. They seemed to like Clair's sister better, or at least to have more fun with her—lots of flirty innuendos. Afterward, Clair always wondered if something involving Nina had happened later that night. Anything was possible with Nina. Even her sensuality recognized no boundaries.

FROM COLLEGE, NINA got a job counseling at Juvenile Hall, which again, made some sort of quirky sense—a way to better care for the remembered girl criminal she had once been or still might be, for all anyone knew. And even without that possible undercurrent, at the very least she would be able to relate to them, girls who had wandered too far down the wrong path; anxious girls afraid to be angry or with no one to be angry at; girls who picked at their skin and gnawed their fingernails.

Clair transitioned into graduate school at the University of California, Berkeley where, in her second year, she met Tom during one of what quickly became clear were obligatory protests. When in Rome. At the end of it, while others were piling up the placards and posters, he had taken her hand tenderly as if they had known each other for years and had been waiting for just the right moment for something that neither had been able to request. "Shall we arise and go now?"

"Okay," she said. Who could resist a man armed with poetry? It made him somehow more masculine, confident enough to summon poesy.

Tom had always been a dabbler but it was a while—longer than it should have been—before Clair learned that she was merely one of his dabbles. She almost didn't care. A tall healthy showman who blew big winds into the small sails of his accomplishments and who spoke in memorized lines that impressed listeners with his eco-socio-politico savvy, he was one of the illuminati among their group. He knew everyone, or seemed to, and at least half of those he claimed to consort with did eventually turn up at one or another party or scene or late-night joint-smoking disquisition where there stood Tom, tossing back the heavy brown forelock of hair, his cheeks a fervorous pink, the thrill of the stage inflating his chest as he boomed out his opening word, "Listen." Sometimes, to make it sound more important, more urgent, he would invoke another language, usually French, even though romanticism was not exclusively a French invention. "*Ecoutez!*" He spoke three languages. He had an amazing memory—verse, slogans, sentences from philosophers lifted from context and cryptically reapplied elsewhere. They listened, his friends, their friends, but it wasn't so easy to remember. The trouble with theories and abstractions like "the physicalist/vitalist conflict" was that something so vast was finally not especially real. What was real was the baby growing inside her.

"Ah, it'll be grand," he told her, adopting, for some reason, an Irish brogue. "We'll have a wee lassie and I'll carry her about on me shoulder, and you can weave posies into her flaxen locks. Jaesus, we've the luck, hadn't we, luv?"

"I'm not done with my degree," she said, surprised that he was embracing her pregnancy and the responsibilities that it bore so easily.

"What's the story then?"

"My degree. Remember, Tom?"

They were sitting in a restaurant in San Francisco along the Embarcadero watching the sailboats beat against the wind that was pushing steadily into the bay. The water was a hard brisk noonday blue, and littered across it were the white sails and the sharply keeled hulls. She guessed that there was a regatta, and in her mind she made it fitting, like a celebration with a special piece of music written for the occasion. *Regatta Sonata for Tom and Clair.* In the middle of the regatta was the abandoned prison island of Alcatraz from which so many had failed to escape. It was too isolated, and the tidal currents were strong—a safe place to be, provided you never wanted to leave. She was thinking about what it would be like to have someone in your life, like a baby, like Tom, who would always be there with you; what it would be like not to be imprisoned on the island of Self. What it would be like to have to remain . . . *pervious*, people swimming in and out of the sea of you, with their needs and feelings and ideas about who you should be; with their soft words and murmuring hands.

Tom slapped the table. "Degree? Scrap paper!"

"Scrap parchment. Please."

He made a gesture with his hand, waving it off. "The degree will wait."

"Not really. I'm on fellowship. There's a time limit to the money."

"Are ye tetched, luv?" He tapped his right temple and peered at her with melodramatic concern, squinting one eye. "Naw, we've got to call 'round the lads and tell 'em the good tidings," he said, cheerfully ignoring her remark. "But right now, let's order up a festive pint."

"Why are you talking like that?"

He smiled winningly. "Oh, I don't know, Irish paps, aren't they the best with babes?" The accent was suddenly gone, and she felt a little bad about spoiling his fun. He *was* fun, and that counted for a lot, didn't it? Her mother adored him; her father seemed to find him entertaining. Nina was indifferent, naturally.

"I haven't heard that. Maybe with babies but there always seems to be a passel of dirty-faced children, all of them hungry and feral, in books and movies."

But mention of movies had put Tom onto something else. "Right now, right this instant, you have Mia Farrow eyes, you know, moody smudges. *This is no dream! This is really happening!*"

"I didn't get a lot of sleep last night."

"No, it's good. That sexy bit of fear and worry . . ."

"Was that from *Rosemary's Baby*? That line?"

He smiled.

"God, Tom, not the best association."

"You still look sexy."

Half-glad that in her particular predicament she was still a sex object, it occurred to her that marriage had yet to be mentioned. Love had, a little too frequently, which seemed to throw it into question. He told her that he loved her at the end of their first date, in fact, and without thinking, all she could say was, *that's not credible.* Lifting her eyes to attract the waitress's attention, she decided that beer was just what she needed, and one wouldn't harm the baby, contingent or otherwise. "If we go ahead with this . . ."

"If? Of course we're having the baby! We'll pour all the wisdom of the ages into him, and he shall bear the torch high when we've departed this vale of tears."

Now the baby was a boy version of Tom striding along a mythic isle, like a Greek god, a stone Hermes in winged sandals and little cap, immortally entitled, munificent, eternity in his unseeing eyes.

"For he on honey-dew hath fed / And drunk the milk of Paradise," Tom recited.

"I don't think that it's exactly a good thing, Kubla Khan drinking the milk of paradise. I think it made him see things. Coleridge was on opium when he wrote that, you know. Mr. Khan was having Mr. Coleridge's visions."

Almost angrily, Tom winced; he hated to be called out about his quotes and applications. "Why is it so hard for you to relax into the spirit of things, Clair?"

"I guess I like them to be real first, Tom. I don't see any point in kidding myself. About anything. A baby is a big deal. The biggest deal there is. Technically, you know, that's our only job here on planet Earth. To reproduce. I'd like to do that job well."

"You're a scientist," he said. It sounded like an insult and a dismissal.

But wanting to salvage his mood, she said, "A scientist who loves you."

His gaze melted a little as he reached over to pat her tummy. "Ah, Clair, sweet Clair." A momentary eruption of the Irish brogue. Still, he wasn't really looking at her, he was searching the negative space all around her, eyes skittish.

"So you really think we can do this?" she said.

"Why not?"

"Well, there are plenty of reasons why not. What we have to decide is if there are more reasons to go ahead with it. With our having a baby."

The waitress came by and he ordered them two IPAs, holding her up to ask about the blue stone pendant she wore around her neck, what it was, where it came from. She glanced over her shoulder toward the kitchen and finally ducked away. The restaurant was busy, exactly the sort of material detail Tom would not notice.

"But, Tom, do you really think that there are enough reasons to go ahead? I mean, enough reasons for you?"

"What man doesn't want his own child?"

"I know you want it, or I think you want it." The little laugh she gave was tinged with frustration as she watched her hand turn the spoon at her place setting so that it faced up, then down, up and down, waiting to be put to some earnest use. "But do you want all that it *means*?" she asked, hesitating to invoke words like commitment and responsibility and ramifications, to measure out the years of a childhood and hold them up beside such words to see whether one outdistanced the other, the years or the words, or whether they became the bound and single force that could carry a child into a happy productive life.

"What it means?" He threw open his arms grandly and she found herself studying his incongruously small soft hands, the twin palms facing her, like the broken halves of some fleshy island fruit. "It means the sun and the moon."

"Diapers and homework, too. It means a steady job and, you know, getting serious about things, Tom."

"If you don't think I'm serious . . ."

"You're serious. It's just that you're serious about, well, a lot of things."

"Passion is a life unto itself."

"We're talking about a life, not a feeling. We're talking about bringing a life into this world. It's a serious deal. We have to think about more than passion and torches and Irish movies. We can't kid ourselves." He was staring into his beer glass, looking vaguely bored and miserable, like someone enduring a lecture on a hot humid afternoon. "Or I can't kid myself," she added, "not about this."

He sighed. "I love you, Clair. Isn't that enough?"

"I don't know."

"Can't that be enough?"

She didn't say anything.

"And I'll love the baby, and *that* will be enough."

"I don't know. It's a life. It's our lives."

"Can't you stop being a scientist just this once and believe in something you can't actually see or measure or dropper into a petri dish?"

A growing breeze was worrying the draped corners of the tablecloth, flipping it about, threatening to upturn the occupants of the table. Shame was some of what she felt, but not all. "Sure, I can do that. I guess I can do that."

"Good."

"You know me."

His smile was forgiving, paternal.

"I just don't like to kid myself about anything. It seems important not to do that. In this world, you know, not to kid yourself, or you end up, I don't know, standing there sort of flat-footed on a corner, alone . . ."

"Nonsense."

So they decided, not according to all the words that had gone unsaid, or to all the years that, really, neither had envisioned or knew how to envision, or to all the experience neither of them could hope to claim, or pretend to have, to go ahead with the baby.

But it turned out that she *had* kidded herself about Tom. She had let herself get into the spirit of him. She had discounted the fact of him.

From the beginning, what she had liked about Tom were his assumptions. It was not often that one liked assumptions, or the people who fostered them, because almost invariably someone ended up mistaken about one thing or another, and that led to embarrassment or cross-purposes or broken hearts. But Tom's assumptions possessed a force all by themselves, and drove otherwise harebrained dreams and schemes along, sometimes right into the arms of reality. Or something approximating reality. It was exhilarating. He had founded a club on campus for all the "lambent flames of intellect," inviting students and scholars from any field to present weekly topics, following which there would be lively conversation along the lines of seventeenth-century English coffeehouses. There was a sign-up sheet, there were light libations, people began to bring food to share, carrots and hummus, chips and salsa, pistachio nuts from the Central Valley. For quite a while, maybe six months, it was a success until the crackpots got wind of it. Soon enough, they and the drug addicts, following their noses, trailed in off Telegraph Avenue and propped themselves up long enough to sour the whole deal. Everyone was too progressive to escort them out, or to suggest that not everyone had interesting things to say, or that one or more might need a shower now and then, preferably now. Or that it wasn't cool to flash knives at speakers speaking their minds. One of the vagrants turned out to have been a murderer. Seriously. The whole deal epitomized Tom's problem. He never recognized limitations. He didn't know how to put on the brakes. He never detected even the faintest whiff of consequences. He was always playing with matches. He was a rotten judge of character or maybe simply no judge at all. In his world, everyone was a potential prophet, an Einstein drop-out, a prince in pauper's rags. Ready, fire, aim.

And so they planned, riding the skyrocket of Tom's assumptions and enthusiasms, to visit Clair's parents two weeks hence and deliver the good news. But on Tuesday of that first week, Henry was diagnosed with cardiomyopathy, a particular form of it caused by alcoholism and requiring, naturally, a total and immediate cessation of drinking. And on Sunday morning, when Louise had gone off for one of her meetings, and Eric and his family were down in St. Helena for mass, and only the winery dogs were around to witness, Henry shot himself in the Morris chair with the TV on in the background and already a glass of the morning's first libation, a Sancerre, on one of the chair arms. He had apparently been reading the harvest and cellar stats on the wine and had jotted down some of his first impressions, which turned out to be his last impressions, his *memento mori*: *perfumy, but flavors not bright—acid too low, surprisingly complicated across the palate; won't live long; no matter—only a Sancerre.*

She had heard it said that there always comes a day of madness and tears, but that day was not the day her father shot himself. Henry's sorrow had been corrosive. He had lost hope, or the conditions that make hope possible, after Tony's death, and thereafter, he had been spared that uniquely human mortification. Hope may have no inherent value, but it attracts healthful agents, and without it there remains only the stone of stone soup. That was hope to Clair, the necessary bit of falsity that drew everything honest and worthy to it. Now she would not have to see her father in his chair surrounded by plates of spoiling food, catalogues earmarking unpurchased items of the highest quality, variously shaped glassware, fingerprinted and empty and attracting fruit flies, and that canvas bag, heavy with hollowed-out portent, slung over one arm of the chair. She would not have to hear the sad insistent chatter of the TV telling the world that everything is okay, the world is as it should be. The world could not be as it should have been for Henry Bugato.

No, for Clair, the day of madness and tears arrived two months later when she spotted Tom with a woman he had dated in the past. He had not tried to hide it or apologize for it. "I love you both," he said with quiet majesty, lifting and dropping his shoulders. His shoulders were big and slightly coved just under the horizontal line of the collarbone as is common among tall people habituated to gazing down. The ordinariness of his shrug, the little incurable narcissistic assumption it contained, combined with her having to look up at him, left her feeling as if it were she who had somehow disappointed him with her small-mindedness and quotidian worries, her lack of generosity, her female jealousy.

Maybe the truth came this way, in blows as tender and familiar as traces of old songs. A voice in your mind whispers, *ah, so this is the way it is, of course, of course* . . . Because she was not surprised that Henry killed himself. And she was not surprised that Tom was sliding out from beneath her, like a city shoe on black ice, impractical, all for show. She had wanted to go through her life safely unaccompanied, and had decided to try the other way, and now here she was with a baby coming and a man going and a father dead. A trinity of truths.

One morning, not too long later, she awoke in her Berkeley studio apartment, which was really just the second floor of a shabby, unspectacular Craftsman near campus. The Arlington bus was roaring north. The homeless had already pilfered recyclable bottles and cans, and now the city collectors were coming by to empty the now-mostly empty bins, their brakes squealing and their yellow lights strobing. The dog walkers were out, gathering up leavings with their hands sheathed in colored biodegradable bags. The before-work joggers were out, too, type As. She could smell the pizza ovens from the Cheese Board warming up for the day. She could hear the renters on the first floor, their aimless yoga music, the opening om. She could feel the nausea forming a glutinous bubble at the base of her throat. *Sternal notch*, her mind whispered. She could see the oak flooring that her bare feet rested on, the dark veins in the wood, the black nail heads; she could see the dust motes along the baseboard crowding into the narrow triangle behind the door where the mousetrap lived, the glob of peanut butter, desiccated and hard, the spring still loaded; she could see the puddled clothing from a week or so of changes and indecision, the second pillow that had ended up on the floor, the book beside it that she couldn't remember trying to read, the box of saltines someone said might help. The window was old, and so she could feel the cold air knife in along the side and bottom edges where the wood sash had long ago contracted. And none of it, not one detail, was persuasive. There was a day waiting all around her, inside her, at the bottom of her throat, in her womb, and yet she could not believe in the waiting day. She could only believe in the day that was over, in the days that were gone.

Then a new sound, the deadbolt, and Nina in the doorway—why was she always in doorways?

"Hello Clairsie."

"Hello Nina."

"Whatcha doing?"

"Nothing."

She started picking up Clair's room, beginning with the box of saltines. "Have you thought about names?"

"No."

"Let's think about names."

Clair tried to look out the window then, away from this person moving about her room, but the morning light was so harsh that she couldn't see anything but the dirty glass and the blinding white day straining through it. "Is that a good idea?" she asked.

"It's a good idea. It's the best thing to do. It's what we're going to do now, you and I."

CHAPTER 9

The sky turns a jaundiced gray, and the pillars of cardon trees, spaced and shaped by aridity, stand like great candelabra, unmoving and anticipatory as the last of the white brushstrokes that are largely ornamental clouds are overwhelmed by a wide, snub-nosed system barreling east from the Pacific. A chubasco. When the rain comes, it comes at once, descending in vertical lines as though each drop has a lead weight attached to it, and it comes in such quantity and so fast that there is instantly so much water on the road that it leaps back up into the air. Bright veins of lightning twist down from the black heavens to the desert, pinkish and direct, and snap a plumb line between one reality and another, immortality and mortality, peace and turmoil. Then a great wall of wind slams into them, battering the side of the van.

They had gone north and west, back toward Guerrero Negro, but not all the way there, meaning to turn southwest at San Ignacio and, later, take a road rumored to be very bad but passable down to the place where PSP planned to expand into Laguna San Ignacio. But now it is impossible to drive, to see, to hear. There is no point in pulling over, for no one, neither they nor any other vehicle, can drive in this catastrophe, and so when Mason stops the van, he simply parks on the crown of the road, such as it is, a faint central welt from whence the water drains to either side into the already flooding ditches where, Clair notices, something furry rushes past—furry and maybe just now still warm but nevertheless already drowned.

Rain of this weight, of this intensity, has always had a strange effect on her. Pounding water. The sound of it, the heaviness, the way it means to obliterate. Inside, she feels herself cowering, breathing fast, her chest caged and straining. The van is making it worse, she realizes, starting to open the door, to run from the storm by running into it, letting herself be dominated by it. But Mason, already perceiving something wild about to erupt just to his right, takes her hand without a word, and then the four of them, Mason, Clair, Rubio, and Marla, sit in the surprisingly humid silence of white noise as the chubasco pummels its way east across the peninsula. Her hand in his feels dangerously safe. To be taken care of . . . how strange that would be. How foreign. How wonderful.

She doesn't want to go on. Everything now seems a great mistake, a monumental mistake. Who are these people? How is it that they are sitting across from them in what amounts to a tin box on a road in the middle of nowhere, in the midst of a violent deluge biblical in size and suddenness? And in a desert that isn't acting like a desert. If this was the first of the plagues, what would be next? Or perhaps this was the second, Mason's back the first. That would mean that there would be eight more to complete the punishment. But what have they done to deserve punishment except to be alive at the same time? That would make life the crime, and death its punishment. Some people could only carry on under the auspice of punishment, people like her father. Up to a point it made living possible.

Once more, she experiences the weird, still-raw understanding of Mason, the new idea of him that Mulegé has exposed. They did stay too long in Mulegé, long enough for her to begin to see the other force that is driving Mason, which is hatred—hatred certainly of his father, hatred perhaps of her as the generalized Other, a witness and a judge; hatred of his mother for the unplanned abandonment with its built-in accusations and condemnations, and its orbiting aftereffects and upshots of accusation and condemnation—and that that force might be what fuels the *other* drive, the one that Clair has always loved: to save the world. But save the world from what? She glances quickly at him, at his profile against the watery glass, and imagines what it would be like to have been Mason as a child trying to reckon the motherless world he found himself in. Only one word comes to mind—wretchedness. Maybe what he wants to save the world from is the wretchedness of his own existence, one that lost a mother and alienated a father. From the world-destroying and otherwise omnipotent force that was Mason the infant, Mason the boy, Mason the young man making his way alone.

How far apart these two drives are, and how powerful, too—hate and rescue, denunciation and salvation. The energy, the fuel, has the same source, but how different their outcomes. Suddenly, she remembers Ethan's worried and jealous-boy words, *Mason is a scourge upon our land*. But Mason isn't a scourge.

Again, she glances over at him . . . those delicate lips with their tiny flaw, a single, almost imaginary undulation, like a skip, not at the corner where it would have been common in an ordinary smile, but just before it, as if hoping for ordinary joy. How she loves the naked intimacy of his face. The absence of apology.

No, it was bad luck, his mother's death, and then the rest of it, and that was all it was. Bad luck. And maybe bad luck, simple, pure, elemental bad luck can compose an isolated moment of force that incites reaction, propulsion, and traction along each line of direction, deviations and repulsions and attractions, too; it's its own little Big Bang, a piece of bad luck there at the beginning of an individual's private universe, radiating out consequences infinitely. One being that he *is* saving the world, a piece here, a piece there—never mind what drives it. This, too, is what she loves about being with Mason—the scale of life, the devotions, the everythings just behind the one thing, and then, too, the limitations, the finite days. Isn't it always easier to love when you know it will end, when you don't have to trust the lastingness of it?

"Oh, for Christ's sake, what timing," Mason says under his breath as he opens the door and passes through the curtain of rain, keeping his back to the van when he empties his bladder. Instantly the rain has soaked through his shirt so that she can see a bas-relief of bones and musculature. It is a fine back, a long trapezoid.

Whatever it is he needs saving from, she knows she can't save him. Even though she is a saver, a squarer-of-accounts and a smoother-of-moods, this is beyond her expertise. Mason's father is dead now, part of Mason's past and part of the Earth's history, and it is not possible to invent history for real lives or to reverse-action *Mason Comstock*, the film. History can be discovered, but not invented. Films can be viewed time and time again until the one thing we keep missing is suddenly, embarrassingly obvious. But no matter what, Mason is stuck with the life that was and is his life.

For the first time, gazing out the window into the lashing rain, at the wind's efforts to flatten and subdue everything in its path, from the ocotillo to the cholla, and even to the lowest of vegetation, a silvery frothing ground cover whose name even she doesn't know, for the first time she questions their future. She thinks she wants it, she thinks it is all she wants, but she can't help questioning it.

Marla begins filing her nails, an act so clichéd that it tilts over into something both farcical and significant, and Clair gives her head a single small shake as if to rattle some sense into what's happening.

For several minutes Mason steeples his fingers and stares contemplatively through the windshield, his very composure making her uneasy as he looks into the heavy torrent, the rain spilling down the glass like water from invisible buckets held by invisible hands over the roof of the van. At last, having sorted and calibrated a collection of thoughts and finding himself bored, he slips one of the brochures he gathered back at the border from the door pocket, unfolds it, reads, slides it across the dashboard, and then reaches for another.

"What day is it?" Clair asks, almost shouting.

"Tuesday," Mason says, not lifting his eyes from the brochure.

"No, what day in Baja?"

Rubio regards her with an uptick of interest.

"Day eight, maybe nine," Mason says. He frowns, either because he's concerned that he can't remember or because he can't tell yet what she's up to, where she's headed with this. "March," he adds, as if making an entry in his journal, "1998. No traffic, rotten weather."

She ignores his joke. "I'd rather be outside. I don't like this. I'd rather be in it. I'd feel safer in it."

He picks something out from under a fingernail and looks over at her through his eyebrows. "Well, you wouldn't be."

Turning his quivering hand up, Rubio says quickly, "You are worried."

"Relax," Mason says. "It'll pass. These sorts of things always do."

"What sorts of things?"

He smiles softly, as if forgiving her.

"There is no cause for worry," Rubio says, shrugging. "A chubasco. They come, they go, it is always *rápido*."

"We've been away a long time," she explains to him, because his gaze is kind, and there is nothing in Mason's eyes now.

Slowly, Rubio nods, and then he lets his head tip to the side sympathetically. Is he embarrassed for her? Does he find her odd and . . . *ethereal*, as others have remarked?

"It's another country," she adds. "It makes it feel longer, being away. My son . . ." She's thinking back over the days, the long hours at the hotel in San Quintin, the gas tank ordeal in Rosarita, the news of Mason's father's death, the days of cocaine in Mulegé, and Mason's back with its appetite for codeine and ice and clemency. She's thinking about Ethan, about little boys and how hard it is to be a little boy with feelings, feelings of loss especially, or feelings of never having had; about boys like Mason, like Ethan, and the aloof form of jealousy that must come from not really knowing what it's like to have what you've never had but know that you ought to have had. A mother. A father. A chance. That was what Tony never had, a chance. Tony was their little Big Bang, the Bugato family's. Ethan and Mason, they each had half a chance. If she and Mason stay together, marry, make a life, form a family, then Ethan can make up that shorted half he started out with. He can piece it together. Whoever gets the whole of anything, anyway? We are all piecing it together, she decides. And what about Nina? Nina with her job at Juvenile Hall, paying damages. How long will it take her to pay back the universe, how much has she managed to piece back together? We start out whole and somehow, unavoidably, collide with life, fly apart, and then spend our lives reassembling ourselves.

At Rubio's feet are several crates of gear and provisions, including one that contains the scotch. With a curiously measured pace, a doctor's pace, a pace that somehow compensates for his tremor by indulging it, he slides it from its spot, and leans forward to pass it to Clair, swinging it bottom-first. She takes a long drink and nods at him as the heat collects at the back of her throat. A moment later he fishes a small plastic bag of coke from his shirt pocket and a blade sheathed in yellow cardboard, and on one of the camp plates stacked in the crate at his feet, he begins chopping up several rocks. The din of the chubasco somehow amplifies the tiny confidential tapping of the blade on the enameled metal plate.

"It's humid in here, don't you think? It feels very . . . close in here," she hears herself say. No one responds. They are in the Vizcaíno Desert too far inland for humidity to be much more than a concept or a rumor from elsewhere—a yearning. The rain is deafening, like military drums, like the sound of something much worse coming their way, an army. Armies of retribution. There are too many of them, too many for the space to contain, too many feelings, too many thoughts, too many little acts ticking away time, Marla filing her nails, one nail, the next, Rubio's hand shaking and the *tap-tap-tap* of the blade, Mason folding and unfolding brochures. Clair has been scratching the inside of her thumb and finally, noticing it for what it is, she sees that she has managed to produce a raw and now faintly bleeding abrasion in the skin.

The sound of water . . .

Taking another gulp of the scotch and setting the bottle very carefully, very deliberately in one of the cup holders, as if she is trying to get away with something, she jerks the door handle and this time escapes into the storm.

Outside she can breathe. Hard rain and hard wind, the booming accusations of thunder, and the sky dark and mean, but at least she's a part of it now. It can swallow her up, and she's convinced that it won't hurt so much, it won't be so confusing if she is part of it, and it is part of her. She does not want to fight this storm, she wants it to defeat her. When it's over, when it passes, there will come the sweet smell of sand verbena, the earthiness of petrichor, the dill-like odor of the faded yucca flowers, all the dormant esters of the desert excited up into the air; there will be the smell of change, too, of one thing having gone on too long and a new thing needing to break through. A purification.

Mason doesn't come for her. He waits in the van, not even looking. She knows this about him, that he is reticent to expose how much he cares about anything, about her. Anyway, she doesn't want him to see her like this, desperate and alien even to herself. Eventually, whatever needed running out of her now run out, she walks back, shivering and empty. A dismal mood has overtaken the van.

"Wow," Marla says with smiling indifference, "that was random." Coke, a delicate dusting of it, coves the opening of her perfect left nostril.

"Nothing's random," Clair says, suddenly repulsed by this woman who hasn't any rudder.

Rubio finds a towel in the jumble of gear and dries Clair's face. He is a mannered fellow, and though manners are not necessarily kind, with Rubio she feels an elegant kindness. But even his courtliness, evidence of a beautiful education, seems an artifact of something tormented. He has had the meanness worn out of him. Or he has managed to resist it. Or it has been reserved entirely for one man, his own father. She closes her eyes so as not to see what's in his, the pain. Under a blanket, she changes into dry clothes.

Mason is silent as he swallows another codeine and tries to shift his back against the mostly melted bag of ice she had situated for him as they were leaving Mulegé. The back is holding its own, neither possible to forget nor so painful that it takes over.

She assumes that he is sore with her for defecting—another idea: that he likes possessing her.

Before the squall passes completely, he turns the key in the ignition and they continue on to San Ignacio. Soon a yellow luminescence sifts through the eastward trailing clouds, and the steamy, still crepuscular atmosphere surrenders within minutes to sharp panes of radiance shattering here and there across the desert. Even the thorns of the cacti are brightly ornamented with clinging drops of rain. Eventually, the sky, emptied of clouds and even of the memory of clouds, is as stark and shocked as the face of a child who doesn't understand what just happened. The *vados* are welling with mud and water, and it takes a long time to reach the town.

From the highway you cannot see San Ignacio until you are almost upon it, for it lies at the bottom of a broad deep green ravine bordered by high mesas. All that is immediately visible is a sea of palm treetops. It isn't until they turn off the highway at a Pemex station and drop down into the arroyo toward the town that they appreciate the surprise and wonder of the oasis—its viridity, its shade, its softness—and the good luck of an oasis to wanderers of deserts. The narrow unmarked street borders a spring-fed lagoon on the Rio San Ignacio, lush and reedy along its banks with the date palms towering just beyond and forming a park of gray, evenly spaced columns through which the umbrellas of palm fronds allow no light to pass. The road continues through the warm shaded endlessness of the columns and then abruptly passes into citrus orchards. Along the way are villagers carrying sacks of goods, a boy pedaling a bike trailing two dogs, a runty horse and rider, chickens, and then at a curve in the road a white wall with the painted sentence, *"Existen tantas cosas que puedes hacer para vivir sin drogas . . ."*—There are so many things you can do to make life a drug-free sport. No one says a word.

At the plaza where the tall mission church predominates, they stop to make a plan. The mission is a handsome Spanish colonial structure of lava blocks, the white plaster weathered by centuries and in patchy retreat from the dark rough stone. The coved windows are small and protective, and the single belfry is high enough to be visible from anywhere in the arroyo, especially from the road that descends into the town. The stone comes from the local volcanoes, Las Tres Virgines, whose conical peaks they saw before leaving the highway. Across from the mission, old laurel trees shade a plaza, its benches still wet and unoccupied. It is all so unexpectedly clean and civilized, the stately mission with its groomed and orderly plaza, everything gleaming, the wind gone, the scene as still as an old painting from a more graceful time.

Rubio leans forward and says to Mason, *"Hermano,* the road will be bad.

Compactado. The soil like this, wet and *compactado*, it becomes very slippery. Rocks too, from the sides *es posible*. We must wait until the morning. Let it dry. Wait for light."

"But your father . . . if we wait, will he still be in Guerrero Negro the next day?"

"He will be there."

"And Yetz. PSP is flying him in tomorrow."

"It is a big place. This scientist, he will have to visit the two big lagoons already in production, and then he will have to come to San Ignacio, too, just as we are, and down the same bad road. He must make his final report to Mexico, to the *Japonés*. It must be persuasive. Everyone is watching."

"Not everyone, but when I'm done, then everyone."

Clair smiles at Mason's confidence and looks away into the plaza where the canopy of trees is so dense that only the smallest patches of sunlight interrupt the otherwise seamless gray of paving stones and raised beds that enclose the enormous laurels. She enjoys his confidence; it is so much more acceptable than her own.

They talk about finding a gas can for the long drive, just in case; about food, about where to stay if they must stay down at the lagoon.

An old woman has entered the plaza from the west side and is shaking out a plastic bag, which she spreads on a bench to create a barrier between her skirt and the wet wood. From another bag, a paper bag, she removes an orange and peels it. The wedges disappear quickly, one at a time, sideways into her mouth, like small tropical fish. Then another orange appears, she peels it, and again, eats it quickly and methodically. It takes only minutes for her to consume five small oranges. Beside her on the dark wood is a mound of bright peels. When it is time for her to go, she stands with some difficulty, cups the peels into her hands and funnels them into the other bag, the one on which she has been sitting, her actions careful and precise, like the actions of someone patiently demonstrating a task to a child—how to eat an orange. It is curious and charming. Suddenly Clair feels happy, as if the bad things are behind now, and simple wholesome things are in order. At the same time, trying to understand, she concludes that the oranges were free, perhaps even gathered from the trees they have just passed, and any other variety of food would have cost money this old woman doesn't have.

"Let's stay here," she says. She would like to stay in this old-world place where things are done in a certain way, small things over and over again, without complaint, without embellishment.

"What's cheered you up?" Mason says.

She shrugs. "Oranges."

"Good enough."

"And let's go into the mission. I want to smell it. It'll be cold, the way they are. There's nothing colder than captive air."

Rubio nods as if she's said something profound.

Presently a man carrying two square cans of water that hang on ropes from a branch born across his shoulder treads along from behind the van. Mason waves out the window to stop him and ask about *cuartos*. The young man nods to a side street, muttering the name of a guesthouse—Casa Molino—and they move the van two blocks and park outside the court-yard wall. Crawling densely across the adobe is a grape vine, its leaves broader than a man's hand, and over the entrance to the courtyard the arbor is so low that they have to stoop beneath it. When Mason remarks in Spanish that they might want to prune, the proprietress says, "This is our home."

"*Bonita*," he smiles.

She is a beautiful older woman with fine features and bright blue mis-chievous eyes and skin that she has obviously kept from the sun, as those who can, do; the upper classes who can avoid the fields, or the true Span-iards for whom the sun is anathema. Clair has seen this combination of dark hair, fair skin, and blue eyes in places like Santa Fe, where descen-dants of the four hundred-year-old Spanish town retain much of their European genetic inheritance and cultural habits.

"You are entering our home," the woman lightly says, as if they haven't been aware and are in need of tutoring. She is filling out their guest cards and not looking at him. "It is good to humble yourself." Now it is her turn to smile as she passes them keys.

Mason replies, "*Claro*," but this time there is a nick of irritation in the way he does not let the word draw out, cutting it off before it might sound easygoing.

Again, the elegant woman smiles, hiding her teeth, satisfied with the exchange.

They agree to meet later, eat early, and turn in so that they can leave at dawn for the drive down to the lagoon. Rubio goes off to find a gas can. Marla wanders in the direction of the *mercado*. And Mason and Clair walk over to the mission. He takes her hand in his and gives it a squeeze. For the moment, everything seems right—where they are and that they are alive together in the world. After all, the scientist in her thinks, you only need two to make a population.

A heavy chain binds the handles of the tall front doors, but they find an open side entrance beyond a small citrus grove and slip into the silence. It is not cold in the church, but certainly cool—cooler than the air outside. Clair drifts slowly up the center aisle, dragging her hand lightly across the backs of the pews, the polished wood darkened at aisle ends from many hands, the kneelers up or down depending upon the politeness of the last to exit, the hymnals in pockets or left on the benches, the old smell of incense that never fails to incite some vague worry, as if there is something she has left undone, or done wrong, or done sinfully. Automatically, she kites up a small prayer for them, *if it is right, only if it is right,* and for the first time realizes that that may be up to her, the rightness of things. Of them as a couple. What she wants to do is to wish openly for Mason, but something in her can't let her have even one unfettered, uncomplicated wish. She has to secure permission from some god or, as Rubio proposed, destino. She can't just want it and then have it. Or not.

Mason wanders along behind, stopping to gaze up at an arched support, hands clasped at his back, and finally joins her left of the altar.

"There's something stricken about churches," she says quietly.

"Well, they did crucify Him, after all." He lifts his chin toward the relatively small cross off to the right of the altarpiece, which features not Jesus but the town's patron saint, San Ignacio de Loyola. Jesus is the size of a sickly teenager, or a midget man, on a stunted cross, a formality in the local constellation of icons and a far more modern piece of sculpture, as if it really had been an afterthought.

"Isn't it gory," she says, "a dying man decorating all the churches of the world? The nails, the blood . . . ? Sometimes they have him holding his own heart."

"A dying man, but a living god. That's the big idea."

"Still, it's twisted, don't you think? This poor fellow perpetually dying up there, and everyone feeling bad about it, never allowed to forget it . . . Talk about a guilt trip."

"I'd say so. If I spent my time in churches."

"Well, I don't either, not now anyway, but after my brother died . . ."

"You had a brother?"

She drops her face toward the stone floor, remembering. "A baby brother. After he died, I spent some time in churches."

"But you don't believe."

"No, I suppose not. Hardly. How could I? How could anyone? Though I'd probably like to. Maybe we'd all like to. But no. It just doesn't make enough sense, does it?"

"So what then, a foxhole conversion?"

"Something like that, I guess, except it was too late."

"But you went to church."

She nods and looks around, as if there might be a way out besides the one that they used to enter. "Maybe just to get out of the house. After Tony, there was a kind of storm, not like a chubasco that comes and goes and leaves everything clean in its wake. Our storm was stalled around us, between us. It was like the air in this church. It was completely silent too, but it also seemed to be screaming in our ears, especially and loudest when we were together. Our storm. Our guilt." From somewhere in the mission they hear a door open and close.

"When someone dies," she says, lowering her voice, "when *anyone* dies, there's always some element of guilt. After all, there you are, you're still alive, you're looking out the window, it doesn't matter at what, you've got the whole world out there waiting for you to come out and play. Except for the storm . . ." Glancing over at the cross, she puffs bitterly. "One way or another, we were all punished."

"Bad luck."

She stares at him.

"I mean, bad luck," he says as if she ought to understand what he means, "it feels as bad as just desserts. In the end it doesn't matter."

She nods, distracted by the memories and thrown off by the word *luck*, by his assumption. "It's funny, how many different ways there are to suffer, to grieve. And you know, there's nothing so personal as grief. Happiness is pretty much the same for everyone. You wouldn't want to have to define people by how they experience happiness. It'd be too generic. A smile, a hug, a goofy dance. It's all cliché. But grief, my god . . ."

He wanders left into an alcove where there is a tray of flickering votaries. His back is to her when he asks, "What did he die of?"

"And not grief so much because of Tony being gone. He was a baby. We hardly knew him. Or I hardly knew him. I mean grief about what it did to us, what we lost between us as a family. The naturalness of just . . . living." She smiles weakly at the crucifix. "How to go outside and play."

Mason turns, faces her, says, "What was it that he died of?" and begins the short journey back to her. Even when he's confined, he likes to keep moving, and this pacing—or sometimes the knee-bouncing or ankle-swiv-eling—is not impatience but energy that has nowhere to go.

She lifts her eyebrows and inhales, then exhales as the words stagger out. "Oh, I suppose . . . us. Anyway . . . afterward, everything was . . . awkward. Just walking down a road . . . it was like we forgot how to do it, we had to think about it, think very carefully because nothing works the way it used to, your feet keep stumbling for some reason, and every step is an act of contrition and you begin to resent them, all the steps, all the things you have to say to yourself, the things you have to do to keep walk-ing."

"It's a long time gone, love. You've sorted it out, haven't you?"

Instead of answering, she comes up with another weak smile. "It's just the church. Being in a church. I'm sorry. I used to spend a lot of time in churches. I said that, didn't I? I'm sorry." She laughs. "Churches."

He places his hand on her arm. "But what caused his death? I'm curious now."

"Oh, you know . . . it was an accident. Household accident. You couldn't say it was anything but."

THEIR ROOM IS a spacious, brightly painted casita opening onto the gardens. The man that they had spoken with earlier is watering plants that grow under the *portale* where the rains, such as they are, and except for the wind-driven chubascos, cannot reach. Clair guesses that he is the older woman's son—same blue troublemaking eyes. Beyond him is a grotto and in it a shrine to the Virgin of Guadalupe enveloped in bougainvillea. Narrow tiled paths wind between the plantings—many varieties of succulents, but also fan palms and plots of decorative banana palms with their cut leaves that seem designed to let the wind through so that it cannot destroy the entire plant. There's some sort of idea in that that she'd like to bring into focus, damaging yourself so that something stronger can't kill you, so that things can pass through . . .

The white curtains are not so sheer that she and Mason can't enjoy the restful blur of the greenery while still lying beside each other, unclothed and half-concealed beneath a sheet. Something has roused a breeze, maybe only the hours swinging down toward dusk, and so there is a lulling verdant shimmer beyond the curtain. The heat has returned. She rolls onto her side, facing away, and nudges up against his hip. He turns reflexively toward her, against her, soon enough sliding lazily into her so that they are coupled but hardly moving, certainly not with any ambition. They are in the time of a relationship when sexual contact is ubiquitous and casual, when a hand, accidentally brushing some curvature, might lead to sex, and that might end up on the kitchen floor or a desktop or a stone ledge in a slickrock canyon.

"You've changed," she says against the pillow. The linen smells of something like incense, but the scent isn't strong enough or steady enough for her to identify. Maybe sage. The Bajacalifornianos throw sage on the fire when they are cooking sometimes, so that it enters the fish or flesh indirectly, with the smoke, and if there are sheets hanging on a nearby line, they would acquire that scent. This is how she imagines the scent has found its way into the bedclothes. This is what she thinks she will remember from the moment, sage and the feel of Mason inside her. "You really have," she insists, though he hasn't disagreed.

"I don't think I've changed. Rather . . . not much."

"You're like a city dweller, you're alone and detached, full of purpose."

"I always have a purpose, guilty as charged."

"But you *have* changed."

"So say you." He moves inside her, hardening, softening, intending nothing more than this languishing and pulsing connection. When he's hard it is a smooth silken pleasant unpleasant pressure that she wants to draw so deeply in that it takes over everything else, and then there is a completeness to the time, to the sensation, a unity of the big dimensions and a falling away of the trivial ones. But when he contracts even a little, then in her chest she feels a catch of anxiety.

"Are we losing each other?" she says.

"Not that I know."

"You are, you know, *changed*."

"The world changed a notch." He softens enough that she can feel him leaving her. "It's fast. It's fast," he says again, talking about the other now, about life.

"Yes."

"Bloody fast. One day dad has you laid out on the kitchen floor, working up your leg this and that way, day after day, forcing it to be what it is supposed to be, new and healthy, on its own . . . all those bloody exercises, the movements, the patterns, and then the next thing . . ."

"He did that for you? Your father?"

"Who else? Who else'd've done it, out there on a Cornish moor a fair stank from the nearest village? Aye, he did it. He did his job *proper*," he says, barking the last word, making a fist in the air. Then quietly, with a strange disappointment, "He always did his job."

"So he wasn't all bad."

"Sure he did my exercises and sure it hurt like hell, and sure, he wasn't all bad. Who is?"

"It's maddening, isn't it, how not all bad we all are? It would be easier the other way."

They lie in silence for a while.

"I think it embarrassed him, having a cripple for a boy," he murmurs. "That'd be why he did the exercises."

"No. He wanted to get you well."

"He could've had me on the parlor floor. There was a rug. But it was the kitchen stone. I can still feel my spine pulling away from it, cold as the grave."

"But he did them, the exercises," she says, trying to recapture the smell of the incense in the pillow linen and the warm smooth filling-up pressure of Mason inside her. "He did the right thing."

"I'm not so sure."

"Why not? That's good evidence. That's reliable data."

"Clair, the only thing I'm sure of," he says with a sigh, "is that that's what you need to believe."

"No."

"Because I've known people who do the wrong thing with gusto."

LATER IN THE plaza, they find a stand and the four of them order fish tacos, sitting on benches and eating without the conviviality that had bloomed so ardently in Mulegé. This time they will not let Rubio pay. It is nothing, anyway—a handful of pesos—and she feels embarrassed that their collective gesture amounts to so little and vaguely worried that Rubio might conclude that they have opportunistically chosen a taco stand to pay back unpayable social debts. Debts, inequalities, favors—for Clair, always troubling.

There is work to do the next day and a long drive and a different order of attention. But early in the morning when they are still dozing in bed, Marla raps on their door and pushes in without waiting for an answer.

"I don't know where he is. He's gone, I don't know where. And they took the stuff."

"Who?" Mason asks, sitting up.

"The men who came last night. They were waiting at the door. One of them followed us into the room. Some kind of official. The other one stayed outside, but this man came in behind us like a, like a . . . dog. The one outside, he's the guy who works here, with the water cans."

Clair has twisted the sheet around her and is sitting up too. "*Stuff*? Do you mean coke?"

Marla nods. For the first time since they've met her, she looks her age, which is very young, and surprised—confused. The shadowed mascara only adds a quality of ruined innocence.

"But they didn't take him, they only confiscated the coke?" Mason says impatiently.

"They knew exactly where it was. I don't know how. How could they know? They asked for my Tourist Card. And they talked to him, outside. Rubio was laughing. Everyone was laughing and no one was happy. The official . . . wait," she waves her hands in a funny confused way, "he was the police chief, there was a badge or something, the other one called him *jefe*, except his shirt was too small, it was worn out, the collar and cuffs, and he was pudgy. He didn't look like police. He looked like . . . , I don't know, a fruit picker. He was the one who came to the doorway when it was over and told me I should move to San Ignacio. *Señorita*, San Ignacio is so pretty, the water, the stars, *las estrellas*, he said. And Rubio, he's standing behind him the whole time with this expression, like, don't say a word, and the *jefe* is going on about stars and dates and how healthy it is with the dry air, and how I should fucking move here and, and . . . I'm not moving here! I'm not moving anywhere. I don't even know what's going on, or why this is happening to me!"

"Of course not," Mason says calmly. "You don't have to, Marla. All you have to do for me now is tell me anything else you heard."

"I don't know, I don't know . . ." She bites the edge of a finger and stares past them at the wall behind the bed. "They mentioned salt."

"Salt."

"I thought it was code. I mean, they took our stuff."

"And?"

"Then someone said PSP."

"PSP."

"Yeah. Everyone in San Ignacio is going to be *rico*, like in Cabo."

"Because of PSP."

She nods. "*Rico* . . . rich, yeah?"

"Yes."

"It's not about the coke," Clair murmurs.

"No, it's not about the coke," he says.

"But why did they take him then?"

"I doubt they did." He gestures, circling his index finger, for Marla to turn as he slips into a pair of boxers and combs his hand through his hair, the other hand pressing into his lower back to muffle the first announcement of pain. "Look, let's just get ourselves together and load up. I have a feeling Rubio will show. We need to get out of here."

Rubio does show only a few minutes after the agreed-upon time of departure. He says only, "Business," grabs his bag, and ducks into the van. His face is entirely shut down. Marla seems to know enough not to ask, though Clair does witness a parody of expressions ranging from petulance to a kind of sodden resentment.

At the edge of town from a building that combines groceries with auto body work, they buy cups of strong coffee, a sack of *pan dulce*, and some of the local orange jam for the fifty-mile journey out to Laguna San Ignacio. The day has begun cool, the air only faintly damp with the night, and the seasoning of the desert is still held within the departing humidity. A flat gray ceiling of clouds spreads over the desert, equally flat to gaze across, but not always flat for driving. Despite the dust, they open the windows, sipping coffee and tearing apart the *conchas*. The road glistens from passing bands of showers, and then Mason slows to let the van find traction, the tires slipping and suddenly biting but generally skittering forward until they reach the dry dirt and gravel again. When the road rises so gradually that the rise cannot really be noticed, patches of larger cacti miraculously appear—cardon, elephant tree, cholla, ocotillo, yucca, desiccated segments of creeping devil—and there is, too, a scatter of dry shrubs and smaller cacti, and sometimes edging the road itself a low ragged fringe of various opportunistic species that have discovered the ditches where the rain collects. But mostly, most of all, there is the impression of a supplicant Earth lying beneath a vast overpowering and incongruously heavy sky. How can something so empty feel so heavy, she wonders.

After an hour or so they stop to relieve themselves amid a jumble of boulders that have collected at the mouth of a dry wash, but when Mason swings the van back toward the road he catches both right tires in the sand, and gunning it, manages to corkscrew a third tire, the left rear, into the sand as well. One tire on gravel is not enough to pull them out. They try laying a thatch of torn shrubbery just against the leading edge of each sunk tire, but as soon as he accelerates the tires merely chew up the vegetation before burying it, and they make no progress out of the wash.

Straightening, Mason says "okay" to no one, to the situation, then tramps from wheel to wheel, squatting beside each and pressing a penknife into the valve stems to soften the tires. The deep sand exposes an intimation of his childhood limp so subtle that it might be a trace or a memory but not really the thing itself. Still, she feels something protective twist up her stomach.

Not wanting the rims to cut the rubber, he has his three passengers stand aside, and then slowly, evenly, he gives it gas and the van crawls out of the sand on not-entirely-flat tires. He has planned well enough to travel with a compressor, which he plugs into the cigarette lighter and then, one by one, re-inflates the tires to less than the ideal pressure but enough to get them where they need to go. The whole process consumes over two hours. But by now the battery itself is low, and it takes a few minutes of nervous *cheppity cheppity cheppity chep* . . . before the engine turns and they are safely back on the road.

Rubio has not done much but pat Mason's back in a gentlemanly way and help in gathering the dried vegetation. He is a thin delicate fellow, like a man still recovering from a long bout of something nearly fatal, and it does not even seem to occur to him to lend a hand except when Mason really can't do what needs doing, like bending to gather branches and dried shrubs. This is another of the mysterious male sorting-out dances that Clair has observed but never understood, the unspoken recognition of territories, the lines not to cross and questions not to ask, the subtle choreography of deeds left undone or left to the other or taken up without question or command.

"I should have had the engine running when the compressor was hooked up," Mason remarks, but she can tell that he is pleased with himself for the sequence of innovations that have freed them.

Clair nods absently. She's thinking about Rubio, what it is about him . . . "Rubio," she says suddenly, twisting around.

His eyes lift.

"Why does your hand shake?"

With a tender curiosity, he studies his right hand. "Oh, I think because it still longs to do what it did not do years ago. I was a boy, *como* Angel. My mother needed me, but I was a boy. *Solamente un niño.* Don Eduardo Cantú, he always came like a chubasco, always with the *acusación*, the . . . accusation. He was gone *mucho tiempo*. Always gone. He did not believe that she had been faithful. What can I do? I can do nada. Nada. I am just a boy."

She doesn't want to know any more, and he is not saying any more either. What more needs to be known? She once heard of a man on a SWAT team, a sharpshooter who developed paralysis of his entire arm because of pulling a trigger that killed a man. There was another, equally strong part of him that objected to pulling that same trigger. To kill. It had been an action taken but fiercely, deeply resisted. Why then couldn't your hand tremble because of actions *not* taken? It was all a matter of conflict—an agony of conflict.

They reach the lagoon long after they had anticipated because of the sand wash ordeal. Not a single vehicle has passed them in either direction. The whales have been heading north, along with the tourists they attract, but there should still be enough around to see and photograph. A litter of shanties and hand-painted signs send them down a fork in the road. Within another few miles, a second sign appears with a primitive whale tail painted on it and an arrow vectoring to the right, the word "Tecate" scribbled across one corner. For a mile or so, they skirt along an upper reach of the lagoon, continuing again until, abruptly, after the empty and endless-seeming unfurling of the road down from San Ignacio, they arrive at a string of thatched huts standing on stilts, facing the lagoon. The water is flat like the land, but silken, a milky gray-blue that mimics the heavy sky pressing down above them. They climb out of the van to stretch their legs. A couple approaches them and, quickly assessing them, they seem to decide that she and Mason are another couple, as they are, and that the other two are still in question as a singular entity. When a couple meets another couple, younger and still forming, they look for themselves at that age. Either the picture recalls something nice, or it explains something that ran aground later on. But no matter, there is the corroborating fact of people still agreeing to come together. To try.

Very soon they find themselves in the couple's plywood, tin-roofed house sitting around a broken-legged table shimmed level with a piece of folded cardboard. "You must come," the man had said. And so they do. The woman moves the kerosene lamp and candles and sets a pan cake in the center, *tres leches*, and then finds paper plates and plastic forks for them, with glasses of the overly sweetened Mexican soda not ever cold or fizzy enough. Mason does most of the talking, but now and then Rubio lends some clarification, because there are dialects and expressions that live sometimes in single villages or within single occupations. Beneath the table, the beaten linoleum, never actually glued down, only cut and laid over narrow boards gridding sandy dirt, has coved toward the center of the room, so that there is a low mound of dirt and sand at the deepest point of convexity, which, Clair thinks, must make sweeping rather easier than usual. Luis is a handsome, tidy man—small precise proportions—with eyes that see distances even when they are looking at the face of the man just across the table from him. His smile is present more often than not. She supposes that his long gaze comes from the sea, from having nothing to stop it from looking farther and farther away. His hands are raw, scrubbed daily in saltwater. He might be younger than fifty, but it is hard to say. They live most of their days outside in this desert beside the sea, these fishermen and whale guides, a life brutal to skin. Josefina, the woman, round and reticent, only nods shyly at anything anyone says, though when they are leaving, she overcomes her reticence and gestures toward Marla's bracelet, a double silver chain from which many charms hang. Josefina seems to think that they are *milagros*. She looks at Marla with grave sympathy, searching for the hidden illnesses and injuries, the inescapable weaknesses handed down from parent to child that might require prayers and miracles. Marla frowns, confused.

"Mementoes," Clair explains. "Mason, what's the word for memento?"

"*El recuerdo.*"

"You see," Clair says to the woman, "she's not sick, she doesn't need miracles, they are *solamente recuerdos* . . . souvenirs."

Josefina smiles broadly, understanding, and eagerly nods to Marla congratulations on her sudden good health, but Marla is impervious to the good will and gives a short mocking laugh as if this woman is not real but merely local color she'd like to get away from now.

The thatched huts up on stilts belong to the couple and their family-run business taking *turistas* out on the lagoon to visit the whales. The rest of the time they fish. Clair and Mason spend the afternoon poking about, Mason with his camera prowling the edges of the lagoon—the tidal flats, the sand dunes, the shell mounds—and Clair making notes about the vegetation along the shore and inland, measuring distances between bands of life, recording assemblages and associations, the human impacts, the meager bids for life that seem nevertheless bitterly triumphant. The wind is nearly constant, a pestering that brings relief from the sand fleas and other insects of the estuary's mudflats, along with the afternoon sun burning a fiery path down the sky toward the horizon. Netting drapes the windows of the huts, bottles of water sit on the table, along with a box of stubby candles; two narrow beds tuck into opposite corners.

How Rubio and Marla spend the rest of the day is not evident, for they do not see them until the next morning. A steady wind had blown most of the night, and something unacknowledged about the place, maybe the austere geometry of the level desert edged against the level sea, had driven them all inside early.

Mason and Clair slice salami and cucumbers, and distribute the discs onto crackers, adding mustard. Dinner from the van's crates of reserves. They drink a bottle of Rioja, saving the last glass to share for after. He prefers to undress her, looking into her eyes. His own eyes are almost expressionless though still available, and in them she thinks that she sees something like reassurance. At first, he is reverent and slow, then a hunger gathers and overtakes him. There is not much trouble with his back, some minor accommodations, and she is hopeful that it is finally getting better. Afterward, lying strewn across his body, she reaches for the glass on the little table, sips, then passes it to him before kissing him. She likes the animal taste of the two of them having been together layered beneath the ripe taste of the wine on their lips. She kisses him again and tips the last of the wine into his mouth.

The tide has come in, and so it is easy to wade into the shallows to wash. Around the moon, a soft halo quickly brightens, and within its bounds, the pale night sky darkens. Lunar halos mean that there are storms nearby, but she can't believe it. The chubasco has passed and though it is cool, the sky is empty and spacious. Between the ringed moon and the glimmering sea, with the water lapping against her thighs, sore in a way that is as pleasing as something wholesome and earnestly achieved, she feels perfectly placed. A part of one and a part of all. She imagines their fluids mixing with the sea, and the sea inside her and outside her, in the past and in the present, primal and yet living and still holding her and all of them; she thinks about the softness of saltwater and the mysterious infinite luxury of his mouth where she keeps losing herself . . . and at this moment, exhausted and so far away from everything she has ever known, hearing the rhythmic palpitations of small waves collapsing onto the sand, and gazing half-seeing into the benign and enormous night at the ribbon of shells along the beach luminescing beneath the moon, the ghostly hull of the panga rocking on the water down shore, at the serrations of the Santa Clara Mountains inked low along the horizon, at the sizzle of stars in the Xanadu dome of night, and the distant golden glow of a candle from Luis and Josefina's shanty house . . . gazing at the incalculable variety of the world, she feels her heart submit to it all and melt with longing. Something vast murmurs to her, something she has waited all her life to hear and that suddenly means she doesn't have to try so hard, or even try at all. A great fatigue rinses through her body, at once vivid and restful, and the pieces of the world seem very big and simple and safely held together.

Filled with contentedness, she returns to the cabana. The darkness inside is much darker than the night. Walls. There are the two narrow cots on either side of the table, and the dull green of the wine bottle where some straying moonlight has landed. Asleep on his side, facing the wall, Mason's breathing is even, claiming something she can't quite name but that feels isolating. An awayness. He has put on a T-shirt and boxers. The thin coverlet is wadded up between his legs to eliminate the angle between hip and knee, putting less strain on his back. In the world outside, the one that she was so much a part of just minutes earlier, she still believes. But she cannot seem to believe in Mason or in their connection. She says *one, two* in her mind, counting the beds, and wishes that he hadn't put on a T-shirt, and wonders why he is like a stranger even when he can't now ever be a stranger. Or maybe only a stranger to whoever it is they are each becoming, or whoever it is they never really knew.

She slides into her bed and stares at the negative white screen of his T-shirt. Probably he will leave her, like Tom, like her father. Anyway, it will be too hard for each of them to stand. Love. He will think that it can't be real, that it's some category of duty or obligation, and she will think that someone else needs or deserves it more. Neither of them will *ever* fight for it.

A CHERRY SUN surfaces above the eastern horizon and quickly lofts up through the pale miasma of dawn and is already above the palmetto thatching of the sleeping cabanas when Josefina slides onto each porch a tray with coffee and a covered dish of warm flour tortillas, a large square of butter on a wooden plate, a ceramic pot of black beans, and bowls of dates, oranges, and mangoes. They can see Luis down the beach, mending a fish net, smoking, his panga bobbing in the shoals beyond the mudflats that were underwater the night before. The air is already warm. The tide is ebbing, releasing the primordial smells of the sea flats, smells that together conjure something holy and essential. Not interested in the food, Rubio wanders down to smoke with Luis. She watches the way they gesture, the native camaraderie. There is a light breeze out of the west and the smell of the sea and of warm, inland, salt flat vegetation like pickleweed and *meado de sapo*, toad piss, that is not always an easy smell, but on the wind where it belongs, is as pleasing as anything natural can be when it is where it belongs. In the morning glare, with yesterday's scrim of high cirrus clouds now thinned away, the water is an opalescent turquoise, not rough but nevertheless constantly in motion as smooth broad undulations that are like the pulsating gills of a sea creature at rest.

Except with Ethan, she does not know where she belongs anymore. She had hoped that belonging would come with Mason, but every day that seems to remain a question. Is it appetite, or is it heart, that draws him to her?

They buckle on the lifejackets Luis has laid out for them and slog through the sandy mud to the panga. Once again, as she had first seen him in a news clipping heading out on a Greenpeace protest in the North Sea, Mason has his Leica camera tucked into the neck opening of his life vest, and that hand, that beautiful, long-fingered, long-feathered hand, is holding on to the gunwale of the panga just as it had been in that earlier vessel on another sea for a different cause. No one tries to talk or seems to want to. It is just wind, sea, sky, a sweetness in the air, the vigorous throb of the engine, the smooth tongue of water between the two unfurling wings of the wake, and then across the water, the bleached and amorphous rim of the lagoon—and farther out, at the broadest reach where it is nearly five miles across, the sea and the land merge into a shimmering band. But to the north and west, something white and blinding: salt. Mason looks across to her and nods. That is what they will see tomorrow when they go north.

The skiff continues. Luis must have a place that he likes, or a place where he has seen many whales this week, because there is no hesitation in the course he has in mind. Twenty minutes later, he throttles down to an idle. Leaning over the side, he raps the panga with his knuckles, just beneath the surface of the water, a patterned call he uses to summon the whales. They do not have to wait long.

Seldom do human beings find themselves able to forget the human fact. In a sense, we are too aware—an awareness that serves the always present hunger, and that hunger invites competition and an even keener awareness of what it means to be human, what it requires, how to best this one, how to breed and keep that one from the same opportunity, how to acquire goods that will provide security or the illusion of it, and so elevate one in reproductive status. Each and every of these pursuits has a greater chance of success with heightened awareness of self and of others, the minute-by-minute maneuvers and adjustments and adjudications of social beings. The mortal dance. The sheer busyness of humanity is part of what keeps us from what might very well be a welcome amnesia. To forget oneself. In a sense, to be liberated from the binds of being and enacting a single selfish clamoring life, rather than all lives bound together. A part of the web of life.

When the whales approach the panga, the calf first, rolling alongside to peer at them with one great ancient innocent eye, the mother just beyond, gentle and watching, Clair manages to forget herself. To forget that she has eyes of her own or hands that are reaching to lay against the calf's soft rubbery skin; forget fear and other feelings that have names; forget history, forget how she looked that morning in the tin mirror nailed to the wall of the hut; forget the smell of Ethan when he's worried, the sound of Mason's quick temper, the shadowed pain in a sister's eyes, forget thirst and the first taste of water, forget all the little live things that she has documented . . . *forget forget forget.*

It is customary to spend no more than three or four hours on the lagoon, but they stay out until late afternoon because they have only the one day. The whales are plentiful, Luis assures them, and so they move from one location to another, watching for their vaporous, heart-shaped spouts, meeting and stroking them, brushing fingers through baleen, gazing into eyes to say what no one wants to speculate or press into words, maybe only to make a marveling and peaceful connection, beyond senses, beyond language. Mason's face is mostly obscured by the Leica as the whales spy-hop, breach, roll, fluke, and generally cavort about the panga, their naturally mottled gray skin patchy with barnacles and lice, their heavy immensity swelling up from the deeps, surfacing, and slowly sinking, like living, shifting features of the marine topography. Every so often, Mason flashes her a smile of boyish excitement. At slack tide, beyond the entrance to the lagoon, they notice a great disturbance of water and whales as two males breed with a very large female, one after another, each patiently waiting his turn, the seagulls and cormorants winging above the commotion. It is easier when there are no currents to deal with, and so the Grays take advantage of slack tides to breed. Along the western shore, for about a quarter mile something green and lush—mangroves—but east and south across the neck of the lagoon, the marsh and mudflats meet the water smoothly, without transition. The winter sun hurries down and finally Luis directs the panga back to his village.

Walking along the shore toward the huts, they swing their arms around each other, she and Mason. Beneath her feet the sand is still warm; she smells mesquite smoke from the meal Josefina is preparing of baked clams, corbina, snook, and sea bass in covered cast iron over a fire. It is getting dusky, the yellow fading from the sky and the indigo of the Pacific west rapidly deepening. The waves are low and small, as though worn out. Clair brushes her head against his shoulder. "I don't know what to say."

He makes a sound with his breath and nods once to acknowledge the day—all of it. "I have a camera."

She smiles. "It's good for the things that are hard to say, isn't it?"

"For anything."

"Maybe. Maybe not. How do you put a fine point on anything with just a picture?"

"Just a picture?"

"I didn't mean it that way."

He glances down at her as they walk along. "Are you jealous of my camera?"

"God, no."

"Let's have a pic," he says suddenly.

"Only if you say what it means."

"Means?"

"What you're taking when you take my picture. What you get out of it. What it says to you."

The Leica is already hiding his eyes. "It says—" and she hears the distinctive *click-click* of the machinery and wishes he hadn't taken what so fixed that eternal half second of disappointment.

CHAPTER 10

Henry's death had a salutary effect on Louise.

There are people who never quite believe in death, who feel somehow that because it is so contradictory to life, a stillness that cannot last beside the stir of being, that it simply cannot really be so. A ludicrous idea. For them, the loss of someone beloved ushers in a living version of death, and gradually they themselves pass into that nonlife, staggered by the reality and never assuredly to reclaim their footing. They sink away from the bright surface of life, like sea creatures returning to the depths. This was Henry. He could not be brought round to the idea of death. It was not persuasive enough, but neither was life after the baby's death, and so he existed, but he did not live. After a while, it wasn't even connected to the baby. The grief that had begun as a violence of feeling, so enormous and vital that it might have been an animal that had run him down, a water buffalo or a big cat—it all faded out and became a hazy aftermath, a lingering cloud of dust, more vanquishing as an absence than it had been as a wild hungry animal taking up all the room in his heart. If asked, Henry would not have been able to say what it was that occupied him after the grief ran off, only that something wild and violent had been there, tearing him apart, and before that, all that made the wild violence possible—that, too, had been there, a great Something. And then, nothing.

But Louise believed in death. By nature, she accepted it, and she also had reason to accept this death. Of course she had loved Henry, especially the Henry before, tall and quick and ready with some witty, good-hearted remark, and when he died she missed his presence dividing up the space in the house and the hours of the day, and how his life, the fact of it nearby, had steadied things the way ballast steadies a ship at sea. But she had been living in the shadow of Henry's grief for so long that it was like some tall gray building across a narrow alley, its pocks and fissures as familiar as the spots and veins on the backs of his hands; that building suddenly gone and now the sunlight flooded across the dusty shaft of vacancy and streamed in through the windows of her life, and everything she had stopped seeing or noticing over the years could be noticed and seen. All those regimented hours, the meetings and workouts, the fundraisers and wine soirées, book-keeping and housecleaning, all the minutes of each day prepopulated and marching along as noctambulant soldiers to a sergeant's command—all had been a mechanism by which she might punish herself for Tony's death and keen in harmony with Henry's misery. In its way, it, too, was a form of death, the orderly marking off of time and action, and no quarter given to waste or accident.

So, after all, it wasn't Nina that she blamed, not after the first shock. It was she herself. The mother. This, too, the girls—now young women—came to realize when Henry died. He had bound them up, all of them, trussed and hung like caught animals swinging over a pit of emptiness, bound them with his beloved grief, his repudiation of death. He had not meant to shame them, but he had shamed them. Without saying, he had nevertheless said, *how can you be happy? How can any of us dare to be happy?* The half-life of his grief was equal to the whole of their collective guilt.

The cardiomyopathy, the drink that he could no longer drink—these were no more his reasons for killing himself than physical trappings are reason to love someone. They merely distract the eye while the secret work of the heart goes on. No, Henry shot himself when that secret work had come to an end, the penances completed, and the austerities endured. At last he could fall into the arms of death, the arms of the great and mysterious Morpheus, keeper of dreams that came true and of dreams that came apart, who occupied that undiscovered country.

But they said it was the drink, it was the cardiomyopathy. You had to hang your coat and hat on some hook, and these would do as well as any. People needed reasons; Henry's brother, Sal, and Sal's family, every one of them Catholic and worried about the soul's journey—they needed a public statement, something to say, for death produced its own genre of slogans. The wine people, they heard the reasons that were offered and checked their own consumption and made nervous jokes about *occupational hazards*, assuming themselves to be exempt. The graveside priest began with the words, "The news is hard," and assigned different reasons to Henry's resignation, the turning away from life, the loss of faith, the lying down in darkness beyond the light of love, beyond the sight of God.

But to the girls it was not important, understanding why; it was only important to mourn, though it seemed they had been mourning a loss years in the making. Time would pass and keep passing, and the details of that passing time were not easy to remember, if they had wanted to remember. The early ones, yes, but after a month or two, everything blurred. The hours drifted behind like leaves in a fall wind, colors faded, edges blurred. The world was losing definition. And then one day in spring, it stopped, it reversed. A first blush of green showed through the long dead gray grass of the hillsides, and something sweet found its way into the air. A scouring away had taken place, and a raw receptivity opened before them.

Clair's body grew with the baby, as if it had come to her from a different planet with different rules of existence. At times, catching a glimpse of herself in the mirror, she felt affronted by the cosmic impertinence of what was happening. Birth.

They bagged up Henry's personal effects, keeping a favorite shirt, an old but elegant watch that had long ago stopped running, a polished slick of Jasper that fit neatly in the palm of an anxious hand, a small carved box in which he kept stamps and paper clips, a JFK election button. Louise carefully folded a psalm book from his youth inside one of his fine Italian ties; Clair took the hawk's feather he used for a bookmark; Nina, the kitschy tower-of-Pisa salt-and-pepper shakers he had oddly found so amusing. The Morris chair, its broad, flat arms branded with the perfect rings of his imperfect ways, glass upon glass, ring upon ring, and the empty eyes their confluences formed—the Morris chair was the first thing to go, even before the gun, which the police had returned to the family, a memento no one wanted.

Three months later, Louise met a man. They had been seated next to each other at one of those tabled events inside a great white traveling tent, chairs listing on spoiled grass, everyone trying to switch place cards. A short pleasant chinless fellow who kept assuring her that he knew nothing about wine—and in fact, didn't—who liked ordinary beer, Wisconsin cheese, and musicals. He was rich and easy about it, so that it did not seem to be part of what defined him; it was just a detail, except that the easiness told just how wealthy he was. Kitchen appliances, the affordable kind—*Happy Chef*—that was where the money had been made. He wore a little teapot of a tummy that attached to the thin rest of him, an accessory he seemed to have developed in order to demonstrate some brand of invincible self-acceptance. His tan was perfect and even. He had just come from Bora Bora, snorkeling.

"Well I like him," Louise kept saying, even though neither of the girls had complained or objected to Mr. Bowden. It was nice, in fact, to see their mother happy, even embarrassed and giddy about things like nail polish and negligees, health spas and hotel stars, aspects of life they never knew she cared for. And, of course, why would she? How could she? Such concerns never came up in what had become her life sentence with Henry. Suddenly she was a woman again, but an exaggerated clichéd version of one, dreamy and unpredictable, not the family employee who could always be counted on.

They were almost exactly the same height, Joe and Louise, which is to say, short, and she was still fit—the effect of all those workouts now having found a grateful bystander—and when they walked down a street hand-in-hand, the length of their strides was eerily matched. The tidy everydayness of them as a couple was both disconcerting and exceptional, and to the twins, the fact of Joe and Louise together was the strongest argument for destiny either of them could have imagined. It now seemed that Henry and Louise had been mismatched from the beginning, and that until an alternative had come along, no one would see or admit it.

So that was three months after Henry's death—Joe Bowden.

Within eight months, Ethan was born. Clair had signed up for Lamaze classes, and had even attended two of the ten, but as soon as she learned that the instructor hadn't ever had a child herself, Clair quit and bought a book. Louise wanted to be present, helpful, involved. She seemed eager to take charge of matters, as she always had with her Teflon can-do attitude. So had Tom—wanted to be present—but he had surrendered that right. Clair was still feeling the need to punish him for having fooled her with his charming game of smoke and mirrors, his flimflamming and gimcrackery, his soppy lines of poetry. A friend from Brown who was working for a small press in the City—she, too, was supposed to be present as the official birth coach. But within minutes of her water breaking, Clair knew that it was only Nina she wanted with her, and so they never called anyone. After all, it wasn't a public event; it was a very private venture, bringing a life into the world. What if there was something wrong with the baby? What sort of debut would that make? And then other people witnessing her disappointment, her first failure as a mother . . . ? Immediately after Ethan's birth, she also realized something as she gazed over at Nina in the vinyl armchair, holding the infant boy while the doctor sewed some of Clair back together. She could see a question in Nina's eyes, *is this okay? are you sure about this?* followed by a tightening, a straightening into something like bravado that hardly lasted and that was more probably pure fear; and at the moment Clair understood that there was something she wanted to give to Nina, a baby having entered the world and at least for the moment, in her charge, in her good arms. Those who had encountered the worst of themselves, or the worst of their perceived selves, were always afraid of themselves more than any other. And one way or another, Clair was always trying to make that up to Nina. To protect Nina from certain stupid presumptive data.

Nina had driven her to the hospital and, throughout the long night, walked her around and around the ward, the nurses having told them that "exercise," such as it was, sped up labor. Twelve hours later, in a rush of pain and chaos knotted tenuously together with artificially meted breath, out slid a small human being, as dark and slick as a grub.

From the beginning, he was a high-strung creature whose charm became obvious only after his personality could express itself. That personality was hypnotically intense and sweet in a dangerous way, because he was always entirely available, present, unprotected. And the way he looked . . . beautiful crushed red lips and plenty of hair, straight as straw, and olive-skinned but pale somehow, even glaucous, as if sickly, he had Clair's litheness and Tom's dark looks with those flashing Kubla Khan eyes. His veins were unusually near the surface of his skin, or his skin was somehow more transparent than the skin of other babies, and so there was a literal as well as a figurative vulnerability to him, as though the least nick might drain him of vitality. His little grip was fierce, and whenever she laid him down, he arched his back in protest, displaying the tiny drum of his torso so that she half-expected him to beat his fists against his chest and declare war. It was six months before he slept through the night, and until that time, he was up four, sometimes five times, needing, wanting. Never in her life had Clair experienced such enormously basic and unrelenting needs, each one of them intensified by a quality that she could only call *worry*. How was it that a child could enter the world already worried about its soundness, already suspicious of its credibility as a holding environment? She thought she was a good-enough mother, not a bad one at least. But knowing something of the world, it frightened her how much reliability Ethan needed. How could she ever be that reliable? How could anyone? And how was it that he had come already knowing that it was all a very shaky proposition, life?

She finished her PhD in Botany, patching it together with a fellowship, a research assistantship, and teaching. By then, Ethan was three. Between Louise, "Pa Joe," as he was now known, plus a four-hour-a-day, five-day-a-week nanny funded in part by Louise, Clair managed life as a single parent. It was two months before Louise could bring herself to hold the infant. There were pastel layers of blankets and clothes, already washed to eliminate the store-bought smell and the sizing, and then neatly refolded and organized in drawers and bins. There was a maple crib with colorful bumpers and pads, a diaper bin and changing table, soft toys, hanging mobiles, a baby monitor, a month's supply of biodegradable diapers—everything necessary and waiting in breathless celebration of the good news coming. Louise spared no expense. The only miscalculation was the gender. The infant clothes and bedding colors foretold a girl. For Louise, a girl would have been easier. And then the baby's arrival, the fuss and worry about feedings and changings and hours of sleep. But she didn't hold him. She took pictures, she gave advice, she carted off the dirty diapers and spit-up towels. One day Clair found her standing over the crib, staring at Ethan while he slept, her eyes moving quickly, randomly, and yet as blank and blind as someone caught in a sudden darkness. It seemed a great debate was underway, so violent and confusing that mere words could not have contained it, a debate that was taking place in some closed-off room of her mind. Ethan let out a sleepy half-hearted squeak and Louise flinched, but the baby resettled immediately, breaking whatever spell his presence had cast over her. Now sensing Clair, she glanced over her shoulder and remarked, "The baby's fine. I just came in to check on him."

"Yes, he's just fine," said Clair. She came alongside her mother, and the two of them gazed down into the crib at the swaddled creature, only his pale round face visible. Peaceful burbling emissions slipped through his wet lips and his papery eyelids quivered with mute absence, and the sleep of death that Henry had chosen was nothing like this scant harried sleep of life.

Louise said, "He wrinkles his brow a lot."

"I know. Is that unusual, for babies to fret?"

Louise widened her eyes and smiled knowingly. "Fret? Or have gas? It's probably just gas."

"Gas is better than God. I sometimes wonder if he's already trying to figure out what kind of universe he's landed in. He does seem sort of . . . anxious."

"No, he's a perfectly normal baby. Look at those fingers . . . those are your fingers by way of Henry. He'll do something with those fingers, something meaningful and precise. He'll be a surgeon, or a sculptor. You wouldn't want to pass up fingers like those."

And so Louise got over her envy, her resentment that a baby boy had come to Clair and not miraculously to her, replacing the one that had been lost. She evolved from *the* baby to *your* baby, and finally, to *Ethan*, the name somehow bringing him fully to life for her and awakening a part of her heart that had been as boarded up as an abandoned mine shaft.

Joe Bowden's easy, pleasant, softly trod path into her life kept her distracted, and not thinking too closely about the past or looking it over to fix it up when some of it could never be fixed up to satisfaction. There were some things that you could never get over, and shouldn't get over, but eventually you did have to get on.

Probably, Louise was not in love with Joe Bowden, but she did love him, and she seemed to love how nice things were around him, his offhand attentions, his funny, trivial topics of conversation, the kind you have when you've had plenty of time to cover the big stuff and all that was left were the idle, summer's-end topics—where, for one, was the best place to display crackers in a grocery store. Even his physical presence was easy. The line between his absence and his presence was a broad smeary transaction, the one sliding into the other without formality or even much awareness. Time, too, seemed to lose its shape, and before long Clair noticed that her mother was now often late, and not late by a regular amount of time, ten minutes or so, which some people adopted as *their* time, *oh, so-and-so is always ten minutes late.* No, Louise was late as the mood took her, or even early. It was not uncommon for Clair to visit home with Ethan and never register Joe's precise time of entrance. He would have come up from the city where his offices were and arrive as if he had always been there, and then they might go off, Joe and her mother, absent-mindedly, as if they had recalled an appointment neither knew the other had made. They functioned like two conjoined water droplets, in and out of each other, flowing one way and then another. And he had the money to support such fluidity.

This began to affect the winery and its smooth operation. So Nina started to spend more weekends up on the mountain, trying to help out, and then she cut back to parttime at Juvenile Hall. Eric was still with

Bugato Vineyards, making the wine. His wife had moved into town with the two kids, using the school and the drive down the mountain as a cover story. Anyway, the kids were in high school, and the mountain had instantly become anathema to the continuous social requirements of adolescence. But Nina's quick relocation from her old bedroom in the main house to the smaller house on the property during her times home told another tale.

In the years of their growing up and going away, of Henry's slow withdrawal, Eric Durand had become famous, his wines, softened with a percentage of cabernet franc so that the bigness of the cabernet sauvignon was managed but not muted, had been winning top honors around the world. There were always a lot of lavish events, winemaker weekends at the Ahwahnee, or dinners at 21 Club in New York, trips to Paris for tasting competitions, consultations in Tuscany where they were beginning to grow cabernet sauvignon and blend it with sangiovese. It didn't hurt that he had a French surname, even though his family going far back had been French-Canadians and he himself, his father, too, both born and raised in California. He was a good-looking fellow, on the tall side, with slow blue eyes. His angular face, often admitting two or three days of beard growth, had a starved quality, as if whatever you had to offer him would be gratefully received though not requested. He often rode his bike—expensive and Italian—all the way west into the Valley of the Moon and then back again in a single afternoon. He did not seem driven to remedy time alone, but whenever there were others around, visitors, friends, he did tend to draw things out. Nina had become especially sensitive to lonely people.

During the cold months when the vines retreated into dormancy, Eric would go away to the winter wine gatherings and events where there were beautiful women in floor-length gowns, meals that went on into the early morning, the big egos of the winemakers and winery owners, and of course, the wine. Eric's wife was a weaver and a knitter, someone who worked in solitude, whose thoughts raveled out like the yarn between her hands. Mistakes could always be undone—that was the beauty of knitting and weaving. She seemed perfectly complaisant about undoing her marriage. She practiced yoga daily, she made her own bread, there was no TV. She was capable of a strange and enviable contentedness, like that of grazing animals or pond fish or readers on long flights.

Eric may not have come to Bugato Vineyards a born leader, he may have felt better off and more comfortable as Henry's right-hand man, living with his quiet wife in the cottage at the lower edge of the vineyards, but gradually, over the years, he had grown into Henry's widening absence. After his death, as it happened for Louise, a vast clearing opened up, and they each flourished like native plants in native soil. It was strange how you sometimes never knew who someone was, or was meant to be, or simply *could* be, until someone proximate died and then could be heard doors flying open, the contents of every room now out for spring cleaning, or out for good.

He was twenty years older than Nina, but, as these things can happen, they fell into the rhythm and direction of each other as easily as making a broad turn on an unfamiliar but plausible road. There was a naturalness about the relationship, the fact of it. No one had expected it, and, at the same time, when it began, it seemed inevitable. Nina did not want children; Eric already had two. And she was more beautiful than ever, as lean as a racehorse, her hair cropped short now and dyed dark and fitting around her oval face like a snappy feathered cloche from the gay nineties, her clear features not so tightly held, not so doll-like but somehow finally mortal, and forgiven of that mandatory crime. She still went to a therapist once a week, but Clair did not have the sense that this was related to the turmoil of the past, rather, to something skinless and susceptible about her that they had all failed to correctly identify. As a child, she had kept this condition well-concealed and safe behind the soldierly arrangement of her toys, the meticulously planned maneuvers of play; she had released it through the reckless adventures of her teens, and later channeled it into those years as a counselor for juvenile delinquents. In other words, she had denied it, indulged it, and displaced it, this one thing that she had sensed about herself—that the world could get in, all the way. It could hurt her. It could take her over. And the meanness of those early years, that was some kind of self-defense—this was what Clair had begun to believe. It might just as easily have been that Nina grew out of it, too.

But how did you grow out of the effects of that meanness? How did you change the concretized patterns of response and adaptation?

There was a man they had known as girls, an old family friend and dairy farmer west in Petaluma—his hip was bad and caused a limp, the result of years of shoving cows into stanchions, and squatting 150 times a day to attach milkers to teats. Sometime in his fifties, he finally had a good hired man, one that he could rely upon long enough to take the two months off and have the bad hip replaced. Afterward, the pain vanished and the limp was no longer necessary, yet he limped, now with a big pain-free grin on his face. The reason for it gone, the old effect was nevertheless so much a part of him that he could not give it up. Henry had once mischievously said to him, "You know, Lawrence, you haven't any use for that limp now."

"Sure, sure, I know," Lawrence smiled back. "But I'm kind of attached to it."

It only disappeared when he danced, the way that stuttering sometimes dissolved in song or in a foreign language.

Maybe Nina had changed, or maybe she had learned to manage the perviousness, or maybe miracles really did happen. What did it matter? Clair could not seem to unlearn the limp, the balancing compensations of their twinship. This was the way they had grown. But not all things that could be called growth were good.

As for Eric, it wasn't long before Nina was the beautiful woman in the floor-length gown beside him. Somehow it all made perfect sense. Nina with Eric in the cottage. Louise and Joe in the main house. And Clair a single parent.

A POSTDOCTORAL POSITION at Stanford sent Clair across the bay to Palo Alto, living in campus family housing. Rarely, she dated. The boy, as one suitor said, was a *glitch*. The lingo of Silicon Valley had already begun to insult the culture, nouns were becoming verbs, little boys were equated with computer problems. It was easier not trying to meet someone. No one wanted to raise another man's spawn was how she explained it. Biologically, it just wasn't good business.

Then, at Stanford following a talk, she met Mason. A panel of ocean-ographers was discussing the state of Earth's waters—islands of plastic bags forming in the Pacific, toxic waste collections near hydrothermal vent communities, species depletions along the British Columbia coast, the pro-posed dumping of the *Brent Spar* in the North Atlantic, the last of these, at that time, Mason's *idée fixe*. He was sitting in the back row under a rumpled felt hat, making notes; she was behind, slightly to the right of him, standing beside the door. She had been late and all the seats had been taken. She felt something coming . . . an *imminence*. She could not now say exactly when or how, but during those two hours she understood that something was approaching, something was about to happen, something singular. The note-making—the avidity of it—the hat he had failed to remove, the careless scarf—it was an unusually cold day—the scuffed black loafers, one of which she could easily study because he had his leg crossed, ankle on knee, and the shoe was protruding past the end of the row. When the older woman beside him rose to leave and then returned, he stood erect and respectful in the aisle, a gentleman waiting for her to safely pass by. But maybe mostly it was his back, the way he held it and adjusted it as if to a shifting invisible weight that he could never hope to lose and maybe didn't want to lose. Yes, he seemed to be a man who accepted burdens and responsibilities. A serious man. Compared to Tom, mature. A lifetime of maturity, she decided. Someone who had never gotten to be a child.

When the Q&A began he stood up abruptly, as if he'd just remembered some place he had to be, and bolted for the exit. Pushing open the door, he glanced at Clair in a way that recognized her, though also in a way that acknowledged not ever having met her, both familiar and alert. She checked her clothes without noting or realizing what she was checking them for and, deciding that she may as well leave, too, to get home to Ethan, she followed the stranger out into the lobby. He might have said *come* with that glance, but it was really only that his departure suggested *departure* as an idea. Justifications piled in, and through the door she went, after the stranger. The heavy fire door sighed shut behind her, a weary, journey's-end sigh, and there was a moment of suspension, a gap in the time continuum, the two of them alone in the unoccupied space and something needing to be said. She wanted to laugh without knowing what about. Her hand flew to her mouth, one finger thoughtfully tagged her lip, and then away it flew.

She said, "You're leaving too." It was an absurd observation—confused, obvious, too personal—a sentence that belonged at the end of a long train of other sentences and associations that they hadn't shared yet and might not ever.

"I was. Should I not?" He quirked his head. She did notice the past tense, a peripheral awareness, enough to keep them standing opposite each other in the lobby. He had been leaving. Now he was not leaving.

She was smiling . . . maybe . . . in any case, something was happening with her mouth. Something beyond her control. It felt wobbly.

"Did you like it?" she asked, not answering his question directly. They were moving toward the double doors that led out to the arcade.

"Like? Hmmmm . . ." He lifted his hat and dragged his hand across the crown of his head, front to back, rummaging through his hair and making an exaggerated pretense of cogitation.

Understanding, she gave a laugh—a cynical laugh—and consulted the tops of her shoes. "Fair enough."

"No good news there," he said, lifting his chin toward the closed door of the auditorium behind them.

"No," she agreed, and made a face, suddenly not sure what she was agreeing to, what he had said, or what it was supposed to mean.

It was then that he looked more carefully at her or, rather, at her hands. They both looked at her hands, which she had splayed before her as if to count off something on her fingers, or as if to try to figure out what the hell they were up to. "What've you got in this?" he asked, indicating the auditorium again. They could hear the Q&A microphone broadcasting the voice of an audience member, followed by a polite eruption of applause. Audiences, even the converted ones, were instinctively oppositional, asking questions designed to put panelists on the defensive and to display their own limited understandings of the topic. It was why, he told her later, that he had bugged out. Vain displays of amateur hour. Mason was confident, frequently too confident, but he was never vain.

"Plants. Lately, island communities. And you?"

"Pics." He framed her face with his hands. It felt familiar, welcome.

"For?"

"Piece about the *Brent Spar*."

She gave a single nod. "Ah. You're a photojournalist."

Then they collided into the awkwardness of time and space, the reality of strangers that they had miraculously slipped out of, and that was now making a belated claim. He took a couple of steps toward a table where brochures and books by the panelists were displayed, stumbling slightly. For that she was glad. For whatever nervousness it might have implied, or simply for a weakness that endowed him with flaws that might put her at ease. He touched a couple of the books, flipped one over, then angled toward the vestibule doors, having pocketed a couple of the free brochures. This was her introduction to Mason's brochure addiction.

She didn't know what else to say, to keep him there, talking, breathing, a rumpled burdened man. This stranger that she knew. This man for whom she had not known that she had been waiting. This sudden intake of air. This flash, this quickening. This splendid stumble. And so she asked stupidly, "Are you English?"

"Former incarnation. And you? Are you English?"

"Very funny." She smiled. "I'm nothing. A California girl, but not the kind they write songs about." She saw him gaze through the glass doors out to the courtyard where tall, well-groomed palm trees stood at attention, aloof and superior and also silly, their fronds bouncing, like a tutu. Was he wanting to escape or just thinking of what to say next? Together they exited to the shaded arcade.

"Well," she said, "well . . ." The floor drew her attention. It was very clean polished stone, great squares with soft swales at their centers from years of weather and the soles of student shoes. She had read somewhere that they had been resurrected from the '06 quake—something she liked about Stanford, the reclaimed materials. The resurrections.

"Mason Comstock," he said, answering a question she hadn't asked.

She had time to think about his name and repeat it in her mind, until she noticed the single raised eyebrow. "Clair Bugato."

Their hands touched, then untouched.

That was it.

Two names. Touch. What good were names when you had no time or place, no plan to meet, no phone number or address? It was just a penny in a pocket, a name, without any value or way of accruing value. You could imbue it with imaginings, though, with secret powers, with comforts you longed to experience, with the camaraderie that mortality besought. With two names you could set in motion an entire world. And you could live in that imaginary world until it came true. As for the touch, it could not be described or measured; it belonged in no known category. It was itself. Something whose existence was both justification and exemption from the time/space continuum. Because it once had been, it still was and would be, world without end.

Several weeks later she saw the photo of him in the paper, camera tucked into his lifejacket, and that beautiful hand feathered over the gunnels, as the Greenpeace boats headed across the choppy sea to the *Brent Spar*. *That hand*, she thought. *The touch of it. Everything about it*. But what was that *everything*? How to account for attraction, to explain the unexplainable. The sharp, rapid, headlong pitch, the familiarity of a complete stranger, the ease and clarity of the fall. The abrupt realization after it's too late to do anything about it. The breathtaking totality. The wild bet.

Once she had read about "search images," how the brain simplifies what the eyes see so as to be more efficient; how mountain lions, for instance, tend to hunt ungulates, which was why there were trail signs warning hikers not to bend over and look too much like a flat-backed, four-legged animal. So maybe it was only that Mason fit her search image—the seriousness, the burdened posture, the inattention to appearance, the restlessness. And maybe it was also because it had been years since Tom, and she was beginning to worry about herself and her failure to fall.

And then they ran into each other . . . a shop that sold fishing licenses and newspapers, cigars, magazines, stale candy. She was buying a tin of Cohibas—*pequeños*—an occasional indulgence developed during her fieldwork in the desert. She liked having a few bad habits. They left her feeling more alive. The shop bell rang, she glanced over, sighting down the long dusky corridor of dusty goods, (it was a narrow windowless shop, the kind that colonizes the alleyway between two existing establishments, larger and taller) and she thought to herself, *what you thought you knew, you lost when he walked through that door.* He was picking up the Sunday *Times.* Coffee in a café afterward. Anyone observing them would have registered a kind of certainty about them, a truth that the facts could not then have justified or composed, but that was nevertheless visible even to a stranger at another table. Anyone glancing their direction would have seen the affinity, the uneasy newness and surprise of joy.

She loved his mouth. She admired his hands. They were capable hands. She had a very clear sense of just how much trouble she was in. If it was going to end, this splendid pending impossible trouble, she wanted to get it over with.

"I have a son," she told him, making her eyes available, prepared for the standard reaction. "He's three-and-a-half."

"Lucky lad," said Mason.

She tried not to smile. "Thank you."

"How is he about sharing his mum?"

She made a question mark with the little straw in the foamed milk of her cappuccino. "I don't know yet."

"How is that? How is it that you don't know if he knows how to share?"

"I don't have a partner, and I haven't met anyone. So Ethan hasn't ever had to share."

"Have you not wanted to meet anyone?"

"Not exactly."

"Have you met someone now?"

"Now I have. Yes, I've met someone."

"I would agree with that," he said, casually looking off in a way that left her wanting him to say more, but knowing, too, that he didn't need to say more.

She picked up her cup to hide her mouth, and her eyes quickly found another table where there were two diners, a mother and her grown son, trying to get through the meal. Clair had been vaguely eavesdropping, cobbling together a narrative—biweekly visit, son pressed against the chair back, gaze flicking around for possible exit points, mother in a floppy hat, turtling her neck forward, gesturing with a fork, nodding in agreement with herself. Was that how she and Ethan would look one day? Strained, politely at odds? *Pro forma* family uttering titular endearments? Maybe. In a two-person equation, things could close up, everything too known and going stale. But add a third and suddenly you had a triangulation. Without that third point, you could never discover the unknown. It was like bodies of water whose outlets had been closed off. They needed oxygen, fresh water, foreign matter. Movement. Even in the making of wine a certain quantity of "material other than grapes," or MOG, was necessary to the health and complexity of the final product.

At that moment, she was happy. Purely, unassailably happy. It was something she noticed, like an object that had attached itself to her. There was happiness on her, a tingling cloak of light. And they were falling. Nothing could catch them, touch them, stop them.

She had to set aside time during each day when she could let herself think about him, because otherwise she would think about him all the time. She imagined scenes, and then, when enough real ones had come to them, she relived them, letting her mind trace the details like fingertips across the illustrated topography of a map, remembering and even revising the flawed particulars, climbing the flat mountains, fording the dry rivers. She indulged in *esprit d'escalier*, rewriting what they had said to each other so that it was better, cleverer, more economical, even excitingly cryptic, to the point that only she and Mason would have understood what was being said. Their language. There were special meanings and even joke phrases that stood in for categories of reaction and single words that represented entire disquisitions.

She was thirty, he was thirty-seven—a seven-year age difference. Seven was a lucky number.

A year and a half passed. Mason was gone a lot. It was the nature of his work. As often as not, he was on another continent or no continent, but unavailable—a Russian icebreaker for weeks as it carved its way through the ice toward the North Pole. That had been one of his ventures. *To-ing and fro-ing* was how he put it. The English and their minimizations. It began to seem that he wasn't taking their relationship seriously. Or that he couldn't take it seriously and do the work the way he wanted it done, which was to say, with a driving commitment to getting it right, not making mistakes, making a difference. Winning. Mason liked to win. He had won her without trying or even knowing that some men did that—tried to win you. He seemed to have simply known something quickly, and then entered into that knowing with an easy confidence, never questioning it, never worrying about its departure, never wondering whether he got it wrong. He hadn't. But now and then it might have been nice to have pretended to have gotten it wrong.

ON THE FIRST day of kindergarten, a problem arose for Ethan—he would not let his mother leave the school. As the entry hall door was closing, she heard a scream that whipped past and then coiled back around her. By the time she had remounted the stairs, he had become a small collapsed heap on the floor, given over entirely to the most extraordinary catastrophe of feeling, his hands like little paws, gripping and releasing the air, his eyes huge and drowning in tears, his mouth a chasm from which sobs broke and spilled. Grabbing the hem of her jacket, he tugged her down though she was already trying to squat beside him, and in his desperation, he caused her to fall gently slowly sideways onto the quarry tile, and then he threw his face against her. "No, no, no, no, no," he cried into her belly. "Don't leave me," he howled. He beat her arms and buried his face so deeply into her that she had to lift her head and consciously breathe.

Children were gathering in the doorways of classrooms, and the assistant principal had shown up, a lugubrious woman in a sad pink pantsuit. "Let's move into my office," she suggested with a gloomy smile, making a lifting motion with her arms, as if scooping up fallen leaves.

For three months, Clair worked at a table in the elementary school library, and twice a week Ethan visited with a child psychiatrist. Eventually, he consented to let her go. Separation anxiety was the diagnosis, with no obvious etiology. For some kids, especially the more sensitive ones, it was harder, the psychiatrist told her. During those three months his high intelligence was officially diagnosed, as if that were the disease, not the anxiety, and then there was a new school, but by then Ethan was submitting to his mother's daily abandonment, and only punishing her during the first thirty minutes of their reunion later in the day.

But his worry, his cosmic and elemental anxiety about the world began to have effects. Clair wondered whether his intelligence was causing all the stress, understanding so much more than his little heart could take. At night, he ground his teeth—deciduous teeth, he informed her, with roots like trees, he added. A visit to the pediatric dentist ended in an all-out steeplechase of two dental assistants, the receptionist, one child from the next chair over, and the dentist himself chasing Ethan around the labyrinth of offices and alcoves where bibbed patients, their mouths already open, vicariously fled with him. He was protective of all his body parts, and no one with metal sticks would be allowed entry into the private domain of his mouth. "You are not the boss of my body," he informed the dentist.

And so they bought a generic night guard at the drugstore and swore off dentists for the time being.

A year later, grade school, and there were more like him corralled into the same classroom. Gifted children, some on the spectrum. Inexplicably there was a higher percentage of Asperger's in the Bay Area. A few of the tech companies even offered weekly support meetings for their employees with Asperger's, given the lure the field holds for the single-minded, the socially uneasy, the OCPDs. But that was not Ethan. He was simply too smart and too worried, now especially about Mason Comstock. The trip to Baja and out to Cedros Island, the two weeks away, the shopping bag of guilty gifts, the postponement of surgical sewing repairs to Mr. Dickens' mouth, the overly cheerful singsong in Mrs. Holian's voice—all had combined to disturb those days before Clair's departure with Mason to Baja. She knew her son, the nervous thoughts, the twitchy distractions.

Now, ten days into the trip and the work that was hers yet to be done out on the island, plus the realization that they would need a few days beyond the two weeks she had advertised to Ethan, she was more than ever concerned about his ability to manage her absence. She was more than ever wondering what she was doing with Mason, and whether or not the heart's investment ever really paid off. And if it did, with what?

ACROSS THE HUT Mason slept, his back to her, the long day of whales and the bounty of seafood Josefina had cooked for them consumed, along with plenty of cerveza. Tomorrow they would drive north to the salt flats. They would find Eduardo Cantú, they would meet Yetz, try to interview him, and, after that, a night in Guerrero Negro before flying out to Cedros. In Guerrero Negro, she could phone Ethan. Everything is going to be okay, she told herself.

CHAPTER 11

It is not easy to conceive of a desert as abundant with life, but even the most lifeless-seeming places, paused over and considered, inspected myopically, reveal themselves to be exactly so—full of life. Not the claustrophobic life that a jungle delivers, but a measured and spaced exhibition of flora and fauna. The difference between a desert and a jungle is that it takes much less effort and fewer blows to kill off a desert plant than it does the flora of the well-watered regions. Water—how much, how frequent—is the first and final determinant. Life exists proportionate to the presence of water, and to a great extent, the resilience of that life depends upon water, too. The bamboo along the Esmeraldas River of Ecuador, though a man may hack it down one day, grows a foot and a half by the next, while the cardón cactus of Baja grows only three to ten centimeters each year. In many parts of the world, aridity is the stressor, the defining agent, gatekeeper, and rule-maker. It governs not just the kind and quality, the shape and texture, the size and spacing of what can grow, but from what that growing thing arises—the soil itself. How many nutrients that soil has to offer: fewer plants cycling through, fewer nutrients. And how stable the soil is—that, too. Fewer plants mean fewer roots to knit that soil together and greater distances between each plant. The sheer ingenuity of desert vegetation to extract, collect, conserve, store, and titrate water to their cellular systems is like something out of a science-fiction movie.

This is why Clair found her way into the deserts to study their flora: fragility, resilience, adaptability. Nowhere is life more cunning than where it must do with less of the one thing it needs most. And there are infinite genetic innovations designed to compensate for the want of water. The creosote bush with its double root system that reaches straight down to capture deep water, and also spreads out from the stalk to capture surface water is so successful at competing for available water that few other plant species can germinate in the surrounding soil. Cirio trees absorb water from coastal fog. Succulents, of which every cactus is a variety, have developed more than a dozen strategies for storing water and for discouraging animals from breaching those stores, strategies like spines. She does not like to think of these plants as drought-resistant or drought-adapted, because that suggests an inequity, a life born to less than its fair share. Even for plants, pity is unwelcome. She prefers to regard their unique talents as forms of efficiency and botanical harmony. That makes it a positive, not a negative that must be got around, or a handicap for which compensations have been developed, like props and limps. To Clair, the Vizcaíno Desert is a museum of design and originality. More personally, it is the ultimate manifestation of wisdom—a theology of landscape.

There is a Buddhist tale that she sometimes thinks of when she spends many weeks in the desert alone. Two seekers travel to the Himalayas to meet the Lama of the Crystal Mountain. This Lama has lost the use of his legs and so has remained at the monastery perched high on a ledge for nearly a decade, seeing only what the windows from his chambers and the view from the ledges permit—the snow-covered peaks, the sheep on the slopes, the small village lining the narrow valley below, and, above it all, the hollowed-out canopy of blue. One of these seekers, curious about the Lama's apparent happiness after so long a time of solitude and silence, and taking in the spare surroundings, imagining the long darkness of winter, the windy silence, and considering the Lama's inability to leave the gompa—this seeker bows and asks, "Rinpoche, how is it for you, here in this place all these many years? Are you not lonely, are you not disappointed, are you not bitter about your predicament? Why is it that you appear so happy?"

The Lama throws open his arms, laughing and embracing the view, his legs having somehow become a general fact in the room, like the air or the light, or merely two sticks of broken furniture. "Of course I am happy here! It's wonderful! Especially when I have no choice!"

This is another aspect of desert plants—of all plants—that she sometimes thinks about: the fact that they can never leave where they are. If they take root in a high crevice, there they must grow and remain until death. Human beings . . . they can move on, bug out, divorce, escape. But the longer she spends with Mason, the more she has begun to think that human beings cannot escape either. Their caves and crevices, their high windy perches and solitary chambers and cold sheets, their locks and bars and half-empty bowls, their pill bottles and whiskey flasks, and even the things that they cannot know because they have never experienced them, but which they can sense like a premonition in the breath before the one that is taken suddenly away—they are all inside, and surely there. Impediments to freedom. Quite often, after a week or so alone in the desert, Clair achieves a deeper level of solitude, one that isn't lonely. People make her lonely. Or people make her aware of loneliness, as if it is something she ought to be feeling, and so she remembers to feel the feeling that, if left unnoticed, naturally lifts away. If there are no people around, she doesn't think much about herself, how she looks, what she is wearing, what hurts or doesn't hurt, or might hurt if she does one thing and not another. She is like the ruined legs of the Lama, a part of the factual world, a thing among many things to notice or not to notice. She worries sometimes that this makes her misanthropic. Each time she ventures into the aloneness, the harder it is to crawl back out of it into the clamor of humanity—to make contact with eyes, to pass a word or two in a store, to stand close enough to smell the unique oil and tang from the skin of another human animal. She has even begun to regard human beings as a mutinous species, one that, without fully realizing what it is doing, is bound to overthrow the vessel of life itself until it sinks back into a primordial oblivion.

Although they have left Laguna San Ignacio early, even before the red sun clears the pale clay-colored mesas to the east, the day becomes so hot so quickly that the sun seems to chase them and bear down upon the van with a pointless show of power. At sunrise, the air was almost sweet, but now it has a burned quality. Around them, the Vizcaíno Desert Biosphere Reserve, a seven million-acre area within the larger Vizcaíno Desert, wavers in and out of reality as mirages deceive the eye. The landscape moves and shimmers, sometimes level, sometimes climbing to rough peaks or tabletop mesas, fading through shades of umber, gray, sulfurous yellow, the dirty pinks and whites of sandstone. Vivid color is provided only by what vegetation there is that can survive so prohibitive a landscape—forests of cardon cactus along the slopes of the Sierra Santa Clara, dwarf shrubbery, occasional mesquite, stunted and skeletal. Peering closely into barrancas and other low-lying areas, she makes out pale stalks of greenery, mostly succulents whose waxy leaves regulate osmosis and retain water.

Mason knows her well enough now to leave her alone when she disappears into a part of the world without humans, but he also recognizes the moment when that disappearing act crosses over into a place where he may have a hard time retrieving her. She can do that. Disappear. She can leave people behind. This is a talent, or skill, or failing—she's not sure what— that keeps her strong. Even knowing about it can be strength enough. But when Mason notices her leaving, the tenderness in that unexpected notice, she has to keep down the feeling that rises quickly and dilates in her throat.

"Where are you?" he asks.

"Here."

"I don't think so."

"Yup. Right here."

Without expression, he sucks the thin emptiness between two teeth. "Right."

"We're going to meet the devil," she offers with false cheer. "All for one . . ."

"Two devils."

"A duet of devils." She smiles with her lips pressed together.

"And one for all."

So, he is worried about her.

Clair glances into the backseat, wondering if they've offended Rubio by including his father in the duet of devils. But he is gazing out the window, his eyes and whatever feeling they hold fading into the distance. Beside him, Marla dozes, a small spray bottle of water listing between her legs, ready to mist and moisten. It is supposed to reach one hundred degrees, and it is only March.

One hundred twenty-five miles to the corporate offices of PSP, and although they have only traveled fifty of those miles, they have already passed seven roadside memorials, *descansos*, the crosses peeling paint and the plastic flowers, once bright tacky artificial colors, now sun-bleached to soft pastels that almost blend into the desert background. Cars pass so infrequently that she can easily imagine how complacent drivers might become, forgetting that someone might be barreling down the next hill, or swinging around the next bend; how close death is, how many masks it wears. And judging by the Tecate bottles and cans along the road, how the tedium of the drive might be relieved by alcohol. These *descansos* are elaborately decorated with pictures of the victim or victims, if it's a double cross, or toys if there were children involved in the accident, a straw hat, a rosary, a twisted bicycle. They all have the plastic flowers and stones encircling or stabilizing the base of the cross, and they all face the highway, calling out to passersby with their short white arms open and imploring. These private sorrows with the exact locations of their beginnings are public lamentations, and so long as they stand beside the road, they suggest no end.

Eleven days, she thinks. That is all it has been. It may as well have been eleven weeks, eleven lifetimes for all the distance it seems they've traveled away from themselves, from the shore of the lives they have known and on which they have walked for decades.

Another *descanso*, this one with a pale doll lashed to one arm of the cross. *Ah*, she should have made the time to sew up Mr. Dickens's torn mouth before leaving. She should have left everyone and everything hale and whole, not in need. She tests the thought, *What if Ethan dies?* She can imagine it, his death, but she cannot imagine the next minute. Or any of the others that would have to follow if she were to go on. You are supposed to go on. Louise did. Loss, according to the shrinks and clergy, is part of life, and getting used to it is what we are supposed to do until we lose the one thing that spares us from having to endure more loss—our own lives. But having lost so much of herself and her childhood to Nina's concerns, Nina's needs, imagined or real, or simply unknowable and therefore unlimited, she does not now think she would be willing to accept another loss. She would not go on. She has a hard enough time trying to identify what she really wants, what she really thinks, so why then learn to lose something or someone she might actually love? There is no one except Ethan to whom she owes anything, and no one who considers her continued presence an uncollected and uncollectable debt. Mason has never behaved as if she owes him anything; he could get on without her. Or is that just something she needs to believe? That he doesn't need her. Certainly, he does not seem to need to commit to her.

She stares out the window at the landscape sweeping by, at the purity of the wilderness around them that is not quite indifference. If there were no examples of life, that would be one thing. But the life, brave and ultimately foolish exertions, changes it. *How trite*, she thinks. *Bravery has nothing to do with it, neither does foolishness*. Life can only do one thing—it can be. That is why there is no bad thing about life ensuring its own being; it is all it knows how to do, all it is made to do, all it can seek to do. To be and keep being, benignly egocentric and self-advancing, but seldom indifferent. Benign tumor, benign use of river banks, benign neglect . . . it is a word too easily abused.

PSP thinks what it does is benign and, up to a point, maybe it is, but the side effects, delayed or covert or denied or simply unfathomable—they are what poisons the meaning of the word. Only a few months ago in December, ninety-four endangered black sea turtles were found floating in the sea off the coast, owing to a brine spill from PSP that raised the level of salinity to lethal intensities. Or so said the accusation. Maybe, in truth, poachers were responsible for the kill—it was Christmastime, and sea turtle is a holiday specialty among Bajacalifornianos, and maybe the Mexican government chose to blame PSP and Washiko, its own minority partner but the one with all the money—indeed, the biggest company in the world, the one that could survive assaults to reputation; blame the foreign company rather than admit that its fishermen broke treaties, especially when Mexico was just then in the process of renegotiating tuna quotas with the US after a nine-year embargo. The turtles were found together and sea turtles tend to be solitary. Perhaps most damning, some of them had been frozen, judging by the accumulation of blood in their ventral region, strong evidence that they had been stored in freezers, plastron-down. And there were no other species of marine mammal or fish affected by the alleged brine dump, which made it easy enough to speculate that, rather than face fines, poachers had dumped the turtles themselves as inspectors approached their boats.

Brine spills did happen, though, and it is useful, Clair tells herself, to conflate old mishaps and future possibilities with dead turtles and accusations. It makes a good story, good exploitable rhetoric. For environmentalists, winning rhetoric is hard to come by. Compared to the timeline of planetary life, human life is nothing, a snap of the fingers, which means that sometimes scientific evidence does not—because it cannot—prove much. The element of time is too constricted, a point, not a continuum, so one is driven to projections, speculations, and educated guesses. *Improving inference*, a phrase she has found herself using. The heat of rhetoric, the high wattage words like *pristine, whale, nursery, decimate, save,* and *threat* sometimes stand in for the science when there just isn't enough to get the job done. *Whale* is the hottest word of them all. Everyone loves whales.

The van swerves left and Mason, one hand on the wheel, brings it back with a disciplinary squeal of tires reclaiming asphalt. The highway is narrow without room on either side for pulling over. Only what had to be paved was paved—two car widths—so there is no margin for error. Mason is a good steady driver, but the codeine has made him fidgety, and now and then the van has been jerking ahead, or crossing the center line, and she begins to imagine what a *descanso* in their honor might look like, what emblems of each of them having loved something or someone would decorate the cross. Mason . . . a camera, his way of seeing and distancing the world, of making his feelings secret, the third dimension in a two-dimension image. Rubio—something of his mother's? Without a thing he must do, a purpose or passion, it would be hard to make emblems of his spirit. There is a ruined nobility about him, a lost-cause quality . . . Marla is a blank. *Wait*—a self-portrait, eyes without pupils, like little orphan Annie's, except that Annie had a soul. But what about Clair? It isn't Ethan or Mason who come to mind, it isn't the desert itself with its exposed anatomy and botanical desperate acts. It's Nina—her face, her voice, her naked eyes.

Soon they begin passing the salt ponds, many dozens of them of varying hues of misty blue, green, pink, and white, each one, from the collection ponds to the concentration ponds to the crystallization ponds, with intensifying salinity, and the whole lot, seventy square miles of them, are patch-worked into the tidal flats and desert between the highway and the Pacific Ocean. With the sun blazing down and the lattice of causeways separating one from another and the persistent wind blowing across the landscape west-to-east, a feeling of futility rushes past them even as, from one of the salt basins adjacent to the road, salt spume as big as hands, as light as meringue, flies across their route. Nearing the town of Guerrero Negro and the headquarters of PSP, where there are even more crystallization ponds, white becomes the only colorless color, so white and so much of it that it forms its own dimension. Beneath the violent noonday sun it shimmers in and out of its opposite, like the peripheral tremor as one gazes at the Arctic snowscape, an incongruous haloed effect of metallic blackness vibrating out from the center of vision. Then, as they approach the town and the open coast, a heavy fog devours the road, so that the white landscape, what they can see of it, takes on a morbid aspect, a shroud laid out in preparation for an immense body that hasn't yet arrived.

The town of Guerrero Negro is a muddled growth of low flat-roofed buildings and signage with a dead-end dirt road parting the town's commerce, a road that, despite the general flatness of the landscape, nevertheless rolls very slightly and drunkenly up and down, as though leveling it out, as easy as that might have been in such a place, called for too much effort. Many of the signs advertising one thing or another—hotels, pharmacy, taquerias—are not actually signs but words painted on the façade of a building and, in one case, on the sidewalls of a permanently broken-down tractor surrounded by several runt goats picking at sparse blades of forage.

"*Llantera*" announce the sidewalls—tire shop. Irony is everywhere. The town has a rushed, compulsory look to it, something that had to be built. Maps of the area before the 1950s do not indicate any town at all. Guerrero Negro began as a company town, a part of the basic plan when the salt-works was built in 1954. Only three years passed before the first shipments left Baja for half a dozen world ports; by then, PSP's little gridded village of cement-block company houses with company appliances and a company store was home to seven hundred or so workers. Now there are a thousand employees in Guerrero Negro and another 325 out on Cedros Island, along with their families. The rest of the town—the motels, restaurants, auto shops, laundry facilities, whatever the company didn't provide and the visitor might desire—is clearly a byproduct of PSP's presence and second-ary needs, plus, the more recent, burgeoning whale-watching industry. There are still only thirteen thousand citizens, because beyond the salt-works and the whales and a scattered and declining fishing industry, there is no reason to be in this place.

"*Bienvenido a Guerrero Negro,*" Mason intones.

Marla rouses herself, squints out the window, and says plaintively, "Are we staying *here*? We're not staying here, are we?"

"It is necessary," Rubio replies without taking his eyes from the window.

"Are you staying here?" she fires at Mason's back.

Before he can answer, Clair says, "Here tonight, Cedros tomorrow."

"Mason?" she says again, ignoring Clair's answer.

So, she is one of those sorts of women.

"Duty calls, Miss Marla." He glances in the rearview mirror to observe her, and Clair looks over her shoulder to see what he sees, the alluring petulance, her lithe figure swagged against the door in a pose of indolent complaint. "We can't all be free spirits."

"What a hell hole."

No one agrees or disagrees. *When you have no choice . . .*

A dense river of fog flows across the street before them, and the front end of the van disappears into it, emerging onto the same dirt strip and gray procession of ragtag businesses. Suddenly everything is feeling ran-dom and wrong. Lost. A dismal sort of longing settles around her. It was the same feeling she had had at the hotel in San Quintin when Mason lay hour after hour, day after day, in bed, drugged and in pain and no less distant than he was during his travels across the globe. What he wants is to save the world, even this one, to heal its wounds and restore the natural balance, and *what I want*, she thinks, is to count its parts, the valiant little sprouts, woody stems, trunks climbing up or out, the wizened and once turgid succulents; to catalogue all the adaptations to circumstance, the necessary distortions away from symmetry. To understand why, and even *why bother.* Guerrero Negro seems an unlikely place to understand anything at all about life, or to document a revolution. But here they are.

She is also suddenly aware that there is another secret element to this trip with Mason, the dark matter that matters more than its opposite, a very much smaller amount of the seen and observable. And while this other matter cannot be seen, it is clearly pushing the seen around. She has been looking for reasons not to stay with Mason. Slowly she has been realizing that he may not be capable of committing to her; that something—guilt, work, a fear of happiness—may keep him forever from her or anyone who might be a *her* in his life. Why, after all, have there been no other women but the one a decade ago who delivered an ultimatum from which he determinedly walked away? As far as Clair knows, she is the second. That's it—two women. But she does not want to feel bad about this potential failure in Mason, does not want to be the reason or impetus for it, does not want to be someone no one wants, the second and last-place twin, the one who cannot startle a self-sufficient man out of his iron-clad autonomy with real love. Love. That is the problem. She is in love with him. *My utter darling*, she thinks, glancing at his hands on the steering wheel. The love, she is beginning to understand, is just as unassailable as his autonomy. At the hotel in San Quintin, at the taco trailer in Rosarito, that first night in Mulegé, she had wanted to flee. But she had not fled. Within her, a battle was underway. And it might not have only to do with Mason, it might have something to do with Nina. With winning. Winning or happiness or even just the bits of what is known as "fun"—they all leave her ill at ease. *My beloved solitude, my dearest melancholia*, she thinks, how meaningful they seem, how reliable, how safe.

Another patch of fog and again they emerge. Emiliano Zapata Boulevard, a grand name for the dusty road they follow through town, soon comes to an end at the PSP company store, which sits between a sad alliance of palm trees overseeing what once must have been grass but what is now mostly hard yellow thatching remembering an original park plan—and, on the left, the gate to the brick-and-concrete offices of PSP. The company logo features a cartoon whale and the letters "PSP." It can't be ironic, but it is so obviously exploitative that she wonders whether the company is even aware of the discordance; whether it actually believes it exists in harmony with the other creatures along the Baja coast, a friend to whale and osprey alike, keeper of the order, and the uberous ubercitizen of planet Earth.

The Director of Operations, Señor Manuel Martinez, promptly appears from a conference room into the dusty front room where they are waiting for him and the promised tour of PSP operations, as instructed by the monosyllabic receptionist. He does not invite them into the conference room with its big colored maps visible through the partly open door, and from which they can hear the murmuring sovereignty of male voices. Some kind of meeting is underway; neither Yetz nor Cantú, he assures them, has arrived yet, but not one of them believes this fabrication. It is just the sort of lie officials deliberately tell to flaunt authority and power, the lie everyone agrees is a lie intended to remind, instruct, and establish hierarchy. But Martinez seems nice enough—short, well-fed, broad of face and generic in expression—a portrait of the company man. His mouth is concise and changeless, his pastel shirt, unlike many of his subordinates, tucked in all the way round his straining girth, though like everyone on the property, he caps his smooth gleaming black hair with a white hardhat before heading into the "yard," handing the four of them identical headgear. It is difficult to conjure a reaction except one of flummoxed compliance. His English is stammered but good. What Clair notices most is that he never gestures. At his sides his arms and hands hang paralytically, separate from the fellow employed to represent Productores de Sal del Pacífico, and hanging as if he had been instructed by an invisible movie director on how not to reveal anything.

"May I take your picture, Señor?" Mason asks at one point, and the man dutifully nods, positioning himself—since they happened to be just passing it—in front of the mountain of salt waiting to be trucked to the pier for loading on barges that will make the fifty-mile journey out to Cedros Island. He looks both bored and proud, a dwarfed spot of color against a vast white scarp of sodium chloride.

"Usually it is others who wish to have a picture," he remarks sourly as he rejoins them. They have offended his pride in PSP.

Rubio catches up with them, stamping out the cigarette he fetched from the van. "Yes, this is my wish. To have a picture with my *hermano* by the *montaña de sal*."

Clair accepts the camera and squints through the lens. A great bird darkens Rubio's face with its wings, a frigate bird so close that she can hear the creak of gristle as it abruptly sheers up and away. She feels obliquely troubled, not by the shadow, but by Rubio's failure to notice it as she waits for it to pass. He seems so unprotected, so pure.

It is one of only three photographs she has ever seen of Mason, let alone taken herself, the two men beside each other, not touching but leaning at the shoulders inwardly, Mason's arms comfortably crossed over his chest and Rubio clasping his own wrist so that one of his hands covers his groin, like a cache-sexe, the two white headless hardhats side-by-side on the salt-and-dirt ground before them. Mason gazes easily and directly at the camera, relaxed with himself. Rubio smiles shyly, the younger brother he has made of himself. The contrast is startling: Mason with his subtle but defining machismo and Rubio who seems not to have been meant for this world.

In the distance to the south, along one of many dirt levees, enormous 120-ton orange trailer trucks haul three giant gondolas of crystalized salt toward the washing facility. Another, there already, is just now releasing its load one bin at a time over the drop zone, never quite stopping, regulating its speed perfectly with the time it takes to empty each trailing bin, and then drawing away, back to the crystallization ponds for another pickup. Every imaginable piece of heavy equipment is at work—bucket loaders, graders, excavators, tractor trailers, and one device that resembles a combine—each one a soldier in Eduardo Cantú's private army of earthmoving equipment. While not the exact same machines that will be used to develop Laguna San Ignacio, if the expansion is approved, they are envoys for the services he provides and the world of which he is master.

They climb into a company van and Señor Martinez drives them from causeway to causeway, crisscrossing sections of the seventy-five thousand acres, pointing out the different saline ponds, the blue ones and pink ones where the salt water gradually concentrates from 3.5 percent salinity to 27 percent before it is pumped into the shallow crystallizations basins to be harvested six months later—eighteen concentration ponds, forty-nine crystallization ponds, countless dikes and gates; the big pumps that draw water from the lagoon and spew it into the ponds at a rate of 530 million gallons per day; the trailer trucks with their twenty-six eight-foot diameter tires and a load capacity of 120 tons; the two years that the whole process takes, start to finish; so many numbers, a mind-confounding manyness, and everything outsized and vast, vastly simple, too, like something from a nursery nightmare where everything is too far, too big, too plain, too blunt, too multitudinal. Almost certainly there will be some sort of cautionary lesson at the end of it all—or there always seemed to be when she was a girl. The horizon loses itself between the pale blue sky and the pale blue ponds, while the green and pink ones create a psychedelic disparity of color-bloc geometry.

Mason takes hundreds of photographs, the discreet shutter notes of the Leica setting off the wind, a wind that never lets up, and at the shoreline near the pumps, setting off the roar of the fifteen diesel engines sucking water from the lagoon into the first of the evaporation ponds. And with equivalent simultaneity, the machines scraping saltpans, the surface miners digging and furrowing salt crystals between milky rills, the conveyor belts whirring the salt along to be washed, sorted, graded, and delivered to the mountain from which it will eventually be transferred to the barges waiting at PSP's own port, Chaparrito, back near the corporate offices, for transport out to Cedros. There the mountain of salt is five times bigger and its port deep enough to accommodate ocean-faring bulk cargo ships. The sky is strewn with loosely mustered confederacies of birds luffing and settling, and beneath the sky breathing with wind and birdlife, in the ponds and flats that surely have no end, at their edges, or in the shallowest ones, more birds are wading, poking about for the tiny sea monkey—brine shrimp—a crustacean that feeds on the algae that gives some of the ponds their pinkish hue. The wide ceiling of the sky claps to the flat earth of colored rectilinear basins, all so absent of the wandering lines that indicate complexity that it cannot be anything but artificial. Yet Señor Manuel Martinez has used the word *naturale* seventeen times, and *orgánico* another nine. She counted. She often hears herself counting, a running mental whisper, and another remnant from childhood that served not only to keep things fair, or as fair as she could stand, but also to calm when calming down was a good idea. She has been counting a lot today, feeling less and less calm.

Back at the offices, before they enter, Rubio pulls Mason aside, away from Señor Martinez. "*Hermano*, what will you say to him?"

"Who? Which?"

Another shadow suffuses Rubio's face, but this time without external source, no frigate bird overhead, only a darkness surfacing from within. "The one I should have killed."

A small burst of breath escapes Mason, tipping his head back slightly, as if he has just seen someone he once knew from long ago. What he says has nothing to do with Rubio's murderous regrets, though the little smile might. "I plan to listen. People make mistakes if you let them speak and you leave plenty of room. They say things they can't hear themselves saying until it's too late. Make a space and, presto, someone fills it with truth."

Rubio looks off across the salt flats, still steadying his one hand with the other, his shoulders so rounded and his arms so closely pinned to his sides that his posture is like the silhouette of a beaten man wearing a blanket against bitter cold, except that the nearly vertical sunlight is unrelenting.

"Why?" Mason asks casually as they head toward the office.

"*Qué?*"

"Kill him."

"For beating her. Many times, he beat her. I am not his, that is what he accuses. And if the wish can make a truth, then that is what is so. I am not his."

"Do you think it's true?"

Rubio shrugs. "*Es posible.*"

"It doesn't matter, does it? Not really."

"It is important to him and to me, for contrary reasons."

CANTÚ IS SEATED, Yetz standing with his back to them as they enter, his fingers playing across a large topo map on the wall, tapping here and there, nodding to himself. It's clear that he has just finished saying something to the earthmover. Short, tow-headed and thin, in khakis and ankle-high boots, Yetz looks more like a boy scout than a world-renowned marine biologist.

"Gentlemen, ladies," Cantú says, not rising, merely opening and closing his hand, the one that has been resting on the table, a large, puffy mitt supporting a knot of silver and green turquoise as prominent as the Papal ring, "sit, please. We have been waiting for your arrival with eagerness."

Yetz pivots around, nods, then returns to the map, extending one index finger straight up as a means of securing their patience while he finishes up whatever he has been doing.

Clair glances at Mason, his flushing face, the surest sign of anger, and one she knows he wishes he could suppress. Mason does not wait well.

"*Hola, mi hijo,*" Eduardo Cantú says. He has a flat mouth whose movements are strangely imperceptible, so it is impossible to resolve intention and distinguish between a smile or a grimace. "You have brought friends. It pleases me to know you have friends, women and men."

"Why would I not have friends? And why do you pretend that you did not know they were coming? I would not be here without them. They are the reason I am here, and no other. Solamente."

"Of course, of course, but these friends, all friends, they change how the world feels at the end of a day when the night is a long road no one has tried to smooth. That is my work, to smooth the roads," he says, turning to the others. "Yes, friends are the lights in the night, much like these here . . . ," he nods royally at Clair and less royally at Marla who stands beside Rubio. "How is your mother, *mi hijo?*" he asks, his eyes still lingering on Marla who for some reason is grinning almost sweetly.

"Better."

"Ah, *bueno, bueno*, and what has made her so?"

"Your absence."

Cantú flicks his eyes toward the scientist at the map, the eyes quickly tracking back to the four visitors and fixing on Mason, though it is Rubio he addresses. "Excellent, excellent. In America I hear it is said . . . ," he pauses to enjoy his own approaching joke, "that the donut hole is proof of the donut. Perhaps she exists because I am gone."

"Certainly she smiles because you are gone."

Seeing anger in someone only recently met accelerates knowledge far more efficiently than the symptoms of pleasure or affection. Hate defines accurately, while love is a blurrier, broader descriptor. Suddenly, with breathtaking clarity, Clair understands Rubio—understands that he must find a point to his life beyond hating his father and that, lacking the necessity of work and having only the idling of drugs and women, of beauty and beautiful places, of fine dogs and wines, jai alai games, soccer matches, slow mornings and cocaine nights, having only the trappings and diversions, hate is the only hard edge against which he can chisel away at himself and carve some shape that produces meaning.

"Your hand, it still moves," Cantú observes, though he is staring at Rubio's face.

Rubio gives the earthmover the benefit of his silence and returns the unwavering gaze, his eyes dark and depthless.

Eduardo Cantú is a big, loosely constructed man with a misshapen nose, also large, and his skin, yellow unlike Rubio's nut brown, transforms this nose into a Yukon gold potato. His lazy liquid eyes are nevertheless alert and above them a receding hairline emphasizes the commanding scarp of his cranium, and his clothes are so nondescript as to suggest disguise. Yet it is his presence, not the presence of the scientist, the visitors, and Señor Martinez, and not the receptionist, a short stout woman who enters and exits like the ghost of a complicit family member, efficiently delivering a tray of small glasses and a bottle of tequila—it is Eduardo Cantú who occupies the room. He takes up the air, shuts out the light from the window behind him, alters the atmospheric pressure. Even when he stands to shut the door, he does not stand but expands upward just as a dark cloud on the horizon grows and looms. Then he shambles over to the door, confident in turf that is not even his, to close it behind the receptionist, not because she has forgotten because she would not have forgotten, but because Cantú wants to illustrate something to them by rising, by passing along behind them, tall and mountainous, by playing at host and servant and minion. All roles his. Then he returns to a chair that is clearly *his chair* now, where he lets one leg languish ever so disdainfully away from its mate while he unstoppers the bottle of tequila not with thumb and index, but with two meaty fingers, pinching the stopper between two knuckles and popping his hand up, once, sharply. There is a vulgar elegance about him. He might be a pimp overseeing a high-end brothel or an assassin carving meat for the family holiday dinner. In a movie he would be played by Orson Welles.

Cantú orchestrates a round of introductions. Clair is still not accustomed to using and hearing *Dr. Bugato* and maybe uncomfortable with Mason's unelevated and unadorned name. She looks away from him, wondering if he is thinking about her—or worse, not thinking about her when her name is mentioned. He is probably thinking about his father, she decides, the man who was, and the emptiness that now is.

"Please sit, friends of my son," Cantú says. To Martinez, he says, "I will pour, *sí?*"

Martinez nods. He seems to enjoy the earthmover's assumption of lowly duties, not realizing that he has been usurped by Cantú's gallant accommodations. Without question, Eduardo Cantú has mastered the subversive power of the helper. This man's care is crippling.

Yetz spins around, ready to join them. In spite of his quick movements, there is an overall rigidity about him, as if he is suffering from a low-grade and unremitting seizure, and when he leans across the table to shake Mason's hand—"Werner Yetz," he says—and only Mason's hand, he bends stiffly at the hip as if it is hinged, straightens, and speaks in a voice that is nearly falsetto—unmistakably one of the voices they had heard through the partly open door before the tour. "Met your writer several weeks ago."

"Yes. He says he has what he needs to do the piece. Probably already finished it, in fact."

"Good."

"I'm following up with the photos, here and out on the island."

"Have you read the article?"

"Not yet."

"Because I didn't get a sense of his final take on the proposed San Ignacio development."

"Hmmm . . ."

"So your photos, they don't necessarily correspond to the contents of the article."

"Oh, I expect they will."

"How's that?"

Mason smiles quickly and unpleasantly. "Intuitive process of concordance."

Small twin clouds of confusion form at the corners Yetz's eyes. He says gamely, "I trust he'll pay attention to the real science and not all this Sturm und Drang. The whales are thriving here in Laguna Ojo de Liebre, Scammon's Lagoon," he adds with an ingratiating smile, assuming he needs to translate for the visitors, "as well as in the two important *bahias*. In fact, calf production is higher in these locations than in Laguna San Ignacio, so there's no basis for the assertion that it's uniquely important to the survival of the species or that it is a so-called pristine place. It's no more pristine than the other breeding locations, especially with the intensity of whalewatching activity. Calf counts are *lower* in San Ignacio. Lower! And the pump noise, I'm sure you're acquainted with that issue, too." He shakes his head. "Pure fiction. There's just no evidence that pump noise disturbs the whales either. It can't. It's too far away from where the whales are or would be if a new evaporative salt production facility goes in. Furthermore, a new study shows that the noise decays to ambient levels with distance from the source. One kilometer, that's what it takes, one kilometer. One! You might ask what they do hear then?" A triumphant smile. "Snapping shrimp. That's it, that's your noise disturbance. Shrimp. Your colleague has the data. Sound evidentiary science will lead him to the right conclusion, not this junk science environmentalists are peddling. Indeed, what could be more natural than sun, water and wind? Ever been out on a boat in San

Ignacio?"

"Yesterday," Clair says quietly.

He glances toward her, dismissively she assumes, then back to Mason. "Well then you know, you all know that the whales keep to the center of the lagoon where the deep water is, and that the land where the saltworks would be is nearly five miles away. They'd have to be using binoculars to see what is claimed to be so disturbing, so disruptive. Your colleague, he's got all this data."

"Does his homework," Mason says, considering Yetz as if he's a specimen.

"But you don't have any idea how he'll . . . present the findings? Or has."

"I couldn't say, Dr. Yetz."

"Werner."

"I couldn't say, Werner."

"Indeed, indeed."

"I'm just the bloke with the camera."

"Yes, right. Keen to have things properly represented, that's all."

"Naturally. Werner."

It strikes Clair as incongruous that Yetz insists on his first name when he studiously avoids the pronoun *I*, but this is a tick that many scientists share as they try to efface themselves to let the research do the talking. She does this herself, but it is somehow more conspicuous with Yetz, as if he is reticent to own the words he uses, preferring to hide in the space where the actor might have been or where he still is, but cloaked, a predicate without a subject, a verb without a noun.

"It's a significant publication. Lot of attention there. Got to get it right, get the facts straight. *National Geographic*. An international podium, I'd say, magazine like that. And at this juncture, it's an international topic. As we all know," he adds with stagy disappointment and grandly opening his arms to include the assembled seated around the table, deciding that they are all on the same page, same side.

"They pay well," Mason says, smiling. "I'm sorry, but you didn't say who pays you, Werner?"

"Pays?"

"Yes."

He looks vaguely wounded, having no doubt assumed Mason knows his credentials, which of course he does. "I'm a full-time researcher with the Hayden Marine Institute."

"And in that capacity you . . ."

"Nooo . . . that would be incorrect. Washiko engaged me as a consultant. Nothing to do with Hayden. Hayden steers clear of these sorts of quarrels. Too emotional, too political and rarely objective."

"Quarrel?" Clair mutters.

"Flew you down, did they?"

"They did, they did." Yetz smiles mischievously, lifting his wispy blond eyebrows to invite them along the twilight halls of memory. "Twenty-five-year-old scotch, shortest flight ever."

"These environmental groups, they buy sentiment and use it to control the perceptions," Cantú interrupts.

"*Sentimientos* are strong," Rubio says. "They are important."

A great sigh escapes Cantú. "*Tú y tu madre . . .*"

"Politics, too," Yetz quickly throws out. "That's always up for sale."

Marla drifts over to the window behind Cantú, then to the water cooler, the maps, but only Martinez, practically without turning his head, follows her slow itineracy as she explores the conference room in a haze of cosmic ennui.

The tray of glasses is circulating the table and when each of them has one, Cantú says "*Salud*" as if it's a question. It would be impossible not to notice Rubio's silent refusal to lift his glass or to remove his gaze from Cantú. At the wall of maps, Marla says cheerfully, "*Arriba!*" obviously hoping something more scintillating will happen now that an intoxicant has entered the dynamic.

Martinez swallows his tequila and tosses up a hand that takes in all that lies beyond the walls and window. "This place, it *wants* to be salt. The sea water, the wind, the sun above, *la tierra plana* . . . uh, the flat land . . . we are only encouraging the natural order. The whales are very happy in our lagoons, very happy. The salt is born when they are here and when they are not here. It is all very *naturale*. We like *las ballenas*. We all like the whales.

Todos. A whale adorns our sign, our clothing. We are proud of our whales. Why would we wish to hurt them? Of course we do not wish to. We are here with them, in harmony."

Eduardo lifts the bottle of tequila, nodding around the room. Once more the glasses are filled.

"There's no doubt that saltworks is a natural process, a green industry. The evaporation index is extremely high here. It's a logical economy for the region," Yetz insists in his helium-tight voice. "And with overfishing, maybe the only viable one now. We've got to stay aligned with reason, not rumors and feelings, and especially not the lies that feelings lead to."

"Before PSP, people got by. The economy, it was not good," Martinez offers. "With the new saltworks, 208 jobs to San Ignacio and the poor settlements around the laguna."

"Half to the Japanese," Clair says. "That's my understanding."

"Maybe so, Dr. Bugato, but 208 is a beginning. There will be more with time."

Abruptly, Yetz flips his hand, as if batting away a fly. "That's not what's at issue here. Beside the point, beside the point. It's the entire holding environment for the saltworks and how it will be affected, if at all. Only good science can assess that. These sociological matters are not part of the equation."

"To the Mexican government, they seem to be important," Mason says. He has shuttered his eyes so that all he can possibly see is the table top where his beautiful, graceful hand reposes directly across from Cantú's, and his face is impassive, a sign that he is summoning hidden forces within his personal dominion to suppress a rising temper.

"You and I both know that if a complaint is filed with UNESCO World Heritage Committee asking it to designate the Whale Sanctuary of El Vizcaíno as a 'threatened World Heritage Site' *before* the EIA can be completed, there will be big trouble. More trouble than a handful of locals with new jobs can justify. It's just bad math, it's bad science. Mexico won't let that happen."

"How sure are you that Mexico cares about those new jobs?" Mason asks.

Yetz is silent. Martinez says simply, "He cares, *el país*."

But Cantú smiles. "The people of San Ignacio are very happy."

"It is only your money that makes them happy. Your bribes, your promises that they will be *ricos*," Rubio says.

Again, Cantú smiles. "Yes, I did hear of your recent visit to that charming pueblo."

"And the people who live on the *laguna*, you buy their land, then you sell to PSP for more."

"*Si, cómo no!* For the saltworks. They will need the land. But if the saltworks do not happen, I lose and they have cheated me and this they know too. It is a good thing to be cheated a little. It is how a friendship is made. *Una alianza*. And there will be the jobs, too."

"Let's see," Mason begins, "Mexico owns 51 percent of the company, Washiko has all the capital. Mexico reaps tax revenue paid by PSP, plus its share of the profits. True. But the end users of the salt, the Japanese and other world-users of the product, all those economic benefits arising from the raw material—not Mexico. Washiko. Raw material is a fraction of the final profit. You know what each one of those new jobs would cost the Mexican government? Six hundred thousand apiece. Sounds like adverse economics to me."

"Not my wheelhouse. Science, that's what matters. That's what *ought to* matter, if we're talking about the planet."

Clair watches Werner Yetz who is busy inspecting the tequila and shaking his head to himself. It occurs to her that he might be an excellent scientist, a man of data and reason. That would be the best thing about him, his objectivity and the soundness of his data—as sound as the limited scope of human time permits. And the worst thing about him may be exactly the same thing—that he's a perfectly fine scientist with sound data leading to reliable, repeatable conclusions, and all of this good science is taking place deep inside his profession, a trench out of which one cannot really see, let alone recognize all the other trenches filled with different people, different ideas, different values. To these other people in other trenches, developing Laguna San Ignacio may represent a bad idea because it's a bad idea to want *more* when there is plenty already. Plenty of salt and plenty of profit.

They may believe that there is an ethical argument to be made for doing nothing. Leaving it alone. But practical people, people of reason, governments and corporations, scientists and politicians, they listen to facts and figures, to tangibles, to things and deeds, to countable entities. At least they can be relied upon. But they cannot see the moral authority of nothing and of doing nothing. How do you count that? They cannot hear an argument beneath which there is nothing that can be tallied or measured or graphed, an argument simply for what *is* and *as it is*. Even as a scientist, Clair herself believes that having no adverse effect does not in any sense mean no effect. And who are they, one brutally copious species, to decide the destinies of so many others with considerably fewer numbers and slimmer margins of error?

"Some of us are talking about planet Earth, but you're not, *Werner*," Mason says in a voice so quiet, so uninflected that the threat is an unmistakable vibration rumbling beneath the table. "Forest and trees."

"Trees?"

"That's all you can see through the fug of that twenty-five-year old scotch. What you don't see is what those trees compose. You don't see the forest."

"The science is good. That's all we have. Science."

"No. PSP is in every other lagoon, every bay. What about leaving one lagoon the way it is now? How about that? Just one. How much profit does it need? It's already the biggest company in the world. What about the aesthetic and moral value of wilderness?"

For the third time since they arrived, Yetz shakes his head, this time as if Mason is childish, idiotic. "Moral value? You don't know what you're talking about. Morality has nothing to do with this. It's not church," he adds, making his version of a joke.

"Not for you. You're just Washiko's high-paid pawn. How much scotch did your science cost them?"

"For Christ's sake, it's a good thing you're just the camera man."

As if on cue, Mason lifts his camera and shutters through a series of pictures of both Yetz and Cantú.

"*Basta!*" Cantú announces. "Now I return to work. And Dr. Yetz has much to do." He rises and everyone quickly drills out of the conference room, except Yetz, who is back at the map, jotting down notes on a tiny pad.

By Mason's van, Cantú takes Marla's hand in his. "I hope we have not molested you with our talk, Señorita."

In her confusion, she says only, "Why . . . no."

Martinez touches Mason's arm before they climb into the van. "Tomorrow you go to Cedros and Punta Morro Redondo, yes?"

"Yes."

"They do not know you are coming."

"Fine. I prefer it that way. Just snap a few pics."

"Good luck, Señor."

Next to the van is a pickup truck, its bed full of tools and amputated bits of machinery, and lying atop the roof of the cab, anxiously surveying them, is a yellow dog of some unidentifiable mix wearing no collar and panting. They've all paused to consider the mystery of this lean young animal with his oversized paws and jumpy eyes on the roof of the truck—there is plenty of shade alongside the office building. "He is afraid to be left," Cantú explains, shrugging. "I feed him now and then. He is not mine." He turns away, heading back to PSP headquarters, humming.

There is little worse than feeding something only occasionally, in whatever guise that food takes, scraps of food or love, money or time. Hope rushes into the gaps and floods the waiting, and of all the pernicious traits belonging to Cantú, this one, this random succor, is the ugliest.

A dry comfortless breeze passes around them as they distribute themselves in the van. Everything has begun to tilt.

They find a motel, one of the newer ones, with bright walls of differing colors, the fresh paint sloppy, and agree that a siesta is in order. She has a good call with Ethan—he has mostly adjusted to her absence and has not yet reached the anxiety of too many days apart, a specific and mathematically predictable number inversely related to geography: the farther away she is, the fewer the number of days before the anxiety begins to eat away at him. There are only three more days of gifts left, and she already knows that three is not enough. They need more time. Maybe she will call Nina, have her take over for Mrs. Holian, have her pretend, as much as possible, to be Clair. Nina is always good with people who have run out to the scared edges of themselves.

Later at dinner in a crowded family-run café, the owner takes a liking to Mason and brings out, unbidden, turtle soup, which they reluctantly eat so as not to offend. Everyone but Marla is subdued, pensive. She's just happy to be away from all the talk, the "blah-blah" as she puts it, wearing a pretty smile, her teeth as white as bleached bones and her eyes twinkling with the foolish triumph of the young. After the soup, they eat well and plentifully—chile rellenos, carnitas, nopalitos, flan with shots of mescal. On the way back to the motel, Rubio reminds them that he and Marla will not go on to Cedros. He has done what needed doing, introducing Mason and Clair to Cantú. "There is *nada* for me now. What did not need *confirmación* is confirmed. *Probablemente*, I will not see him again. He is bad."

"I made the same decision with my own pater."

"Yes?"

"I believe the last words I spoke to him as the door was closing was 'bugger off.' That was twelve years ago. Twelve blissful years. The day before we left for Baja, he died."

"*Muy nuevo . . .*" Rubio pauses to study Mason. "Do you feel . . . *el remordimientor?*"

"God, no. Don't regret a bloody thing."

In silence, they park behind the motel and climb out into the warm dusky night that brings the scent of evening primrose and sage. Clair is tired, and this conversation is too important to have or to hear in this state. And now she has just learned exactly when Mason's father died and very likely what really precipitated the back issue sending Mason to the chiropractor, an injury that has menaced his body ever since and that has not so subtly confounded the trip.

Rubio places a hand on Mason's arm to delay him. "Truly, *hermano? Nada?*"

"I don't know . . ." Mason gazes out into the dimming desert that manifests the landscape of perpetuity, of things that never find their ends, of problems that never die, of dreams that can't possibly come true but that the dreamer keeps dreaming. "We never talked. We might have talked, but I wouldn't let him. If he had apologized . . . but he didn't. I didn't let him, or we didn't talk, or I was just as afraid of that as I was sure that I was better off with the other. With hating him, with no apology, with hating myself for the same reasons he hated me. Maybe we had a lot in common, the old sot and I. Hell, it's complicated. I didn't do anything, and it broke everything. In my case, original sin was literal. I was born." His voice sounds slow and clogged. "Never really had a mum. That's all right. Who needs mothers? Tell you what to do, right?"

"I love my mother. I am devoted to her. Because of her I am *invencible*."

"Invincible? Ha! Maybe so, maybe so . . ." He seems to consider this possibility with all seriousness.

"*Sí. Esto es verdad.*"

"Right. I think I may believe you." He offers a wistful smile. "In any case, or in my case, it's too late. All of it. *Demasiado tarde.* I am not invincible." In the deepening darkness, he smiles again—a flash of teeth. "*Ve con Dios*, right?"

Rubio strikes a match that flicks an inky shadow into the small recess that is the cleft in his chin, while illuminating the halo of heavy dark curls and the hand that quivers to the dancing flame as he lights a cigarette, offers it to Mason, then lights another for himself. Mason smokes when he's worried. Marla has already gone to bed, and Clair, leaning against the door to their room, waiting to enter with Mason, is only a forgotten witness to the two fates raveling out before her.

"*Si, claro, con Dios.* We all go with God."

CHAPTER 12

T hey mount the stairs into the C-47, exhausted from the heat and the long wait, too long to have been believed if they had not just endured it with the other passengers, though they seemed largely indifferent or used to it. Presumably because they are Americans, they are the last two on the tarmac. The door is at the rear of the plane, so that when they enter the cabin they do not at first see the other passengers or where they might find seats; they see instead, directly in front of them, the vats of entrails and the quarter side of beef wrapped in burlap still swinging gently from the hook and ring, like a man hung by the neck, then, closer to where the remaining seats begin, the bushels and baskets of fresh goods and the sacks belonging to the passengers, mostly plastic shopping bags, plus one young goat, a baby carriage, and, in a wire cage, two clamorous chickens. An unpleasant, half-raw, half-cooked smell hovers over the food, which has already developed orbiting flies. And why not? It has been sitting in the heat for hours. There are only two seats left, at the front of the plane and facing backwards toward the other passengers. Before they can begin to make their way forward, Mason correctly reads her intentions, sets his mouth, and takes her arm with force, propelling her ahead of him and up the narrow aisle to the seats. Even though it is aggressive, it is also somehow reassuring. The other passengers have fallen into silence, trying not to watch them. She ducks into the seat against the window, as greasy as the inside of a meat case, and lowers her eyes. *This is a meat case*, she thinks, staring down the length of the metal tube they've all willingly scrambled into. Everyone is solemnly watching them, as if they have been convicted of a crime and are only here to be sentenced.

All her life has been like this, waiting to be sentenced.

Glancing down, she sees in the narrow space that their feet have woven between the feet of the couple opposite them, that she and the women are in sandals, and that both of the men wear cheap athletic shoes, equally worn and formerly some other color, which has devolved to a unanimous ashen brown.

The rear door is still open. They are not yet trapped.

After five minutes pass, a fit young man threads his way up the plane. He is wearing khakis and an old-fashioned leather bomber jacket, a long filmy white scarf, aviator shades. Oh, he's handsome, too, with gleaming white teeth and short thick black hair, smooth as an eight ball, beneath which the happy, confident smile of a flimflam man bears him forward, this teenager dressed up as a WWII pilot fresh out of central casting.

"*El piloto*," Mason mutters, making little effort to stifle a guffaw.

As they had during the boarding process of the two gringos, the other passengers follow the pilot to the cockpit, this time with shy admiring eyes. Indeed, the force of this admiration seems to have generated a small updraft that gently lifts the loose end of the white scarf into a carefree salute as *el piloto* drops, smooth as a dancer, into the captain's seat, swipes off the white scarf, and dons headphones. No such entity as a co-*piloto* materializes.

Once the propellers choke and cough awake, spinning to a blur, and the noise and the vibration overwhelm the cabin, passengers begin to talk—not the two facing Clair and Mason who continue to watch them blankly, a talent that calls to mind eternity. When the C-47 labors up off the runway, they finally hazard a look out the greasy windows, in part because, turning west, the plane cants so sharply over the blinding blue water that for a few minutes they are hanging above the windows and have no choice but to look out and down. The beef has pendulated toward the rear door and the open bins of food have crept across the aisle, and the goat, tethered to the back of the last seat is practically floating, but all goods slide back to their original positions when the C-47 rights itself and settles into a deep, steady, grumbling drone, resigned to its duty.

"A real workhorse, these C-47's," Mason says into her ear. "Go anywhere, do anything."

"Really?"

"Reliable as they come."

"How do you know? How is it you know everything, Mason?"

"Been in half a dozen. Hardly need a runway. Field'll do fine. Even an ice floe, landed on one up in the Northwest Territories."

She considers his yellow shirt, the one from Morocco, wishing she didn't like it, didn't love him. Love was the worst sort of burden . . . the mistakes, the memories . . .

"You called it Aero Fatale back at the runway."

He flashes her a crazy cheerful smile reminiscent of the smile he sported among the boojum trees when he was goofy and enchanted. "That was before we successfully lifted off."

"This whole thing, it's . . ."

"Dodgy?"

"Yes, dodgy. Worse."

"Bog-standard for the C-47."

"But a real workhorse."

"Right."

She places her hand over the side of her face as much to conceal her fear from the other passengers as to try to make herself heard, and leans into him, smelling his skin, its familiar salty oil, and then, faintly, the orange he ate earlier. "It's hard to breathe. I want to get out of here. I have a son. I shouldn't be taking these kinds of chances. The kind of chances you're always taking, by the way. I don't know what I was thinking or what I'm doing here, what we're doing. Anymore. What are we doing? What the hell are we doing? Nothing is making sense to me anymore."

"Don't get hysterical, Clair." He registers not her but their audience of two across the way and gives a little smiling nod that seems to say, *everything's okay over here.*

"Hysterical?"

"Forty-five minutes. You can manage that."

What she thinks is *go to hell*, but what she says is nothing because that has always been the only option—protecting Nina, sparing her father, deceiving her mother, humoring Tom, coddling Ethan, avoiding colleagues, and, with Mason, suppression. She has next to no experience with *no*. Escape into stoical work, into a university three thousand miles from home, into hard routines and self-sacrifices, into shapely clouds of deception. That has been the pattern: smoke and mirrors, then the disappearing act. Some part of her has always thrived on deprivation, the worst being the deprivations of fraud. Now it seems impossible to know who she really is. She has spent so much time giving each person in her life a different face, depriving herself of the kind of self-knowledge one can only glimpse in the eyes of others. That is what fraud does, it deprives you of yourself.

But to say, *no, I don't like that, no, I don't want that, no, that's wrong, no, go to hell* . . . what was she afraid of?

The low altitude and slow, 160- miles-per-hour speed, the heavy drone, the airless heat, the suffocating smell of raw meat and wilting vegetables, the blue grave waiting below, the implacable eyes of the other passengers who belong and know that they, these Americanos, do not belong . . . it's impossible. Now she is trapped, trapped in the experience.

Closing her eyes, pretending to doze, she counts long breaths backward from one hundred, makes it to seventy-three, opens her eyes and counts windows, hats, the rivets marching out to the wingtip . . . they are still alive, the plane has not yet plunged them into the Pacific, she can see and smell, touch and hear . . . *hear what?* Again, she leans into Mason, listening for his breath, lost in the drone . . . but she can feel his chest rising, falling, the warmth of skin . . . and then suddenly, the dun-brown and sulfurous landscape of Isla Cedros erupts beneath them, the southernmost reach of the island and from above, a manifestation of Hell. She can see why the locals call their home *El Piedron*—the Rock. Sharp, jagged ridges, precipitous declines, rocks and talus, desertic soil unrelieved by anything that doesn't look burnt and forsaken, then the great, regimented massif of salt, each mound flat-topped and broad—all of it runs like fast-forward film across the porthole windows of the C-47 as it sweeps down and around, bouncing onto the short runway and coming to a perfunctory stop. Someone opens the rear door, an attendant she has not noticed seated in the last row, and the rickety metal steps are folded down to the tarmac. Passengers collect their bags from the back of the plane and scatter, most to the company town of El Morro adjacent to the runway. There is only one taxi in Cedros, an old brown and yellow Chevy station wagon with fake wood panels and a chassis suspended so low that, as it approaches, she can see it shaving the crown of the dirt road. A tall lopsided man with half an unlit cigar pinched into the corner of his mouth emerges from the driver's seat and limps a few steps toward them, waving his arm in a wide arc, exchanges a few words with Mason, and finally accepts payment in advance, clearly more than he takes from the three other passengers. Everyone piles in for the short six-mile ride into Pueblo de Cedros. On the way they deliver a fellow passenger to the salt docks where one of the mountains of salt—its scale, its purity, its whiteness—is so staggering that it's ominous. At the same time, and as real as its physicality avows, it seems abstract, something dreamed up by a roomful of faceless conspirators a world away.

The next two passengers climb out beside a shack on the outskirts of the pueblo and the driver, Señor Aquilar, instantly lurches up to speed, what has so far been something close to hurtling. Looking back, she can barely make out the shape of the two men enveloped in a cyclonic whirl of dust. It's funny, how they watch the taxi with an awesome longing as it flies away, their mouths softly open, as if it might have taken them somewhere else, somewhere that belongs to the land of improbable dreams.

Everywhere she looks—up the hillsides, into the barrancas, beside the road—garbage. Though they are fairly certain that the island only has rooms, Mason still asks the driver about a hotel. He shrugs and dully replies, "*No hay.*"

"*Nada?*"

"*Solamente cuartos.*"

"Okay."

In answer, the driver flings his left arm out the window and turns abruptly, descending into the pueblo down a wide dusty main street littered with goats, children, and other citizens of Cedros going about their afternoon business. At the bottom end of the road is the harbor with its crook-armed breakwater and beyond, Bahía de Sebastián Vizcaíno. The village is a squalid growth of one- and two-story box structures, some with second-floor railed balconies, none with vehicles of any variety that look functional. In front of the shanties and houses are oil drums overflowing garbage, broken remnants of one thing or another, and in the dirt itself, stains that may be oil but are more likely evidence of the wash tubs and piss pots emptied over the railings or out an open window. The driver takes a right into a narrow alley that dead-ends at Casa de Huespedes Aguilar, another two-story building but this one is either in the process of being completed or was abandoned at the minimum stage of construction. Some walls have wood siding painted baby blue, some have only tar paper held in place with occasional boards and a handful of nails. It takes no measurable intelligence to deduce that the taxi driver, Señor Aquilar, with his widely swinging, boisterous arm, has some financial interest in the Casa de Huespedes Aguilar.

If the woman at the desk, a small sewing table in actuality, is surprised to see two Americanos, she makes no indication. She seems to have no age, expressions, thoughts or feelings. Even when Mason speaks Spanish to her, she is unmoved by that ability, taking cash in advance for their four nights and leading them in silence to their room, handing them a key for a lock that doesn't lock in a door that is wonky and that can easily be shoved open. Finally, she points with grave formality to the only truly finished and even elegant item in the establishment, a sign that hangs over the entrance hallway that reads *Quede estrictamente prohibido ingerir bebidas alcoholicas y toda clase de drogas en los cuartos.*

"It is strictly forbidden to ingest alcoholic beverages and all classes of drugs in the rooms," he reads aloud for Clair's benefit and adopting a comically serious tenor.

There are four rooms in the guesthouse. The one assigned to them is on the second floor up a set of dubious wooden stairs that, inexplicably, begin within a small area surrounded by a picket fence and gate.

The toilet is in a room the size of a phone booth and offers only a hole in the ground and half a roll of toilet paper sitting at the bottom of a yard-high stick. The shower is so spacious it might be meant for communal washing except that there is only one source of water, a pipe that protrudes from a hole in the wall and, they are informed, there is water only in the mornings. The walls are peeling turquoise paint, and the drain in the center of the floor is clogged with a sodden brown muck bristling with hair. There is no hot water. Somewhere a sink must exist, but they have not yet located it. The electricity works from 6:00 AM until noon and, later, from five to eleven in the evening. Their cubicle contains two cots lined up less than a foot apart, between them one dirty window the size of a shoe box, plastic paneling made to resemble wood, and for each cot, one sheet, one brown synthetic blanket, one pancake pillow. Nothing pretends to be clean, which is somehow a relief.

With them they have an aluminum camera case and a small duffel, having left the rest of their belongings in the van, which Mason arranged to park at the motel under the shade of a massive ironwood tree. He was concerned about all the used rolls of film, keeping them out of direct light and as cool as possible during their time on Cedros. Where a long lens is usually secured in the molded foam of the camera case, Mason has stored a bottle of tequila. As the door closes behind the woman, he removes the bottle and shrugs, bunching his lips. There is nothing to say. He hands Clair the bottle, she drinks and hands it back to him, watching for him to finish so that she can have a second shot at it.

"Let's walk down to the harbor, get some air."

She nods. "How will we get out of here?"

"We will."

"But how? How do we call the taxi, how do we get back to the airport?"

"I made an arrangement with the driver. He will come for us on the morning of the fourth day."

"Do you believe him?"

"He named a restaurant. I saw it as we drove down the main street. Fausta's Cocina."

"Fausta's," she repeats, committing to memory a life-saving password.

She keeps her arm knotted in Mason's as they slowly march down the main street, passing through one bad smell after another and conveying with them a ring of silence that extends five yards in every direction. Once they have traveled far enough away from the last idle assembly of residents, voices resume behind them though they are watched for a long while, and never feel relieved of menacing assessment until they reach the harbor. Here the smells are worse, an amalgam of rotting flesh emanating from several dead and bloated seals bobbing up against the breakwater and the cannery, Productos Pesqueros, a cooperative for the island fishermen whose blue corrugated buildings take up the curving inner reach of the jetty as it connects to the shore. Behind and beneath it all, the metallic smell of deep water. The largest of the fishing boats are either anchored along the break-water or tied up to the rickety pier, while the smaller *lanchas* dot the open water of the harbor. The wreckage of a power boat is strewn among the rocks of the south seawall. Up the dark beach the highest tides have left a long rippling signature of plastic bottles and garbage, kelp, fish net, and whatever other flotsam has found its way to Isla Cedros. A greasy sheen makes floating puddles of color on the sea surface as the afternoon light fades behind a flat insipid haze.

All day long she has been hot, but now she shivers against Mason's arm and wonders how they will make their way across the next long hours, long days in this ramshackle pueblo. At sunset, the wind comes up, and they turn to make their way back to their cuarto. The two towers of the Catholic church, Parroquia Nuestra Señora del Carmen, on the hill above the pueblo catch the rosy light as if to refute all that lies at her feet, the dilapidated houses and shanties, the clouds of dust, the sagging electrical lines, the garbage everywhere, the misery of the paint colors whose insistent variety communicates an altogether different failure—the failure to refute a collective truth. Everyone, every house and boat, every dirty child and scabrous dog, every man's lidded inspection, and every woman's dull eyes—all seem to be suffering the same ailment. Poverty. And with it, some mix of distrust, aggression, and indifference. Life is very cheap on Cedros.

The light deepens to a fuchsia, and the whole town glows, but the effect is not enough to transform the visual depression to something even vaguely appealing. It just looks incendiary, like the last burst from a burning heap. When an ashy dusk descends, they have a hard time finding the alleyway to the guesthouse, but she remembers the smell of old urine and fuel, maybe heating oil, the decapitated and wheel-less body of a red car at the corner, and, on the other side, the same diapered child sitting on a cinder block by the door of what looks like a body shop, banging a plastic bottle against the ground.

There are two cantinas in town, Fausta's and another that has no name but that the woman at the sewing table tells them is located on Avenida de la Verdad, a grand name for the dirt path that runs parallel to the main street from the hill down toward the water. In the night sky hangs a bitten yellow moon, but what illumination it might offer seems incarcerated within the small, damaged circle of itself. Instead, they rely on the lights in the shacks and houses on either side casting a hopscotch of pale smudges that guide them toward the nameless café.

"We're still being watched," she tells Mason.

"Sure."

"It feels very . . . anatomical."

"There's a whorehouse at the top of this street. That's why they call it Avenue of the Truth. Maybe they think I've purchased you."

"What? Why?" In the darkness, for a moment, she can see his teeth.

"You're wearing shorts. Mexican women don't wear shorts. Not the kind you marry."

"It was hot today. It's still warm, in fact," she says defensively. "And why didn't you tell me about the whorehouse? How do you know about it?"

"The writer. He thought it was a hotel. It's right up there lateral to the church, probably so that guests can blunder from one to the other without having to catch their breath." He laughs. "The salvation of the confessional. It's a very devout country."

"Yes, I know, but this isn't funny. You should have told me about the shorts. I don't like being watched . . . that way, you know, it's unsettling."

"Aren't you used to it by now?"

"Because I'm white?"

"Because you're pretty."

"Why is it your compliments always sound so uncomplimentary?"

Mason is spared from having to come up with an answer by the appearance of two men staggering out of what can only be the nameless cantina. The light inside is fluorescent, as gray and examinative as a morgue, the room a crowded checkerboard of Formica tables each one occupied except the one just vacated by the two staggering men. The walls are barren. A low bar with stools faces the kitchen, and the backs of the men seated at it shift when they enter but do not turn. A girl with menus points to the empty table, which she quickly wipes using a crumpled napkin left by one of the men. She and Clair are the only females in the room. They sit and study the menu cards. Now and then someone says a few words to someone else, but mostly the room is silent except for the muted *tap-tap* of flatware on hard plastic plates, the *clink* of beer bottles on Formica, the hiss of food in a pan from the kitchen. They order beer and some of the local calico sea bass, which, it turns out, is the only item available on the menu card anyway. When it arrives with a pile of Mexican slaw and hot tortillas, several of the other customers turn to keep an eye on them as they eat, a diversion that soon bores them.

Before they are more than a couple of mouthfuls into their dinner, a gaunt, wild-eyed man lurches over to their table and begins to gabble in patchy English, about what it's hard to say. At first she is pleased that someone will talk to them, but she soon realizes that there is something off about him. His hands are black with grease or soot, his face smeared with the same substance, his hair is stiff and matted off to one side, like a salute. He's holding forth about a tree, a tree that lives in Santa Barbara where he has traveled. "*Estados Unidos*," he pronounces with pride.

"The fig tree," Mason says.

She looks at him as if he's just as crazy as their visitor.

"A Mortan Bay fig tree from Australia. Been there over a hundred years. It's famous. You should see the roots, like Medusa's hair. All exposed."

The man is still gesturing and talking enthusiastically with his new friends, about jail now, which either he was in or is about to go in, it's not clear, and how the fig tree, the magical fig tree, *mágico*, saved him, or will save him. Whenever Mason throws out a word in Spanish, the man charges into turbulent English to return the volley. Maybe the other diners are amused that their version of a town idiot has cornered them, or maybe they are embarrassed by this representative of Pueblo de Cedros, but not a single man even glances their way now. When the check arrives, they hand the pesos directly to the girl and duck out, tramping back up Avenida de la Verdad with the zeal of penitents who have seen enough truth.

All night long, in the room next to theirs, through the single-ply walls of the cuartos, they hear men, how many they can't tell, playing some kind of game with dominoes that involves slamming the tiles violently to the floor at random intervals. Each time it happens she starts awake and thinks about the aptness of *bones* for dominoes. Later, she hears voices down below and then a new sound. At the base of the rickety steps leading up to the second floor, within the picket fence, two goats have been penned, and long into the long night their bleating accompanies the clattering dominoes to form a tribal concordance that agitates her dreams.

The next morning, exhausted, they prepare for the hike up Mount Cedros, normally a three- to four-hour trip, but because Clair plans to lay out plant transects, it will take twice that. They will do the lower two today, the higher ones closer to the summit tomorrow, and the last, easy ones at sea level at the end of the third day when Mason will photograph whatever he needs at the Punta Morro Redondo docks. In a small bodega they buy chips, packaged ham, oranges. As they are heading up the main street toward the trail, a man passes them balancing on his head a broad wooden board bearing cookies and bread. Women from the houses emerge, make their choices, pay, and disappear back through the dark doorways. Mason stops the baker to buy the pink and yellow *polvorones* that are lighter than shortbread but sweeter, popping one in his mouth.

They continue climbing.

The first thousand feet above the town glitter with broken glass, evenly distributed as if it has been decoratively applied. On the glittering scarp, garbage—all manner of garbage, from cradles to cars, TVs, scrap metal, cans, chairs disgorging stuffing—anything a human society might use up and discard. Nothing is sorted, and no one has attempted to confine the refuse. It looks as though someone tossed it out the window of a speeding car, except that much of it is sizeable and will take many, many generations to degrade. The worst of it has been tumbled down a long, deep arroyo that abuts the trail for a while, but the surrounding landscape is quickly catching up with the arroyo. Some of the disassembled vehicles have graffiti spray-painted onto their panels. Beside the worst of the scattered garbage is a feckless sign that reads *"Prohibido Tirar Basura"*—littering prohibited.

"A little late," Mason grumbles.

At an elevation of a thousand feet, they leave the trail, hike thirty steps north-northwest and measure out the first transect. After documenting its location, Clair drives four metal tent stakes into the soil, marking a three-meter square grid, while Mason runs the cord from stake to stake. Then they stand back and consider what lies within the grid, Clair listing each plant in her field book, Mason photographing the entire grid from different angles, and adding close-ups of the plants that are not readily obvious or that are likely unique to the island. She snaps off a few leaves from each of the variant species and tucks them into small, individual, plastic specimen bags. Between them the silence is both intimate and fluent. They have always worked well together, intuiting small needs, and because of this single unexpected gift, the kind one never thinks Life even knows about, let alone gives, it is her favorite time with him, easy and companionable. The task or job is irrelevant, the commonality of the goal what matters. Within an hour, they have dismantled the transect, returned to the trail, and continued up the steep flank of Cerro Cedros.

They climb another thousand feet, checking the altimeter, locate a second transect site in what seems a pristine quadrant of terrain not far off the trail, and set up the grid. After tabulating the flora circumscribed within the three-by-three-meter square, they take a simple lunch.

"What a wretched species we are," Mason remarks, flicking orange seeds into the desert.

"The garbage."

"All of it. The garbage, the mad men with their magic trees, the bloated thugs like Cantú who tear it all up, the scientists thinking they know. And then us. We're sure, we're *positive*, we can do something." He spits out a seed. "We can't do bugger all. We're the spanner in the works. Human beings. What we need is a good plague."

"You're tired."

"Shouldn't I be?"

"Of course. And your back . . ."

"My back. Let's hang it all on Dr. Bonebreak's ministrations."

She makes a quick decision to change the subject, which was ranging into too wide a space, one that might not find its borders. And she hadn't even mentioned the death of his father. "When will you photograph the docks? After the last transect?"

"Maybe not. Maybe not bother, you know?" They are sitting on the thick horizontal branch of a dead elephant tree, looking east down the mountain and across the bay toward the Baja peninsula. He has been fiddling with a length of straw, drawing circles in the dirt, poking at a lost ant, sending it back where it came from, or in any case, away from him and his food. "Hardly much point in anything, after all is said and done. Nothing changes. No one sees the light before they die. They just die in darkness, having added to the trash and subtracted species, and the world becomes less habitable, less diverse, less resilient, less of a world. Everything we do or think we can do . . . ah, it's just a botch job, Clair. It's all botched." He looks away, swiping at his eyes.

It will make it worse if she reaches out to him, so, instead, she considers the leaf of a *Dudleya pachphytum*, endemic to Cedros, the leaf as small as the tip of a finger and just as softly plump, like most succulents, full of conserved water, preparing for a future. *The future . . .* "Maybe," she says, "maybe so," feeling ill, as if they've both contracted a mysterious sickness. Hope is draining from them, blood from a deep wound. It's easy to feel hope when that's what it is—a feeling. But what if it has to be a duty? What if that is all that's left, all that can carry you forward, duty, not feeling? And for what perform that duty? Why bother? as Mason asked.

Maybe he's feeling bad about his father, too.

The next day they hike directly up the trail to what will be the third transect and eat tortillas with slices of cheese while they tabulate species. The dominoes were silent the night before, and the bleating goats murmured quietly behind the curtain of night, so at last some sleep. Mason had declined the shower, but Clair stood shivering before the metal pipe and let the cold water come, even while she worried about the unidentifiable muck on the floor and her bare feet and the impossibility of cleaning anything. They've been sleeping in their clothes but everything still feels filthy.

By noon they reach the summit of Cedros where the native island pines grow, surviving on the fog from the west. Cool and windy, the clouds sweep by, enveloping them, and in the soothing damp air the work goes quickly. On the way back, among an outcropping of palms at the bottom of an arroyo, they come upon the caretaker of the springs that supply the pueblo of Cedros. It is hard to tell how old he is, his skin is so weathered beneath his straw hat, but his white moustache is neatly trimmed, a perfect trapezoid, and he holds his head at a proud angle, gazing down at them, though he is shorter. His eyes are small and dark, with whites that do not show, like the eyes of dog. He's been loading his burro, in a hurry to get back to town, and clearly not interested in talking with what he probably assumes are tourists. But when he notices the backpack, he stops to ask Clair whether she has been collecting.

Mason tells the man that they have gathered a few specimen leaves from native plants for scientific purposes.

"Soon," the man tells them in Spanish, "you will need a permit for such actions. You will need a permit to come to the island, a permit to take plants, a permit even to take pictures," he adds, nodding at Mason's camera and cinching another strap on the burro. "We are not a playground to foreigners. This is our home."

"But no such permits are required now."

"No."

"And by what authority? What agency?"

"*Secretaria de Medio Ambiente y Recursos Naturales.*"

"Secretary of Environment and Natural Resources," Mason explains to Clair.

"Finally," she says. "Bueno," she adds, nodding to the man.

He looks over at her, his bead eyes shining with hatred. "*Pronto,*" he tells them, holding up two fingers. "*Dos años.*"

"But not now," Mason repeats.

The man shakes his head once, sharply, and finishes loading up his burro. "No, now you may still take. Take plants, take pictures, take as you always take. But one day, it is time to give."

"That's what we're trying to do," Clair says, glancing quickly at Mason to translate. It's obvious that Mason just wants her to drop it, but she gives him another look and he says, "Señor, we're doing this to help. This woman here is documenting plant species, to understand and preserve them, and, well, I'm trying to stop PSP from hurting the gray whales in Laguna San Ignacio. This is true, Señor."

"PSP . . . ," the old man says pensively, "my son works on those docks. He has many children." Before starting down the trail, he turns to warn them. "Do not leave any garbage in our home."

"No," Mason says, dropping his eyes and finding something on the ground that prompts a faint smile.

The man lifts his chin. "You are amused, yes?" Now he raises a single finger, pointing at heaven. "Do not be amused. We have changed. And the garbage you and your country send to us, it still comes with the rivers, it falls from the sky, it crawls onto our beaches. Today this happens. Today and all the days behind and the days to come, we receive your garbage. The border is nothing but a false promise."

"Yes, that's true," Clair says. She understands some Spanish but cannot speak it, and this inability has become maddening. She wants to say more, to explain, and in her words, not Mason's. He is always less agreeable.

Mason looks solemnly at the man and nods once. "You're preaching to the choir, Señor."

"Um," he says without drawing it out, an acknowledgment but no more. Well, what did they expect, *thanks*?

Once again, it is Nina who crowds into her thoughts and with Nina, feelings of remorse and guilt, of so much having drifted into the razed landscape of time where what comes too late can never take root; the only thing that will grow is regret.

That night a violent windstorm lashes the island. Dust scours the tiny window of their cuarto, the cheap walls cry and creak, and up the hill the church bells riotously clang. At the height of the storm, long after the power has been off, they notice lights outside. Venturing down the stairs and out to the main street, they discover that vehicles have lined up with their headlights trained on the water inside the breakwater where moored boats are pitching and plunging like toys in a child's tub. One vessel, a tourist's sailboat, white and gleaming, has broken loose from its mooring. Between the long cones of headlights, they watch it toss itself back and forth toward the breakwater and the instant it strikes the rocks the villagers send up a cheer, honk their horns, flash their lights. She had thought that the vehicles with their lights were lined up to help, but now she realizes that it is a local sport, watching boats throw themselves onto the rocks. In the lights, they can just make out the dark shapes of two people crawling out from the hatch onto the seawall, and someone running along the path toward them.

THE NEXT MORNING at dawn, Mason leaves with his camera, having hired a *launcha* to tour the island's coastline and, in particular, to bring him alongside the salt docks at Punta Morro Redonda. He was giving up just the day before, he had asked *why bother?* but a stubborn commitment to his calling and to his best weapon, a camera, sends him almost without awareness out to do his job. His duty. Duty can survive even the loss of hope. When he returns—later than planned—he's fired up about the vessel docked at the southernmost point on Cedros, a 260-meter dry bulk carrier ship that dwarfs everything around it except the mountain of salt pouring into its cargo holds. Apparently, some of PSP's dockhands yelled at them to move away, to stop photographing, but it wasn't until one of them threw something that the hired man in the stern swung the tiller and motored them back to Puerto Cedros. The size of it all, the *scale*, he tells her . . . that alone will sway attitudes. And so, Mason has regained his footing. He has forgotten about his father, his back, Cantú, and Yetz. He has taken refuge in the one thing that always offers refuge, his art and the work it does. He has stopped looking like a boy resigned to the departure of someone he loves.

WHERE THE TEQUILA was stowed in the camera case, he now tucks the rolls of film. They finish up the last of the transects and turn in early.

On the morning of the fourth day, they gather their small assortment of belongings and walk to Fausta's Cocina. A quiet morning, soft and sunny. On the front step of the café, a barefoot girl of six or seven sits, her legs neatly folded beneath a dirty flowered skirt and her hand resting on the head of a brown dog sleeping in the warmth. Clair smiles down at her as they enter, and the girl with her dewy eyes looks up and returns the smile. It is late—most of the villagers have already dined and departed. Only one table is still occupied, a man and probably his son—they are wearing shirts embroidered with the same leaf pattern.

They order eggs with beans, which arrive in a vegetable scramble, along with steamy, cloth-wrapped flour tortillas, but Clair is feeling so anxious about the taxi driver showing up that she manages only a few bites. Mason methodically consumes his entire breakfast, asking for butter and salt for the tortillas, and not two but three cups of coffee. The driver is supposed to arrive at 9:00. At 8:45, they pay and go out front to wait. The girl is still sitting beside her dog, staring east across the street to the shadowed side where an old man is mending a fish net stretched over a trough, the rest of the net wadded behind him in the dirt. Where they are the sun is higher now, the light still soft and pale as flax. Now and then, one or another woman tosses a bucket of liquid over the second-story railing of her house—urine, dishwater, water for scrubbing floors—it's impossible to tell. At 9:05 the driver has still not arrived. By 9:10 Clair urges Mason to go back to the cuartos in the event Aguilar decided to pick them up there. Uncharacteristically, Mason readily agrees, which is when she realizes he is almost as anxious as she is to get off the island. His tall, long-legged figure scissors quickly down the street and around a corner, his torso leaning forward at a slight but stiff angle and his yellow shirt like a torn-away piece of the sun.

Another ten minutes pass and the sun's warmth on Fausta's side of the street is growing in strength, which time has honed to a sudden keenness. Her cheeks are burning and the long pants she's wearing to avoid the stigma of the shorts are beginning to cling. Half-mad with worry, she drops beside the girl. Within a few minutes, the girl stands and steps backward to face her from the street. She reels off something in Spanish, too fast for Clair to understand, but she does pick up one word, *perro*, and knows that the girl is telling her about the dog still sleeping peacefully in the sun a foot or so away. With indecipherable meaning, the girl's plump fingers wriggle along with her words and grasp toward the dog, and finally, Clair feels bidden to pay closer attention. From one of the sleeping eyes, she notices a trail of ants at about the same time she hears the girl use the word *muerto*. She realizes then that the dog is dead, that it has been dead, but only recently, and that no one entering, exiting, or working at Fausta's, no one passing on the street, no one cares that there is a dead dog on the front step.

She gasps and jerks away from it. Across the street the old man smiles with a mouth unexpectedly packed with bright white teeth.

Coming from the direction of the cuartos, the station wagon careens around the corner, Mason in the front seat, batting his arm out the window to hurry her over. Up she flies, stumbling toward him, falling into the backseat with the camera case and duffel bag, her heart hammering inside the cage of her chest and the girl waving gently after them in that curious way of children, squeezing the air, as if trying to hold it, or them, in place.

The driver turns and laughs at Clair's expression before gunning it up the street. Tapping the fingernails of one hand against the fingernails of the other, Mason monotones a remark and the rest of the journey to the airstrip is as silent as a deathwatch.

This time there is no waiting, and there are empty seats that face forward. A number of the passengers wear shirts with the PSP logo sewn into them. Someone takes their two bags, the fancy camera case, and the small duffel, and pushes them into the rear of the C-47. Not even the one-by-one excruciation of ticket inspection is required for the return flight. If you come to Cedros, you will surely go.

NOTHING ABOUT THE flight back frightens her, or if it does, or could, or would have in former times, just days earlier, those concerns have slipped from the bottom of a list that gets shorter each day.

They are becoming the simplest versions of themselves.

She can see now how difficult it would be to astonish the people of Cedros, and how, after only a short while, it would take more to astonish her, too.

THE VAN IS still where they left it, parked under the Ironwood tree at the motel, and though it has been conspicuously ransacked, the only things missing—probably because the man assigned to ravage their belongings could not resist the basic instincts of utility—are the Coleman stove and every single roll of exposed film that Mason had carefully stored under the rear bench, out of the direct sun, in a box, beneath a blanket. The only thing that was everything.

Pinned beneath the windshield wiper is a matchbook with a single word scrawled on its inside cover—*vete*. Go away.

None of this is surprising, really. None of it astonishes them.

The only truly surprising thing about their return to the peninsula is that atop the van, high enough that someone must have lifted it, is the yellow dog, the same one that had lain, sphinxlike, atop Eduardo Cantú's truck.

Mason looks as placid as a monk as they finish assessing the van, invite the stray into the back, and wordlessly climb in. Before driving off, he pauses, stares through the windshield, reaches behind for his camera case, and opens it. There is nothing in the slot where he had stowed the film from Cedros. It's all gone. All of it.

CHAPTER 13

"Where are we going?" she says.

"Unclear."

But without hesitation he turns west onto Emiliano Zapata toward the saltworks, drives two miles, passes through the gate, by the empty guard booth, and parks at the offices of PSP. The receptionist recognizes them and tells them that Cantú and Martinez are out at base dock 3, that she will telephone over there. But Mason explains it's a little surprise, *una pequeña sorpresa*. His voice is charming; he makes a joke and she smiles, giving directions. It's a fifteen-minute drive southwest to the dock.

"I don't know what you're doing."

"Um."

"What are you doing, Mason?"

"I'm going to retrieve my film."

"It's gone, and you know it. It's long gone. We have to forget this. We'll make another trip, or someone else will. The magazine has other photographers, it doesn't have to be you. And we need to get home. I have to get back to Ethan, and we're already late."

"It won't take long."

"What?"

"Leave it, Clair."

"What won't take long?"

"Getting the film back."

She considers him, feeling a sadness. "Mason, the film is gone. It's nothing to them. They're just messing with you. They know it'll keep happening. Everybody's in this fight, the NRDC, the global scientific community, the press, all the celebrities and artists and politicos . . . everyone."

"Without the film, *I'm* not in it, Clair."

"They're just fucking with you. Don't you get it?" she shouts. "You're nothing to them!"

He glances at her, startled, as if she's someone else.

"They're fucking with you!" she repeats.

"So, I'll fuck them back."

Moored alongside the dock is an enormous oblong barge from which a range of peaked mountains rises as the conveyor system disgorges a bright white stream of salt. Several parked trucks line up opposite a low building.

Mason stops, turns off the engine, and for a minute or two, they listen to it tick. He seems to be watching the door of the building, but it's also clear that he's intently, blindly thinking. The door opens, two men emerge from its shadow. Cantú, Martinez. They don't notice the van stopped about fifteen yards away, they're talking, walking toward one of the trucks, Cantú gesturing with the back of his hand as if outlining steps in a process, Martinez in a baseball hat, his arms just as inactive as when they first met him. Ducking into the truck, Cantú powers down the driver's side window and it's then that he notices Mason striding toward them. Cantú opens the truck door, he's straightening just as Mason arrives and with a sudden pivot, delivers a short, quick uppercut that staggers Eduardo Cantú back against the door frame. Martinez, scrambling around the front end, uses his torso to shove Mason away, reserving his arms for helping his colleague to steady up onto his feet. There's a bloody cut along his jaw and a volcanic look in his eyes that's almost instantly replaced by a languid squint of appraisal and a slippery half-smile.

"Too many things matter to you, Mr. Comstock."

"My film."

Clair has grabbed his arm to pull him away, but two men in company shirts materialize, pushing her off and forcing Mason into the backseat of one of the other trucks.

LA POLICÍA WON'T tell her much of anything, except that, yes, Señor Mason Comstock is there somewhere in the recesses of the Criminal Justice buildings, the *Centro de Justicia Penal de Guerrero Negro*, and to come back mañana.

In the morning, nothing has changed.

"Doesn't he get a call?" she asks.

"Not today. *Solamente* Tuesdays and Thursdays."

"What?"

"Two days in the week."

"But you haven't charged him. And they stole his film, all of it. For the article he's working on, for *National Geographic*," she adds, as if it lends importance, as if it changes and strengthens the spell that will magically release him.

"*La prueba del crimen, Señorita*. We will require that if you are accusing Señor Cantú." He pauses to rub his chin. "And there is still the assault."

"Proof? But *they* have the proof." Or rather, they didn't, they don't. No one has the proof because there is no proof that anyone has stolen Mason's film, or even that the film ever existed.

The officer puffs his lips and shrugs, a tired, middle-aged man in an old job that he knows too much about. Even the gel in his hair isn't fresh, has begun to stiffen and lift.

For a full two minutes she stares at him, stymied. Taking a deep breath and slowly exhaling, something cold and metallic drains from her mind down into her body and instantly hardens into resolve. A younger officer winds through the back of the room, glancing at them, then continues out into a yard surrounded by mostly windowless buildings, one of which must contain Mason. As soon as he is gone, Clair unzips her purse and removes her wallet, but before she can pull out the cash, all that she has, the man shakes his head sadly, even kindly. "It is PSP, Señorita. It is Don Cantú. I would like to accept your gift, this is very generous of you, but . . . Don Cantú. *No es posible.*"

From the payphone at the motel she mangles her way through Spanish to reach the US Consular office in Tijuana. A woman takes down the information, including Mason's Tourist Card number and date of entry into Mexico, and promises to track the legal proceedings and to urge a *just and speedy* outcome. "But you say there was an assault?" the woman asks.

"Yes, yes, they stole all his film. They destroyed his work. It was just once that he hit the man. One punch, and anyway, Mason was provoked."

"Of course. Well, the Consulate will keep track of the case, I assure you. A speedy outcome," she repeats.

No es posible, Clair thinks, sighing, hanging up the phone. None of that will happen. Even exceeding the in-country dates on a Tourist Card will land a visitor in jail, often indefinitely. "A revenue garnering device," Mason calls it, the bribery system, the entrenched corruption.

The next day will be Tuesday when Mason can call her, or she can call him, but she's unwilling to wait that long. Instead, she telephones Rubio Cantú, the presumed son of the so-called victim, finds him through the proprietor of the first restaurant, El Farolito, where they followed Rubio in Mulegé, where they sat with the baffling crucifix, and with Marla, equally baffling, as Rubio finished up his business for the day.

After offering commiserations, he says, "I have friends."

"Friends."

"An organization," he corrects, because—she knows this—he will be honest. He is honest.

"I already tried to bribe them," she confesses. "Maybe it wasn't enough money, maybe the officer knew I didn't have enough."

"Money is not always *la solución*, Clair."

"Okay," she says simply, not wanting to know what the solution is, or how it will be managed, or what sort of dark path she's on now, or even whether it will cause more problems for Rubio with his father. All she knows is that she will do anything to get Mason out of jail and out of Mexico and back home with her. Whatever it takes.

"By tomorrow," he tells her. "This will be finished tomorrow." His voice is calm enough to cheer her a little. She wanders around the town, buys tacos from a food truck, stops at a market, then returns to the motel room. *Tomorrow*, she thinks.

Having no one to talk to and nothing to do except worry, she spends what's left of the afternoon trying to coax the stray into a friendship, using scraps of meat from the tacos she couldn't finish and a dish of dog kibble the local market displayed on a dusty shelf between detergent and diapers. They didn't have a collar or a leash, but a kerchief and a rope serve well enough. It's nice to have something living in the room with her, something breathing. He has beautiful eyes and his name, she's decided, is Chance, for now he has one, and, after all, it's the one thing everyone needs, a chance. Even a second chance.

No matter what, she will have to talk to Nina tomorrow, to make arrangements for Ethan after Mrs. Holian's time runs out, but she can't yet say how many more days this will all take, not with any certainty. If Rubio's plan fails, she will just keep at it, keep pushing, keep on.

The night is long and raw. There were coyotes behind the motel, digging through garbage, and Chance was just as restless as she was. Planning to head over to the police station when they open, to collect Mason and escape Guerrero Negro, to believe in Rubio, to trust his assurances, she is packed and ready thirty minutes early. The room is dark and stuffy. Opening the door to let in the light and the morning air, she sees him scudding across the parking lot, leaving a low fuzz of dust. Mason—hollow-eyed, agitated, his movements jerky—throws one arm around her and quickly pulls it back, grabs her bag, and hurries her out to the van.

And just like that, it's over.

SOMEHOW SHE EXPECTS the town of Guerrero Negro to be different, to acknowledge and even respect the changes that have gathered like new ghosts behind them, but it is the same grubby scatter of low buildings parted by a wide straight road so typical of the desert, the same words painted directly onto storefronts and businesses stating in plain language what might be bought or done beyond the shadowed entries leading inward, away from the light. All the rush, the bluntness of boom towns and company settlements, is emphatic and unmitigated.

But it ought to be different, it ought to look different and feel different, as different as she feels now within herself. The sameness is an affront. If Rubio were here . . . *but what? What if he were here?* She glances behind to where he used to sit . . . *how soon he became familiar* . . . across the jumbled bags and gear, into the dusky reaches of the van, her eyes following the six-foot path she and Mason made when they had shoved their things against the side wall, back to where Rubio used to sit. *How easy it is, familiarity, when someone you don't know but instantly recognize at last arrives. How soon he became dear.*

Now, on the bench seat, the yellow dog sleeps. A young male, reasonably healthy despite the ribs, feathery fur, eyes as round as pennies with a dark copper color, hopeful brows peaking above a gaze like the gaze of the ancients. The first thing Mason told her two days ago, when they lifted the dog from the top of the van and put him in the back, was not to name him. The plan was to take him to Ensenada where in the larger population the animal might find a home or at the very least, more plentiful and regular scraps.

"Who do you think put him up there?" she asks Mason.

"A gift from Cantú, I'm guessing, by way of one of his henchmen."

"And the matchbook?"

"That too."

"*Go away.* That's what we should have done, you know. You know that."

He grunts softly, reluctant to be wrong, to be someone who makes mistakes, especially big ones.

"I wish we could go south to Mulegé to thank Rubio in person, but we can't."

"Yeah, I know."

"We'll see him in Palo Alto," she says, remembering the future visit that they had all eagerly conceived before parting on the morning Mason and Clair headed out to the airstrip for the flight to Isla Cedros. She imagines Rubio Cantú at the house in Palo Alto, easily picturing him in the elegant

Spanish-style home with its wrought iron and spreading oaks. "But right now we can't backtrack, we have to get to the border."

"No kidding."

"Because what if someone changes their mind? There are the checkpoints, and the ones going north are much worse than southbound."

"I know, Clair. Do I look stupid?"

At the crossroads they pull into a store and Mason returns with beer, two bottles of what she supposes is the cheapest tequila on the shelf, a brand she's never seen before, and some lime soda to stand in, apparently, for margarita mix. She doesn't bother asking about the quantity of alcohol or whether it has to do with his arrest or his back or his father or his film because she doesn't have whatever it would take to analyze whatever he might say and the feelings it means to hide. And anyway, right now, she doesn't care. It's Ethan's voice she needs to hear with an ache that radiates as though some essential body part has been numb for weeks and has just now painfully awakened. He hardly seems real to her, it has been so long, or at least no longer real in this world. A pale abstraction. But first she has to call Nina and arrange for her to take over for Mrs. Holian so that Clair can tell her son what to expect and when and with whom because he is such a stickler for details.

In the doorway of the store, two men watch them back up to leave. A boy squeezes between them, wraps his arm around the leg of one of the men, and with the open contemplation that mimics his elders, carefully monitors their departure.

Little boys . . . It occurs to her that not once, not ever, has Nina taken care of Ethan. It has just never come up, what with Nina's travel schedule for the winery and Louise always eager to babysit, the long drive up to Napa, back down . . . *But that's just ridiculous*, she hears herself think, and then tries to retrieve the muffled thought that led to the internal response, something that bobbed up from the deeps and then just as quickly subsided. What was it that she was thinking? What is it that everyone has always in some way been thinking, so much so that it's like the unique and unidentifiable smell that a house acquires over time, its own smell characterizing that house and no other?

At the far edge of town they stop at the Pemex station to fill up and to use the pay phone. By way of an awkward and uncertain negotiation between numbers, operators, and languages, she is finally connected to Nina whose voice with its familiar flat inflection is startling, as if it's only a recording of Nina made before something catastrophic happened. Before everything changed.

This is new, this understanding of how things can change—really change. They've been changing all along in the deep water where the cold currents run, but on the surface everything looks the same, even is the same for a long while, long enough to deceive anyone wanting to deceive himself, except that all the while the surface has been thinning and tearing until that deep cold-water current pulls everything with it and runs into the future with the whole sea fast behind it.

"Clair, are you back?" Nina says. A cool quick gust of words. She sounds worried; it's not like her sister to worry.

"No, and I won't be back, not for two more days, maybe three. Ethan doesn't know yet, and Mrs. Holian can only be there one more night."

"You want me to tell mom to go down?"

"I was thinking maybe you could take him, you know, for a change."

"Are you sure?"

"Yes, yes, I'm sure."

"You've never asked before."

"I haven't?" Clair stares across the station to where Mason is pumping gas. A hot wind twists up pieces of garbage just beyond him, and he's studying something absent in front of his face, his expression lost in the shade beneath the station awning. Beyond it, past the line defining shade to sun, the light is like a flashing knife.

"Never."

In the back of her throat, a sound like a tiny siren develops along a wire buzzing between her inner ears, and the phone itself has begun to feel like one end of a tin-can phone system, both parties pretending to hear what the other is not really saying. "I guess not," she says, shrugging as if there is someone nearby who can see her and confirm that this data is obviously of no import.

"I always figured you were nervous."

"What about?"

Silence.

"Don't be ridiculous, Nina." She closes her eyes to un-see something, or to hide, according to the logic of a child, from the whole world. When she opens them, the transparent coffin of the phone booth amazes her, the floor constricted by perimeter sand and compacted trash; in her hand, the receiver is so sticky and unclean, so revolting that she almost drops it. How had she ended up here, confronting this most particular of particular thoughts, the most deeply submerged—and decades late?

"Is that what I'm being?" Nina asks, "ridiculous?"

"No. I'm sorry." A sigh. Long ago Nina developed a habit of bluntness that never faded away, part of a no-hiding policy learned in therapy, but it was something you never quite got used to. Human beings are creatures of masks and manners, essential to getting-along. If you pretend, maybe it will make it so, at least in some reality.

Nina's voice is slow and level. "It was an accident."

"It was, and I know it, and I've always known it."

"I was five."

"We were five."

"The faucets . . . I didn't know how to work them."

"Why would you?" Clair says, her voice breaking. "It was a terrible accident, but . . . for a while, they just . . . they didn't seem to know how to deal with that. It was too, too . . . mundane almost, too stupid." Turning her back on the station, she gazes through the dirty glass of the booth out across the empty desert, searching for something she can't even name. "Accident! How could such a terrible stupid thing happen? You couldn't call it an accident, not at first, because that just didn't seem enough, it wasn't worthy of what happened. But everyone knows it. And I've always known. And mom and dad . . . it was an accident."

"Clair . . ."

"Look, I want Ethan to be with you. I do. That's what I want. We look alike, and it'll reassure him." It occurs to her that it might reassure Nina, too, a thought that churns up the old sadness in her stomach. Nina, the question of Nina—that has always caused the most trouble for Clair. Nina is the riddle Clair could never solve, whose control she could never escape. If you start out at the same time, if you look the same, there's an assumption of equality. Even guilt must be equally assumed.

"We look a lot alike," Nina says, emphasizing *a lot*.

"You didn't like that when we were kids."

"No."

"Why not?"

"I didn't want to be a *we* or *the twins*. It's not all that easy to compete with a twin. It's like beating yourself."

"You did like to win."

A burst of static and she's afraid Nina has hung up, but soon enough the line settles. "Anyway, what I want, what I'm asking, is for you to take Ethan until I get back," Clair says, involuntarily shrugging again. "You're my sister. His aunt," she adds with a blink of wonder.

"I'll be there first thing."

"Good."

"But everything's all right in Baja," Nina tells her, again without inflecting a question.

"It's been a strange time."

"Mason."

"Why do you say that?"

"The man has a temper."

It's true. She's always tried not to notice how much of him is made up of anger. She's always thought or hoped that it was something only she could tame, not so much to flatter herself but to extol their love. The love was what mattered, the third dimension between the two of them. It would fix everything, wouldn't it? Distracted, she murmurs, "Yeah, he does," half expecting that admitting a thing diminishes it.

Also, it has always been convenient to regard anger, strong anger, as being confined to the male of the species.

He's in the driver's seat now, waiting for her.

"But you're both all right."

"It's been a rough time. His back . . . and then, or before that, actually, just before, maybe the day we left, or the day before, but anyway, right around then, well . . ."

"What?"

"His father died."

Nina emits a sound, a kind of low *huff* that seems to come from her gut, as if a bird has flown into the softest part of her. "The father he hates."

"That one."

"So . . ."

"Right. And there was an incident, too. I'll tell you about it when I get home."

Clair can see Mason open a bottle of beer and take a sip without tipping his head back, just lifting the bottom of the bottle and staring through the windshield, drinking the way someone drinks when they are up to no good, casting about for trouble. He looks like the driver of a getaway car. And in fact, that's exactly what it is.

"Listen, Ethan will probably ask you about the gifts, one for every day I'm gone, but things took longer."

"Of course," Nina says easily.

"He might not see it that way. He knows they were guilty gifts, but . . . I don't want to let guilt keep me from living my life anymore. Plus, he likes to think I'm perfect. Or maybe I do." Again, she sighs. "I'm done with that."

"Why did you try?"

Clair laughs and it sounds so good that she feels the sting of tears. "Well, someone had to try to be easy for everyone else's sake. Maybe it seemed a logical way to protect everyone, not just you."

"Well, *I* always hoped you'd develop a flaw. Or even two, you know, for my birthday present. Our birthday," she adds.

"Ha! Well, you get your wish." A pause. "And that's another thing I get. I get to wish, Nina, I get to want. I'm tired of the other, whatever the other was. Self-censorship, maybe, and too much accommodation. It's hard to keep up, and it takes a hell of a toll. Pretty soon you don't know *how* to want, let alone what to want."

"We have a lot to talk about," Nina says simply.

The Pemex station is empty except for their van, so when she hears the blast of the horn she knows it's Mason, and quickly says goodbye, but not without telling Nina not to bother about the daily gifts. "He'll just have to take it on faith," she says, "I'll be back." Leaning out of the booth, she raises her hand and spreads her fingers to indicate five more minutes.

Ethan's voice, high, lucid, sweet, even his anger with her, it's all thrilling, so full of life, so furious with love and need. If she could, she would hug herself just to have something to do with all of what she feels, the bursting, flying-away sensation, the uncomplicated joy. A deep breath rushes up, expanding her lungs as she says his name again as if to remind her son who he is, that she is his mother, that they will be together soon. "Ethan," she intones, writing his name in the dust on the little, triangular shelf beneath the phone box, "I adore you."

THEN SHE AND Mason are back on the road, retracing the miles north up the narrow empty highway, dropping into the *vados*, climbing the grades, swerving to miss the bands of wandering cattle, so lean and with horns too wide for the chutes in a meatpacking plant. Here they must be butchered individually and by hand. *Better*, she thinks. All murder should be personal.

An hour or so north, she tells Mason she's hungry. He says that he's not.

Another hour north, they encounter the first checkpoint at the junction of Mexico Route 1 and the road that heads east out to Bahía de los Ángeles. But it is unattended, and so they keep going. Soon after, having eaten hardly anything of what remained of the snacks in the van, nothing really, she insists that they really need to stop for lunch. Like all the other villages, the next is hot and dusty, an exhausted hallucination beneath the mid-afternoon sun. Nothing looks open or occupied, but there is a small building resembling a café—abandoned gas pumps out front, a flat roof with broad eaves, vertical strips of cloth swishing from an open doorway, a few parked cars, and just over there, a small, hand-painted plywood sign that advertises "Gas–Food–Laetrile"—*Gas* has been crossed out.

She opens the passenger door. "Aren't you coming?"

"Not hungry."

"But you'll come in with me."

"Not hungry."

She glances down at her shorts, then shifts her eyes over toward the obscure figures dining behind the windows, worrying that they are watching her. Somewhere, music—Mexican pop. The sun's heat is searing against the back of her legs. "I'd rather not go in alone."

He shrugs and takes a swig from the tequila bottle. A fly has taken shelter in the van, its desultory buzzing articulating the silence.

"What's the matter with you?"

"Absolutely nothing. I'm not hungry, and I like it where I am."

"I don't speak Spanish."

"Pity."

"What's going on?"

"You want to eat. I don't. Happy to wait."

"Why are you being such a jerk? After everything that's happened?"

"I'm not hungry, that's all."

Not once does he turn to look at her. It's as if she no longer exists, or as if he's trying to make her disappear, this person he claims to care about.

"That's not all, not at all! You have to stop this." Closing the door, she glances over her shoulder, then makes a show of staring at him through the open window, hungry enough to think she can go in, or at least bluff. But there's no question of her going in alone. He knows she won't, and he doesn't care. She knows that, too. Even in America she won't eat alone in a restaurant. It would make her feel pitiful, and she can't stand pity.

Since Cedros . . . no, since they left home, he has been shredding, piece by piece. Maybe he is becoming someone he was all along—or someone changed she does not now want to know. That can happen, people can change and break time into two halves, before when there was weight and meaning in the smallest of things, when everything seemed to have something to say to them, something important and particular to them—and after, when it is like the dangerous vacancy of the next morning, the light too bright, the color gone, and time opening before them, ringing with silence and starkly unassigned. A stranger in the next seat.

When she consigns herself to the van, she joins Chance where Rubio used to sit. "Forget it," she says to the top half of Mason's face in the rear-view mirror, to the duplicate glare of spectacles, the nullified gaze. "Just keep going." The dog is skittish, but already less afraid than he was, and she rests her hand on the seat between them without triggering a back-and-forth agitation of eyes and head as he reflexively checks for an escape, but his body still trembles occasionally. Cantú might have calculated that he was delivering a burden to them, to people who care about too many things, even while to him, with his haphazard feedings and listless engagement, the dog was nothing. This must have been some of what Rubio experienced as a boy.

Nevertheless, now they are saddled with the dog's fate. The fate of a dog named Chance.

She opens a beer, swallows some, stares out the window.

ONLY A WEEK ago in the warm darkness beneath the palapas on the cliff overlooking the Sea of Cortez, the moon a spill of milky radiance on the sleek black water below them, Rubio said that he liked the two of them together. "But not apart," he had added. "Apart, there is *la pobreza*."

"Poverty?" Mason had said, as though Rubio had not found the right word.

"*Sí, sí*, poverty. A thing missing. One without the other cannot speak. Not of truth."

Under the palapas she could not see Mason's expression and was glad for that, yet she decided—perhaps only because it was a nice thought and now and then that was okay, wasn't it?—she decided that he wanted to take her hand as much as she, his, to seal Rubio's words, and so that together they might be rich and stand for something true and speak with one voice. A world without love . . . why, it was just a tattering of pretense. And the loneliness, the feckless methods of refuting it, the self-trickery . . . No, someone must love, another must be brave enough to accept love, and both must be willing to lose it again and again, to trust in it as though leaning into the wind to be held up by it.

Behind the tinted windows of the van, she considers herself as if from outside, looking in at her own veiled form as a woman newly in mourning, hair uncombed, eyes too big, alone and despondent, unaccustomed to demanding or even asking for what she wants, lost in loss. And up front, an angry, equally isolated man, getting drunk and already gone away from her. Into a self-made world of punishment.

At the El Rosario checkpoint, a soldier in camouflage carrying an automatic weapon peers into the van. *"Adonde va?"* he asks Mason.

"San Diego," he replies.

"De donde viene?"

"Mulegé, San Ignacio, Guerrero Negro . . ." In the sideview mirror she can see Mason smile. *"Muy bonita. Y las ballenas . . ."* He opens his arms to indicate something enormous.

"Armas y drogas?" the soldier asks impatiently.

"No," he says, producing a sound of surprise and gentle complaint, as if he's been insulted. *"Vacaciones,"* he adds, gesturing toward the clutter of gear in the van, and Clair sitting quietly on the back seat beside the dog.

The soldier backs away and waves them on.

A nearly identical exchange transpires at the Maneadero checkpoint, except this time the soldier opens the side door of the van to make an inspection, paws through a few items in the crates and under the seats, opens the glovebox, pokes into the seatback pockets and, regarding her with a certain curious disapproval as if the absolute mess of their domestic effects is her fault, he gives his head a single shake and slides the door shut. She can hear him laughing with another soldier as they drive away.

It is close to nightfall by the time they reach Ensenada. Four hours driving without speaking. It had not been so hard, after all. She sat in the back, defeated but at peace, her heart a stone in her chest. If he glanced at her in the rearview mirror, she did not know or would not have known. She had made no effort to see his eyes, not because she was afraid, but because she had decided not to care. She can do that, decide not to care.

Now at last he has conceded the need for them to eat, but they can't agree on which of the many tawdry establishments lining the main road, Avenida López Mateos, they should stop at— one is too empty, one too close to the traffic, another seems to cater to drunk American weekenders, the place on the corner is clearly exclusive to locals, and on they go until finally they pull to the back of a crowded parking lot behind one of the bigger restaurants to give themselves over to an argument that flared minutes after they began to speak to each other and that really has nothing to do with where to eat or if to eat or why to eat.

She tells him to control his voice, that he's upsetting Chance.

"And why in God's name did you have to name the cur?"

"Cur?"

"I told you not to name it."

"He's a he, not an it."

"He. I could have lived with that. But you had to name him."

"I didn't have to, I wanted to."

"What? For the length of two days? You want to form a relationship for two days before you abandon him to this shit-hole? Brilliant. They'll probably eat him, you know. Meat is not so plentiful in Baja as it is on the Great Plains of America." He booms his voice so that it sounds like a travelogue voice-over, mocking a country he has adopted and actually loves.

Looking over at Chance, Clair gently strokes his flank, the only quadrant of his body that he has agreed she can touch. He's young enough not to have developed any of the skin diseases that the older strays have, diseases that leave raw patches and scabs; he's still a pretty creature. His ancient copper-penny eyes regard her, afraid but hopeful about her intentions, though evidently disappointed in the world he's already encountered.

"Why not call it dinner? Had a friend who named his steer Dinner and one day it was." A phony laugh. He swigs from the bottle of tequila. In the dimming light his skin is pale, his eyes muddy, his yellow shirt jaundiced.

"Dinner is a label, not a name. It would be like calling you Photojournalist. A name is how you build a relationship. It's learned."

"Next thing you'll be naming the whales. There's the ticket. Why not name the gray whales?"

"I don't want to tame or train a whale. But a dog . . ."

"It's not going to be your dog, it's going to be no one's dog. It's damned cruel to name it when tomorrow morning you're going to leave it off by the side of the road. You've said it yourself, no one wants someone else's spawn."

"He's not my child."

"Shouldn't have named it, that's what I'm saying. That's all."

"You said 'it' again."

In silence he stares through the windshield into the twilight, over the metallic glow of dozens of parked cars that together form a cold checkered dystopian stage. The van is at the rear of the lot, on a rise backed up to a cyclone fence, and the stage below them seems set for a modern play whose themes they won't understand. Finally, he mutters, "It was good enough for me."

"What was?"

"It."

Forward to the back of his head, to his halo of hair, the glint of the transparent bottle, his long fingers around it, the flash of the white-faced watch, and beyond, past Mason, through the windshield at the guttering of the day into the welling night, the dull pewtered candescence of the air itself . . . at that ghostly tableau, she stares, and that is the moment she remembers a funny little addendum to one of his childhood stories.

Long after his mother died, when Mason was thirteen, his father remarried, a woman who dutifully assumed the role of stepmother. Emily was eighteen and ready to fly the coop, which she did when the new wife, Honora, showed up with her matched Samsonites that included a cosmetic case the size of a badger. But Mason could not escape his father's new bride or the new world order she brought to their Cornwall estate. It wasn't clear initially that he altogether wanted to escape her. A mother might have been nice, even an artificial one, and even one so late as this one. Honora took her job seriously but not, as her name might have implied, honorably. Thirteen can be a difficult age for boys, especially ones who have beatified their dead mothers and vilified their living fathers. For all concerned, it was not an easy adjustment.

Honora kept a diary, a holdover from her years in boarding school. When she died, only two years after her arrival, of a marvelously stealthy blood clot—she had been a smoker—Mason and his father sorted through her earthly goods together, in a state of disbelief, but not particularly keen feeling. One morning he could hear his father in the bedroom, hitherto as silent as the reaper himself had been, chuckling over some of the diary entries. At last he couldn't keep the source of the humor to himself and handed the small pink book with its juvenile lock and key to Mason. In its pages, amidst a swarm of exclamation points, Honora wrote regularly of her new charge, young Master Comstock. From the very first entry she refers to him as *It*. *It left a right mess for me at the dinner table again!* Or, *They've telephoned from that fancy school about It—another cock up!* One of the last entries read, *Three more years with It. Three!* Well, she was wrong about that.

It grew up and went off and, as is said, made a name for himself.

In the course of Clair's memory about Mason and naming, there comes literally, and with comical drama, a knock on the door. The passenger door. The door opens as if on its own, and a short woman leans in across the empty seat. It is now fully night and the only illumination that can reach them strains from the back windows of the restaurant across dozens of parked cars and reaches them in a weakened condition. All that Clair can tell is that their visitor is not that young and not distinctive, someone you would not recall even if she brought you food in an expensive, once-a-year restaurant, or dressed a painful wound beneath fluorescent hospital lights. A little dumpy, a little tired-seeming, something comforting and maternal about her. She says a few words to Mason in Spanish, her voice also ordinary and not in any way alarmed or apologetic, as Clair assumes it ought to be because she has also assumed that there is some emergency, some need, maybe a ride somewhere, a dead battery. A handout.

Mason says something back to her. She says something else. And then he lifts his right hand and jerks his thumb over his shoulder toward where Clair sits in the murky recesses of the van, and angrily grunts, "*Mi esposa* . . ."

Peering in, the woman's eyes widen enough to project two small white rings; she scrambles backward, closes the door, and scurries off across the silver stage.

"What was that?" Clair asks.

"She thought I was alone."

"And?"

"And interested."

"Oh."

It's the last thing they need. A reminder that everything is temporary, anyone can be bought, Clair is replaceable, invisible, a part of the background, sitting beside a stray dog with a bellyful of emptiness, or beside a sister who insists on more, or behind a man who can't love enough; a reminder that he can betray her this way, or some other way, and so easily; that nothing is impervious, not them, not their love; that the world can get in, it can simply open the door . . .

They give up on food altogether and navigate back to the road, passing through the city and alongside the harbor before reclaiming the highway north toward Tijuana. Without consulting her, he takes the emptier alternate route that edges the Pacific. She really doesn't care. Leaving behind the stench of the fish processing plants and the glare of city lights, they disappear into the shroud of night. The water off to their left conjures an unseen but nonetheless discernable impression of vastness, and she wonders about the moon, about when it might light a path to the horizon and beyond into another day. Now, only the tiny green lights trapped inside the dashboard and the searching beams of the headlights lead them on. For ten miles or so they follow a wide, divided highway, obviously new but so short a distance that the optimism about Ensenada's economic future it anticipates seems naïvely boastful. Soon, when the highway narrows, she loses awareness of other cars and accepts that there can't have been any, that they are alone.

The argument that began without cause escalates to a full fight, except that he acts as if he can barely summon any interest in it, and she is so desperate to understand why he's behaving the way he is that her eyes are spilling hot tears. "I can't trust you," she finally cries. "I can't trust you with me, with my heart, my dreams . . ." *And Ethan*, she thinks. *My son.*

"You still do that, dream? How quaint."

"Don't be this way."

"But I'm good at it. Have been from the get-go."

"You're trying to drive me away. This is deliberate," she says, realizing the truth of the words as soon as she says them. "You're being a hateful bastard. It's sadistic, and you're trying, you're actually trying."

"Not so. I come by it naturally."

"You're throwing in the towel . . ."

"What's this?" In the darkness, the road unraveling before them, his question sounds genuine. Not sarcastic, not dismissive, not contemptuous.

"Us. And the photographs . . . you're acting like it's all over, like there'll never be another job, another battle. You've decided to let your father be right. All he ever said about you, all he accused you of, and having to be a parent, the resentment . . . all of it, you just bought into it. He died and you pay that debt by declaring him right. Making him bigger than he was. So this is how you plan to punish yourself. You've been waiting for this day all your life, to give up hope, to accept defeat. This is your day of defeat. It started with the photographs of your mother in the hamper, the ones he got rid of, and it's ending with the photographs here, and yeah, Mason, they are gone. Long gone. And this is how you plan to cure yourself of the old guilt. It's perfect, isn't it?"

"You're barking mad."

"Great plan. Are you losing hope because of something you think you've done or someone you think you are? Can't you see what you're doing?"

He tosses something at her, his glasses. She pinches them off the rug and tucks them in a cupholder. "Okay," she says quietly, adopting Mason's own toneless delivery, "now you literally can't see. Pull over."

He swerves to the side of the road, gropes around for his glasses, and finally says, "Give them to me."

"Cupholder."

In a stifling silence they sit while the world around them gradually makes itself known. The random little sounds from the engine, the thunder of big surf from over the cliff, one wave, then another and another, measuring out time. A soft fresh saline smell, primordial and enveloping; also something resinous—rabbitbrush. In fact, no one passes on the highway. They are alone in this world. Very quietly, she says, "I know what you're doing, Mason. You're buying the line the same way I bought the line about

Nina and me. I've been living that line, the line about her guilt and my own guilt about that line. And then the guilt I only now understand is because I've betrayed myself buying everyone else's line, and I'm guilty about *that*, about never getting to be, or letting myself be, Clair. All of me."

He does not respond or even move. He's just a blacked-out shape—head, part of an arm, right hand clenched on the edge of the seat.

"Maybe you never really wanted to save the world, maybe you were trying to save yourself somehow. That's a tall order. Didn't you kill your mother and make your father an enemy?" Out the window the empty gray road lines up along the cliff, and in the theater of her mind, she sees everyone she's ever known walk up to the cliff edge to consider the waiting sea. "Are you going to say anything?" she asks.

"Doubtful."

"So you're not even going to talk now."

"We're not talking. *You* are lecturing."

A claustrophobic panic seizes her. At her feet are the crates where they had once stored provisions, filled now with camping gear, used propane tanks, beer cans, chip bags, and other empties, trash. Suddenly all she can think about, all she can bear to think about, is food. It's simple, it's urgent, it's absent. She can deal with that, simplicity and urgency. Thanks to Mason—or to Nina or to a lifetime of passivity—she hasn't eaten all day and the anger about that, about everything, supercharges this single need. Maybe they overlooked something, a tin of almonds or some dried salami, crackers. She drops to her knees and begins pulling things out of the crates, tossing them against the van wall, and it's not long before she's throwing one thing after another at the wall. A whimper as Chance crawls under the bench seat, and though she can't see his eyes, she's convinced he's watching her with fear.

Mason tells her to stop.

"Should I leave you alone?"

"Sure."

And that is what she finds herself doing, grabbing her duffel and stumbling across the highway in the night to the cliff edge. It's not as steep as it looks from the road, and she manages to scramble down, rolling the duffel ahead of her until they both end up in the sand. Under the night sky stung with stars the sand is very white and seems to go on forever in opposite directions. Behind her, the cliff. The sea is a great black wall that has just fallen back, the bottom edge where the surf crashes, torn up and anguished, rushing at her feet, sinking away, the luminescence paling to nothing until again it explodes, a shock of white, followed by the trailing, hissing darkness. Beyond it the ancient wall of the sea lies in ruin. And all around, night dilates like an enormous pupil. She thinks the word, *alone.* Then, *not big enough.* This is the aloneness she's known most of her life, the one that does not call up tears or reproaches; it's there behind everything, behind the great black fallen wall of the sea, behind the things you desire and cannot have, the call you make that goes unanswered, the heart you love that will not feel. She senses a knowingness, airy and vast, surrounding her, widening and widening without remorse. It is comforting in a strange effortless way, a thing that she doesn't have to fight or defy. She has only to settle with it, as with a great priceless debt. She is alive. The life she has belongs to her and to no other.

She leaves her sandals with the bag at the base of the cliff and walks off in one direction, north. The sand is deep and soft, the beach declining toward the water, and when the waves spill across her path, they quickly shrink back, like penitents. She's just walking, that's all. Her toes fit around the wet sand, clutching it, and the muscles of her calves ride high and taut, like fists, and her back arches with pleasing effort. It's easy to breathe, so easy that it is a feat she notices, the effortlessness of it. Nothing more than this is worth caring about. And it is worth caring about. It all comes to this: sand, sea, night, a sky waiting for its moon. Breath.

About Mason, she feels nothing. Nina, too—nothing. Ethan is a single word-thought: safe.

Each breath is huge, so huge and coming so effortlessly fast that one by one they lift her a little off the planet.

So strange . . . as recently as two weeks ago, she did not know that these people existed. Rubio, Marla, Eduardo Cantú, Yetz, and all the rest, the charming and forthright Daniel Markovsky, Angel with his mangoes, Señor Aguilar . . . his amusement, his sinister indifference, the kind couple at the lagoon, the officer at the border, the old roué with his prowling eyes, the caretaker of the springs, the parking lot prostitute, Fausta's little girl . . . She had known Mason, the Mason in California at the talk where they first met, and the brave man in the newspaper clipping, clinging to the gunnels; she knew the Mason who made a single call from a Russian ice breaker. A call to her. The Mason with his clever hand between her legs. Mason cavorting among the boojum trees. But she does not know the Mason in the van at the top of the cliff who drives her away. She does not know this man, but she sees what has brought him to this place.

Going away is easy though.

She did not know about the landscape of salt that kills and preserves at once. Maybe that is what people who love each other do, because love is contrary, killing what it most wants to preserve.

She had not fathomed the kinship with whales, but it did not surprise her.

And justice. Justice especially. She could not have understood how just human beings want to be, and what distortions that need grows in the human heart, how rotten the harvest, how thin the fare, how bitter the taste.

Guilt. One way or another it bends everyone to its will. That will . . . *it's to justice!* she thinks with a start of something like pride. Meanwhile, justice is too often defeated, because the same guilt that drives us toward justice is also the mechanism of distortion. We spend our lives trying to make up for crimes we may not have committed, or people we were told we had become, or mistakes that might have been the mistakes made along any extraordinary journey.

CHANCE FINDS HER first, trotting up and tapping the back of her leg with a wet nose. She leans down to make a chalice of her hands, conveying good intentions, and this time when he backs off it's only a foot or so. To the east, a young moon rocks up and briefly rests like a cradle on the cliff edge. The eye of the night contracts. Trudging through the wet sand toward her, a dark figure against the flat and infinite sea forms a vertical line that grows bolder as it nears. By the time Mason reaches her, the moon is already sailing over the water, a small empty luminous dory, so small and with so far to go that she can feel her heart clench with feeling.

He lays his arm across her shoulder while his cupped hand turns her back, and Chance races ahead of them through the lapping, penitent sea.

A LATE AWAKENING, the light complete. Around the bench seat, hinged open into a double bed, their untidy belongings crowd. *The untidy heart*, she murmurs to herself. Fur and dog breath, salty skin, ocean, sage, sun-struck asphalt. Seagulls calling. The lullaby of surf. An old cotton sheet crumpled against her bare shoulder. Warmth from the next body. Cool air through the open window. A morning.

"Thank you," he whispers.

"For . . . ?"

"Coming back with me."

"I would have."

"Good." Her head, resting on his chest, gently rises and falls when he takes a single, careful breath—in, out. "Good," he says again.

Someone else, someone cleverer and wiser, a therapist or an old aunt, the guru on the mountaintop, someone else might have said that they should not be together; that it would not work, he was too much this way and she too little that; that there was baggage or neurosis, willfulness or passivity, a selfish heart, a stifled heart. Someone outside might say that it will never turn out well and that to spare themselves or save themselves, they must keep looking. Someone on the outside could make all such manner of admonitory remarks, and they might probably be correct. On the inside . . . on the inside, there is all the love. And love writes its own story.

They sort themselves out for the drive north, and when they roll onto the highway, she turns to ask him what it was that he called her. "Back in Ensenada, at the parking lot."

"What?"

"What did you say to the prostitute to send her away?"

"Ah!" He smiles grandly and opens his arm as if he's introducing her to someone important, but also as if it's obvious. "*Mi esposa.* My wife!"

ON THE OUTSKIRTS of Tijuana they buy burritos from a roadside stand and from the *mercado* across the street, a can of wet dog food to go with the stale kibble from Guerrero Negro. The strays they've seen, their limbs twisted with malnutrition, look terrified. One was hairless. Without talking about it, it seems they've decided to try to keep Chance with them.

At the US border, they are pulled over. Everyone is being so polite that Clair grabs Mason's hand as the border patrol agent, a chubby boyish fellow with pinked cheeks who is trying to appear detached, leads them beyond a bank of cubicles into a small conference room. At the end of a long table, alone and nibbling at the skin around her polished nails, is Marla. For a second she glances up at them with hope, and then immediately seems to decide that they will be of no use to her. Basic fear has replaced her soft-eyed regard of lazy indifference.

No one bothers greeting. It's as if this room, this meeting . . . all of it has been part of a plan.

Another agent enters and spends a generous amount of time examining their pieces of identification and writing things down on a tablet in miniature capital letters. A thorough man, he's in no hurry, fit and clad in an expertly ironed uniform, silver weaving through his closely clipped hair suggesting experience, blunt fingers, a clean straight mouth unused to expression.

The first thing he says is, "We don't normally care about their people or what happens on the other side." He lifts his chin once southward, looking exclusively at Mason, then gives his shoulders a dismissive shrug. "Not technically our business." Tilting his head a little, he sends his eyes to the ceiling, puckers his mouth, sighs. "But someone wants to cross a T and dot an I. And, you know, the Mexicans . . . they have a hard time saying they don't know. They want to say they do, or maybe imply they do, even when they really don't know or don't even want to know. Too complicated." And on he goes, punctuating each sentence with a small-muscle gesture or action that exquisitely embodies content.

Yesterday, when they were driving in silence up the Baja Peninsula, about the same time that Marla was on an overnight bus headed for Los Angeles, Rubio Cantú was found floating in the mangroves of the Mulegé River estuary. The roots of the mangroves stand above the water, and the trees seem to grow up on a tangle of stilts, the chaos of so many roots forming a perfect cage. Even though it took the fisherman several hours to report the body—he wanted to finish his day's work—the body was still exactly where he spotted it, prisoned within the mangrove roots. The typically rotten bacterial smell of the mangroves easily concealed the body's earliest putrefaction. It had probably been there since the night before.

Marla has already experienced the news and the questions, the terrible tale, and merely stares down at the table, picking at her nails in a state of dozy apprehension as if the story might turn out differently this time. Except that it won't ever because it can't ever.

Did they know Rubio Cantú? They knew him, yes? How long had they known him? Did they know anything about his death? What was Mr. Cantú's line of business? Ah, a man of means . . . but any hobbies or sidelines? There are so many hobbies a man might have these days, a man who frequents two countries.

By the time they reach the point in their story where they caught a flight back from Cedros, another agent—a woman—enters to confirm that they were indeed on Isla Cedros four nights and were logged onto a mid-morning flight back to the peninsula three days ago. So even though no one checked their tickets, their presence had been duly noted.

No one mentions the two nights that Mason spent in the Guerrero Negro jail. Or Rubio's role in his release. Or the organization, as Rubio called it, that was instrumental in that release, probably a cartel and probably the one based where they are right now, in Tijuana.

The whole interview takes less than an hour. Less than an hour to tie up the loose ends, answer the unanswerable questions, solve the final riddle of a man's life. There is no evidence of foul play. The agent seems to experience salacious pleasure in the opportunity to use this phrase, *foul play*. "No foul play," he repeats, rediscovering this new pleasure, like tart candy, in his mouth. Probably the young man drank too much tequila and fell in the river. It happens. There will be no autopsy. The family does not want one, and the Mexican authorities are apparently mostly uninterested in the circumstances of this young man's death. The family is the mother, "a religious," according to the agent, and the father is "some kind of big shot." There may be a half-brother somewhere, but so far no one has been able to locate him, or cares to—a "no-good." By common knowledge, everyone understands what this means.

Stricken, Mason and Clair retrieve the van parked in the impound lot behind the border patrol offices. It's not possible to say for certain whether or not their things have been searched through again; everything is already chaotic. Chance is still there, cowering under the back bench seat. Had they missed him, or did they just not care? When they approach the actual borderline, the boy agent with his pink cheeks and labored detachment waves them across, visibly disappointed in the outcome.

After she had been removed from it, Marla's bus had continued on to Los Angeles. Clair and Mason were prepared to give her a ride north, but on the US side, after making the short walk across the line, dragging her expensive roller bag, she ducks into a black town car, which, they later learn from Daniel, had been sent to meet her by her attorney father. It was Rubio who had put her on the bus from Mulegé a day and a half earlier. Then he went out and managed to die.

AS A CHILD you expect things to change because you yourself are changing so quickly, so frequently. You buy new clothes because the ones you were wearing only a few months earlier no longer fit. You start a new grade, a new job, you make friends easily with little attention to fitness or commonalities. It's all timing and circumstance. It's all chance. Maybe a bit of intuition. You haven't had an opportunity to identify preferences or develop discretion because your character is still as malleable as clay. It has to be because things change so blindingly fast. You yourself change, over and over again.

When you are young, loss is a shallow occurrence, washing in and washing out. It's nothing to plunge through the light easy currents to the next patch of dry ground and survey the scene for what will likely be your opening steps away, toward yet another patch of ground. Another destiny. But for whatever genetic dispositions formed your personality at birth, it's almost an accident how destiny is made. Those endowments of birth that left you adventurous or retiring, sunny or dark, quick or dull—they set the first stones, and from that a life is built with plenty of jerry-rigging as needed.

But when you grow up and become accustomed to the same sizes, the same friends, the same job and interests, gradually and without noticing it, you forget how to lose. After a while, it all begins to feel imperishable. The very fact of your life seems just that—a fact. You can practically rap your knuckles against it, it's so solid, so immediate. You've grown accustomed and that can lead to flawed assumptions. Things, people . . . all falsely permanent. What there is to lose now weighs more. It can take you down, it can even sink you. Rarely you meet someone as you might have as a child, a new best friend, for instance, and then lose them. The adult sensibility doesn't know how to lose this way especially, a way that is like the way children lose for its being so ephemeral, so soon, but now from the perspective of an adult who regards life as a permanent fact. How often do you meet a friend for the first time and then lose him almost immediately? Such a thing draws on both the brisk losses of childhood and the slower, profounder sensibilities of an adult, so the loss is the loss of the child's age, quick and indecently detached, but to the adult experiencing it, a hard shock.

She hopes that it was at least personal, Rubio's death. Not a drug deal gone south, not a drunken fall. That he knew exactly where guilt lay and that he had a little time to imagine true justice. She hopes that his hand didn't tremble. That his father was not involved. She's glad that the buzzards couldn't have gotten to him through the roots of the mangroves. She wishes that this strange feeling of rejection, this disorientation would release her and let her crawl up on some sandy bank out of the tumult of the fast current to catch her breath.

Beside her, Mason drives toward Daniel's in Laguna Beach two hours north. Tomorrow they will make the rest of the journey home. After the border he had tried to talk, he had said, "He lived in a certain world," his voice graveled down with feeling.

"We all live in a certain world," she had said, crying, "we're in that world."

And then they gave in to silence.

From time to time, she looks over at him with wonder, this beloved creature who is at once a man and a place. The place she sits beside. For the first time in her life, she doesn't feel what she only now can name, what was all the years long, a homesickness.

Daniel is standing on the threshold of his bungalow when they pull in, waiting for them, like a parent waits for late children. Helplessly, his palms open, his head falls to the side. "My poor friends . . . come in, come in. We'll sit in the back, we'll talk. I have food."

AFTERWORD

In 1994, Exportadora de Sal, S. A., (ESSA), jointly owned by Mitsubishi Corporation and the Mexican government in a 49/51 percent split, announced plans to build additional salt evaporation works at Laguna San Ignacio along the Pacific Coast of Baja California, one hundred miles south of the existing saltworks in Laguna Ojo de Liebre. The new solar salt facility would be even more massive in scale than those in operation at Guerrero Negro, entailing 116 square miles of dikes and evaporations ponds, in addition to a mile-long dock for loading salt onto barges that would then be towed out to the deep-water port at the southern tip of Cedros Island. Estimated production would be about seven million tons of salt annually. These proposed saltworks would be developed in the last uncompromised breeding and calving waters of the California gray whale, part of a UNESCO-designated World Heritage Site located in what is known as the *buffer zone* of El Vizcaíno Biosphere Reserve, Latin America's largest wildlife sanctuary. Laguna San Ignacio is one of only four saltwater lagoons in the world that gray whales use to reproduce, and the only one left that is still pristine. At that time, ESSA was the biggest saltworks on the planet and the salt it produced was among the purest, used for everything from agriculture and food production to chemical and industrial purposes, from road salt to plastics to glass.

The 1994 proposal for the new salt operation was submitted less than one month after the California gray whale had been removed from the endangered species list, having made a long and nearly miraculous recovery back from the brink of extinction in 1946.

In their initial Environmental Impact Assessment (EIA), ESSA and Mitsubishi claimed that the proposed site for the saltworks consisted of "wastelands with little biodiversity and no known productive use." It was a 465-page plan of which only twenty-three lines addressed possible impacts on gray whales. One year later, in 1995, Mexico's National Institute of Ecology rejected the EIA submitted by ESSA, declaring the expansion incompatible with the UN World Heritage designation and Laguna San Ignacio's status as a protected place. ESSA went back to the drawing board, planning this time to address environmental issues.

Meanwhile, a coalition of environmental groups formed, including the Mexican *Grupo de los Cien* (Group of 100), led by Homero Aridjis, the renowned Mexican poet, and numerous members of the international environmental community—Greenpeace Mexico, the US-based Natural Resource Defense Council (NRDC), the International Fund for Animal Welfare, and others. Together with scientists from around the world, this coalition fomented an intense and acrimonious campaign to prevent ESSA's incursion into Laguna San Ignacio. Environmentalists were concerned that boat traffic, noise, oil spills, brine dumps, and increased water temperatures might drive the whales away. ESSA countered by saying that the new saltworks would create two hundred new jobs, as well as wetlands habitat for birds, and that it would bring electricity, running water, and other basic services to the impoverished fishing villages scattered around the lagoon.

The opposition campaign employed a wide range of tactics, some of them involving the relatively new phenomenon of the Internet, but all of them focusing on the charismatic California gray whale. The NRDC sent out millions of direct mailers, collected millions of dollars in donations, more than doubled its membership, and, with the help of other conservation organizations, arranged for full-page ads in newspapers that listed thirty-four scientists, nine of them Nobel laureates and Pulitzer Prize winners, who signed a letter arguing that the saltworks posed "an unacceptable risk" to the lagoon's ecology and wildlife. Toward the end of the five-year-long battle, forty-six California municipalities and fourteen pension and socially conscious mutual funds boycotted or divested in Mitsubishi. Nearly a million letters from protesters around the world were sent to ESSA and Mitsubishi, and another three hundred thousand to the Mexican government. Billboards were erected in Mexico City, decrying the potential assault on Laguna San Ignacio and its whales. Actors, politicians, and other international celebrities weighed in.

Undeterred, Mitsubishi began preparing its second EIA with a list of new studies required by the Mexican government, spending two million dollars, committing four years to multifaceted studies and engaging highly respected scientists to conduct the investigations. On the other side, a team of UNESCO scientists conducted its own studies at the existing saltworks on the northern lagoon of Ojo de Liebre. In the end, both groups arrived at similar conclusions: that the saltworks were compatible with whale breeding and calving and would not adversely affect other marine or terrestrial species of plants and animals or damage the area's ecology. Negative environmental consequences at Laguna San Ignacio would evidently be confined to the landscape on the north side of the lagoon where the vast evaporation ponds would be excavated.

In 1997, in the midst of the ongoing studies, there was purportedly a toxic brine spill from ESSA's existing saltworks that resulted in the deaths of ninety-four endangered sea turtles. This had the effect of supercharging an already highly charged campaign. Environmental coalition members submitted a formal complaint to Mexican authorities and later, in June of 1998, requested that UNESCO review the situation at El Vizcaíno Biosphere Reserve and the Whale Sanctuary during their next meeting in Kyoto, Japan. The coalition of environmentalists failed at that point to obtain an "in danger" designation for the biosphere reserve, but two years later, at the meeting in Morocco, they succeeded. Later evidence showed that the turtle die-off was likely the result of poachers dumping their catch overboard as inspectors approached.

Finally, on March 2, 2000, then-President Ernesto Zedillo of Mexico held a press conference to report the abandonment of ESSA's plan to construct salt operations south into Laguna San Ignacio.[1] He based his decision not on potential harm to whales or other wildlife in the Reserve, which he insisted would not have resulted from the development, but on the belief that a seventy-five thousand-acre saltworks would change the landscape "in a place unique in the world both for the species that inhabit it and for its natural beauty, which is also a value we should preserve."

ESSA believed that winning the fight depended on the science. But for environmentalists it was a fight as much about conservation ideas, invoking the "precautionary principle" which affirms that there may not be enough data to state definitively that environmental damage *won't* occur, so caution or outright rejection are the best options. It was about leaving a wild and undisturbed place as it is if only because it is just that, wild.

1. James F. Smith, "Activists Break New Ground to Help Shake Off Saltworks Project," *Los Angeles Times*, April 23, 2000, https://www.latimes.com/archives/la-xpm-2000-apr-23-mn-22581-story.html.